"I'll walk along with you."

"Oh, that won't be necessary," Kate responded quickly. Too quickly, she realized as his flinty, unnerving eyes narrowed. If she weren't so bloody nervous, she might have laughed at the way her imagination was running rampant: comparing the man to wild animals and warrior Scots, for heaven's sake. Alec MacKenna, she reminded herself, was just a man. The same as any other.

"It'll give us a chance to discuss Legends Lake," he said. "I'll bring you up to speed on his problem."

"Oh, there wouldn't be time enough for that on such a brief stroll," she said in a blithe, airy way she was far from feeling. "Go along with the others, Mr. MacKenna. Truth be told, I'll be needing a bit of time to gather my thoughts after my little altercation with Brian."

"You didn't really . . ."

She realized he was on the verge of asking her if she'd actually committed an act of magic. Then he shook his head with obvious disbelief. "Never mind. It's not important."

While he stood there for a moment longer, looking at her hard and deep, Kate, who definitely didn't want to get into an argument, managed to resist informing him that protecting the tree might not be important to him, but was gravely important to the faeries. As well as everyone who would have had to drive along that cursed roadway.

"Well." He seemed momentarily transfixed, almost, Kate considered, as if he were under a spell. One she certainly hadn't put upon him. "I'll meet you at your farm, then."

Accolades for JoAnn Ross and

FAIR HAVEN

"Not only does JoAnn Ross provide her usual impressive blend of tender warmth and fascinating characters, but she also adds a colorful dash of the supernatural. The talent for great storytelling is obviously embedded deep in Ms. Ross' bones."

—*Romantic Times*

"With writing as fresh as the heady scent of the first daffodils of spring, JoAnn Ross takes readers to a place close to heaven on earth. . . . Ross produces one delightful page after another, one unforgettable story after another. You'll tuck Michael, Erin, and Shea in the place in your heart where hopes and dreams are safely kept—alongside the belief in all things magical."

—CompuServe Romance Reviews

"In *Fair Haven*, JoAnn Ross returns to Ireland she knows so well that readers will feel a sweet mist on their faces as their hearts are warmed by the lyrical sound of the Irish brogue. *Fair Haven* will touch readers' souls like no other book this year. Have the tissues handy, you will bounce between tears and laughter. . . . Put this on your *to buy* list now, because this book will sell out fast."

—Romancing the Celtic Soul

"As magical as Ireland itself. . . . A masterpiece of writing from the heart. . . . Storytelling at its all-time best."

—*The Belles and Beaux of Romance*

"This follow-up to Ms. Ross' highly popular books *Far Harbor* and *Homeplace* is sure to please readers immensely. . . . Another wonderful story from this talented author!"

—*The Old Book Barn Gazette*

FAR HARBOR

"An enchanting and warmhearted sequel to *Homeplace*. The lives of these special people are played out beautifully on the pages of this touching and exceptional novel."

—*Romantic Times*

"A powerfully moving story of intense emotional depth, satisfying on every level. You won't want to leave this family."

—CompuServe Romance Reviews

"This story is a wonderful relationship drama in which JoAnn Ross splendidly describes love the second time around."

—Barnesandnoble.com

Books by JoAnn Ross

Homeplace
Fair Haven
Far Harbor
Legends Lake

Published by POCKET BOOKS

POCKET BOOKS
PROUDLY PRESENTS

BLUE BAYOU

JoAnn Ross

Available soon from
Pocket Books

Turn the page for a preview of
Blue Bayou. . . .

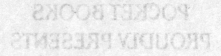

BLUE BAYOU
JoAnn Ross

Available soon from
Pocket Books

Turn the page for a preview of
Blue Bayou...

By the time Dani finally escaped her depressing meeting with the fire marshal, the sky was darkening, the only visible light a band of purple clouds low on the western horizon. She'd forgotten how quickly night came to the bayou. As she steered the rented boat through the labyrinth of waterways, fireflies lit up the waning twilight while nutria and muskrats paddled along, furry shadows in waters as dark and murky as Cajun coffee.

Bullfrogs began to croak; blue herons glided among the ancient cypress which stood like silent, moss-bearded sentinels over their watery world. The boat's light barely cut through the warm mist falling from low hanging clouds; when the ridged and knobby head of an alligator appeared in the stuttering glow, looking like a wet brown rock amidst the lily pads, Dani's nerves, which were already as tattered as a Confederate soldier's gray uniform, screeched.

"This is nuts." If she had any sense at all, she'd cut her losses now and return to town. But she'd already come this far, and unless both her internal homing device and the boat's GPS had gone entirely on the blink, she couldn't be that far from Beau Soleil.

Dani checked her watch. Despite the way the isolation and deepening shadows had seemed to slow time, she'd been out on the water for less than half an hour.

"Five more minutes," she decided. If she hadn't reached Beau Soleil by then, she'd turn back.

A moment later she came around a bend, and there, right in front of her, was the Greek Revival antebellum mansion. Dani was glad she'd undertaken the nerve-racking trip tonight; as bad as the plantation house appeared, it would have been far worse to first see it again after all these years in the hard, unforgiving glare of southern sunlight.

The double front entrance harkened back to a time when if a suitor happened to catch a glimpse of a girl's ankles, he was duty bound to marry her. In a typically southern blend of practicality and romance, the house had been designed with dual sets of front steps—one for hoopskirted belles, the other for their gentlemen escorts. The ladies' staircase had crumbled nearly to dust; the other was scarcely better, held up as it was with a complex design of Erector set–style metal braces.

Beau Soleil had survived being set on fire by the British in the War of 1812, cannonballed, then occupied by Yankee soldiers—and their horses—during the War Between the States. It had also stood up stalwartly to numerous hurricanes over its more than two centuries. Seeing the once noble plantation house looking like an aging whore from some seedy South Louisiana brothel made Dani want to weep.

It had dawned on her belatedly, after she'd left town, that her plan to catch Jack unawares could backfire if she came all the way out here only to find the house dark and deserted. But she'd been so frustrated that she'd acted without really thinking things through. Which she'd been doing a lot lately, with admittedly mixed results.

The flickering lantern light from the upstairs windows of the once stately house was an encouraging sign as she eased the boat up to the dock that was still, thankfully, standing. It appeared to be the same dock her father had paid Jack to build the summer of her seventeenth birthday, the summer her carefree, youthful world had spun out of control.

She tied up the boat with a long ago learned skill some distant part of her mind had retained, and studied the house. Amazingly, most of the centuries-old oak trees had survived time and the ravages of storms; silvery Spanish moss draped over their limbs like discarded feather boas left behind by ghostly belles. She lifted her gaze to a darkened window on the second floor. The years spun away as she envisioned the reckless teenager she'd once been, climbing out that window to meet her lover. Her skin, beneath her white T-shirt, burned with the memory of Jack Callahan's dark, work-roughened fingers encircling her waist to lift her down from that last low hanging limb.

"A smart *fille* like yourself should know better than to sneak up on someone at night in this part of the country," a deep, painfully familiar voice offered from the blackness surrounding her.

Dani yelped. Then hated herself for displaying any weakness. Splaying a palm against her chest to slow her tripping heart, she turned slowly toward the gallery.

He was hidden in the night shadows, like a ghost from the past, with only the red flare of a cigarette revealing his location.

"You could have said something. Instead of scaring me half to death."

"If I figured you and I had anything to say to one another, I would have returned your calls." His voice was even huskier than Dani remembered. Huskier and decidedly uninviting.

"So you *did* get my messages."

"Yeah. I got 'em." Although night had dropped over the bayou, there was enough light shining from the windows of Beau Soleil for her to see him. He was wearing a gray Ragin' Cajun T-shirt with the sleeves cut off, a pair of jeans worn nearly to the point of indecency and cowboy boots. He was rugged, rangy and, dammit, still as sexy as hell.

"But you chose to ignore them."

He took a swig from a long neck bottle of Dixie beer. "Yeah."

Well, this was going well. "I happen to know your mother taught you better manners."

"I was never known for my manners. Drove *Maman* nuts."

That was certainly true. He'd been known throughout the bayou as Bad Jack Callahan. A devil in blue jeans with the face of a fallen angel. "I was sorry when she died."

Since Marie Callahan had been the closest thing to a mother Dani had ever known, sorry didn't begin to describe it. Especially since the Dupree family housekeeper had only been in her late forties when breast cancer claimed her life. Dani had swallowed her pride and sent Jack a brief handwritten note of sympathy. He never responded. Nor did he return home for his mother's funeral, something which surprised even his most stalwart detractors, who'd reluctantly admitted that despite his wild devilish ways, Jack Callahan had always been good to his *maman*.

"Yeah. I was damn sorry, too." He sighed heavily as he flicked away the cigarette, which flared in a sparkling orange arc that sizzled, then snuffed out when it hit the water.

After polishing off the beer, he tossed the bottle aside, pushed himself to his feet and came down the stairs, crunching across the gleaming oyster shell walk on the loose-hipped, masculine stride that had always reminded Dani of a swamp panther. Now, as he loomed out of the blackened shadows, his tawny gold predator's eyes gleaming, the resemblance was a bit too close for comfort.

He'd always been outrageously handsome and the years hadn't changed that. But time had carved away whatever bit of softness he'd kept hidden away deep in his heart. His full sensual lips were drawn into a forbidding line and a savage slash of cheekbones cut their way across features far more harshly hewn than they'd been when he was younger.

His hair appeared nearly as long as hers and glistened darkly with moisture. It flowed back from his strong forehead and was tied at the nape of his neck in a way that made her think of the pirates who used to escape to Blue Bayou after raiding Spanish merchant ships in the Gulf. Taking in the surprising gold earring he hadn't owned when she'd known him last, Dani decided that all he was missing was the cutlass.

Dangerous was the first word that sprang to mind. Maybe Bad Jack Callahan himself didn't present any danger to her, but the unbidden feelings he'd always been able to stir in her certainly could be.

"You shouldn't have come here, Danielle," he said bluntly.

He'd said those same words to her once before. Warning her off. Dani hadn't listened then, nor could she now. "You didn't give me any choice, hiding away out here in the swamp like some mad hermit trapper."

He didn't respond to her accusation. Just gave her a long, deep look. Then grazed his knuckles up her cheek. "You're bleeding."

Her skin felt as if he'd skimmed a candle flame up it. Dani took a cautious step back, lifted her own fingers to the cheek she belatedly realized was stinging and had to remind herself how to breathe. *In.* "It's undoubtedly just a scratch from a tree limb." *Out.* "This isn't the easiest place to get to, with the road gone." *In again.*

"Flooding from last season's hurricane wiped out the road. Since the place was already crumblin', the parish commissioners didn't see any reason to spend public funds to rebuild a road to make it easier to get to some place no one ever wanted to go anyway."

"Which, from what I hear, suits you just fine. I suppose you would have been happier if I'd gotten lost coming out here."

Jack shrugged his broad shoulders. Then gave her a censorious look and cursed. *"Sa c'est fou."* He may have stayed away from the bayou for the past dozen years, but apparently he hadn't completely abandoned the Cajun patois he'd learned from his Acadian mother.

A welcome flash of temper scorched away her nervousness. She lifted her chin. "I've done crazier things."

He laughed at that. A rough, humorless sound that came rumbling out of his broad chest like distant thunder. "I sure as hell won't be arguin' with that, *chérie*."

Dani was not foolish enough to take the endearment to heart. Hadn't she heard him call his old bluetick hound, Evangeline, the very same thing?

"We were both damn crazy that summer," he mused aloud, with something that sounded a bit like regret.

But *he* was the one who'd deserted *her*. If he'd regretted his behavior, he could have called. Or written. Instead, he'd disappeared off the face of the earth.

"I'm not here to talk about that summer."

His eyes, which had seemed to soften a bit with remembered affection, shuttered, like hurricane shutters slammed tight before a storm. "Then why are you here?"

Good question. If it'd been only herself, she would have slept on the street rather than come crawling to Jack Callahan for anything. But she had her children to think of. Innocent little boys who needed a roof over their heads. There was nothing Dani would not do for her two sons, including winding her way through inky black bayou waters risking gators and heaven knows how many different kinds of snakes to beg this man for help.

"You seem to have hired every available construction worker from here to Baton Rouge."

"As impossible as it may be for you to fathom,

sugar, this place is even worse structurally than it looks. It's a smorgasbord for termites, half the roof blew away in the last storm, the plumbing's flat rusted through, and what the inspector laughingly referred to as an electrical system is a bonfire waiting to happen. I could hire every damn construction worker from Lafayette to New Orleans and probably still not have a large enough crew to finish the work in this lifetime."

"Perhaps you ought to just build a new house that won't give you so many problems," she suggested with openly false sweetness. She still hadn't gotten used to the idea of Jack owning her family home. The home her father had recklessly risked, then lost.

"And let the bayou reclaim Beau Soleil? Not on your life."

The force in his tone surprised Dani. "I never realized you felt so strongly about it."

He rocked back on his heels as he looked up at the once magnificent house draped in deep purple shadows. For a fleeting second, his tawny eyes looked a hundred years old. "Neither did I."

"Well." That unexpected bit of honesty left Dani at a momentary loss for words. She reminded herself of her mission. "I need a carpenter, Jack. And I need him now."

He gave her another of those long unfathomable, brooding looks. Then shrugged again. "I don' know about you, but I skipped lunch today to meet with a pirate who calls himself a septic tank engineer and I'm starvin'.

"I've got some chicken in the smoker and after we take care of that scrape on your face, you can peel the shrimp while I make the roux. Then we can pass ourselves a good time over some gumbo and jambalaya and see if we can come up with a way for both of us to get what we want."

Determined to settle her business, Dani forced down her concern about getting back to town. Marie Callahan had once told her that the way to a man's heart was through his stomach. At the time, since she'd been sleeping with Marie's son, Dani had known—and kept to herself—the fact that Jack's other hungers had held first priority.

Still, perhaps he might be more amenable to negotiation after a good meal. Even one he'd cooked himself.

"That sounds like a reasonable enough solution."

A white sickle slice of moon was rising in the sky as they walked in silence toward the house, the bayou water lapping against the raised narrow pathway. Dani had just about decided that the rumors of Jack as a dark and crazy swamp devil, living out here like the fabled *Loup Garou*—a legendary evil shapeshifter that was the bayou's answer to the Abominable Snowman—were merely gossip, when he suddenly crouched down and plunged his hand into the inky water. The violent splash sent a flock of ducks who'd been sleeping in the nearby reeds exploding into the sky, firing the night with a dazzling shower of falling stars.

"*Bon Dieu*," he murmured. "I've never seen the ghost fire so bright." He brought up a broad, long fingered hand that glowed with phosphorescence in the purple velvet dark surrounding them. Sparks seemed to fall back into the water as he stood up again. "You still set this bayou on fire, *mon ange*."

His feral gold eyes drifted down to her lips and

lingered wickedly for what seemed like an eternity, as if he were remembering the taste and feel of them.

He moved closer. Too close. But if she tried to back away, she'd risk falling into the water.

"I'm not your angel," she insisted, even as erotic pictures of them rolling around on a moss-stuffed mattress flashed through her mind, making her breasts feel heavy beneath the white T-shirt that had been pristine when she'd begun her long, frustrating day but was now clinging damply to her body. Although it had to be at least ninety degrees, with a humidity equally high, her nipples pebbled as if she'd dived naked into the Arctic Ocean. She dearly hoped it was dark enough for him not to notice.

It wasn't. "You can lie to me, sugar. You can try to lie to yourself. But your pretty angel's body is saying something else. It remembers, she. The same way mine does."

Dani managed, with herculean effort, to drag her gaze from his, but couldn't resist skimming a look over his broad chest and still flat stomach, down to where his erection was swelling against the faded placket of his jeans.

"See something you like, *chère?*"

Heat flooded into her face. "You know how it is," she said breezily. "You've seen one, you've seen them all. It *is* comforting to discover that not everything around Blue Bayou has changed. You still have sex on the mind."

"*Mais* yeah," he countered without an iota of apology. His wicked eyes glittered with predatory intent as they took a blatantly male appraisal from the top of her dark head down to her sneaker-clad feet. Then just as leisurely roamed back up to her face. "The day

I stop reacting to a desirable woman is the day I tie some weights around my neck and throw myself in the bayou as gator bait."

Dani was no longer a virginal Catholic girl experiencing sexual desire for the first time. She was a grown woman who, in the years since she'd left home, had married, given birth to two children she adored, and was the first divorcée in Dupree family history. This bayou bad boy leering at her should not make her stomach flutter and her pulse skip. It shouldn't. But, heaven help her, it did.

As they resumed walking toward Beau Soleil, she vowed not to let Jack's still powerful sexual magnetism turn her into some fluttery, vapid Southern belle who'd swoon at his feet. Or any other part of his anatomy.

But when he put a casual, damp hand on her hip to steady her as she climbed up the braced stairway to the gallery, Dani feared that if she wasn't very, very careful, she could discover exactly how dangerous supping with Blue Bayou's very own homegrown devil could be.

Look for
Blue Bayou
Wherever Books Are Sold
Coming Soon
in Paperback from
Pocket Books

ALSO AVAILABLE FROM
USA TODAY BESTSELLING AUTHOR

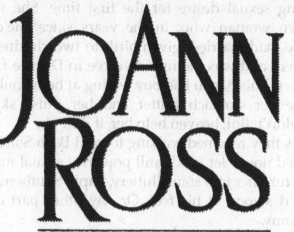

JoAnn Ross

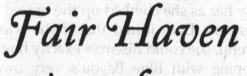

Fair Haven

Far Harbor

Homeplace

POCKET BOOKS
A VIACOM COMPANY

3106

JoAnn Ross

Legends Lake

POCKET BOOKS

New York   London   Toronto   Sydney   Singapore

This book is a work of fiction. Names, characters, places and incidents are products of the author's imagination or are used fictitiously. Any resemblance to actual events or locales or persons, living or dead, is entirely coincidental.

An *Original* Publication of POCKET BOOKS

POCKET BOOKS, a division of Simon & Schuster, Inc.
1230 Avenue of the Americas, New York, NY 10020

ISBN: 978-1-4516-5555-1

First Pocket Books printing August 2001

10 9 8 7 6 5 4 3 2 1

POCKET and colophon are registered trademarks of Simon & Schuster, Inc.

Cover art by Gregg Gulbronson

Printed in the U.S.A.

To Jay,
as always,
with all my love

LEGENDS LAKE

1

ALEC MACKENNA was a gambler by nature and by choice. On any given day, a Thoroughbred trainer could stand at the pinnacle of success in the morning, only to plummet to the depths of despair by sundown. Alec had always found that risk part of the appeal. Yet, when he rolled out of bed before dawn on that fateful morning, falling from grace was the furthest thing from his mind.

The sky outside his hotel room window was the color of spilt ink; rain streaked down the glass, blurring the city lights in the same soft-focus way Hollywood cameras photographed aging movie stars. Born and reared deep in the embrace of the hazy green Appalachian mountains, Alec didn't like Florida.

It was too flat, too warm, and too damn bright. Day after day, the sun blazed unrelentingly down from the wide endless sky, tanning locals to the color and texture of beef jerky while exposing the sad seediness lurking just beneath the pastel Art Deco seaside landscape.

Five days ago, a tropical storm blew in from the Caribbean, colliding with a cold front swooping down from Tennessee's Great Smoky mountains.

Clouds gathered on that first day, a few at a time—

like crows flocking on a telephone wire—just as blue-haired snowbirds were settling poolside for their afternoon canasta games and gossip sessions.

As the afternoon sky grew darker, worried mothers called their children indoors. Golfers in checked pants and cleated shoes hurried off rolling greens, knowing that standing out on a golf course while holding a metal club could turn a man into a human lightning rod.

On the second day, the steely Atlantic surf swelled; seabirds were reported to have been seen flying backward and migrating whales began riding the breakers inland to beach themselves on the glistening pearly sand.

Then the storm stalled, closing down over the south coast like a heavy iron manhole cover. Nerves jangled, tempers flared, yet still, despite the thickening mud at Gulfstream Park racetrack, Thoroughbreds pounded the turf, as they'd been doing each winter for more than sixty years.

As he walked across the paddock, Alec frowned at the turf, which, after four days of nonstop rain, was a quagmire.

"We're moving the Orchid Handicap to the main track," the race steward informed him when he checked in.

The filly Alec had trained to run in today's prestigious Orchid Handicap hated racing in mud. The fact that the track appeared nearly as bad as the turf did little to ease Alec's mind as he entered the shedrow. Usually the rich, familiar aromas of hay and horse would lift his spirits. Not today.

Lady Justice had left hay in the net from the night before, a sign she was nervous. The last time she'd run in mud, she'd barely avoided what could have been a fatal accident when a horse stumbled in front of her in the stretch.

Since fear served as a prime emotion in prey animals, motivating them to flee from predators, Alec was concerned that the incident had been programmed in the filly's memory, encouraging her to relate today's rain with that other near disaster. Rather than breeze her as he would have done on any other race day, he settled for having her walked around the shedrow. Her nerves were palpable, sparking in the thick moist air like downed electrical wires.

Making his decision, he headed over to the sleek orchid and white-painted grandstand clubhouse complex, finding the filly's owner in the Turf Club.

"Surely you're not suggesting we scratch?" Douglas Wellesley shot Alec a sharp look over the salted crystal rim of his Bloody Mary glass.

A senior partner in a silk-stocking New York law firm whose grandfather had once been elected governor of Connecticut, Wellesley had entered the horse business with the same intent with which he entered a courtroom: to win. That need, which went all the way to the bone, was something Alec and the attorney shared. The difference was that while Alec was driven to win, he wasn't willing to achieve victory at any cost.

Knowing Wellesley wouldn't appreciate the premonition prickling at the back of his neck, Alec stuck to facts. "She seems to be favoring her right hoof."

She'd suffered a hoof bruise two weeks ago. From what Alec had been able to tell, she was fully recovered, but if there was an outside chance she wasn't back to one hundred percent, he damn well didn't want to race her. Racetracks were unpredictable at best; running a horse that was less than sound was definitely stacking the odds against you.

"Of course you called the track vet."

"Of course." Calling for a consult had been the racing equivalent of a Hail Mary pass.

"So? What did he say?"

"*She* couldn't find any outward sign of injury, but—"

"Then we're not scratching."

"Lady Justice hates mud in her face."

"Instruct the jockey to have her break out in front and stay there. Then she won't have to deal with mud."

The filly had never been a horse to break for a lead and hold it. She liked to bide her time, watching for an opening, then slipping through the crowded pack at just the right moment.

"This horse is talented. She has the best gift for spotting an opening than any I've ever worked with. On the right day and the right track, she can run with the best of them. And win. But her kick is only good for an eighth of a mile. There's no way she can hold a lead for a grueling twelve furlongs. Asking her to do it in mud is flat out impossible."

"I didn't hire you to make excuses." The older man's voice turned as hard as his marble gray eyes. "I hired you to win races."

"I believe I've done that." Alec left unsaid the little fact that under his training, Lady Justice had gone undefeated as a two-year-old, winning the Eclipse award as America's top juvenile filly.

"The Orchid Handicap is the most prestigious distaff race in the Florida racing season. I intend to be standing in the winner's circle when it's over."

He'd certainly dressed for the occasion, trading in his usual pinstriped suit for charcoal slacks, a custom-tailored brushed wool blazer and silk Hermès tie. Alec gave the attorney reluctant points for somehow managing to still appear patrician in the orchid purple jacket.

"You're being extremely well paid to stick to the original battle plan: today's Orchid, the Burbonette Breeders Cup at Turfway, the Apple Blossom at Oaklawn, finishing up with the Kentucky Oaks. Then the horse can rest on her laurels all she wants when I set her to breeding champions."

Deciding that this wasn't the time to resume the argument that the filly loved racing too much to be turned into a broodmare at a mere three-years-old, Alec stared at Wellesley, who stared back. Finally, feeling as if he were eight-years-old again, facing down some bully on the playground who'd called his father a drunk, he broke the stare and looked out the window to the sloshy track.

Alec knew how addictive the exhilaration of watching your horse come in under the wire first could be. To some, winning became like a drug in the blood; they couldn't get enough of it. He'd long ago accepted that his own reasons for needing to win were more complex.

"There'll be other days. Other races."

"I don't give a flying fuck about other races. At this moment, I'm only concerned with the Orchid Stakes."

"This isn't some New York City courtroom where you can manipulate the jury with legal sleight of hand and mental gymnastics. You've got to play the cards you've been dealt, and if you insist on running that horse in this weather, I'll quit."

It was not a bluff. Alec refused to take into consideration the exclusivity agreement he'd signed with Wellesley last year, which resulted in the only horses currently boarding in his training stables belonging to this man. Even as he admitted to himself that there wasn't any real reason to keep the filly off the track, and that throwing away what most trainers would consider a dream job working for a man with seemingly bottomless pockets might be considered reckless, Alec couldn't force Lady Justice to run a race that wasn't hers.

Douglas Wellesley's mouth thinned. "The horse runs as planned."

"Guess I'm out of here, then." Alec turned and strolled out of the restaurant.

He might not be officially Lady Justice's trainer, but that didn't stop him from hanging around long enough to watch the outcome of Wellesley's arrogance.

Despite the miserable weather, the mood at Gulfstream Park remained unrelentingly upbeat. Umbrellas popped up all over the infield grass like mushrooms, conversation in the stands buzzed like a swarm of hornets as tips were traded, odds debated. At the betting windows, business was so fast and furious horseplayers found it difficult to hear over the sound of money being exchanged.

Rumors of the race being called due to rain swelled from shedrow to the clubhouse to the grandstand. Ten minutes before post time, the downpour lessened to a drizzle, causing the stewards to gather and confer over printouts of satellite weather photos.

A ten-minute delay was called. Then another. Then, finally, as the crowd who'd come here today expecting pageantry began to grow impatient, the signal was sent to the saddling paddock that the race would take place.

A voice boomed over the loudspeaker, announcing the beginning of the post parade. Despite his misgivings, the sight of the magnificent four-legged athletes—all gleaming muscle and lithe grace—parading by on their matchstick legs, the colorful silks worn by their jockeys brightening the gloomy day like a rainbow, sent a surge of pure adrenaline through Alec's bloodstream. The familiar thrill was quickly replaced by an ominous dread as Lady Justice passed by the grandstand.

It was obvious that the filly didn't want to be here. Rather than her usual joyful prancing, she was plodding through the motions like a workhorse weary of the plow, head down, jet black tail hanging limp, nearly trailing in the mud. She was equally reluctant during her warm-up gallop around the track.

And then it got worse.

Displaying a temperament Alec had never witnessed, she refused to enter the starting gate. They tried putting a hood on her, which only made her more anxious.

Alec rubbed the back of his neck, which felt as prickly as if he'd walked through a spider web as he watched the track officials coax, cajole, then split up, some in back pushing, others in front pulling, literally wrestling the filly into the starting gate. They quickly slammed the back gate behind her. Having seen other Thoroughbreds become violent in such situations, Alec held his breath, then let it out on a long slow *whoosh* as she appeared to have accepted her fate.

But still he watched.

Waited.

Worried.

The gates sprang open. "They're off!"

Hooves pounded, mud flew, the bright hues of the silks blurred in the mist. Alec cursed when Lady Justice missed the break. The rest of the horses, which had broken in a tight pack, began to spread out. Lady Justice remained dead last.

"Come on, sweetheart," Alec murmured encouragingly over the roar of the crowd. "You can do it. Just run your race and you'll be fine."

Johnny Devaroux, the veteran jockey from Louisiana's bayou country Alec had hired to ride the filly today, knew her well enough to let her relax, keep her off the pace and allow her to close at her own speed.

She was at the rail, boxed in by three horses in front of her and another on her outside, making Alec wonder how the hell she'd be able to get through the traffic when it did come time to make her move.

Then, as she made the far turn, Johnny found a sliver of daylight. Eager to escape the mud flying in her face, the filly exploded through it.

Her closing kick had the crowd on its feet as she accelerated dramatically, pounding her way from the back of the pack, streaking past the other horses, going from last to second place in record time. Her long legs lifted, stretched, pounded. Her head was thrust forward; her tail streamed out behind her like a jet flag as she dueled with the leader, neck and neck.

It was the most remarkable comeback Alec had ever witnessed. Her magnificent heart and the desire to win were proving stronger than her hatred of mud.

They were nose to nose.

She forged ahead and was flying down the final stretch when a single ray of sunshine streamed through a break in the bruise-colored clouds, casting a shadow from the timekeeper's box atop the stands.

Startled, the filly did what came naturally: she tried to jump it, her speed causing her to land on her foreleg in a way nature had never intended. There was a massive gasp from the crowd as she went crashing down. Screams as she somersaulted into the rails. Weeping when she struggled gamely to her feet, the foreleg that had snapped just above the fetlock swinging hideously, uselessly.

Alec jumped the rail and was running toward the

horse when the track crew leapt into action. An outrider managed to immobilize the stricken filly while high screens were erected around her. The waiting ambulance raced toward the scene.

When Alec reached the horse, she whinnied weakly.

"I know, baby." He stroked the velvety dark face of this horse he'd begun training shortly after her first birthday. "You never should have been out there." His voice cracked. A ball of crimson mist rolled toward him from the infield. He managed to ignore it. For now. "But you've never run a stronger race." He didn't need to be a vet to know that it was also her last.

She whinnied again, softly, raggedly, as if pleased by his approval.

The ambulance arrived. The veterinarian emerged, face grim, bag in hand.

Alec pinched the bridge of his nose to stem the hot moisture threatening at the back of his eyes as he knelt beside the filly who possessed worlds more heart than its wealthy Yankee owner ever would.

It did not take long. Lady Justice breathed a short, shuddering sigh. A filmy mist rose from her body and drifted off over the track like a freed spirit. After they'd loaded her into the ambulance, Alec gave the filly one last caress. Then, without a word, headed to the Turf Club.

He found the attorney in the bar, staring at the television screen. The camera had moved back to a long shot, panning the obviously stunned crowd that was watching the catastrophe unfold with the same ghoulish compulsion that made drivers slow down to gawk at accidents.

"I suppose you're here to gloat." Wellesley tossed back a martini and signaled to the bartender for another. "To rub in how, by not scratching the horse, I'm out a goddamn fortune."

Myriad responses reverberated in Alec's mind, but not one of them could do justice to the powerful emotions battering at him. Guilt, as bitter as bile, backed up in his throat. His hands balled tightly; disjointed, painful memories flashed like strobe lights; the red mist returned, shimmering in front of his eyes.

The collision of fist against bone reverberated all the way up his arm to his shoulder. Alec felt as if he'd just hit a brick wall. But, sweet Jesus, the unmistakable sound of that patrician glass jaw breaking was satisfying!

Without a word, Douglas Wellesley crashed backward off the stool and landed in a graceless heap on the floor.

Ignoring the excited buzz of conversation, Alec left the clubhouse.

He did not look back.

2

Castlelough, Ireland

THE DAY WAS COMING to an end. The world had slowed, then seemed to pause, as Kate O'Sullivan strolled on the sea foam-kissed beach with her children. The brisk air was tinged with the scent of salt and sea and romantic, faraway places. In the distance, the Aran Islands gleamed with a golden light and beyond them, far over the horizon and across the Atlantic, was America.

Although her day had been a vexsome one, Kate had no trouble summoning up a smile as she watched her four-year-old daughter, Brigid, dancing across the sand, whirling and spinning to music only she could hear over the sigh of the sea. She could have been a wee faerie sprite, performing a good-bye dance to the day.

The sun slid silently into the great wide sea like a molten copper coin, the shimmering light surrounding them turning Brigid's bright red curls to flame. Kate took a moment to sing her own brief, mental song of farewell to the sun, thanking it for having graced her day, even as troublesome as it had been.

"How did your meeting go?" her eight-year-old son, Jamie, asked.

"Not as well as I'd hoped." Kate sighed at the memory.

He looked up at her, concern showing on his small, freckled face. "The government is still about building the road?"

Wealth brought in by Eurodollars had Ireland on a building spree. Highways were being constructed all over the country, new red lines appearing on maps that hadn't changed for decades, going every which way and that. With a speed that was decidedly un-Irish, stone walls were being knocked down to widen country lanes, hedges trimmed back, land taken from farms that had been in families for generations, all in the name of progress.

Even though she knew that easier access to the more profitable commerce centers of Cork and Dublin could help unemployment here in the rural west, Kate had nonetheless been saddened by the changes. But she'd mostly held her tongue. Until the highway planning commission had made one fatal mistake.

"It appears they believe they'll be building it."

"Did you explain how if they cut down the tree, the faeries will get angry at losing their home and curse the road, and make those who drive on it crash?"

"I did, yes. And told them more, as well."

"And they didn't listen?"

"Every last one of them let me make our case." *The faeries' case*, she thought with a frown as she dragged her hand through long black hair, harkening back to an ancestor who'd been part of an unsuccessful attempt of the Spanish Armada to land on Irish shores. "And then, when I was finished, didn't they all laugh?"

"That's because they don't understand."

She smiled at his earnest tone. "They don't want to understand, because they fear it's old-fashioned to believe in such things."

"But you'll make them believe, won't you, Ma?"

"I certainly intend to do my best."

There'd been a time when she wouldn't have considered standing up and speaking before the county council. A time when she dare not even go into town for fear of the gossips *tsk-tsk*ing about the new bruise from her husband's hand on her cheek. Then there were always those few outwardly pious souls who'd eye her with open suspicion, obviously fearful that the town's most infamous pagan might suddenly turn into a screeching banshee and put the evil eye on them.

"Brigid," she called out to the child, who was getting too close to the incoming tide for comfort. While her marriage had been a drastic mistake, her children were Kate's treasure, more precious to her than emeralds or gold. "Come here, darling. It's nearly time for supper."

They were walking back along the cliff, near the pre-Christian circle of stones where her ancient druid ancestors had once gathered to practice their magic, when Kate was buffeted by a strong gust of wind.

She glanced back toward the sea and, for an instant, was startled by the dazzling, heart-stopping sight of the great sea god Manannán mac Lir galloping his steed Splendid Mane over the copper-hued waves.

The vision was so clear she could actually see the setting sun flashing off the god's magic mail and breastplate. The two magic jewels in his helmet momentarily blinded her, forcing her to shield her gaze with her hand.

"Ma?" Kate could just barely hear her son's worried voice over the thunder of Splendid Mane's hoofbeats and the fearsome pounding of stormy waves against the ancient cliffs. "What's wrong?"

She blinked to clear her mind's eye of the unsettling scene. "Not a thing, darling. I just thought I saw some seals out in the water."

"Could they have been selkies, do you think?"

" 'Tis always possible." Still a bit unnerved, she managed a faint smile at his mention of the mythical seal women. "Which means we'd best be hurrying before they'd be luring my handsome son to his doom beneath the sea."

"You don't have to worry," he assured her as they continued back down the narrow winding path toward the house she'd been born in. The house her father and grandfather and generations of Fitzpatricks before them had grown up in. "I won't ever be leaving you."

Kate was on the verge of reminding Jamie that as much as she was in no hurry to lose her son, the day would come when he'd marry and begin his own family, when she was distracted by an uneasiness in the breezy, salt-tinged air, so pungent she could taste it.

She glanced up at the sky and saw the flock of geese returning home from the south, later than usual, flying in a broken pattern that was an omen of discord. As they entered the slate-roofed farmhouse by the kitchen door, another gust suddenly blew through her, icy and foreboding.

The winds of change, Kate thought. Then shivered.

Two months after the tragedy at Gulfstream Park, Alec was working in the small private family cemetery, where, surrounded by a short wrought-iron fence, gray stones chronicling two centuries of the American branch of the MacKenna family tree gathered together in neat lines.

The oldest grave belonged to Angus, the family patriarch. A canny Scot from the Highlands with a fondness for horseflesh and an unmatched talent for making sour mash whiskey, Angus had arrived in America in the mid-seventeen-hundreds. Family lore had him one step ahead of the law, who had a warrant for his arrest. The way Alec had heard the story, Angus had continued to insist to his dying day that the Thoroughbred he'd sold to an Edinburgh physician wasn't really stolen at all, but merely liberated from a wealthy English viscount who'd sorely mistreated the poor animal.

He'd been assigned to the cavalry corps during the American Revolutionary War. When the war ended, he used his mustering-out pay to buy two mares and a stallion, then wandered down to the green hills of southeastern Kentucky, which reminded him of his beloved Highlands, where he supplemented his fledgling horse business by selling whiskey made from the secret MacKenna family recipe he'd brought with him from Inverness.

The currently empty barns on the property attested to later generations having inherited Angus's appreciation of horseflesh. For a time it appeared as if Alec's father was going to turn out to be the most successful trainer in the family. But a fondness for gambling, along with an addiction to the family recipe, proved his undoing. Alec had been fifteen years old when his father's infamy ruined the MacKenna name in racing circles and cost a brilliant stallion his life.

Fortissimo, trained by John MacKenna, should have won the Derby that year. In a business rife with stories of the million-dollar colt that couldn't run and the fifty-thousand-dollar one that could, the chestnut stallion was a five-thousand-dollar miracle. Along with the ability to run faster and farther than any horse on the track, he had the mental toughness needed to endure the pressure of competition and the soundness required to stand up to the physical rigors of racing.

On top of all that, he possessed the one aspect that couldn't be bred for, the single thing that welded all those other necessary attributes together into a champion: Fortissimo had class. With a capital C.

It was class that had him winning even when he drew the worst gate position; class that kept him running in any weather on any track; class that enabled him to overcome any adversity fate threw his way and that same class that prevented him from ever making a mistake in a race.

He could have easily been the greatest horse of all time. Had John MacKenna not fallen deeply in debt to a Las Vegas bookmaker. When offered the choice of having his own legs broken, or Fortissimo's, he'd condemned the horse in less time than it took to roll a pair of dice.

In the end, he'd chosen an alternate method to control the final outcome of the race: shortly before post time, he administered a massive injection of amphetamines into the Thoroughbred's bloodstream, causing the stallion to literally run his huge heart out before he could cross the wire.

Inverness Farms had survived a civil war, two world wars, and numerous recessions. There had, of course, been those who'd moved away from the mountain, as Alec himself had done in his younger years. After his father's death, he'd returned home and worked like a demon to pay off John MacKenna's creditors—both legitimate and those shadowy, mob-connected individuals—and keep the land in the family. During his years away from Kentucky, the desire to establish his own stables had served as a lodestone, keeping him working steadily toward his lifelong goal.

These recent years, all his profit had gone into up-grading the barns and creating a state-of-the-art train-ing facility. His plan was to work with other owners' horses for another year or two, while putting aside his share of earnings to buy the best horses he could af-ford, sired by stallions who'd already proven them-selves to be winners. Then he could begin training his own Thoroughbreds.

The day after the Orchid Handicap, a trailer had ar-rived at Inverness Farms to take Douglas Wellesley's remaining horses to another training facility in New York state. Alec had expected that. It was when he started making calls to owners who'd tried to hire him in the past that he discovered that knocking the Yankee attorney off that barstool had sealed his fate. The horse business was mercurial enough; owners preferred trainers they didn't have to worry about slugging them. Especially when the trainer in question came from questionable stock himself. Because of the unprece-dented financial outlay these past years, Alec's bank ac-count was running low; his plan was running on fumes. If he didn't latch onto another training job soon, he might lose the land to taxes. Which would, in turn, cause the speculators who'd already tried to buy the land to swoop down like vultures and turn the moun-tain into another damn vacation condo development.

"And wouldn't that set old Angus spinning in his grave?" he muttered as thunder rumbled over the mountain.

Kudzu was threatening to devour the dour stone figure guarding the MacKenna patriarch's grave. The angel had been missing a wing for as long as Alec could remember; supposedly it had been knocked off by a huge oak limb during a winter ice storm back in 1873.

He'd get another horse, Alec vowed as he attacked the ravenous vine with a vengeance. It had taken Alec a decade, but he hadn't lost his legacy after his father's arrest. He was damned if he was going to lose it now.

"Pete sent me out here to get you," a voice behind him offered grumpily.

Alec rocked back on his heels and looked up at his fifteen-year-old going-on-thirty stepdaughter standing beneath an umbrella imprinted with Van Gogh's sunflowers, finding it difficult to reconcile this petulant teenager with that little girl who'd giggled when he'd lifted her onto the back of the patient old mare he'd bought for her fourth birthday.

Her hair, which had once fallen to her waist in a shimmering platinum slide, had been cut short and dyed a fluorescent magenta shade never seen in nature. It was standing up in nail-like spikes that looked hard enough for some mystic Swami to lie down on.

More spikes on what looked suspiciously like a dog collar encircled her long, slender neck. A glittery sweep of metallic eyeshadow appeared to have been laid on with a trowel and beneath her ankle-length black wool coat she was wearing a skin-tight scarlet sweater that stopped just short of her pierced navel and, despite the winter weather, red leather shorts that rode low on her slender hips and looked as if they'd been applied with a paint sprayer.

Alec recalled, with vivid clarity, the day Tammy Sue Burdell had sauntered into his second-year Spanish classroom wearing a pair of hot pants made out of some buttery soft material that resembled the chammy he used to dry the pickup truck he'd bought used from Tammy Sue's daddy, Dan-the-Man Burdell, who'd played offense linebacker for the University of Tennessee and owned the only Ford dealership in this remote corner of the mountains.

The shorts had hugged Tammy's crotch and revealed a tantalizing view of the smooth ivory cheeks of her young firm ass. As she'd walked past Alec to take her place across the aisle and two seats ahead of him, the blood had shot straight from his head to his groin. Since it was impossible to conjugate Spanish verbs when you were suddenly stuck with grits for brains, Alec failed that day's midterm exam. He hated the idea of any pimply-faced kid getting a boner looking at Zoe.

"What's up?"

Seeming determined to torture him by deliberately taking her own sweet time, Zoe sighed and held her hands out in front of her to examine impossibly long artificial fingernails lacquered in copper glitter.

When he'd first learned that his ex-wife had died, leaving her daughter without any blood relatives to take her in, Alec had immediately flown to Switzerland, foolishly believing Zoe would be glad to see him. But it turned out that the kid hadn't exactly shared his fond memories of the six years she'd lived at the farm. Or if she did, scared and angry as she was, she'd refused to admit it.

Still, he'd been optimistic. While the little he knew about teenagers could fit on the head of a pin and still leave room for a thousand dancing angels, he earned a very good living coaxing two-thousand pound, highstrung Thoroughbreds into doing what he wanted; how hard could it be to keep a one-hundred and ten-pound teenager in line?

Damn hard, he'd discovered during the past six months she'd been living on the mountain. A silver cross had joined the other two earrings adorning her left earlobe. Perhaps she was thinking of taking up religion. At this point, Alec wouldn't object to Zoe joining a convent. In fact, now that he thought about it, hadn't he heard rumors of a cloistered order hidden somewhere deep in the hills of North Carolina?

"You have a phone call," she announced. Her petulant tone suggested that she'd been interrupted from something far more important than fetching her stepfather, who obviously didn't have enough sense to come in out of the rain.

"Would you happen to know who's calling?" he asked with a patience he was a long way from feeling.

Another long sigh. More checking out of fingernails. Her shoulders lifted and dropped in a shrug that managed to be both dramatic and uncaring at the same time. It was a gesture only a teenager was truly capable of carrying off.

"Pete said it was some lady you used to work for in Lexington."

Pete Campbell was more than just a business partner. He was more of a father than Alec's own had ever been while alive. "Winnie Tarlington?"

Another shrug.

"Okay." Curiosity spiked. "I'll be right in."

"I suppose she wants you to go train another stupid racehorse for her?"

Alec caught the hint of worry edging her churlish voice. Looking at Zoe now, hunkered beneath the cheery umbrella that was such a contrast to whatever dark inner demons she'd been fighting, he saw not the sullen, body-pierced teenager who could have starred in an MTV video, nor the angry would-be juvenile delinquent who'd gotten away last month with a stern warning after her first—and pray God, only—shoplifting charge.

What he viewed was a confused, abandoned, lonely

child whose young life had spun out of control when her mother had fallen off a yacht in the Mediterranean and drowned six months ago, proving that T. S. Eliot had been wrong about April being the cruelest month.

"Winnie's been out of the business the past couple years. But even if she does have a line on something, you don't have to worry about me taking off and leaving you."

"Like I care. I keep telling you, I can take care of myself."

Alec resisted, just barely, from pointing out that she'd been doing a pretty piss-poor job of that. He returned to the house and picked up the receiver Pete had left on the kitchen counter.

"Hey, Winnie. How are you doing?"

"Still kicking." The rain had the wires crackling a bit, but her voice sounded far younger than Alec knew her to be. "And, from what I hear, a great deal better than you."

Alec wasn't surprised that she knew of the change in his circumstances. The horse world was a closed, incestuous environment where everyone made a point of knowing everyone else's business.

"Not that the horrid Yankee didn't deserve getting knocked on his keister," she continued. "After what he did to that sweet filly. In fact, I would have given anything to have seen you break his jaw. . . . But I didn't call to gossip. I have a horse I want you to train."

"I thought you'd gotten out of the business."

"So I keep trying to tell myself. I swore, when I sold off the horses after Palmer passed on two years ago, that I was getting too old to ride that crazy roller coaster. Then I stumbled across a Thoroughbred that will make the world forget Go For Broke."

Go For Broke had been Alec's ticket to the big time,

the Thoroughbred's speed, stamina, and unrelenting heart coming together in a remarkable union that had made Alec the youngest Triple Crown-winning trainer in racing history. For a brief time, he'd been king of the world.

Unfortunately, that same year his wife had taken off with a sleazy European duke she'd met at one of the Derby parties. The stallion came up lame in his first race as a four-year-old, but was still living a peaceful, and Alec assumed, happy life at stud, adding his remarkable genetic makeup to future generations of champions.

"This horse is magic. I tell you, Alec, the stars smiled on me the day I claimed him for a song."

"You claimed him?"

"I know, I know. You don't usually find champions in claiming races. But no one picked him up in the Keeneland sale, so his owner decided to try that route. And am I glad he did, because this big horse is greased lightning in a bottle. Why don't you come by the farm tomorrow morning and get a look at him in action?" The excitement in her voice reminded Alec of that first time they'd stood side by side and watched the yearling Go For Broke run. "I'll be there."

3

As HE DROVE down from the mist-draped hills early the next morning, Alec tried to temper his enthusiasm.

Had it only been two short months ago when every sunrise offered new challenges, when his days were brimming over with opportunities for achievement beyond anything all but the most ambitious man could have imagined? And he'd admittedly been an ambitious man, determined to outrun his father's legacy. Unfortunately, those days seemed to belong to a different lifetime.

Yet, Alec asked himself, as he had for the past sixty days, given the same circumstances, would he have done anything different? He rubbed his knuckles, as if unconsciously recalling that satisfying punch.

Hell no.

The answer, as always, kept him from indulging in an unproductive pity party. He'd been down before. And each time he'd come crawling back up. Racing was a business of pinnacles and valleys. Having always considered safe another word for boring, Alec wouldn't have wanted it any other way.

As he approached the bluegrass country of Lexington—once referred to as the Athens of the West—his headlights cut through the predawn gloom, illuminating the lush landscape of paddocks, pastures and dry-laid rock fences. Even as Alec admired the bucolic scene, he was grateful Angus had chosen the untamed hill country to make his home. There was something about those ancient mountains that stirred Alec's soul every bit as much as the sight of one of his Thoroughbreds crossing the finish line in first place.

The sun was rising in a pale-pink silver light as he recognized the black Kentucky oak plank fence bordering the pastures of Tarlington Farms. He stopped at the tall gate—with its wrought-iron curlicues and stylized TF—and announced himself on the intercom. Buzzed through without hesitation, he continued on, the pea gravel of the long winding driveway crunching beneath his tires.

Winifred Tarlington was wealthy enough to still be sleeping amidst silk sheets in one of the ten bedrooms of her restored white-columned antebellum mansion. But Alec knew her well enough not to look for her at the house. He climbed out of the truck and headed down a lane canopied by stately old oaks toward the shedrow. It was a walk he could have made blindfolded.

"Well now, you don't look nearly as bad as I've been hearing." Winnie approached, as reed slender as a jockey. Indeed, in the pearly dawn light she could have been mistaken for a young jockey, rather than the wealthy, ninety-year-old woman Alec knew her to be.

"Let me guess. Word is I've pretty much gone back to my roots and turned into a hillbilly redneck right out of *Deliverance*."

"That's pretty much it." She looked up at him, her eyes bright and touched with both concern and humor. "You don't look like you've been drinking."

"It was my daddy who was the drunk."

"And wasn't that a crying shame. With all his God-given talent and potential?" She sighed and shook her head. "Well, there's no point in crying over spilt milk. Because speaking of potential, I want to introduce you to my new baby boy who's going to make the world forget Secretariat. Maybe even Go For Broke."

Her green eyes sparkled with enthusiasm and intelligence. Since the woman definitely had a mind of her own—as did he—their time together hadn't always been easy. But it had been profitable for both of them. And enjoyable.

Legends Lake was still in his stall, already saddled and polishing off his breakfast. He nickered softly at Winnie, who told him how beautiful he was and rubbed his broad nose with a blue-veined hand while Alec's heart sank.

The only thing this horse had in common with Secretariat was his gleaming dark-red color. A true champion was lean, well-muscled, approximately sixteen hands high, with a strong, straight neck, a well-balanced V-shaped chest and a confident demeanor. Like Secretariat. Go For Broke. The unfortunate Fortissimo.

Legends Lake, on the other hand, was too tall: nearly seventeen hands, with lean flesh stretched over long, angular muscles. If he'd been a man rather than a horse, he would have been Ichabod Crane from *The Legend of Sleepy Hollow*.

"Good-looking horse," Alec said blandly, fighting back his disappointment.

"Liar. He's admittedly got more conformation faults than Carters has liver pills. But aren't you the one who's always said that you don't go to a stakes paddock to study textbook conformation?"

"Point taken." Alec gave the horse a slower, more judicial appraisal.

"He's got a gorgeous heart," Winnie offered into the silence.

"His feet definitely aren't textbook." One turned out, the other in.

"They're not that bad. At least they're pointed in the same direction, which is what's important." She opened up the stall door, drew the horse out. "Why don't you withhold judgment until you watch him walk?"

Despite his less than perfect feet, the Thoroughbred had a good strong stride. Of course that didn't mean he could run worth a lick. Alec continued his examination, beginning with the hooves, working up the pastern, the ankle, the cannon bone, and onward up the leg. Despite gawky first appearances, the horse's balance, symmetry, and alignment were all within acceptable bounds.

"His chest is awfully narrow."

"That's better than too wide." True enough. A too-wide chest tended to throw a horse's balance off.

"He's got a nice enough neck," Alec allowed.

When he stroked that long thin neck, Legends Lake lowered his head, inviting Alec to scratch his forehead, which he did.

"Granted, his head isn't real pretty," Winnie admitted.

"People get too hung up about that." He skimmed a hand down the front of the long, homely face, satisfied that the horse's broad nostrils would allow plenty of air into his lungs when he ran. "Always falling for the big-eyed, pretty face." The same way men tended to do with women.

Legends Lake might not have the huge, thick-lashed show eyes that looked good on television, but they were intelligent and calm, without any of the white showing that might suggest he'd be flighty.

"He's got champion breeding," Winnie assured him.

As she rattled off an impressive bloodline, a faint voice of reason in the back of Alec's mind pointed out that potential champions didn't end up in claiming races. They were pampered, syndicated, only run in the most prestigious races, then retired to stud farms where they continued to earn their investors big profits.

"That's royal blood all right. But is he sound?" Even the greatest bloodline couldn't always prevent a horse from ending up with a weak immune system, which could prove deadly, given all the viruses running rampant around racetracks.

"I have his vet records," Winnie answered. "He's never been sick a day in his life."

"So, what were you doing in a claiming race anyway, big boy?"

Alec skimmed his hands along the horse's bony body, stroking, checking for hidden flaws. All the time, Legends Lake continued to munch from a block of fresh green alfalfa hay while watching the newcomer with interest.

"How do you run on mud?"

The horse snorted. His ears pricked up even as he chewed. He was obviously listening intently now.

"Doesn't bother him in the least." Winnie reached into a pocket of her corduroy barn jacket and pulled out a quarter of apple, which the horse's huge yellow teeth delicately plucked from her outstretched palm. "Which, I suppose, is to be expected since he was born and bred in Ireland. Wet-weather racing runs in his veins." Winnie called over a young woman who'd moved in to clean Legends Lake's stall as soon as he'd been taken from it. "This is Julie. She'll be riding him today."

Alec and Julie exchanged hellos, then she led Legends Lake through the shedrow. He walked with confidence, the unnaturally long stride revealing enjoyment at the opportunity to stretch his lanky muscles.

"This doesn't exactly look as if you've retired," Alec said as he viewed the exercise riders breezing the horses around the oval dirt track.

Thoroughbreds were trotting in one direction, cantering in another. Early morning steam rose from their backs; fog curled like white satin ribbons around their fetlocks.

"Since I already had the setup, it made sense to go ahead and board a few horses. Gives the Horse Center down the road a bit of competition and keeps us all on our toes."

In the center of the practice track, a pair of mallards floated on a small pond. In a few months the winterbare bushes would be a riot of blooming watermelon pink azaleas and snowy rhododendron. The show of colors echoed that of the Tarlington silks that Winnie had chosen when she'd first come here as a young bride, whose only prior experience with horses had been reading *Black Beauty* as a girl.

She'd learned the business well. But more importantly, she honesty loved and respected the horses that had made up a stable renowned for winners.

Even after she climbed up on the bottom rail, the top of her head didn't come up to Alec's shoulder. It seemed she'd shrunk a bit since he'd last seen her. But she definitely hadn't lost any of her spunk.

"This is Dan Jordan." She introduced him to a young man in his early twenties, who was already at the rail, watching the morning exercise, stopwatch in hand. "He's been helping me out some until I could get you on board."

"I haven't agreed to train the horse yet," Alec said mildly. The truth was that two months ago he wouldn't even be considering taking on such a tall, lanky bag of bones. Which just went to show, he considered grimly, how far he'd fallen.

The handsome young face immediately lit up like a beacon in the gray gloom. "It's an honor to meet you, Mr. MacKenna." His earnest, soft drawl brought to mind South Carolina's pine-scented red clay lanes and hoof-churned, rose-beige sand tracks. "I've been in racing since I turned twelve and started as a hot walker at Dogwood Stables, where my daddy was barn foreman. But it's not often that I get to meet a legend in person."

The words, which were obviously meant as a compliment, had Alec feeling older than the mud the horses were currently plodding through.

"Secretariat was a legend. Citation, Exterminator, Man O' War, and Go For Broke were legends. I'm merely an unemployed trainer."

"Not for long," Winnie offered. "That damn Yankee lawyer may think he's in tall cotton after temporarily driving you out of the business, but Legends Lake is your ticket back to the big time. And think how grand you'll feel when this horse beats the socks off Litigator in the Derby."

Litigator had been Lady Justice's stablemate. A huge, strong bay Thoroughbred with an iron constitution, he was being touted as the favorite to win this year's Kentucky Derby. It was a Derby victory Alec had, just sixty short days ago, planned to be a part of.

"Did you set things up as I instructed?" she asked Dan.

"Yes, ma'am, Miz Tarlington. Everyone's just waiting for you and Mr. MacKenna."

"Why don't you drop the Mr. MacKenna?" Alec was feeling older by the moment.

"Geez, that'd be a real honor, Mr. uh, Alec."

Alec managed, just barely, not to roll his eyes. He turned his attention back to the track, realizing that the horses were being led into a portable starting gate.

"You're going to race them?" This definitely was not a typical morning breezing.

"We've arranged a special event in your honor."

Legends Lake was not showy; he did not prance or toss his head as Go For Broke had always done. He just calmly walked into the gate, not so much as sidestepping when the back gate was shut behind him. Then he stood patiently, waiting for the more skittish horses to be led into place. His eyes were nearly at half-mast, making him look as if he were about to fall asleep.

Terrific. If this horse really did represent his only opportunity back into racing, Alec was in deep, deep trouble.

Finally the bell rang, the automatic gate sprung open, and they were off.

Legends Lake burst from the gate like a giant arrow released from a greased bow. Reluctantly impressed, Alec reminded himself that a lot of horses broke fast, only to fall behind by the backstretch.

But this didn't prove the case with Winnie's new favorite. He ran like the wind, long lean muscles rippling. When he was in motion, relaxed, obviously enjoying himself, ears pricked forward, hooves pounding in perfect rhythm, throwing mud up behind him, it was almost possible to forget how ugly he was.

Two other horses moved forward, one on the outside, the other on the inside, trying to cut Legends

Lake off, but it was as if they didn't exist. He could have been all alone, streaking across open pastures, or, Alec considered, considering his birthplace, the rolling green fields of Ireland.

Alec didn't need Dan calling the time; the stopwatch he carried in his head told him that the horse was running a remarkable pace for mud.

As the Thoroughbred came down the stretch, giving no sign of fading, a gray gelding managed to come up on his outside. Putting on a burst of speed, Legends Lake went from turbo-drive to warp speed. His lanky legs stretched even longer, rising and falling like powerful pistons.

"I wouldn't have believed it if I hadn't seen it for myself," Alec said to Winnie, who, oddly, despite the colt's considerable lead, appeared to be holding her breath. "You're right. You've definitely caught yourself lightning in a bottle."

Alec knew trainers who'd run over their grandmothers to have the opportunity to work with this ungainly appearing, three-year-old phenomenon.

That's when it happened.

Legends Lake blew his cork. With no motivation that Alec could see, he suddenly reared, threw back his head and wildly pawed at the air. Julie jumped off his back as deftly as a gymnast dismounting from the vault and managed to roll out of the way just before the Thoroughbred began streaking toward the four-railed infield fence.

Seeming unsurprised by this behavior, the riders atop the other horses steered their mounts away from what could have proven a disaster.

Alec drew in a harsh breath and watched, unbelievingly, as the horse cleared the fence with a good six inches to spare, then, chased by whatever inner demons haunted him, streaked across the infield, flying over pond and bushes before finally coming to a halt. If he'd had brakes, they would have squealed in protest at such a sudden stop.

He spun and faced them, brown eyes huge and showing white, his wide nostrils flared.

Mystified, Alec turned toward Winnie. "What the hell just happened?"

"I guess I forgot to mention that he also jumps fences."

4

UNABLE TO RESIST an animal in obvious distress, Alec climbed over the fence and slowly approached the horse. Legends Lake was shaking so hard Alec feared he might actually fall over. His ears were pinned back and the whites of his eyes were visible as he snorted through flared nostrils. His tail was kinked, his muscles rigid.

From the beginning of creation, animalistic instincts had been geared toward either fight or flight. The horse, having learned in the early dawn of its existence that flight beat fight, ran, not because man had trained it to, but because it was its nature.

At this moment, as he approached Legends Lake, it was more than obvious that every ancient escape instinct in the Thoroughbred's body was on full alert. His flanks shone with sweat, his muscles quivered.

Still, Alec didn't pause. He kept moving forward, talking quietly, soothingly, as he might to a small, frightened child.

"Hey, big boy . . . What's the problem?"

He held out his hand, allowing the horse to get a sniff of him, but was not surprised when, instead, Legends Lake shied away and went trotting across the infield where, in another month or so, the bluish-purple spring buds would give the Kentucky grass its famous blue-green cast.

"Didn't feel much like crossing that finish line today, huh?"

The colt spun back toward him, lowered his head. He snorted a warning, his breath coming out in white puffs, like dragon smoke.

The exercise track was located in the midst of yet more acres of fenced pasture. Sweeping the meadow with a judicial glance, Alec decided that if the horse did get it into his head to jump the far fence, he'd still be fairly safe. For now, at least. Unfortunately, there was also the danger of him breaking his leg or neck on a fence plank if he did bolt. Deciding that the prudent thing to do would be to let the Thoroughbred calm down a bit, Alec slowly, deliberately turned his back and returned to where Winnie was waiting.

"I take it he didn't behave like this during the race where you claimed him."

"I swear there wasn't a single sign of any trouble."

"Not even coming home? How did he load?"

"As easily as he entered the gate today. Walked right into the trailer as if he knew it meant he was going home. And the drive back here from Turfway didn't affect him in the least."

"So when did you discover he plays steeplechase?"

"When I decided to run him at Hialeah. I'd hired Dan to serve as interim trainer, and everything was fine on the way. And when we got down to Florida, he settled right in. Didn't he, Dan?" she asked the younger man.

"Yes, ma'am," he seconded her claim. "He ate well, breezed great—"

"And behaved exactly like the champion he was born to be," Winnie broke in. "He led straight out of the gate, just like today, and held it until he took it into his head to jump the fence at the far turn."

"Christ." Alec decided that the fact he hadn't heard of the chaos that must have ensued revealed exactly how far out of the mainstream he'd become in a mere two months' absence from the track. "Was anyone hurt?"

"Not a single horse or jockey, thank God, which is undoubtedly the only reason the race stewards let us get away with a severe warning. But they warned me that any repetition will result in him being banned from the track for life."

"That's only fair, Winnie."

"I know." Her gaze shifted across the infield to the obviously disturbed horse. "I'm afraid he didn't help his case any when it took another hour to get him quieted down enough to walk him back to his stall for the medical exam," she admitted. "Which, by the way, turned up negative for any foreign substances.

"We brought him home that same night and he settled right down as soon as he was in the trailer and didn't give us a moment's trouble. In fact, he travels better than any horse I've ever seen."

Alec was mystified. "Who was his trainer at the last place?"

"Bobby Jenkins."

"Well, hell." When the trainer had died of a heart attack while bidding on a Florida-bred stallion at January's Keeneland sale, few had mourned his passing.

"I know what you're thinking," Winnie said quickly. "Bobby didn't have the reputation for being the most soft-spoken trainer in the business—"

"That's putting it mildly. Look, I don't have any problem with people practicing their religion, even if it involves chanting mantras or sticking pins into voodoo dolls." Actually, Alec knew a very successful jockey from the Dominican Republic who was rumored to do exactly that. "But I have a helluva lot of problems with any guy who's chosen to train racehorses taking that biblical statement about men having dominion over animals too damn seriously."

"He did win the Belmont last year."

"A chimpanzee could have won the Belmont with Proud Dancer. That horse was bred for endurance, not speed. Which is one of the reasons why it hadn't so much as placed in a race before taking the Belmont."

"And hasn't since," she allowed.

"Well, at least now we know why he was in that claimer. Your horse has a major mental problem."

"Why do you think I called you?"

"I'm a horse trainer. Not a miracle worker."

"From what I hear, you're not exactly in a position to be choosy these days." When he didn't immediately answer, she placed a coaxing hand on his sleeve. "Legends Lake could become a real legend, Alec. A horse people talk about for generations. But he needs—no, let me rephrase that—he deserves the best."

"Dammit, Winifred!"

Legends Lake, hypersensitive to the smallest nuance, immediately cantered around the pond to the other side of the infield.

"You saw him," Winnie continued to press her case. "He runs like the wind. A horse like this doesn't deserve to end up as dog food."

"I've never known you to be an alarmist. We both know that doesn't have to be his fate. There are a lot of other options: dressage, jumping, even trail riding."

"Those opportunities aren't open for stallions. I'd be forced to geld him."

"True."

"Then I'd lose him as a stud horse."

"True again. But if gelding him opens up other opportunities—"

"No." Clearly primed for battle, she tossed up her chin and squared her shoulders. Winifred Tarlington was certainly not the easiest in a long line of owners Alec had worked for. She was, however, the one he most respected. "I'm not gelding Legends Lake. We just need to figure out how to get his head straight."

"We? You've had a good run, Winnie. A great run. Why would you want to take on a problem like this now, when you should be sitting back, enjoying the fruits of all that labor you and Palmer put into building this place?"

"Because, although I hate to admit it, I'm not as young as I used to be. In fact, I'm getting damn near ancient. Since Palmer and I were never blessed with any children or grandchildren to pass the business to, rather than let the government end up with all we built—" her wave encompassed the track, the barns, pastures and the magnificent house that always reminded Alec of Twelve Oaks—"I decided to divvy things up while I'm still kicking. . . .

"So, here's the deal I'm offering: If you can keep Legends Lake from being permanently banned from racing so he can win the Derby, I'll deed you fifty-percent ownership the minute we get to the winner's circle. And bequeath the remaining fifty percent to you in my will."

The offer was more than tempting. It was astounding, especially considering the fact that there weren't a helluva lot of other owners bidding for his services right now. There were, unfortunately, a great many catches. Beginning with ridding the horse of his screwy steeplechase tendencies.

Even if he could pull that off, winning the Kentucky Derby was never guaranteed, no matter how much natural ability a horse might possess.

"Hell, why stop at winning the roses? Why don't you shoot for the Triple Crown while you're at it?"

"Actually, now that you bring it up, I firmly believe that together, you and Legends Lake can pull off a Triple Crown sweep. But I didn't want you to feel overly pressured at this stage in the game."

Alec couldn't help laughing at her cockeyed optimism.

"Why don't you speak with Legends Lake's breeder," she suggested. "That way you can ask any questions you want about his breeding before making up your mind."

It was, Alec thought, a valid suggestion. "I assume you have his number?"

"Of course. And it happens to be a she. Kate O'Sullivan, from County Clare. Her maiden name was Fitzpatrick."

"She's Joseph Fitzpatrick's daughter?" The man was a legend, having been the best in the business during his lifetime.

"None other. She's gaining a reputation as a top breeder. Of course, I'll pay all expenses if you decide it's necessary to take Legends Lake back to Ireland."

"Not that I've agreed to take the job, but for the sake of argument, why would I want to risk making a problem horse worse with an overseas trip?"

"Because Kate O'Sullivan could be a huge help. She's supposed to have a near miraculous gift of communicating with horses."

From what he'd seen, Alec figured that if he were to take on the job, they'd need a miracle worker.

"You needn't worry about the trip making things

worse. I told you, the horse is the best traveler I've ever owned."

"You know I don't respond real well to outside pressure."

"Then don't give me your answer now," she said, appearing to know when to stop pushing her case. "Why don't you go on back to your mountain, sleep on it, and I'll call you in the morning. Meanwhile, would you be willing to help us get him back in the stall?"

It was not easy. It took nearly two hours for the horse to trust Alec enough to be led back to the shedrow, where once back in his stall, he turned as docile as a newborn lamb.

All during the drive home, Alec weighed the pros and cons of taking on Legends Lake's training, reminding himself how Winnie had believed in him when nearly everyone else thought that he'd end up no better than his alcoholic criminal father. Along with giving him the opportunity to become rich and famous, the Lexington horse owner had also provided the key that had allowed him to overcome—at least until the incident at the Gulfstream Turf Club—the snobbery and exclusiveness of the horse world. And for that he'd always owe her.

The dream came shortly after midnight, stealthily creeping into Kate's mind on padded cat feet. A horse—as white as the nearby cliffs—galloped across a misty meadow starred with fragrant white flowers.

The Celtic mother goddess, Etain, was riding bareback, her long fingers tangled in the silky mane, her hair streaming out behind her like a gilt flag, the muscles of her strong bare thighs pressed against the horse's flanks. The pounding rumble of the horse's hooves, as it raced over flower jeweled meadows and green and gold hillocks, drummed like a goatskin bodhrán.

The scene shifted, like tilting, changing facets of a kaleidoscope, and Kate became the one riding the magic steed, which was no longer white, but a deep chestnut that gleamed like red fire. As they raced the wind it was her fingers clutching the mane, her legs tightening against the horse's sides, her body becoming one with the magnificent stallion, her spirit becoming one with his powerful strength, grace and speed as they left the bounds of the earth.

Another tilt. Now there was a man seated behind her on the horse, his body pressed against her back, hard and strong, and so very male, as the three of them—man, woman and steed—moved as one, soaring over the glowing ball of fire that was the sun.

5

"So?" PETE CAMPBELL DEMANDED, looking up from the stew he was stirring.

"So what?" Alec pulled a beer from the refrigerator.

"What's the story of this horse Winnie latched onto?"

Alec popped the top on the can and took a long swallow. "He's a natural."

"Sounds like I hear a *but* in that statement."

"He's about as ugly as homemade sin." He grabbed a piece of freshly peeled carrot. "And off in the head, to boot."

"He jumped clean over the fence?" Pete asked after Alec had described the race. Brown potato peels had begun flying a little faster into the sink.

"At that moment, I think he could have jumped over the moon." Alec snatched another piece of carrot.

"You keep eating my vegetables and there won't be any left for supper." Pete moved them to the far side of the cutting board with the flat edge of the knife. "That explains what he was doing in a claimer."

"Yeah." Alec wasn't surprised Pete had hit on the crux of the matter so fast.

After all, the robust man with the formerly fiery

hair that had faded to the color of rust and freckled face wreathed in wrinkles from years spent outdoors, had undoubtedly forgotten more about training horses than the collective wisdom of all the other trainers currently working the circuit. High blood pressure and three heart bypasses had forced Pete Campbell into semiretirement, but Alec still valued both his friendship and his opinions, which he never bothered to sugar-coat.

"The horse is glitchy. But Winnie's right about him being born with the urge to run flat out in his blood." He reached for another piece of carrot, caught the look in Pete's eyes and took another swallow of beer instead. "I've never seen a horse with so much potential."

"More than Go For Broke?"

"God, yes."

They were both silent. Thinking. Considering.

"Sounds like you don't got much choice." Pete dumped the carrots into the bubbling dark brown beef stew.

"That's pretty much what I was thinking. Which is why I'm going to turn Winnie down."

"Wrong choice."

Alec tossed down the rest of the beer, crushed the can, then threw it in a high looping arc into the trash. "What the hell do you expect me to do?"

He yanked open the refrigerator door again, reached for another beer and because this time he felt need, rather than thirst, settled for a Dr. Pepper instead. Alec knew from firsthand experience that the one thing his stepdaughter didn't need was an alcoholic for a father.

"It's only been six months since Zoe lost her mother," he pointed out when Pete didn't answer.

"From what you've told me, Liz hadn't been around for that little girl all that much since she ran off from here with that no-account French count six years ago."

"He was a duke. Or an earl."

"Or maybe the duke of earl," Pete suggested dryly.

That earned Alec's first real smile of the day. "Could have been," he agreed.

"Ever think she feels guilty about disrupting your life?"

Alec took a long swig of Dr. Pepper. "If she does, she's either hiding it pretty deep inside her, or she's one helluvan actress."

"Probably a bit of both. Besides," Pete continued doggedly, "from what I've been able to tell, your act of martyrdom hasn't exactly turned this family into *Father Knows Best*. The kid looks like she's auditioning for a job at that massage parlor across the county line, the one everyone, including the sheriff, knows is nothing more than a hooker hangout."

"Zoe has a lot of pent-up anger and resentment to work out," Alec repeated what the school-appointed shrink had told him after the shoplifting incident.

"So did you," the older man reminded him. "Once upon a time when you were her age."

That was true enough. Alec had just turned fifteen when he'd left Kentucky in the middle of the night after Fortissimo's collapse. He'd ended up in Louisiana, land of King Cotton, black gold, yellow catfish and a passionate horse-racing tradition going back to the days of French possession.

Lying about his age, he landed a job as a hot walker in Folsom, just north of New Orleans across Lake Pontchartrain. His job, for which he was paid below minimum wage, was to cool the horses down after their morning exercise runs.

It had been Pete who'd found him sleeping in an

empty stall, taken him under his wing and literally turned his life around.

"I was lucky. I had you."

Alec thought of what might have happened to him if Pete had called the cops that night he'd shown up at the track to check on an ailing filly.

Instead, the older man had taken Alec home with him, where his seemingly unflappable wife had immediately run the filthy teenager a bath and fed him supper. It might have been only tuna casserole and sweet tea, but Alec hadn't had a meal since that he'd enjoyed more.

Jenny Campbell had passed on eight months ago, leaving her husband of fifty years as rudderless and lonely as Alec had once been. Which was why it had seemed perfectly natural to invite Pete to come live here and help build his dream stable.

"And Zoe has the two of us. So, she'll be fine."

"I told Winnie I needed to sleep on it."

"Why don't you do that?" Pete suggested easily. Too easily, Alec thought. "And while you're sleeping, you might want to consider that the girl's mood might perk up some if her daddy wasn't so miserable himself."

"I'm not miserable."

Pete shrugged his huge shoulders. "Wouldn't want to call any man a liar. But if the way you've been these past weeks is what you'd call a good mood, I'd sure hate to see what a bad one looks like. You know what you said about Winnie's colt being born to run?"

"Yeah."

"Well, you might be able to lie to yourself, boy. But not to old Pete. You're feelin' about as low as a snake in a rut, and things aren't going to get any better around this place until you're back doin' the work you love."

He put the lid on the kettle and turned down the flame to a high simmer.

"You were born to train horses. I've known that from the first day I saw you gentling that filly who'd tripped coming out of the gate at Louisiana Downs. I told Jenny that night that I'd never laid eyes on a kid with more natural horse sense.

"You've got a bunch of Angus MacKenna in you, Alec. Racing is in your blood as much as it is in those Thoroughbreds. So how about doing us all a big favor and quit trying to be some clone of Cliff Huxtable and whatever the name of that guy was who played the know-it-all stepfather on *The Brady Bunch*."

"So why don't you just tell me what you really think?"

"Haven't been a lot of owners knocking at our door since you knocked Wellesley off that barstool. Seems this Legends Lake, glitchy as he is, might just be your last chance."

Alec was not yet prepared to admit that he was down to last chances. "The season's just beginning. There's still time for something to turn up."

While Pete mixed up some dumplings to go with the stew, Alec went upstairs to call Zoe to dinner. She was talking on the phone, as she seemed to do most of the time.

"He is so rad, Jen!" She giggled, sounding much more like a normal teenage girl than the petulant Lolita wannabe who'd called him to the phone. "Of course Alec doesn't know. Are you kidding? My stepfather is as straight as they come. He'd freak if he even saw Jake's tattoos.

"Oh, God, they are sooo cool, Jen. He's got this dragon on his right arm that looks just like it's breathing real fire. And a killer devil with the weirdest red eyes that look like they're glaring straight at you on his left biceps."

It took an effort, but Alec managed not to freak. Not quite yet, anyway.

"The first time I kissed him I thought I'd faint. Or maybe melt . . ."

There was a nerve-racking pause.

"Of course he uses his tongue! God, Jen, he's not some immature high school kid. He's nineteen. He knows what to do with a woman."

He was *not* eavesdropping, Alec assured himself as Zoe continued to enumerate all Jake's less than honorable attributes. The kind guaranteed to strike terror in the heart of any parent.

The hell he wasn't.

Assuring himself that as her stepfather and legal guardian, it was his duty to protect a defenseless child, Alec learned that Jake wore a black leather biker jacket over the tattoos, had a pierced tongue, for Christ's sake, and heaven protect them all, the bastard had dared to invite Zoe to run off to California with him.

Zoe, apparently, had decided to do just that.

The tattoo-painted, metal-pierced, hog-riding gangster—who undoubtedly also dealt dope, Alec thought darkly—was after Zoe the way a fox stalked a chicken who'd wandered too far from the pen.

The terrifying thing about it was, short of locking her in a closet for the next few years or getting out his grandfather's old Winchester 30-06 and waiting beneath Zoe's window for the cretin to show up, Alec couldn't think of much he could do to stop her from making a disastrous mistake.

He could try to talk some sense into her. Share some wisdom born of his own youthful mistakes. But if earlier attempts at conversation were any indication, his parental words of warning would undoubtedly fall like small stones into a deep dark bottomless well.

Opting for action over talk, he went back downstairs to his office and used the second line to place a brief, but highly satisfying call to the local sheriff's department.

6

THE FOLLOWING MORNING, Alec took the piece of paper with Kate O'Sullivan's phone number on it and placed the call to Ireland.

"Well, I expect there's only one answer for it," she declared in the musical cadence of the Irish west after he'd explained the problem.

"And that is?"

"You'd best be bringing him home. So I can get to the bottom of what's bothering the poor dear horse."

It was definitely a long shot. Alec didn't have an iota of proof that Kate Fitzpatrick O'Sullivan would be any better able to figure out what the hell was wrong with the horse she'd bred than he could.

Alec didn't believe in magic. But having stabled the horse at her stud for its first year, she obviously knew the colt better than anyone else. If he could find a way to calm Legends Lake down enough that he could be trained to win the Derby, Alec would have taken him to hell to make a deal with the devil himself.

"I'm not going," Zoe declared after Alec had broken the news that they were going to Ireland. The magenta spikes may have deflated a bit in the night, but they had enough goop on them to keep them from moving when she tossed her head.

Trying to conduct the conversation on more level ground, he sat down on the end of the bed. "You know, you might just have a good time in Ireland."

"Yeah, sure. When I'm not playing Little Bo-Peep with all the damn sheep and being dragged to all those Catholic churches for confession, I'll probably have a fucking dandy time."

Even knowing that she was trying to shock him, Alec found it disconcerting to hear the F-word coming out of those same lips that had once so sweetly kissed him good night.

"Do you have anything all that important to confess?" he asked casually. "Other than the shoplifting?"

"No."

"Well then, I guess you can take that stop off your itinerary."

"Why can't you just leave me here? I can take care of myself."

Alec resisted the impulse to point out that she hadn't been doing a real bang-up job of that lately. "Sorry. Where I go, you go. That's the deal I worked out with your probation officer."

"I'd rather kill myself than go off to some boring, dead-end place like Ireland."

"You're exaggerating." He reached out and took her hand. "About the suicide. Aren't you?"

"I might not be." She snatched her hand away, refusing to look at him. "Suicide is, after all, a popular choice of my generation."

"Zoe."

He didn't bother to censure the concern in his voice. The odds were she was merely jerking his chain, looking to get a reaction. Well, if that's what she wanted, that's what she was damn well going to get. This was too serious a matter to bluff.

"Tell me the truth. Are you even a little serious? Because if you are—"

"I'm not going to kill myself, okay?" She was out of bed and across the room in a shot, the long legs revealed by the oversize nightshirt reminding him of a filly's. "I wouldn't give everyone the satisfaction of getting rid of me that easily," she said out the window toward the weathered blue mountains.

Anger. Pain. Need. They were all there, surrounding her like a dark force field so strong Alec could almost reach out and touch it.

"If I thought staying here would be a good thing for you, I'd turn down the training job in a heartbeat, Zoe. But there's just too much bad stuff going on in your life right now, what with the shoplifting—"

"They have stores in Ireland," she reminded him pointedly.

Another threat. Unspoken, but heavy enough to hover in the air between them. "True. But Jake MacAllister isn't in County Clare."

Her head spun back toward him. He watched the comprehension dawn in expressive eyes that looked as if they'd been lined with lumps of Appalachian coal. "You listened in on my private phone conversation!"

"Not on purpose," he hedged, wondering who was the liar now. "I came upstairs to tell you that supper was almost ready and—"

"You eavesdropped!" She was looking at him as if he were no better than pond scum. "You invaded my privacy."

"Accidentally," he stressed yet again. "But to tell you the absolute truth, I'm glad I overheard you talking about him. The guy's trouble, Zoe."

She raised her chin. "Maybe I like trouble. Or maybe I'm bad. Did you ever think of that?"

He gave her a long look and wondered if he looked as miserable as she did right now. "Nah. I don't think so. But Jake is, Zoe."

"You don't know him," she repeated stubbornly. Petulantly.

An instinct Alec didn't even know he possessed warned him to tread carefully. The last thing he wanted was to create some Romeo and Juliet forbidden love scenario that would have her more determined to run off with the guy.

"I know his type. Guys like him hang around the track. They may be more into horses than Harleys, but at the core they're pretty much the same."

She glared at him, then turned her back, giving him the silent treatment. Alec waited. Dust motes danced in the sunshine slanting through the window, a woodpecker hammered away at the eaves and a mockingbird hidden in one of the Southern pine trees sang its morning song.

"Pete'll have your breakfast ready any time." He stood up and had reached the open door when he paused.

"By the way, you don't have to worry about Jake showing up before we leave."

"Why not?"

"He was picked up last night. Seems he had some methamphetamine on him. Quite a lot, as it turns out. Enough that the sheriff is holding him on suspicion of possessing a controlled substance for sale."

The nice thing about settling down in the homeplace where you'd grown up was that you could call upon those old connections. Alec had gone to school with Sheriff McCall; in fact, he and Jeb McCall had smoked their first cigarettes behind Jeb's daddy's tobacco barn the summer they'd turned twelve. With that shared history, it had only taken a single call to accomplish the protective maneuver.

Zoe impressed him, just a bit, by cursing at him in French, then German, then, just in case he hadn't gotten her drift, in English.

Alec was halfway down the stairs when he heard the unmistakable sound of a water glass hitting the doorframe. Then shattering. Next something that sounded like a book thudded against the wall.

"Sounds like a real doozie of a grand mal tantrum," Pete said over the screams coming from upstairs when Alec entered the kitchen. The father of now-grown daughters, he appeared to take Zoe's temper in stride as he shoved a mug of coffee into Alec's hand. "You're doing the right thing."

The usually unflappable older man flinched, just a little, as the slamming of the bedroom door shook the two-hundred-year-old house.

"I sure hope you're right." Alec took a long drink of Pete's high-octane brew and idly wondered if Kate O'Sullivan's magic touch worked on teenagers.

In the end, they decided Pete would stay in Kentucky, preparing for the stable of Thoroughbreds Alec still optimistically hoped to acquire. Since, despite her recent rebellion, Zoe was an honor student, the principal agreed to a lesson plan she could study on her own while in Ireland, which would save the hassle of enrolling her in school for the short time Alec planned on being out of the country.

Visibly sulking about having been dragged away from her planned assignation, five days after Winnie's phone call, Zoe studiously ignored Alec on the flight to Ireland. From the time they left the house, she kept her Discman earphones on, her magenta head bobbing to whatever sounds were undoubtedly destroying her eardrums.

Once on the plane, she continued to treat him as if he didn't exist, burying her slender nose in the stack of glossy magazines she'd packed into her warning-flare-orange backpack. The magazines boasted bright covers featuring young, all-American models who could have appeared in an ad promoting the wonders of milk while screaming fluorescent script addressed some apparently vital teen girl issue.

Are you ready for SEX? Ditch the doormat! Love your body now! To be or not to be—a VIRGIN! Priss-Proof Prom—Frocks that Rock!

Other than wishing Zoe would actually want to do something as normal as attend a prom, Alec found little comfort in the topics offered.

At least he'd gotten her away from that tattooed and studded Harley Romeo. Maybe not in the logical, talk it out way that Ward Cleaver or Ozzie Nelson might have done, but at this point in his life, when some aliens on a planet in a galaxy far far away seemed to be zapping Zoe's frontal lobe with random particle beams, Alec decided to be grateful for small favors.

His small satisfaction disintegrated when he was greeted after clearing customs by a tall, dark-haired giant.

"Welcome to Ireland." The man held out a huge, work-roughened hand. "I'm Michael Joyce, a friend of Kate O'Sullivan's. I own the farm that adjoins her stud. I've come to fetch you and your horse."

"Mrs. O'Sullivan didn't come herself?"

"Oh, Kate's a bit tied up at the moment, but she'll

be greeting you and your daughter personally at the stud once she takes care of unexpected business."

The horse breeder was not making the best of first impressions. But having come all this way, Alec had no choice but to continue on to the farm. After introducing Zoe, who loftily informed the farmer that she was *not* Alec's daughter, it was time to load Legends Lake into the trailer Michael Joyce had brought.

Fortunately, Winnie hadn't been exaggerating about the colt being a good traveler. He came off the plane as if he'd just taken a quick little jog around a track rather than flown across the Atlantic, practically prancing into the trailer without a moment's pause.

"That went well enough," Michael said.

Alec murmured an agreement. If he hadn't actually seen it with his own eyes, he never would have believed that the cheerful, personable horse was the same terrified one who'd jumped that fence.

They climbed into a truck that smelled of wet dark earth and the burning peat that drifted on the winter breezes this time of year in the west of Ireland. Between the two men, Zoe slouched down, her eyes hidden by a pair of oversize sunglasses as she tuned them out.

Alec's early irritation about Kate O'Sullivan's no-show at the airport faded as the road twisted through a maze of hedgerow-separated fields, over narrow stone bridges, through the center of the tidy medieval town of Castlelough—the brightly painted shops reflecting a Celtic optimism in this land of soft days and rainy nights—and out again, past whitewashed slate-roofed houses, peat bogs and enchanting winter gold hayfields lit with silvery, pale green frost in the shadows where the sun had yet to reach.

"I've visited here before," he said to Michael, who was driving with one huge hand casually draped over the top of the wheel. "But the scenery always catches me by surprise."

" 'Tis a grand place, that's for sure." Michael frowned briefly, thoughtfully. "There was a time when I didn't appreciate it. When I was younger and felt a need for adventure."

"That's probably natural," Alec allowed. Hadn't he once felt the same need to leave his mountain home? Of course, he'd also been running away from his father's reputation as much as running *to* anything in particular.

"Especially for those born on an island. But I've traveled the world and now, like the prodigal son, I've come home, taken a wonderful woman to wife, have a darling daughter who holds my heart in her wee hand and most days I forget that dark time away from home."

Alec suddenly recognized both the name and the face. "You're *the* Michael Joyce. The war photojournalist."

"That I am." The fleeting frown suggested that this may not be one of the giant's favorite topics.

"I have one of your books. The one on Bosnia. I remember thinking at the time I bought it that if only it could be sent to every leader in the world, it might go a long way in stopping wars."

"Ah, now isn't that a lovely thought? Unfortunately, experience, along with the tragic history of my own country, has me believing that it would take more than a book of photographs to stop men from trying to kill one another over a bit of land or ideology. Especially—"

He suddenly broke off his planned statement. His curse, while in Irish, needed no translation.

Alec followed Michael's frustrated gaze across a field to where a lone tree clung to the edge of a cliff. Stopped a few yards from the tree was a huge yellow bulldozer. Behind the bulldozer stood at least a dozen men wearing white hard hats. Between the huge machine and the tree stood a single woman.

"Bloody damn. I was afraid of this," Michael muttered.

"Afraid of what?"

Michael sighed wearily as he pulled off the road onto a bit of grass that was fortunately not bordered by either hedge or stone. Since Irish drivers were known for speeding as if they believed their narrow curving roads were NASCAR racetracks, Alec definitely wouldn't have wanted to risk parking the horse trailer on the dirt shoulder.

"I was afraid she'd get it into her foolish, stubborn head to make a grand stand." His brogue, which hadn't been all that pronounced when they'd met, had thickened.

He reached down, grabbed a 35mm camera from beneath his seat, then opened the driver's door. "It appears, Mr. MacKenna, that you're going to be meeting our Kate sooner rather than later."

7

"KATE?" ALEC NARROWED HIS EYES at the lone, rebellious figure, clad in a long red wool cape adorned with swirling Celtic symbols. "That's Kate O'Sullivan?"

"That's herself, all right." Michael sighed heavily. "She's a lovely woman, our Kate is. As close to my heart as me own sister. But I wouldn't be denying that she does tend to have her own unique way of stirring up trouble." Flinging the camera strap over his shoulder, Michael began trudging across the field.

After instructing Zoe to stay put in the cab of the truck, Alec quickly caught up with Michael Joyce.

"What's she doing out there?"

"Would you believe me if I told you that she's rescuing faeries?"

"You can't be serious." Terrific. He'd come all this way across the Atlantic Ocean to hand Winnie's precious horse over to a madwoman.

"No Irishman would ever jest about faeries."

"Surely you don't believe in them?"

"Now, I'm not saying I do. And I'm not saying I don't. But having an open mind, I tend to avoid the subject. The trouble is," he explained as they grew close enough to hear the sound of a male voice raised in obvious frustration, "Kate not only believes in their presence, she's elected herself their champion."

Okay. That was it. If he had a lick of sense, he'd have Joyce take him straight back to the airport, get on that plane and return to the States.

"She's fighting for faeries?" a young female voice asked behind them.

Alec glanced back over his shoulder and saw Zoe struggling to catch up with them, which was not all that easy since her boots, with platform soles that had to be at least three inches high, kept sinking into the damp meadow.

"Aye, that she is," Michael said.

"By standing in front of a bulldozer?" Alec asked.

"The county government has decided to move this road closer to the cliff." Michael lifted the camera and snapped a few photographs of the standoff taking place. "The thought being that it'd bring more tourists in to take the drive, you see, like the Ring of Kerry."

"So?"

"So, if they keep to the original survey, they'll have to cut down that hawthorn tree."

"She's making a stand for one damn tree?"

"Not just any tree. You see, Mr. MacKenna, in these parts, this particular hawthorn tree is considered by many to be an exceedingly special tree."

The motor drive of the camera whirred as he shot more photographs. Even as frustrated as he was, Alec couldn't help noting that the giant handled the camera with the same ease Alec himself felt when dealing with a bridle and reins.

"A tree where faeries dwell," Michael continued. "So, naturally, following the druid path as she does—"

"Are you telling me that Kate O'Sullivan is some sort of witch?" Alec cut him off abruptly.

"Cool," Zoe said.

Alec shot her a warning glower that suggested that he, for one, found nothing cool about this news flash. Uncowed, the teenager folded her arms across the front of her black coat and glared right back at him.

Shaking his head in mute frustration, and biting back a string of curses, Alec marched away from the group and approached the woman he'd begun to hope might help him solve Legends Lake's mental problem. Instead, he was discovering that Winnie's crazy bargain horse had been bred by a mad, reckless witch.

"It goddamn figures," he muttered. So far, everything about the colt was turning out to be as screwy as hell.

"You do realize that you're outnumbered, don't you?" he asked, forgoing any conventional opening conversational gambit.

She didn't so much as bother to glance his way. "Now isn't that a matter of opinion?"

"Actually, it's a matter of size. If the driver of that bulldozer—which, in case you haven't noticed, outweighs you by several tons—gets tired of this fool standoff, you're going to be in a world of hurt."

"If I allow these men to cut down this tree, far more people will be harmed, Mr. MacKenna."

"You know who I am. So I guess I'm supposed to believe that you're psychic as well as being a druid Irish witch?" Frustrated and jet-lagged, Alec didn't bother to conceal his sarcasm.

"As a matter of fact, I *am* fey." She shot him a quick glance. "But that wouldn't be how I know your name. Didn't you get out of Michael's lorry? And didn't I, myself, send him to fetch you from the airport?"

"I was expecting you to meet us."

"I was expecting to do exactly that." She turned back to facing down the bulldozer driver. "Until I learned that the roadway commission had chosen today to commit infamy."

"And here I thought you Irish were supposed to be masters of understatement. I fail to see how cutting down a single tree can be construed as infamy."

"What if it were your home?" Eyes as deep and blue as a mountain lake, fringed with a silky jet crescent of lashes so thick he wondered how she could keep her eyes open, bore into his. "Would you, perhaps, take matters a bit more seriously?"

"Well, of course, but—"

"There's no *but* about it, Mr. MacKenna. Whether you choose to believe me or not, this is no ordinary tree. It's home to beings far older than all of our ages combined multiplied several times over. And I'll not stand by and allow some foolish government agency to destroy it and send all those dispossessed spirits out into our world to seek their revenge by creating mischief and mayhem upon the innocent people of this county."

The man atop the bulldozer roared with laughter at her heated pronouncement. "You're not only fey, you're daft, Kate O'Sullivan."

She spun back toward him, hands splayed on her hips. "There are those who'd be thinking that," she allowed. "And isn't it one of the kinder things some of the good, supposedly pious people of this county might say about me.

"But daft or not, that doesn't stop you from being in the wrong, Brian Doyle. You yourself grew up in this selfsame county. Would you be forgetting how the American owners of that auto factory in the North were so arrogant as to think they could cut down a hawthorn to make room for their factory? I suppose you'd be trying to tell me that it was only a coincidence that very same factory collapsed? Surely you'd be knowing that what you're wanting to do is foolhardy."

His ruddy complexion deepened. "I'm only doing me job."

"If that's the case, perhaps you should be seeking a different line of work."

"God Almighty!" He literally threw up his hands. "I'm beginning to understand why Cadel was always so vexed with you."

Her eyes flashed sparks. The fire in her cheeks heightened, though watching her carefully as he was, Alec thought that she paled a bit at the man's remark.

"I shouldn't be surprised, you standing up for your own cousin that way, but you have no business bringing my husband into this discussion, Brian." Black hair swirled out as she tossed her head. "What's happening here today is a matter between the two of us—"

"And the entire fecking Irish roadway department," he reminded her.

"Fine." She tossed her chin exactly the way Winifred Tarlington had, when Alec had suggested gelding Legends Lake. "Why don't you turn that big yellow machine around, drive back into town, ring up whatever eejit planned this roadway in the first place and tell him to stop hiding behind his big wide desk and come out here in person so I can explain why this ill-conceived enterprise is fated to failure."

"Jaysus!" He yanked off his hard hat in order to drag his hand through his copper bright hair. He shot a hard look at Alec. "Would you be talking some sense into this woman?"

"Since we just met, I doubt if anything I might have to say would make a difference."

The one thing Alec didn't need was to get into a battle with some government agency. He'd bought enough Irish-bred horses for clients to have learned that Ireland's bureaucracy could have as many twists and turns as a Celtic knot. Nothing in this country, including its people, was straightforward, which had always been part of its appeal.

Until now.

Brian's curse was harsh and suggested that he'd just reached the end of his rope. "I'm giving you one last chance, Kate."

"You can give me a million chances, Brian. Then a million more after that. And still I won't be moving."

"We'll see about that." His glower darkened as he switched the key, bringing the bulldozer to roaring life, causing it to belch like a fire-breathing dragon.

"Aye, we will indeed," Alec heard Kate murmur over the deafening engine.

She lifted her white arms—which, while slender, were well-muscled from a lifetime of managing horses—toward a sky that, with the exception of a few scattered clouds hovering out over the sea near the horizon, was as clear as pale blue glass.

Then closed her eyes and began to chant in a language Alec took to be Irish.

The bulldozer inched forward.

She paid no attention as she stood her ground, moving uplifted arms in wider and wider circles.

Alec watched the standoff, unable to believe that one of the hardheaded individuals wouldn't back off. He hadn't seen such a foolhardy display of recklessness since the time he was five years old and a passenger in the car when his drunken father had played chicken on a suicidally narrow curving mountain road with a truck carrying huge pink slabs of Tennessee marble.

Brian Doyle kept advancing with the bulldozer.

Kate O'Sullivan kept chanting.

The temperature dropped a bit as first one cloud, then two, trailed across the sky like a veil draped across the morning sun. When a deep shadow fell over the rolling landscape, Alec glanced up, watching in disbelief as, impossible as it had to be, Castlelough's witch appeared to be gathering up the clouds in her graceful, beringed hands.

The other men began to mutter to one another and shake their heads. A few stepped back. One older man, whose face had been weathered by years and a lifetime spent outdoors in the elements, made a sign of the cross and began murmuring a Hail Mary.

Still Brian moved forward.

Still Kate gathered her clouds.

A day that had been bright and sunny when Alec had arrived turned cold. A brisk wind picked up, coming in from the sea, tinged with salt and something else.

Magic? Alec wondered. Then castigated himself for even considering such an impossible thing.

This was Ireland, after all. Rainy, wet Ireland. If you didn't like the weather, all you had to do was wait ten minutes and it would change. Which was all that was happening now, he assured himself.

"That's so awesome," Zoe breathed, obviously enchanted.

Alec would have been pleased that she'd finally found something to capture her interest, were it not for the fact that the idea of Zoe as would-be witch was even worse than her current teenage temptress persona.

"It's meteorology."

"I never saw any TV weatherman do that," she retorted.

Even as he resisted accepting the possibility that it had anything to do with Kate O'Sullivan, Alec couldn't help noticing that the temperature was now a good twenty degrees colder than it had been when he'd first walked out of the terminal at Shannon airport. And dropping.

The clouds, which only minutes earlier had resembled the fluffy white sheep grazing on hillsides, turned first silver, then darker yet, as if being tarnished by the elements. The sun became more and more obscured until it finally disappeared altogether. All that was left was a faint, stuttering glow edging those threatening gray clouds.

Time seemed suspended.

Brian's square, pugilist's jaw was clenched.

As were Kate's fists.

Indeed, every muscle and tendon in her body seemed to be straining, reaching for something. But her expression remained strikingly, eerily calm. And, Alec noted, supremely confident.

He felt it first. A prickling that had the hair on the back of his neck and his arms standing on end.

Then he tasted it: a faintly sulfurous flavor on his tongue.

He heard it next: an unmistakable hum and crackling overhead like the sound the heavy power lines back home made when dampened by morning fog.

And then, although in upcoming days he'd try to convince himself that what happened next was only his imagination, Alec saw it: a jagged bolt of lightning shot out of the center of the amassed clouds, striking the ground mere inches from the front of the bulldozer with a force that made the earth tremble.

The construction crew scattered, running back to their cars and trucks parked at the edge of the field as if chased by the hounds of hell. Cursing, Brian leapt from the seat of the bulldozer, falling onto his knees as he hit the ground.

"Keep your fecking tree, then," he shouted, scrambling to his feet and following the other men in their dash to safety. "It makes no bloody difference to me."

"Tell the highway planners what you saw here today," Kate called after him. "Warn them that worse will occur if they're so foolish as to defile sacred lands."

That little matter taken care of, she turned back to Alec, with an odd serenity that suggested that what he'd just witnessed was nothing more than a dream. Only the heightened color in her cheeks and the bright sapphire gleam in her eyes remained as proof that it had been all too real.

That and, Alec noted with stark surprise, the small burned circle of blackened turf directly in front of the still idling bulldozer.

8

"WELL, NOW THAT THAT LITTLE MATTER has been taken care of, I suppose it's time for me to mind my manners and apologize for not meeting you at the airfield, Mr. MacKenna," she said. "As you could see, a bit of an emergency came up. However, since Brian and his boys have gone, we can be getting on to the farm and—"

"I'm not certain that's such a good idea."

"Alec!" Zoe wailed.

"Don't tell me that a little demonstration of Mother Nature's powers can have you risking Legends Lake's well-being?" Kate asked mildly.

The question was softly issued through voluptuous lips that appeared to come by their deep rose color naturally, but there was nothing seductive in her tone. Alec could recognize a challenge—a dare—when he heard one.

"As important as the horse is to me, my daughter is more important."

"Dammit, Alec!" Zoe wailed again. Michael Joyce put a calming hand on her arm. She furiously shook it off. "I keep telling you, I'm not your daughter. And I'm not your fucking responsibility!"

Kate moved her gaze from Alec to the teenager. Her smooth expression showed neither shock nor disapproval of Zoe's language.

"I don't believe we've been properly introduced," she said, as if they were meeting at a Junior League tea party rather than on the edge of an Irish cliff where a possible display of black magic had just taken place. She extended her hand. "I'm Kate O'Sullivan. And you'd be—"

"Zoe Poullain."

"Ah. What a lovely name." Kate's smile was warm. Alec could have ceased to exist. Every atom of her being was directed toward Zoe in much the same way as she'd concentrated on gathering the clouds earlier.

"My first name is Greek," Zoe divulged with a sudden shyness at odds with the angry, profane teenage shoplifter who'd gotten onto the plane in Atlanta. "It means *life*. My last name is French. My father was a famous Formula One race-car driver. He died before I was born. In a race in Brazil."

"Well, now, isn't that a shame," Kate said. "Would you be knowing what your father's family name means?"

"No."

"As it happens, I do. It means a horse breeder. So, it appears you and I have something in common, Zoe Poullain."

"I don't know anything about breeding horses."

"Perhaps not consciously. But bloodlines are magical things, Zoe. The secrets of all the people who've come before you are buried deep within your bones. Why, I've no doubt that a deep and abiding knowledge of horses is just lying there, waiting for an opportunity to come out.

"Which is why it's so wonderful that your—that Mr. MacKenna," she corrected, deftly avoiding a conflict by referring to him as Zoe's father, "has brought you here. Do you believe in fate, Zoe? Destiny?"

"I don't know." But Alec could tell that she was fascinated.

"Well, as it happens, I'm a firm believer in the concept," Kate said cheerfully. "I also believe that it's obvious that your personal destiny has brought you here to Castlelough." She turned back to Alec. "As your destiny has you bringing Legends Lake back home again."

"The only reason I'm here in Ireland is because you bred the horse. I figured you might have a handle on how to cure him of his problem. If he's not overbred, that is," Alec couldn't help tacking on.

"The horse is not overbred," she responded, with a serenity that seemed designed to mock any attempt he might have been making to raise her ire. "As for solving his problem, I'll have to be seeing him to do that, now won't I? Why don't we postpone any further discussion until we get to my farm?

"My sister-in-law, Nora—who was once married to my late brother"—she elaborated—"stopped by this morning with some spice cake for our tea. Nora's a marvelous cook. You're in for a treat."

As they walked back to the parked truck, Alec watched Zoe hanging onto Kate O'Sullivan's every word and decided that perhaps she was truly a witch, after all. Because she certainly appeared to have cast a spell over his stepdaughter.

Although Kate would fling herself off the cliff before admitting it, especially to such an ill-tempered man, the first sight of Alec MacKenna had unsettled her. The Yank was as lean as a winter wolf and looked as if he could be just as dangerous. His hair was the color of midnight over the Burren, his flint gray eyes as chilly as the clouds she'd gathered to send Brian and the others on their way. His jaw was firm and square and echoed the hard stubbornness of his openly disapproving gaze and the hard line of his mouth. She suspected if those firmly cut lips did ever curve upward, his smile would be distinctly predatory.

The air around him was every bit as charged as the lightning bolt she'd drawn from the clouds. It took no imagination to picture him clad in the MacKenna tartan swinging a claymore in the heat of battle. He would not be an easy man to work with. Nor an easy man to know. He'd especially not be an easy man to love.

That errant thought, appearing from out of the sky that had turned a wide clear blue again, struck a startling note in her mind and caused a chill in her heart. She stopped dead in her tracks and stared at his broad back.

He'd continued on approximately three meters when he apparently realized that she was no longer with them. He turned and pinned her with a look that she hoped would not see too much.

"Something the matter?"

"Oh, no," she lied, forcing her expression to one of supreme calm even as her heart was hammering like that of a spring hare.

Once, long ago, wolves had prowled Ireland, all gray and silver and black, with yellow eyes that could see in the dark and sharp canine teeth that could rip a stag's throat open with the same ease as Kate might bite into a ripe blackberry.

The wolves were no longer, but the lesson early man had learned from them remained in the hearts of the humans left behind: It was dangerous to allow wild things to sense your fear.

"My farm's just over the next hill; I'll walk home and meet you all there."

His unnerving gaze zeroed in on hers. This was a man, Kate realized, who took nothing at face value.

Which undoubtedly was one of the reasons he'd garnered such success at such a relatively young age.

"I'll walk with you."

"Oh, that won't be necessary," she responded quickly. Too quickly, she belatedly realized as his flinty, unnerving eyes narrowed.

If she weren't so bloody nervous, she might have laughed at the way her imagination was running rampant: comparing the man to wild animals and warrior Scots, for heaven's sake. Alec MacKenna, she reminded herself, was just a man. The same as any other.

"We can discuss Legends Lake," he said. "I'll bring you up to speed on his problem."

"Oh, there wouldn't be time enough for that on such a brief stroll," she said in a blithe, airy way she was far from feeling. "Go along with the others, Mr. MacKenna. Truth be told, I'd be needing a bit of time to gather my thoughts after my little altercation with Brian."

"You didn't really. . . ."

She realized he was on the verge of asking her if she'd actually committed an act of magic. Then he shook his head with obvious disbelief.

"Never mind. It's not important." He seemed momentarily transfixed, almost, Kate considered, as if he were under a spell. One *she* certainly hadn't put upon him. "Well then, I guess I'll meet you at your farm."

"Within ten minutes," she promised.

"Ten minutes American? Or Irish?"

Despite the strange way her nerves were tingling, as if a bit of lightning left behind from her standoff with Brian had slipped beneath her skin, Kate laughed. Obviously the Yank horse trainer was acquainted with the old Irish saying that when God made time, he made plenty of it.

"I realize you're a man accustomed to dealing with

time in increments of a thousandth of a second. While I can't promise to be that prompt, I can assure you that barring any further emergencies, I'll make it to the farm under the wire."

"Fine."

He swept a brief look from the top of her head down to the toes of her boots. If he had been under any type of spell, it had obviously lifted because now he was radiating a disapproval so strong she could sense it the same way she could sense a storm building out over the sea, or the first buds of spring beginning to unfold themselves deep within the peat dark earth.

If he was trying to annoy her, he'd chosen the wrong day. Despite her unease, Kate was feeling almost invincible. After all, she'd faced down not only Brian and his snorting, growling yellow bulldozer, but the entire Ireland highway commission, as well. Surely one ill-humored Yank wouldn't prove that difficult to handle.

"Then I'll be seeing you there," she said. "Oh, and if you'd please be leaving Legends Lake in his trailer? I'll want to see how the horse unloads."

Lifting up her skirts a bit, she turned away and began cutting across the stone-bordered field. It took every ounce of self-restraint Kate possessed but she managed, just barely, not to give in to the temptation to look back.

Kate O'Sullivan's stud was nestled in the lee of a hillock like an infant held in the crook of a mother's arm. At first glance, Alec thought it looked vaguely familiar, but decided that it was only because it looked like every postcard of Ireland he'd ever seen.

There was an aura of peaceful harmony surrounding the stone house and barns. Horses roamed the pasture, cropping the grass, and at the edge of a sparkling, reed-fringed lake, the crumbling ruins of an old, moss-draped Norman castle stood like a silent sentinel of times long past.

"Nice castle," Alec said.

"It's falling down," Zoe countered.

"Aye, more's the pity," Kate, who'd arrived just in time to hear the muttered comment, said. "There are similar ruins all over our country, of course. Yet I will admit to a fondness for this particular one. When I was a little girl, I used to sneak away there to visit with the Lady."

"What lady?" Zoe asked with obviously reluctant curiosity.

"Oh, she's a lough beastie, and there's a story, which I'll let my son, Jamie, once he gets home from visiting his cousin, tell you about—how she came to live in the lake."

"A beastie?" Zoe echoed. She shot a sharp look Alec's way, as if to ask *Did you know about this?* He shrugged. "Like the Loch Ness monster?"

"A bit, though I certainly wouldn't be calling our darling beastie a monster. Nor is she as famous as Nessie, of course, but we're fond of her just the same."

Alec suddenly recalled why the Fitzpatrick farm looked familiar. "This is where that horror movie, *The Lady of the Lake,* was filmed."

"It is, indeed. Didn't my own sister-in-law's husband write both the screenplay and the novel on which the movie was based?"

"You know Quinn Gallagher?"

"I do. He lives just down that very lane. Nora, who made the spice cake for our tea, is his wife. And Michael"—she nodded her dark hair in the giant's direction—"whose family has owned that castle for all these centuries, is Nora's brother. Which makes us all related in an Irish family sort of way."

She smiled up at Michael, warmth in her clear blue

eyes. "I'd be owing you my gratitude for fetching Mr. MacKenna and Zoe. You're a darling to take precious time away from your work."

"No problem. Besides, with Erin away at her medical convention in Cork, and Shea spending the night with your Jamie and Brigid and the other kids at Nora's, I was finding myself a bit at loose ends."

Her laugh reminded Alec of a silver flute. A magical flute, he considered, recalling that strange incident in the field. For a suspended moment this rather fey female reminded him of the faeries she'd seemed determined to protect.

"How lovely that a man who pledged himself to the fatherless existence of an Irish bachelor farmer could be at such loose ends without his daughter and new wife." Her blue eyes twinkled merrily up at Michael.

"It's a surprise to me, as well," he agreed with a wry grin.

"And isn't life filled with surprises?" Kate said. "Which is why we must keep our hearts and minds open to them."

She turned toward Alec. "And now that we'd all been properly introduced and gotten our getting acquainted chatting over with, I suppose we'd best be seeing to Legends Lake."

She walked over to the horse trailer. "Does he still travel well?"

"If this trip is any indication, I'd say yes."

"Well, now, isn't that some good news, at least."

She opened the back of the trailer and walked up the ramp on the left side until she was standing at Legends Lake's head. Alec heard her murmuring to him. He couldn't understand the soft, soothing Irish words, but apparently the colt did because he nickered and began nuzzling at the buttons between Kate's breasts.

She laughed softly, reached into a hidden pocket in the scarlet cape and pulled out a bit of sugar, which he took, with equine grace, from her palm.

Seeming to prefer to give the horse time to remember her, to realize that he'd returned to the farm where he'd spent the first all-important year of his life, Kate took her own sweet time.

"He's ready now," she announced approximately ten minutes after she'd gone into the trailer. "If you could all just be backing up a wee bit, I'll be bringing him out."

Backing a horse out of a trailer was often as difficult as convincing him to enter in the first place. But with Kate at his head, Legends Lake managed the maneuver without any difficulty.

"I'll be wanting to take him to the paddock."

When she began walking briskly away from the trailer, apparently expecting him to follow, Alec reluctantly decided this was not the time to get into a turf war about which of them would be in charge of the horse's rehabilitation.

Kate led Legends Lake past a stone barn that looked as if it had been built back in the seventeenth century. The horseshoe painted on the wooden molding around the open door and a second, whitewashed story were more modern touches.

"I have his old stall waiting for him after he has a bit of a run," she told Alec. "I thought he'd be more comfortable in familiar surroundings."

She opened the gate and slipped off Legends Lake's bridle. He took off like a bullet, tossing his mane, galloping joyously over the pasture, obviously relieved to be able to stretch himself at last and release his pent-up energy in a burst of speed.

"I spent most of last night, when I wasn't fretting about Brian and his bulldozer that is, pondering on how best to handle his problem," Kate said as they watched the stallion run. "I finally decided that it would be best if I had a clearer idea of what to expect when we took him out to run on the track tomorrow."

"I told you, he jumps fences in the middle of a race."

"But not all the time?"

"Not according to Winifred Tarlington, his new owner. She has a horse farm in Lexington. That's in bluegrass country."

"Having been in the horse business all of my life, I know where Lexington is, Mr. MacKenna. I also know of its famous blue grass. In my opinion, it is not nearly as beneficial to horses as our own rich grass, which, for the point of this argument, is neither here nor there.

"I also know of Mrs. Tarlington, who won your American Kentucky Derby with Go For Broke, who, if memory serves, was trained by none other than yourself, before you apparently retired from the horse business a few months back."

"I didn't exactly retire." He was trying not to argue with the woman, but she was beginning to grate on his nerves. "I may have taken a brief sabbatical, but I haven't quit. In fact, I've been thinking about doing some breeding myself."

"The Fitzpatricks have always welcomed competition," Kate replied smoothly. "Though breeding horses is a great deal different from training them, which you'll no doubt discover for yourself if you give it a try. However, it sounds as if you've come out of your brief retirement—sabbatical," she corrected smoothly, "to train Legends Lake."

"I'm only considering training him at the moment. He's not what I'm used to working with." Alec knew that he was risking being laughed back out of the business when and if he showed up for the Derby with the tall, bony horse in tow. "Though he does appear to have possibilities."

"Possibilities?" The pride was back, burning like a white hot flame. "And they accuse us Irish of being masters of understatement. Legends Lake is a natural, Mr. MacKenna. He carries the love of running in his blood and the strength of thousands of years on Irish soil in his bones.

"Even a rock-headed Scot such as yourself should be able to look beyond the package and see that you've got yourself a champion. One who could set a new standard for all the generations of Thoroughbreds who come after him."

"I may be a bit hardheaded, but I'm an American. And, as I said, the horse has possibilities. But he doesn't have a snowball's chance in hell of winning even a rural stakes race unless I figure out what the hell makes him glitch out."

"Have you established any pattern?"

"No. Winnie contacted his first owner, the one who bought him from you originally, but he swears he never had any problem."

"Well, that's obviously a lie, since it's undoubtedly why he put him in a claiming race," Kate said with ill-concealed disgust. "I contacted him as well, the moment I got off the phone with you. At the time I sold him, I believed Legends Lake was going to a single owner. That's certainly what he told me when I asked for his credentials."

"By credentials, you're not speaking of his bank balance."

She lifted her chin. "I do not breed my horses to be treated poorly, Mr. MacKenna. I asked for references, as I always do, and the ones I received, many from people I'd done business with in the past, settled my mind, despite some lingering doubts.

"Unfortunately, he'd no sooner taken ownership when he created a syndicate of mostly absentee owners. They, in turn, hired one of you Yanks, a Bobby Jenkins, I believe, to be the trainer, then left him alone."

"Too bad you couldn't have foreseen *that* possibility in your crystal ball, or whatever you use to tell the future."

She ignored his sarcasm. "I also did some checking on Mr. Jenkins and discovered some disturbing stories."

"He used to have a fair winning percentage. But personally I wouldn't hire the man to muck out a stall. He died recently."

"That's what I was told," Kate confirmed. "So there's no one but Legends Lake to tell us what's happened to make him explode."

"I've seen this kind of behavior before in horses that were overbred."

"I'm not saying it can't happen from time to time, but I assure you there's no overbreeding done here at this stud. Didn't the French quartermasters travel all the way here to Castlelough to purchase Fitzpatrick stock for Napoleon's elite cavalry corps?"

"That was a long time ago."

"Precisely the point I was making. We've a fine long reputation for breeding champion Thoroughbreds that has continued to this day. Even, if I may be so bold as to say it, grown."

The Irish people may be known for their cheerful gregariousness, but Alec had dealt with enough of them over the years to know that their pride was a fierce flame of a thing. "Granted. But there's still something wrong with the horse."

"If there is, and I'm not agreeing you're right, mind

you, whatever happened was done by some man's hand. After Legends Lake left Castlelough."

"I'm not discounting that possibility, either."

"He truly never displayed any fear during the year I kept him here at the stud. I do wish I knew if he'd developed a pattern," she murmured.

"After watching him go bonkers, I wasn't all that willing to risk him breaking a leg with another test."

She angled her head and gave him another of those searching looks. "That's very thoughtful of you."

"It doesn't have anything to do with thoughtfulness. Look, Mrs. O'Sullivan, I'd had a bit of bad luck lately and this horse, as screwy as he is, could just possibly be my ticket back to the big time."

"And that's important to you," she guessed.

"Hell, yes. It's the singular most important thing in my life, what I've worked toward since I was a fifteen-year-old hot walker. While Legends Lake might not look like much—"

"Well now, won't he grow into his height once he has a few more months on him."

"That remains to be seen. Personally, I wouldn't bet my stud on it, if I were you. The thing is, the horse could be as ugly as a plugged nickel and still be worth millions. But only if I can prevent him from getting banned from racing for life. Because if that happens, all the grand bloodlines in the world aren't going to be able to keep him from ending up in a damn Alpo can on some supermarket shelf."

She didn't respond to that same overstatement he'd scolded Winnie for making. But he sensed her attempting to determine whether he was as coldhearted and venal as he'd just made himself out to sound.

They stood there, remaining silent, as Legends Lake, seemingly oblivious to the heated discussion concerning him, ran off the excess energy that had built up during the long overseas trip. His mane flowed in the breeze, his incredibly long legs ate up the ground.

"He may be glitchy," Alec said, "and he's sure as hell the homeliest horse I've ever seen, but I have to admit he looks good when he runs."

"He may be not as striking as some, at first glance. But his heart is that of a champion.

"Ever since neolithic people brought the first ponies here, Ireland has always had a marvelous climate and soil for rearing horses. We've lots of limestone; this creates a great amount of minerals coming through all our green grass, which makes for good, strong legs."

She turned to Zoe. "The Celts invaded with battle chariots drawn by hot-blooded horses five hundred years before Christ was born. As has happened all through this country's history, those invaders became settlers, allowing the blood of their fiery mounts to meld with that of our indigenous ponies.

"Successive tides of Vikings, Normans, English, and, of course, St. Patrick and his Christianity, each changed the hearts and minds of our people a bit, yet one thing has never changed. For all these thousands of years and hundreds of generations there's been a strong bond between the Irish and our horses."

She glanced over at Alec and lifted her chin. "Horses like Legends Lake aren't merely symbols of our heritage, they define us as a people."

Alec may not be thrilled at working with a woman who appeared to be as loosely wrapped as Kate O'Sullivan was, but he couldn't deny that her love of horses was all too obvious. As was her pride in being a part of their world. It was appearing less and less likely that she'd overbred Legends Lake. Still, it remained a possibility he couldn't overlook. He owed Winnie too much to allow this self-proclaimed druid's enthusiasm to cloud the analytical part of his mind.

"You've had a long and tiring trip," Kate said. "Why don't I show you to your rooms, where you can wash up and take a bit of a lie-down, if you'd like, while Legends Lake begins to settle in."

"I don't want to put you out," Alec repeated what he'd told her when they'd made plans for his arrival. "We're more than willing to stay at a hotel."

"As I assured you, there's no need. Castlelough only has the single inn, and even if it wasn't booked to the rafters for the annual step-dancing competition, the cost would be dear and it's a bit of a drive to be making back and forth each day. No, it makes much more sense for you to stay with the children and me.

"There's a small apartment over one of the barns that I've been using as an office. I'm sure you'll find it quite comfortable. And I've already prepared a room for Zoe," she said with a smile toward the teenager.

"What does your husband think of this arrangement?"

Alec recalled the bulldozer operator mentioning something about problems between Kate O'Sullivan and her husband. He had enough troubles without landing in the middle of a domestic dispute.

"I've never had any idea what Cadel would be thinking from moment to moment. But your staying at the farm won't be of any concern to my husband, since he no longer lives here. And hasn't for several years."

"I'm sorry."

"Wouldn't you be the only one who is?" she responded shortly, effectively cutting off any further conversation about her obviously failed marriage.

"Our rooms have a connecting bathroom," she said to Zoe. "I hope you won't mind sharing it."

"I had to share with six girls at school."

"Well then, this should be an improvement," Kate declared easily as she began walking back to the house with the teenager, once again leaving Alec to follow.

The bedroom was simple, but not without its appeal. In spite of her determination to hate everything about Ireland, Zoe was charmed by the white lace curtains at the window and the dried wildflowers blooming in the earthenware pitcher atop a weathered chest. A green glass dragon perched on the windowsill, while a trio of small winged horses ran across the top of the pine dresser.

The single, iron-framed bed was draped in a crocheted coverlet that had either been dipped in tea or was really, really old. From the sepia tint to the collection of framed family photographs atop the dresser, Zoe guessed the ivory hue of the coverlet was due to age. The bed was piled high with lacy, feminine pillows that appeared to have been made of scraps of old clothing. One triangle of pink lace stimulated bittersweet memories of the dress she'd worn at her mother's wedding to Alec. The flower girl dress was one of the few things she'd taken with her when they left for Europe.

Her mother had insisted that she didn't want any reminders of her second failed marriage, but that hadn't stopped Zoe from rolling the fairy-tale princess dress up as tightly as she could, hiding it beneath her nightgowns, and smuggling it away from the mountain. She'd slept with it under her pillow for months.

More modern photographs of what appeared to be local life—children playing on the beach, horses trotting across meadows, the castle ruins gleaming like burnished metal in the coppery glow of a setting sun—hung on the white plaster walls.

She sank down onto the mattress and stared out the window toward the pasture, unable to remember the last time she'd felt as carefree as Legends Lake looked. Nor could she remember the last time she'd been happy.

Yes, on second thought, she could. She'd been nine years old and living in the rolling blue Appalachian mountains with Alec and her mother.

When they'd first arrived in Europe, Zoe had hoped that her mother would realize what a loser that stupid duke was and take them both back to Kentucky. Later, after realizing that she might actually be stuck in that old-world nunnery, she'd had a brief flirtation with religion.

Every morning, the first words that sprang into her head when she woke was a fervent prayer that Alec would come and rescue her, like some bold knight in shining armor riding a white steed like in all the fairy tales. The prayer was also the last words she whispered into the lonely darkness before she fell asleep.

And all day, every day, while she struggled with long division, conversational French and German, the obligatory catechism classes and tried not to fall into a coma during afternoon benediction, she'd recite the words over and over again in her head. But when God hadn't seen fit to answer that one simple request, she'd come to the conclusion that the only person in this entire world she could count on was herself.

She'd met Jake three weeks ago, the morning after she'd been caught lifting those stupid earrings she hadn't even wanted from Wal-Mart. She'd given the school security guard the slip and was hitching her way into town to get a butterfly tattoo on her ankle when he'd offered her a lift on his Harley. He was dark and dangerous and when he kissed her, tasting of beer and pot, Zoe was able to put the obvious disappointment she'd seen on Alec's face when he'd arrived to pick her up at the sheriff's office out of her mind.

Jake had assured her that she'd love northern California, where he had some friends who supposedly had a primo patch that brought in big bucks, but since she didn't do drugs and didn't expect to be staying with him all that long either, Zoe hadn't cared where they went. Just so they got the hell out of Kentucky before Alec gave up on her and sent her back to those Nazi nuns.

But now he'd screwed up her escape plan by bringing her here to Ireland. Short of swimming across the Atlantic Ocean, she couldn't figure any way to get off this damn island.

"I hate him."

Even as she threw herself onto the pillow, Zoe gave Alec reluctant credit for patience. Ever since he'd shown up at the school to bring her back with him to the only home she'd ever known, the home she once would have given anything to return to, she'd been behaving like the bitch juvenile delinquent of the world, but nothing seemed to faze him.

Not smoking in her room, even after he'd asked her not to, her dyed hair, makeup, or slut clothes. He hadn't said a word about the navel ring she flashed at every opportunity and although he'd grounded her after the shoplifting, he hadn't said a word about wishing he'd never brought her back from Switzerland.

"He probably just doesn't give a shit what you do," she muttered to herself.

But that wasn't really true. She'd seen the silent disappointment—and frustration—in his eyes. But amazingly, no matter how far she tested him, he still hadn't sent her away.

"It's only been six fucking months, stupid."

Six months that had, though she'd just as soon slash

her wrists as admit it, been the best she'd had in a long time. Which only made her feel guilty, since she wouldn't even be with Alec if her mother hadn't fallen off that yacht and drowned.

"Don't get used to it," she warned herself.

If there was one thing she'd learned in fifteen years, it was that nothing ever stayed the same and happy families were only some stupid Nick at Night fantasy. There was no way, in a million—a gazillion—years, she could ever be perky, perfect Marcia Brady with her two perky, perfect parents.

"Hell, you're not even pukey whiney Jan."

She was swiping at the moisture streaming down her cheeks when a thought occurred to her, like that bolt of lightning Kate O'Sullivan seemed to have pulled out of the clear blue sky. So long as she was stuck with him here in Ireland, Alec was also stuck with her. He couldn't send her away. At least not until he and Kate—who was actually pretty cool and sure didn't look like any wicked Grimms' fairy tale witch—got that stupid horse's head straightened out.

As Legends Lake galloped across the pasture, with the crumbling ruins of the castle and a sparkling blue lake in the distance behind him, Zoe did something she hadn't done since she was nine years old.

She folded her hands in the shape of a steeple, the way she'd been taught by the nuns in Lucerne. Next she squeezed her eyes—which were swimming with hot tears—so tightly shut that white spots swirled like paper-winged summer moths behind her closed lids.

Then she sent a small, desperate prayer heaven-ward, this time not asking for her stepfather to ride to her rescue, but instead begging God to freeze time.

9

SINCE IT WAS THE OFF-SEASON for racing, Kate had arranged for the use of a nearby turf track. The morning after the MacKennas' arrival, they gave a docile Legends Lake his first workout. He breezed beautifully, again and again, exactly like the champion she'd bred him to be, without a single problem.

The sight of the big Thoroughbred she'd brought into the world running with the soft air whistling through his mane, his long legs stretching, hooves throwing up turf, warmed Kate from the inside out, leaving her oblivious to the drizzle that threatened to turn a soft day into a wet one.

"We'll try again tomorrow," she suggested as they returned the Thoroughbred to the barn.

"We don't have that much time to screw around," Alec countered. "Even if the damn horse *does* break his habit of leaping fences in races, he's still going to need intensive training. The Derby's only a few weeks away."

"I'm aware of when your Kentucky Derby is, Mr. MacKenna."

"Then you know that time's running out on us. We

obviously are going to have to try him in a racing situation."

She sighed, knowing that he was right. "Tomorrow morning, then."

"Fine." He looked at the horse with something that appeared a great deal like disgust and picked up a towel.

"I'll tend to that," Kate said.

"He's my responsibility."

"Your responsibility is to train him to win races. Mine is to get him to trust me enough to tell me what's wrong with him. I'll be better able to bond with him if we have some time alone."

He gave her a long look. "All right," he said finally. "Since you're the one with the supposed magic touch, we'll play it your way. For now." He walked out of the barn without looking back.

Rude, impossible man. Shaking her head with frustration, Kate took a towel and curry comb and began drying and grooming the remarkably placid colt. Five minutes later, she heard the engine of the car she'd loaned Alec start up, then watched as he roared past the barn, down the dirt lane to the roadway, headed toward Castlelough.

She stroked Legends Lake's long neck. "He doesn't begin to deserve you, darling boy."

The Thoroughbred whinnied what Kate took for agreement.

Much, much later, Kate was in the kitchen, preparing supper, when the all too familiar harsh sound of heavy boots striking the wooden front stairs caused gooseflesh to rise on her arms.

She'd heard of post-traumatic stress syndrome. But until Erin O'Halloran, who'd spent years as war zone physician, had come to Castlelough and married

Michael, Kate had believed such things only happened to soldiers who'd fought in wars or people who'd survived catastrophes such as earthquakes or plane crashes. When Erin diagnosed her with PTSD, Kate began slipping away twice a month to visit a therapist in Galway, where she'd learned that many battered wives suffered with this syndrome.

He's not Cadel, she reminded herself as she overheard him knocking on his stepdaughter's door, the murmur of what appeared to be a one-way conversation, followed by a short, pungent curse. She heard the front door open again, then close on something close to a slam. Watching him stalk back to the apartment over the barn, Kate continued to remind herself that this gruff, uncommunicative man was not her abusive husband. Still, she was immensely relieved when both Americans chose to spend the evening in their separate rooms.

He declined supper, brusquely informing her that he'd eaten in the village. Zoe refused to come out of her room, but Kate noticed with satisfaction that the pan-fried chop, fresh vegetables and roast potatoes she'd left outside the bedroom door disappeared. Kate's mother had always professed that the way to a man's heart was through his stomach; hopefully the theory would prove true for sulky teenage girls.

The second night of the MacKennas' stay at the stud, Kate tossed and turned, unsuccessfully chasing sleep. Despite the night air outside the house being chilly enough to sketch frost pictures in the corner of the windowpanes, she was uncomfortably hot. She threw off the quilt and was in the bathroom, getting a drink of cool water from the tap, when she heard the muffled sound of weeping coming from the other side of the door.

She lifted her hand to knock, then paused, suspecting that the teenager wouldn't welcome a witness to her unhappiness. Still, unable to ignore a child in distress, she turned the brass knob and discovered the door unlocked.

Her heart turned over at the sight of Alec MacKenna's daughter, curled up into a tight little ball of misery. Sighing, Kate sat down on the edge of the narrow bed and silently stroked her hunched back.

"Go away," Zoe sniffled.

"I will. As soon as you assure me that you're not ill."

"I'm not." The words were muffled by the down pillow her face was buried in.

"I'd be more relieved if you'd be telling me that to my face," Kate suggested reasonably.

Zoe mumbled something she couldn't quite catch. Kate stayed where she was, her hands stroking, soothing, as she might a distressed filly.

Finally, the child flopped over onto her back. Her eyes, in the moonlight streaming through the lace curtains, were red-rimmed and swollen in her puffy face. "I hate it here."

"I can understand how you'd be missing America."

"It's not that. I miss Jake."

"Would Jake be your boyfriend?"

"Yeah." Kate thought she detected a wee bit of doubt in that declaration but decided it was no time to address it.

"As I'm certain he'd be missing you," she said, even as a vision of a long-haired young man—his body adorned with blue and red tattoos—playing billiards with a blonde in an impossibly short skirt flashed through her mind.

"Alec brought me to Ireland to break us up."

"Perhaps he thought he was doing what was best for you."

"He never cared all those years I was stuck in Europe. Why should he now?"

"It's difficult for parents and children to know what's in each other's heart. But I have the sense that your stepfather loves you a great deal."

"Then why did he let my mother take me away?"

"I wouldn't be knowing that." Another tear trailed down the thin, sad face. "Have you asked him?"

"No."

"Perhaps you should. Sometimes, even when a parent loves a child, family strife can cause a rift."

Zoe swiped at the tears with the backs of her hands, looking more Jamie or Brigid's age than the fifteen years Kate knew her to be. "Is that how it was with your parents?"

She sounded as if she was hoping for a sad tale. But Kate wasn't prepared to lie, not even if it could soothe this poor miserable girl's troubled heart.

"I was close to both my parents. I suppose that's because we shared so many of the same dreams and desires. We were, the three of us, comfortable and happy with our lives here in the west. Yet my older brother, Connor, ah, wasn't he another story altogether? From the time he was a young boy, he and my father were at odds.

"While the stud's always been successful enough, there's no denying that there were years when the money was tight and even during the good times, we never had enough for luxuries. Which was fine enough with me, because I've always been happy enough so long as I had a few horses in the barn and grain to feed them. But from Connor's earliest days, he was determined to leave this place." Kate frowned at the memory of her golden, star-crossed brother. "To outrun and outride our rural poverty and become rich and famous."

"Is he rich?"

"He was, for a time. He was a famous steeplechase rider—the best Ireland's ever produced, some say. He was well-known on the European circuit, but unfortunately lost his life when his horse failed to clear a wall in Brittany."

"That's just like my father dying in his car wreck."

"It's much the same," Kate agreed. "He came to see me that last day. I was cleaning out the stalls when I felt someone behind me, and there he was, standing in the door of the barn, as close to me as you are now, with the sun shining behind him, making it look as if he was wearing a halo.

"His hair was hanging down in his lively eyes as it always did, and the wicked, teasing smile on his handsome face was the one I knew well." Kate felt her heart clench just a bit at the memory. "Connor always reminded me of a pirate. Bold and dashing and restless as the wind, he was. At first I thought that he must have lost in an early round and returned home early. But of course, that wasn't the case at all."

"It wasn't?"

"It was not. I realized what had happened when I went to give him a hug, don't you see, and he held up a hand to keep me in my place. My feet could have been nailed to the barn floor, it was that impossible for me to move."

"Wow," Zoe breathed, seeming to momentarily forget her earlier distress, which had been Kate's intention in telling the tale. "Weren't you scared?"

"Of me own brother? No. But I was so very sad. You see, I'd witnessed his accident in a vision, but had no idea of how or when it might take place."

"Did you warn him ahead of time?"

"I did. But Connor was a brash, stubborn man, overbrimming with self-confidence and would be hearing none of it. When he stopped me from touching him, I knew the worst had happened, just as I'd seen it, and now he was coming to bid me farewell."

"That's really sad." Zoe's eyes, surrounded by black smudged mascara, glistened. Kate worried that she'd inadvertently caused more tears.

"Aye. But in its own way, it was special, too, since Connor had come to tell me in death what he said he wished he'd told me in life, that he loved me dearly and a lad couldn't have wanted for a better sister."

Her voice cracked, just a bit. Kate struggled for composure and won. "He asked me to watch out for his wife and baby, which, of course, he knew I would without him asking, Nora having been my dearest friend for all of my life. Then he leaned forward and kissed me, just a brush of his lips against my forehead, as light as butterfly wings, it was."

Kate brushed an equally tender fingertip against the teenager's forehead. "Then, with his good-bye said, his spirit faded away, like morning mist beneath a summer sun."

"Wow," Zoe repeated. Kate could practically hear the circuits whirring in her head beneath the now-flattened magenta spikes. "Is it true, then? What those men said? Are you really a witch?"

"There are some who'd be calling me that," Kate allowed mildly. "And I wouldn't be arguing the label. However, in reality, I'm more druid than witch."

"What's the difference?"

"It's a bit complicated, but basically a witch casts magic spells. I don't possess the power to do that and would not if I could. Yet I've always been more in tune with nature than some. Me mother said that I could hear the leaves unfurling from the seed pods in the darkness beneath the turf before I could walk."

"Did you really make that lightning bolt come down?"

"Aye. Oh, I wouldn't have hurt Brian, mind you. But there was a point that needed to be made. And even without the faeries to deal with, his foolish road could never possibly conquer the earth, even if he'd succeeded in building it."

"Why not?"

"Because Man, Earth and the Otherworld must constantly be kept in balance, and those things made by the hands of man can never rule over nature. What do you suppose would have happened if the highway construction crew had managed to uproot the tree and spread their asphalt and concrete along the cliff?"

"They would have killed the tree?"

"No. Because no matter how hard man may try to conquer his environment, mere human actions will never halt the ongoing force of the land. Wouldn't the roots continue to grow in the darkness beneath that road? Wouldn't they continue to press against the surface until finally breaking free so they can lift their bright green faces to the sun, the fire of all creation?"

"I've seen that," Zoe confirmed breathlessly, seemingly enthralled by thoughts she'd never before considered. "Roads and parking lots where grass and weeds have broken through."

"Of course you have. Every entity in the universe must remain free to be itself. And in the end, nature will always prove victorious."

"What else can you do? Can you cause an earthquake? Or a hurricane? Can you start fires?"

"Would you have me be putting on a show for

you?" Kate's smile took the bite from her words as she smoothed her palm over the child's spiky hair. "Two other things you must know about druids is that, first, we only answer the questions we choose to. And second, such powers are a sacred trust and not to be used lightly."

Zoe appeared to consider that. "Okay. But you said you saw your brother. Does that mean you can tell the future? Like those psychic hot lines on TV?"

"Not exactly. Now, I wouldn't be one to be putting down anyone's natural abilities, but from what I've seen, those individuals mostly appear to be taking money for telling people what they truly want to hear in the first place."

"I called one once."

"Did you now?"

"Yeah." Zoe sighed. "My mother and I had a fight about me wanting to leave school and go live with her right before she went off to Greece. Then she drowned before I could apologize for the things I said that night."

"Ah, darling, of course she knows that you're contrite." Kate's heart went out to this poor lost girl. "A child is always foremost in a parent's mind. Even when there are differences and arguments. Death doesn't change that."

"Do you really think so?"

"I do, indeed. Modern society believes death is the last thing. But in truth it's merely a cobweb we pass through." She pointed out the window at the silver moon that was floating in the midnight sky. "That moon will get smaller and smaller until it vanishes from our sight. Without it, the night appears a dark and frightening place, yet is the moon truly dead, never to return again? Or isn't the dark moon merely a passing phase of the bright, which will return again to light our sky and our lives."

"I don't think my mother's going to come back."

"Perhaps it's her destiny to move on."

"She was already real good at that." Zoe sighed. "Could you speak to her for me, like you did your brother? Could you tell her that I'm okay?"

"If I were your mother, I'd much rather be hearing such news from you."

"I don't know how to talk to the dead."

"Of course you do. It's no different from speaking with the living. Just open up your heart and she'll hear you. And if you keep your heart open enough, you'll be hearing her responses to you, as well."

"Really?" Vast hope shimmered in that single word.

"I promise." Kate straightened the sheets, and tucked her in, as she would one of her own. "Now, why don't you be getting some sleep? You know, I was having a thought while I was brushing my teeth tonight."

She waited for Zoe to say something. But the teenager seemed to be retreating back into her mutinous, silent mode.

"I was thinking that I'd probably be needing a little help with your da's horse." She was encouraged when Zoe didn't correct her unintentional slip, reminding her that Alec was her *stepfather*.

"You want me to help you?"

"If you'd like. After you get your studies done each day."

Zoe thought about that for a moment. "I don't know anything about horses."

"Ah, I told you, darling, it's in your blood." She bent and brushed her lips against the girl's temple.

"I don't know if Alec will let me."

"Why don't you be leaving the MacKenna to me? If

he doesn't immediately take to the idea, I'll be putting a spell on him."

"I thought you didn't do spells."

"Isn't there always a first time for everything?"

Her words earned a smile. Oh, it was faint, sure enough. But, Kate thought with satisfaction as she returned to her own room, it was a start.

10

KATE WOKE IN A BAD MOOD. Despite having stuffed
her pillow with soothing hops and sweet woodruff,
she'd spent a restless night chasing sleep. Finally, as
the moon had ridden higher and higher in the night
sky, she'd slipped downstairs and brewed herself a
cup of lemon balm tea, which finally allowed her to
drift off to sleep sometime before dawn. But even that
short rest hadn't helped, since it was filled with
dreams in which she was doing all sorts of hot, erotic
things with the American.

Obviously the lemon balm had affected her
strangely. "I must have made it a bit too strong," she
decided.

Despite her belief that dreams were communica-
tions from the Invisible World, Kate could not believe
they actually had anything to do with the Yank himself. It had been a very long time since she'd had such
a visceral reaction to a man. Even as she continued to
find those images unsettling, Kate assured herself that
she should be relieved her horrific marriage hadn't
killed every bit of womanhood she possessed. It was
encouraging to discover that after all she'd suffered

with Cadel, she could respond to a man in such an elemental, female way.

Not that she intended to get involved with Alec MacKenna. After all, by both the laws of Ireland and the Church she was a married woman. And would be for more than two years to come. Divorce may now be possible, but it wasn't easy. Nor quick. So, while she wasn't about to complicate matters by having herself a flirtation with the Yank trainer, perhaps someday, once she was legally free, she might consider taking a tumble.

She'd willingly surrendered her virginity to a man she'd believed at the time she loved, only to realize later that her poor brain—and several other vital body parts—had been bedazzled by clever words and thrillingly wicked touches.

She'd married out of duty to her family and her unborn child to a man she'd neither loved nor desired. But at the time she'd not had a plethora of choices. The truth was that while Cadel had not been in the market for a wife, the stud had proven an appealing enough dowry that he'd agreed to make an honest woman of her, thus saving the Fitzpatrick family from the shame she would have brought them from giving birth to a child—by a Yank, for heaven's sake!—out of wedlock.

Now, as the mere memory of those dreams seeped into her veins like warm honey, Kate reminded herself that even though sometime in the future she might be willing to engage in a passing affair, she had no intention of ever again giving her heart to any man.

She was, after all, a modern woman of the new millennium, on her way to becoming one of the first divorcees in Ireland. Surely in this brave new world, which allowed females such freedom not known since the ancient days of Celtic Brehon law, women were once again free to separate love and sex.

For a modern woman, she was certainly a pitiful sight. Kate groaned as she looked at herself in the mirror over the sink. The flesh beneath her eyes was puffy and appeared to be bruised. If she didn't get some decent sleep soon, she was going to resemble Echtga-the-Awful, the underworld hag for which Galway's Slieve Aughty mountains had been named.

She dressed and went out to the brood barn to check on her favorite mare, who'd been born on this very stud. It was the mare's first pregnancy and Kate was pleased she was progressing nicely.

"You put Guinness in her feed?" a deep voice rumbled behind her.

"Aye." Kate kept pouring the creamy, black-as-bog-water stout into the alfalfa. "I do. Hasn't it been prescribed by doctors for old people and pregnant women for two centuries?"

"Surely not these days."

"Surely so," she responded easily. "We've also given it to our pregnant mares three times a week since the eighteen-hundreds. It happens to be full of vitamins. Indeed, its creamy head is due to local seaweed, which is filled with nutrients and gathered on our own beach." There had been times, during lean years, when the extra income from that seaweed had paid for feed.

"I doubt its popularity has anything to do with it being a good source of vitamins."

"I suspect you're right, Mr. MacKenna."

He shoved his hands into the pockets of his jeans—which fit his long legs very nicely—rocked back on the heels of his boots, and looked around the brood barn where the visiting mares, along with her own, were stabled.

It consisted of several large stalls, outdoor pens where the would-be mother horses could be corralled before and after breeding, along with a covered breezeway she'd added two summers ago.

"Is that the breeding barn on the other side of the breezeway?"

"It is. We keep three stallions of our own at stud, as well as a number of visitors whose owners have hired us to make a match. More and more of the breeders are going to artificial insemination, but despite understanding a need to keep up with the times, I prefer the old-fashioned way."

"If horses could talk, there are probably a great many stallions who'd thank you for sticking with tradition."

"And what makes you think they haven't?"

She'd meant it as a jest. But obviously he found nothing humorous in her light statement. His face shadowed. "Who's this?" he asked in a not at all subtle move to change the subject from her claim of equine communication.

"Nora Barnacle." She stroked the pregnant bay mare's nose.

"Named after Joyce's wife?"

"Why, yes." She couldn't quite conceal her surprise. "I wouldn't think that many Americans would be acquainted with James Joyce."

He shrugged. "Traveling the circuit, I didn't have a lot of time to make new friends. A guy I worked for turned me on to books when I was in my teens, so I used to spend most of my spare time reading."

"Isn't that fortunate for you. Books can be a grand companion." Kate was surprised he'd chosen to use his free time in solitary pursuits. Knowing how easy sex was to be had on the racing circuit, she had no doubt any number of women would be more than willing to help him wile away his free hours.

When an unbidden and certainly unwelcome vision flashed before her eyes, a steamy scene from last night's dream of rolling around with this man amidst tangled sheets, both of them as naked as the day they were born, Kate felt hot color flood into her cheeks.

She knew that most of the people in Castlelough would describe her as calm and collected, the type of person one would choose to ring up in an emergency. *Oh yes,* they'd undoubtedly say, *Kate O'Sullivan may be a witch, but she's certainly a level-headed one.*

What no one—with the possible exception of Nora Gallagher, who could not be closer if she was a blood-born sister—knew was that all Kate's life she'd been in constant war with her emotions. Emotions that ran too close to the surface. Wild, unruly, reckless emotions she fought to control now.

She rubbed her cheek against the side of Nora's face. Horses had always calmed her. As it seemed, she in turn, calmed them. "Nora's by Rebel's Rogue out of Patrick's Prize."

"That's quite a bloodline."

"Aye. It is."

Alec had observed the color flooding into Kate's face and was amazed that there was a woman left anywhere in the world—even here in Catholic Ireland—capable of blushing. Kate O'Sullivan was no innocent virgin. She was married, with two children who'd arrived home from their aunt Nora's home last evening.

The little girl, Brigid, a red-haired charmer, had chattered away like a magpie, filling her mother in on her adventures. The boy, Jamie, had appeared more quiet and a great deal more serious than his sister. That could be due to their difference in age. Still, there'd been something familiar in the boy's sober blue eyes when Alec had first come into the room. A wariness Alec remembered all too well.

The flush faded and she seemed to relax again, laughing lightly as the mare nibbled her shoulder. She was dressed in an Aran sweater that came nearly to her knees, faded jeans and scuffed boots. Certainly not the garb of a faerie, yet there was something ethereal about her, almost as if she could be concealing a pair of gossamer wings beneath that heavy cream-hued sweater.

"The stallion who sired her baby is Fenian, whose first two colts have already proven themselves on the track and the third, a yearling, looks to have grand potential," she continued, unaware of Alec's uncharacteristic flight of fantasy. "He's one of our more successful acquisitions."

"How many foals do you deliver in a given year?"

"This baby, which will be the final one of the season, will make a grand total of forty I've brought into the world this year."

"*You* brought into the world? Yourself?"

"I've had help with some of the more difficult births, but isn't this my stud? People who bring their horses here and put them in my care expect me to be the one to tend to them."

"Sounds like a lot of work."

"Ah, but surely you yourself know that it isn't work when you love what you're doing."

"Point taken. You've got a nice setup."

"Thank you. I hope to build a separate foaling barn this summer."

"All the new business you'll get when Legends Lake sweeps the Triple Crown should pay for any system you want."

She tilted her head and looked up at him. "That's quite a goal you've set for the colt."

"He's capable of that, and more."

"So long as you can get him to stop jumping fences."

"So long as *we* can get him to stop jumping fences."

"Would that be meaning that you're beginning to accept the idea of us working together?"

"It would be meaning," he said, tossing her Irish syntax back at her, "that I don't see how either of us has much choice in the matter. Because whether we like it or not, Mrs. O'Sullivan, we both have a helluva lot riding on this horse living up to his breeding."

She studied him for a long silent moment. Since she seemed to be choosing her words with care, Alec waited her out.

"If I were to ask you something, would you answer me truthfully?"

"I don't lie."

"I thought not." She nodded, seemingly satisfied. Her intelligent gaze lifted to his. "Are you typically as rude as you've been since arriving here in Ireland?"

Who the hell ever accused the Irish of being incapable of a direct statement? With those big lake blue eyes looking up through those incredible lashes at him, Alec would have found it impossible to not tell the truth.

"No. Not rude. I suppose I can be impatient. Brusque at times. And stubborn. People have, on occasion, even accused me of being conceited, but a close friend of mine once pointed out that it's not bragging if it's the truth." He waited for her to smile at Pete's old adage. She didn't. "But rude? No."

"I see." She glanced out the open barn door, toward the paddock, and beyond, to the mist-draped lake and the castle ruins. In the dawning light he could see a pair of swans, one black, one white, floating on the glassy waters. She began shredding a piece of straw with long delicate fingers he found easier to envision strumming a gilded harp than pulling a foal from a twelve-hundred-pound horse.

The west was beginning to awaken. A ribbon of rose appeared at the top of the eastern mountains; lark song floated on the cool morning air. Alec heard the lowing of cattle and the baas of sheep in distant meadows. Kate appeared to be a woman comfortable with silences. He liked the fact that she didn't feel the need to fill every conversational pause with words.

She turned back toward him. "Then the only thing I can conclude is that it must be *me* who has you behaving so uncharacteristically." She ran her fingers down the front of Nora's face again. "Is it that you don't like me?"

"I don't know you," he pointed out.

"True enough. Nor have you made the slightest effort to become acquainted." She held up a slender hand. "I'm sorry. Please forget I said that. It was rude of me."

"Hey, I'm the one who's rude, remember? Besides, it's the truth. My daughter and I have been lousy houseguests. You've every right to be pissed off."

"I'm not—" She paused. "If I'm to request honesty from you, the least I can do is return it. In truth, I suppose I am a wee bit irritated with your behavior."

"Only a wee bit?"

"All right." She tossed her head on a flare of frustration. "Perhaps more than that." Her gaze slid back to the castle. Toward the plump and seemingly contented mare. Then, finally up at him again. "I'm not exactly what you were expecting, am I, Mr. MacKenna?"

A bark of a laugh escaped at what had to be the understatement of all time. "No, Mrs. O'Sullivan, you definitely are not."

"You believe that I'm fey."

"I believe that *you* believe you are," he corrected. "Since you stated that fact for yourself out on the cliff."

"Aye. I did. And, since it appears that, like it or not,

we're destined to work together, you may as well know from the start that I *am* fey. I see things, Mr. MacKenna, before they happen."

He folded his arms. "What sort of things?"

"Random events. Some good, some bad. Before I'd even begun first form at Holy Child School in the village, I saw a black wreath on Mrs. Callahan's door. Two months later she dropped dead of a heart attack while weeding her cabbage patch."

"Was she old?"

"She was. In her nineties."

"Hell, then her death couldn't have been that much of a surprise to anyone. You would have been at the age when you probably first began to ponder the concept of death. It's not so farfetched that you'd put those feelings onto an elderly person you knew."

"I admire your argument, Mr. MacKenna, since it was the same one me own father made at the time. Though I am surprised you'd claim to be knowing anything about childhood development."

"Zoe and her mother lived with me from the time she was four years old until she was nine. We had a barn cat—an orange tabby she named Marmalade— die when she was about the age you would have been when you imagined—"

"I did not imagine. I *saw*."

"Whatever," he said with blatant disbelief. "We had a proper funeral for the cat. I made a small wooden coffin with wood milled on our property, Zoe and her mother made a small headstone and we buried him in the MacKenna family cemetery." He smiled a bit at the memory. "Then we all sang 'Amazing Grace.' "

"It sounds like a lovely funeral. That was very kind of you."

"It wasn't that big a deal."

"I suspect it was to your stepdaughter."

"The point I'm trying to make is that for a week after the cat's funeral, Zoe kept insisting that Marmalade came in her window every night to sleep with her."

"Perhaps he did."

"Perhaps you weren't paying close attention, Mrs. O'Sullivan. The cat was dead."

"Its body was dead. But not its spirit. Isn't death merely a shadow we pass through on our circular journey from the Unknown to this world, then back again? An incident—even a miracle—in the midst of our never-ending lives?"

Damn. And here he'd begun to think that she was a reasonably sensible person. A bit quirky, perhaps. But not mad. Once again Alec worried about the wisdom of trusting Winnie's horse—the Thoroughbred in which he had a potential fifty-percent stake—over to this retro Irish flower child.

"I didn't think pagans believed in miracles."

"I'm reminded of their existence on a daily basis, whenever I look at my own children and realize that they, like all children of this world, were born of a man and a woman coming together, minds, hearts and bodies joined as one, allowing life to flow through them and in them. And from this passion, nine months later, another child arrives from the Unknown. What could be more miracle than that?"

"Childbirth is special," he allowed. "But when you die, you become nothing but dust. Dust to dust, ashes to ashes. You live, you die, then it's over."

"Did it ever occur to you that perhaps you've gotten the message wrong? That the reason for burial is to allow the discarded body that has hosted the spirit to return to the earth, the Mother from whom that flesh was born?"

Alec raked a hand through his hair. "Look, if it makes all you New Agers happy to think that—"

"There is nothing *new* about my beliefs, Mr. MacKenna." Both her back and her tone had turned to steel. "Indeed, my Celtic religion, which teaches us that time is a curve, a continuous link without beginning or end, goes back three millennia here in Ireland." When she absently ran a fingertip around the curving symbols etched into the silver oval she wore on a ribbon around her neck, his attention was drawn to her long slender throat.

"I've nothing against any organized religion. Heaven knows, my own faith carries its own rules and prohibitions. What bothers me about modern beliefs is that so many of them require us to believe that this one, fleeting lifetime is all we're given. Which, in my view, tends to make people more inclined to grasp all they can, while they can, even at the expense of others."

When her words had him thinking of Wellesley's abuse of Lady Justice, Alec forced the bitter memory down. The early morning hours, when most of the world was still asleep, had always been Alec's favorite time of day. A time when he could enjoy the sight of horses running in the misty air and not have to exchange small talk with anyone. Morning conversation was definitely not on his hit parade of favorite things to do. As for discussing religion at any time of day, forget it.

"Did it ever occur to *you* that just as the human race has given up living in caves and hunting woolly mammoths, we've moved past worshiping trees?"

"Druids do not worship trees. We worship *amidst* trees. There *is* a difference. Indeed, the very word *druid* translates to 'having the wisdom of the oaks.' " She paused when he didn't respond to that claim. "I can see that you're not believing me."

Alec figured that it didn't exactly take a druid seer to read the skepticism on his face.

"While I don't usually share my experiences with those not close to me, and I certainly don't concern myself with attempting to convince skeptics that their views are narrow and shortsighted, let me tell you another story," she suggested.

"Isn't that what the Irish do best? Tell stories," he elaborated at her questioning look.

"Yet another tradition that goes back to the Celts," she agreed pointedly, refusing to smile. "When I was a teenager, the same age as your Zoe is now, Nora Gallagher—she was Nora Joyce then—and I were picnicking on the beach with Devlin Monohan and Peter Quinlan one lovely summer afternoon.

"Peter was as handsome as an ancient king, and the lad all the girls attending Holy Child School daydreamed about when we should have been keeping our minds on studies. As the sun sank into the sea, I could sense that he was about to kiss me. A kiss I had, in truth, been waiting all day to give him."

"And then he keeled over and died?"

She frowned. "Here I am, sharing the most private part of myself, and you refuse to take it seriously."

"Sorry." He gave her a go-ahead gesture. "Please continue."

She nodded. "I will . . . Just when Peter's lips were a mere breath from mine, I viewed, in my mind's eye, little Kevin Noonan floating facedown in the surf. I'd just managed to call out a warning to his mother, who was packing their dinner things away into a wicker basket, when a white-crested wave swept the toddler off his feet and began pulling him back out to sea.

"Fortunately, Mr. Noonan, who was closer to the surf, was able to get to him in time, and except for swallowing a bit of salt water, the child was fine."

It was, Alec allowed, an interesting anecdote. But he didn't believe there was anything psychic about it.

"Peter was getting ready to kiss you. You glanced out of the corner of your eye to see if anyone was watching. Perhaps because you didn't want the townspeople to see you kissing a boy and tell your parents."

"My parents would hardly have been surprised by that, Mr. MacKenna. Seeing as they'd certainly been young themselves and undoubtedly had stolen kisses on that selfsame beach."

"Ok, perhaps you *did* want people to see you."

"Why would I be wanting people to see so personal a thing as a kiss?"

"If you're looking for privacy, a public beach sure isn't the place to find it. If Peter was as good-looking as you say—"

"He was, indeed. The most handsome boy in Holy Child School."

"At that age, it stands to reason that you'd like to show off a little. To let everyone see that of all the girls in Castlelough, *you* were the one who'd managed to land the hunk."

The quick flush of color in her cheeks suggested he wasn't far off the mark. "Wouldn't that make me very shallow?"

"It'd make you a kid. You're supposed to be shallow when you're fifteen."

"I should have realized that you're an expert on teenage girls. Seeing how your own relationship with your stepdaughter appears to be going along so splendidly."

"Things have been a little rocky. But we'll work it

out. Somehow . . . So," he said, returning to the original topic, "while you were sneaking a look around the beach to make sure you had witnesses to this long-awaited kiss, you caught a glimpse of this kid, whatever his name was—"

"Kevin Noonan."

"You saw Kevin Noonan toddling down to the sea by himself. Your vivid imagination, along with a natural human instinct to protect a defenseless child, kicked in just before the wave washed him off his feet. That's all it was."

She sighed. "You're a hard man, Mr. MacKenna."

"So they say."

Actually, there were a few other names more often used to describe him, not all of them flattering. Believing that being single-minded and competitive were admirable attributes rather than character flaws, Alec had always considered the names used by his detractors a compliment. It was probably good for her to know that if they were to have any working relationship, she couldn't expect him to stand back and let her cast her spells, or voodoo, or whatever she did on Legends Lake.

"Would they be correct, then?" she asked. "Those people who call you hard?"

"If refusing to accept pretty illusions as reality makes me hard, then I suppose they're right. If wanting to do anything—short of breaking the rules or endangering a horse—to win makes me hard, yeah. If expecting my horse to be the first across the finish line makes me hard, I damn well wouldn't want to be any other way."

"Well, that's certainly to the point."

"I don't believe in dancing around a subject. So, tell me, did you get your kiss?"

"Ah, and isn't that the regrettable part of my little

tale? After actually witnessing the ability that he'd heard rumored about me over the years, Peter—who according to his mother was destined for a life as a cardinal in Rome—feared he might be risking his immortal soul by publicly kissing a girl who possessed such devilish arts. . . . He did, however, invite me to go down to the caves with him one night the following week."

"The caves?"

"They're carved out of the cliff by the sea. In the olden days they were used by smugglers trading French brandy for Irish fish and horses. In more modern time, they're where boys might be taking girls they don't want to be seen in public with."

"Peter may have been a hunk. But he was also a jerk."

Her lips curved in a faint smile. "He was young, no more than seventeen himself. Afraid, and at the same time intrigued, by the forbidden idea of dating the Castlelough witch."

"I suppose it would be too much to hope that he's now a potbellied farmer, saddled with a fat, ill-tempered wife, countless shiftless relatives and a passel of wild kids."

"As it so happens, he's a priest in Limerick. I've run into him from time to time and he's apparently become more broad-minded as he's grown older because while he hasn't brought up the subject, we've shared some lovely chats."

"That's real open-minded of him." For some reason, Alec was really pissed off on her account. Perhaps because she was so damn accepting.

"I'm told the unmarried girls, and not a few of the married women in the parish, refer to him as Father-What-a-Waste."

As irritated as he was, Alec laughed at this. She

smiled in response, a true smile that lit her eyes and turned them the remarkable blue of the lake, whose banks the Joyce castle had been built on.

Her gaze turned earnest. "My purpose in telling you these stories, Mr. MacKenna, is to try to explain that I certainly did not ask for this ability, which, in truth, at times feels a great deal more curse than gift. It was passed down to me by an ancestor on my grandmother's side, Biddy Early, a healer who practiced white magic for those who came to her with problems.

"Since there's no way to send back my inheritance, I've come to accept it as part of who—and what—I am. It's no different from my having black hair or blue eyes. Or being left-handed."

If it were true, he suspected it would be a helluva lot different. But since he refused to believe it was the case, he saw no reason to argue a moot point.

"I'll accept that you believe this. I'll also give you points for seeming to be well-grounded, in spite of your belief system."

"Perhaps *because* of it," she murmured.

"Fine. As I said, your beliefs are your own business. But I still have one major problem with your *inheritance*."

"Oh? And what would that be?"

"Not *that*. *Who*. Zoe. She's at an impressionable age, admittedly has some problems right now, and I damn well don't want her glamorizing what you do and—"

"Be swayed over to the dark side?"

It appeared he was not the only blunt speaker in the barn. "I was attempting to put it a bit more diplomatically, but, well, yeah."

"You don't like me very much, do you, Mr. MacKenna?"

"As we've already established, I don't know you. Nor do you know me."

"Well, that's certainly true enough. Since my gift is only a part of what I am, let me give you a bit more information about myself: I'm a horse breeder's daughter who could ride before I could walk. I've sat up nights in freezing weather with mares who are about to foal; I've had ribs cracked from being kicked by a mare in heat, and before we began padding the breeding stalls, I had my wrist broken when an overeager stallion knocked me against the wall.

"By the time he died seven winters ago, my father had taught me everything he knew about horses. Everything his own da had taught him. During my lifetime, I've acquired my own knowledge as well, and although I wouldn't be one to be heaping pride on myself, there are few in this country, even among those working in the lofty environs of the National Stud, who would be better with horses than I am.

"There are, admittedly, those few gossipy old souls in the village who might warn you against being in the company of a witch. I follow the old ways because they seem more natural to me, but I do not recruit impressionable children into my coven, not that I even belong to one, because I prefer solitary practice.

"Witches are not humpbacked, hooked-nose, wart-faced crones who cackle over cauldrons bubbling with concoctions of dragons' teeth and eye of newt. I do not dance naked in the moonlight and I've never put a spell on any person.

"Though there are a few I can think of who would have only been improved by being turned into toads," she tacked on as an afterthought.

"Too bad," he said, when she paused to take a breath. "Oh, not the toad thing," he elaborated at her questioning look. "Though I can certainly think of a few people myself I wouldn't mind that happening to." *Wellesley for one.* "But it's a bit disappointing to hear that you don't dance naked in the moonlight." He skimmed a quick, but thoroughly masculine look over her. "That would definitely make my time here in Castlelough more . . . interesting."

He'd expected her to blush again. Instead her gaze hardened. Her full, unpainted lips firmed.

"My husband may no longer live here at the farm, Mr. MacKenna. But I am still a married woman. And, since it takes five years to become divorced in Ireland, will remain married for another two years. As Peter learned for himself, simply because I do not happen to be a practicing Catholic like most of the rest in Castlelough, I'm not after romping in caves, or haystacks," she added with an upward glance, "with any good-looking male in trousers who happens by."

"I'll keep that in mind."

She gave him another long deep look, then nodded. "Fine."

"Well then, since we have that little matter settled, there's something else."

"Oh?"

"Since we're going to be spending a lot of time together over the next few weeks, it'd probably be easier if we dropped the formalities." He held out the hand he hadn't bothered to offer when they'd first met on the cliff. "I'm Alec."

Unlike her countrymen, whom Alec knew were capable of holding grudges for centuries, Kate didn't seem to be inclined to stay angry.

"Good day to you, Alec." Her voice was rich and warm. "And I'd be Kate."

She slipped her hand into his. Her skin was as soft and smooth as it looked, but his thumb brushed against a ridge of calluses at the base of her fingers.

Her bones were slender and felt about as light as a bird's, yet her breeding work meant that she routinely handled a thousand pounds of aroused stallion. He suspected the slight kink in her wrist came from that time she'd mentioned, when she'd been slammed against the breeding wall.

Kate O'Sullivan might look and smell like some mythical faerie who dwelt in magical Irish hawthorn trees, but there was no denying that she had a close acquaintance with hard physical work. The barns she'd shown off with pride were as up to date as his own. That the modern equipment was housed in century-old barns appealed to the part of him that had insisted on upgrading the Inverness Farms buildings, rather than razing them and building new, which would have been simpler and cheaper. He'd kept those old weather-hewn barns with their stone foundations partly because of a sense of history, continuity and for aesthetic reasons, but also because he'd always been intrigued by contrasts.

As they drove the few kilometers to the turf track, while he knew it was dangerous to allow his mind to go in that direction, Alec decided that Kate definitely fit that description. Her detailed breeding records, kept in a thick leather-bound journal and backed up on the hard drive of her computer, revealed that in business the woman was practical and efficient, with the exception of those rare instances she'd admitted having trusted her instincts when matching two Thoroughbreds. Checking the records of the offspring of these hunch matches revealed that her instincts, thus far, had proven to be excellent.

But then, complicating the picture of this calm, intelligent, hardworking woman, was that passionate druid faerie protector he'd met on the cliff. Where the hell did *she* fit into the picture?

Contrasts layered upon yet more contrasts, all wrapped around a charming female enigma. That was Kate O'Sullivan.

They turned off the road onto a narrow lane. As she downshifted for the washboard ruts, Alec was drawn to the sight of the hand curved over the black knob of the gear shift and found himself wondering what those long slender fingers would feel like on his body.

11

LEGENDS LAKE

Kate O'Sullivan.

the gear shift and found himself wondering what

"Mr. MacKenna? Alec?"

She'd parked beside the shedrow, cut the engine
and was now looking at him curiously. "Would there
be a problem?"

"No." He blinked and the provocative, unbidden
image of her shiny hair, draped over his naked chest
like a long black veil, evaporated.

Christ. Didn't he have enough troubles, with Legends Lake and Zoe? There was no way he was going to
allow Kate O'Sullivan to become yet another problem.

She'd arranged to have a group of local breeders
meet them at the track with horses. They ran two mock
races, four and one-half furlongs each, around the oval
turf track and both times Legends Lake broke first and
held the lead, crossing the finish line ahead of the others. Mentally in sync with the stallion, Kate experienced the thrill of the races as if she were Legends
Lake: The breeze feathering her hair could have been
that rushing through his mane, the drumbeat of her
heart the pounding of his limestone-strengthened
hooves throwing up clods of dew-moist turf, the
sound of the nearby surf, the roar of the crowd, his

pleasure as he streaked to the finish ahead of the others, *her* pleasure.

He was more than the champion she'd been hoping for when she'd arranged the match between his parents. Legends Lake was magic.

"We'll try it again," Alec said.

Kate refrained, just barely, from asking who died and made him Emperor of the Realm. She looked up at the sky where a handful of small gray clouds was drifting by. "It looks as if it might rain."

"I watched him run in mud and it didn't bother him. Besides, the track is turf."

He spoke with the unyielding confidence of a man accustomed to having his orders obeyed, which wasn't that surprising, given his winning reputation. But she'd promised the others, who hadn't been all that happy about helping out some wealthy Yank horseman, that it would be a short morning's exercise session.

Summoning up her brightest smile, she went over to attempt to coax them into compliance. Since Castlelough was located in a Gaeltacht part of the country, where despite the old British penal laws, the native language had never been allowed to die out, Kate knew that Alec couldn't understand their Irish conversation. But she suspected that he could well read the frowns darkening the ruddy faces.

"Haven't we done enough humoring of your mad Yank for one day?" Kevin Murphy, who owned the bay gelding who'd come in a full two lengths behind in second place, complained.

"He's not my Yank. And aren't you being well paid for your time and effort?"

"Money isn't everything," the wealthy farmer she suspected still had the first pound he'd ever made said.

"Of course it isn't," she soothed, encouraged by the

fact that not everyone shared Alec MacKenna's mercenary attitude. "But you'd be doing me a great personal favor, Kevin. I'm trying to protect the reputation of the stud, not just for my da's memory, but for Irish horses in general.

"If this colt gets banned from racing, people might not want to buy a horse with the same bloodline, which could affect any breeding potential from that colt of yours that's showing so much promise. Since he and Legends Lake share the same dam," she reminded him pointedly.

"That would be of no concern to me," Michael O'Bannion gruffly entered into the discussion, "since none of my horses have any link to that of your Yank's."

"He's not *my* Yank. And that doesn't matter, Michael. Since we all know how a brush—even a false one—can spread a wide swath. You could end up getting unfairly tarred with the rest of us. If you won't do it for me, at least do it to uphold the grand tradition and protect the future of all of Ireland's horses.

"Over the centuries, when others have looked down their noses at us for one reason or another, the entire world—even our former enemies—has acknowledged Ireland's reputation for breeding champion horse stock. Surely you would not let us lose that? Because without our horses,"—she threw out her arms—"what are we?"

John O'Neill laughed at her fervor. "Ah, Katie, child, what a fine heartfelt speech. Why, if I'd closed my eyes and imagined your voice two octaves lower, I would have thought I was hearing the dear departed Joseph Fitzpatrick himself."

Her father and John had been closest friends for more than three decades. John had been the best man at her parents' wedding and was her godfather. In the interconnected way of small communities, she'd once had a wild schoolgirl crush on his nephew, Brendan, who owned the Irish Rose pub, and John's eldest son, Patrick, a solicitor in Galway, was handling her divorce.

"Does that mean you're agreeing?"

"For you, lass," he said. "And for your father's memory, God rest his soul."

"God rest it and keep it," the other two men murmured automatically.

"We'll also be doing it to uphold the grand reputation of Irish horses," Kevin Murphy added, revealing that it had been her final argument that had swayed him.

"But we'll do no more than one last run," O'Bannion stated firmly.

She smiled in gratitude. "Thank you."

"No thanks necessary, darling," John said. "But know this one thing, Katie. We are *not* doing it for your Yank."

Pleased to have won their cooperation, Kate decided against pointing out yet again that the MacKenna was not *her* Yank.

She walked back over to Alec, who was standing there, arms folded, waiting with an impatience that shimmered around him in a bright red aura.

"They'll be staying for one more run," she reported.

"Thanks. I was watching you win them over. If you ever decide to give up breeding champions, you'd probably make one helluva politician."

Such simple words. Yet it was lovely hearing them. Not that she'd be caring for compliments from the American, Kate lied to herself as the horses were led back to the portable starting gate for the third time this morning.

It was just that it had been a very long time since she'd received a compliment from any man other than

Michael, Brendan O'Neill or Quinn Gallagher, none of whom counted, since she and Michael were more like brother and sister, having run barefoot in the fields together when they were still in nappies. Brendan, who'd been her brother's best friend, had become hers as well and was as dear to her as Connor had been, and Quinn was obviously besotted with Nora.

Kate wondered what it would feel like to be so adored, then shook off the slight depression, reminding herself that she was not divorcing Cadel in order to start up with anyone else. She was divorcing him because she wanted to ensure that the harsh and brutal alcoholic was out of her life forever.

"He certainly doesn't look nervous," she ventured as Legends Lake calmly awaited the start of the race.

"Hell, he doesn't even look awake."

"No doubt he's conserving his strength."

Alec's pointed look suggested that she might be overdoing the optimism.

The colt broke as he had the first two times, flying out of the gate like a bullet shot from the barrel of a gun. His muscles bunched, rippled, then stretched with a power that literally took Kate's breath away. His already long stride lengthened, the clods thrown up by his hooves striking the chests of the horses behind him.

Kate unconsciously grasped Alec's arm. "He's glorious."

"You won't get any argument there."

He'd no sooner agreed when, faster than a breath, quicker than a heartbeat, it happened. The colt reared, clawed his front hooves in the air, dropped back down to the turf and took off streaking across the track.

A scream lodged in Kate's throat as she watched him leap the rail fence and keep running, approaching a stone wall without so much as slowing. The rider,

Johnny Doyle, cousin to both Brian of the hated bulldozer and her own husband, was hanging on like a cockleburr. Her grip on Alec's arm tightened.

"Hell," Alec muttered.

It was all happening too fast. The wall was too high, Legends Lake was running too fast. It was, Kate thought, like watching two freight trains speeding toward each other on a single track. The outcome was as inevitable as it was impossible to change. With fear thundering in her ears, remembering all too well that vision she'd had so long ago of Connor failing to clear just such a wall on a faraway Breton coast, Kate braced for tragedy.

Later, she would try to convince herself she'd imagined it. Surely no horse, none of this mortal world, could have achieved such a feat. But for one suspended fleeting moment, Kate could have sworn she was watching winged Pegasus soar over the wall without so much as breaking his stride.

The knocking on the door was driving Zoe crazy. "Go away," she called out for the umpteenth time in the past ten minutes. She turned up the volume on her Discman. But she could still hear it.

"All right. I'm coming!" She tossed aside the book her literature teacher had assigned—coincidentally, *The Crucible*, which Zoe found ironic since she was currently staying in a witch's house—stomped across the wood floor, unlatched the lock and yanked the door open.

"What do you want . . . and who are you?" she asked, staring down into the unfamiliar freckled face of a kid who looked to be about eight or nine.

"I'm Jamie O'Sullivan." He moved aside so she could see the child behind him, who looked like a small, red-haired doll. "And this is my sister Brigid. We live here. In fact, you're sleeping in my room."

That explained the collection of American baseball cards she'd found in a shoe box in the closet and a plastic model of a dinosaur in a drawer.

"Mama fixed it up to be pretty for you," the doll piped up. "Because you're a girl."

"I didn't know. Look, if you want it back—"

"Oh no," he said quickly, paling so that the freckles on his face stood out like small copper coins. "Ma'd be getting angry at me if I made you feel unwelcome. Besides, I like sleeping up in the attic. It has a grand view of the castle."

"Yeah, I saw the castle."

"That's one reason we knocked on your door," Brigid said in a clear, sweet voice. "To ask if you wanted to go there with us."

"You want *me* to go with *you?*" Oh God. If there was anything more pitiful than being so bored and hard up for company you were actually considering playing with a couple of little kids, Zoe didn't know what it was.

"You wouldn't have to be walking all the way." The boy's eyes were the clear blue of the alpine lakes Zoe remembered from Switzerland. She could see his mother in those eyes. And in the little girl's full rosy lips.

"We could take my pony cart," Jamie pressed the invitation. "My ma made us some sandwiches before she left with your da."

"Stepda," Zoe corrected absently. "I mean stepfather. And shouldn't you be in school?"

"It's Saturday."

"Oh."

Obviously, she'd lost track of the days during her self-imposed solitary confinement. She chewed a ragged purple fingernail and considered her options.

Riding around in a pony cart with a couple of little kids definitely wasn't her idea of a cool way to spend a Saturday.

On the other hand, the trouble with sulking in silence was that it got to be a real drag after a while. Her feelings were still all tangled up in a huge knot and there were so many of them—anger, frustration, fear, love—jumbled up inside her she could hardly think straight.

She was more than ready to come out of the bedroom, but since Alec had given up asking, she hadn't been able to figure out how to pull it off without looking as if she was surrendering and giving him the upper hand. Still, as nice as this room was, she was getting sick and tired of looking at the same four walls.

"Maybe we'll see the lady," Brigid said.

"Your mom said something about her."

"I'll tell the story if you'd like to be listening."

Zoe glanced around the room again. Then looked out the window where green fields and the glistening lake beckoned. Her shoulders lifted and dropped in a shrug meant to show them how little she cared. "Might as well."

"Oh, it's a grand story," Brigid said on a bit of a lisp as she grinned up at Zoe. "You're going to love it!" She looked up at her brother. "Now you can ask her for your notebook before we go," she prompted.

"Notebook?" Zoe asked.

"It's beneath my mattress," he mumbled, obviously embarrassed.

"It's his spy notebook!" Brigid announced loudly.

"Spy notebook? Like double-oh seven?"

"A bit like that," he confessed. "I got the idea when I read *Harriet the Spy* for a book report in school."

"I read that." Zoe remembered finding in the poor

little rich girl a friend she could not only identify with, but trust.

"Did you like it?"

"It was okay, I guess." She did not divulge that for the six months after having read the book, she'd walked around with a notebook and leaky pen, recording every observation, searching for patterns that might explain her unhappy life.

"I liked it a lot. Even if Harriet was a girl, she was a good spy."

"Jamie's going to be a spy when he grows up."

"I said I *might* become a spy," he corrected his sister. "I like writing things down," he told Zoe. "So maybe I'll be a writer like Uncle Quinn."

"And write about spies," Brigid suggested as Zoe obligingly lifted the mattress, allowing Jamie to retrieve the blue spiral-bound notebook.

Fifteen minutes later she was bouncing down the lane in a horse-drawn cart filled with little kids. They'd stopped along the way and picked up a red-haired girl named Shea who was introduced as Michael Joyce's daughter.

Then they made another stop for another boy and girl. As they continued on to the lake, Zoe was relieved she didn't know anyone in Ireland. She'd never live it down if anyone from school saw her with this bunch of Irish munchkins.

"Rory's da makes movies," Brigid told Zoe, after their cousin joined them with Celia Joyce, who was introduced as Rory's aunt, but looked about the same age. "He made the movie about the Lady when I was just a wee girl, and we all went to the pre—pre—"

"Premiere," her brother filled in as she struggled for the word.

"That's it." She nodded and beamed up at Zoe. "It

was in Dublin and we all got dressed up in our Sunday clothes and flew on our very own airplane."

" 'Twasn't really our airplane," Jamie qualified. "Quinn only hired it for the weekend."

"Sounds rad," Zoe admitted.

After breaking up with the duke, her mother had, for a while, dated an actor she met at the Cannes film festival. He'd been totally stuck on himself and Zoe had hated him as much as he'd hated her. He'd sure never taken them to a premiere party. Rory's dad, on the other hand, didn't sound like a Hollyweird phony.

"Quinn is really, really nice," Brigid said. "Mum says he doesn't act like a famous Hollywood person at all."

Zoe was startled to hear her own thoughts spoken in a clear bell tone tinged with its Irish musical cadence. She looked at Brigid.

The little girl looked right back at her.

And in that brief exchange of silent communication, Zoe realized that Kate O'Sullivan wasn't the only druid witch in the family.

"He's like a regular person," Jamie agreed. "Didn't he come on the father-and-son trek with us?"

"That was fun," Rory said.

"Until you thought you got the leprosy. . . . It was really sunburn," he told Zoe as Rory flushed scarlet.

"It *could* have been leprosy," Rory muttered.

"If he did get the leprosy, Erin could have fixed it," Shea said. "She's my new mum," the girl informed Zoe. "From America, just like Rory's da. And she's a doctor. She helped make me better when I had my brain tumor."

"You did not," Zoe challenged.

"I did," Shea said earnestly. She bent her head and parted some fiery curls. "See, that's where they cut into my head and took it out."

There was indeed a network of raised red scars. The thought of anyone drilling into her skull made Zoe's stomach slip over. "That must've really hurt."

"Oh no, because Dr. Jess, who's Erin's best friend, gave me a shot that made me go to sleep before the operation. And Mary Margaret was watching over me. She's my guardian angel."

Zoe rolled her eyes but, not wanting to get into an argument with a little kid who'd nearly died, didn't bother to respond.

12

LEGENDS LAKE was shaking with what appeared to be stark fear, just as he had that first morning Alec had watched him blow at Tarlington Farms. He pawed the ground and snorted, running away whenever Alec attempted to approach. Having always prided himself on his ability to handle horses without force, Alec's frustration escalated as the colt demonstrated yet again that he was not the least bit eager to be captured.

"Let me try," Kate suggested after the Thoroughbred had worked himself into a lather.

"Be my guest."

She slowly approached. Just as he'd done with Alec, Legends Lake would wait, visibly trembling, trotting off whenever she got within arm's length. Three times she attempted to approach the horse; three times he bolted. Seemingly undeterred by her failure, she continued to talk to him in a low, soothing tone one might use to calm a frightened child.

"Last time he pulled this, I finally got him to come to feed," Alec suggested.

"Let's save that for a last-chance solution," she said mildly.

"Hey, it's your call." So long as she didn't make things worse.

She stopped about six yards from the horse, crossed her arms over her chest, then lowered her head and drew in her shoulders. Visibly smaller, she then turned as still as one of the stone statues of the Virgin Mary found at crossroads.

The horse snorted. Pawed the turf. Snorted some more.

Kate didn't move. Indeed, from what Alec could tell, she was barely breathing.

Legends Lake trotted toward her. Head down, she didn't appear to notice. The horse moved closer. Still she didn't move.

He stopped, ears pricked, every flight instinct obviously on full alert as he watched for her slightest movement.

Nothing.

He licked his lips. Then began to inch toward her.

Still she stood there, head and eyes downcast.

When he was only a few inches away, close enough for her to reach out and grasp his reins, the colt snorted again and trotted away. When he got to the edge of a small pond, he stopped, then spun back around.

If the horse had been seeking attention by running away, he definitely wasn't getting it. Indeed, Kate O'Sullivan appeared to be in another world, far away from this Irish turf track.

He tossed his mane. Neighed. Appearing to lose his patience, he lowered his long head and charged right at her in a full blown, ears back attack.

"Get the hell out of the way!" Alec shouted, sprinting forward to head Legends Lake off. The other men, who'd stayed to watch the battle of wills, were right behind him.

Kate didn't appear to hear him. Nor did she appear to be aware of either the men or the charging horse. The colt closed in, swerving at the last minute, but not before coming within millimeters of her slender body.

"Christ." Alec took a deep breath and instructed his heart to begin beating again. "Okay. That's enough humoring him."

"Please," she said on a voice so soft he could have been imagining it. "Just let it be."

"Right. Like I'm going to stand by and watch you commit suicide just because you're too damn stubborn to admit that this horse is too far gone for even you to help."

"You're wrong."

He'd just opened his mouth to argue when the stallion charged again, twelve-hundred pounds of furious horse headed right at her.

"Goddammit!" he shouted at both horse and woman. When the idiot female seemed unprepared to move, he grabbed her and shoved her behind his back.

This time Legends Lake skidded to a halt in front of them and reared up, front hooves high and ready to strike. His high pitched whinny rent the air.

That was when Kate did what was either the most foolhardy or bravest thing Alec had ever witnessed. She slipped from behind him, lifted calm blue eyes to wild brown and continued to stand her ground.

Legends Lake dropped back down. Shook his large head. Then stood absolutely still.

She was speaking to him, soothing Irish words that rode on the soft breeze like a low hum. The two of them could have been in their own private world. Seeming oblivious to anything but the horse, she began walking away from the men, the horse watching her every move.

"That woman is flat-out nuts," Alec muttered, hating the way his heart still felt as if it were going to pound its way out of his chest.

"Some might say so," O'Bannion agreed. "Others around here might call it something else."

"Such as cursed," Kevin Murphy grumbled.

"The girl is no more cursed than you or I," John O'Neill insisted. "Yet she does have a near magic way with horses. As her own da did, and none ever called him cursed."

Murphy frowned at the comparison. "Because *he* didn't go around the county claiming to be a witch."

"She has Biddy Early's blood. It's not surprising that she would be inheriting The Sight," O'Neill pointed out. "I don't recall you turning her away when she showed up with that ginger tea when Maeve was sick as a dog with the morning sickness last spring, Kevin Murphy."

"There'd be not a shred of proof the tea made any difference."

"True. And likewise no proof that it didn't."

"Mam says Maeve would have gotten past the babe sickness without the tea. Like all women do."

"And felt a great deal worse in the meantime. If you ask me, Kevin, your only problem with Kate is that she finally wised up and threw your nephew out of her house the way she should have years ago."

"Divorce is a sin."

"Now, I may not know my catechism as well as some, but surely wife-beating is a far greater transgression than divorce in God's eyes."

Alec hadn't been listening all that closely to the argument, more concerned with the stubborn, foolhardy woman's safety than gossip about what magical powers people in the village might believe her to possess. But that statement caught his attention.

From what he'd seen, Kate O'Sullivan was a strong, independent woman with a mind of her own. The idea that she'd allow any man to strike her, not just once, but from what O'Neill was implying, for several years, was difficult to believe. Still, the guilty dark flush rising from Murphy's collar suggested that O'Neill's accusation may well be true.

Reminding himself that he had no desire to involve himself in this woman's marital problems, Alec turned his attention back toward the standoff, watching as she reached out and stroked the stallion's long neck. Legends Lake snorted again, but this time the sound was lacking the earlier threat.

The Thoroughbred drew closer yet, allowing her to stroke the white blaze running down the front of his long face. Alec waited for her to reach up and grasp the bridle that was now within reach, but she surprised him yet again by turning her back on the horse and walking away.

"What the hell is she doing now?"

"Just wait," O'Neill suggested. "Watch a true horsewoman spin her spell."

Kate was walking back toward them, Legends Lake following, as obedient as a pup brought to heel.

"We'd best be getting him back to the stud." Her calm tone belied the fact that she'd just risked her life. "Then I'll try to find out what's wrong with the poor dear."

Alec was struck with the thought that she'd only been in that field with the horse because of him. Because he'd been so damn eager to crawl his way back to the top he'd been willing to do anything—risk anyone—to get there. Residual fear from having watched her nearly stomped to death metamorphosed into an anger that was easier to deal with than guilt.

"That *poor dear* could have stomped the life out of you."

"Oh, he wouldn't have done that." She reached up and tossed her arm around the horse's neck as it stopped beside her, seeming to wait for her next move. "Would you, darling boy?"

The Thoroughbred nickered in what sounded like agreement. He was much calmer than he'd been when he'd bolted, yet looking at him closely, Alec viewed a glint of red in his eyes that suggested lingering danger.

"What the hell is it with you?" His temper was hanging by a single ragged thread as they walked the colt back to the trailer. "Are you some sort of damn adrenaline junkie? Or do you just have a death wish?"

She glanced up at him, clearly surprised by the force of his tone. "Of course I don't. Why would you be asking that?"

"Because in the few days I've been here in Ireland, I've watched you face down a bulldozer and a crazed horse." The words were forced through clenched teeth. "Both of which could have easily crushed you."

"Standing in front of the bulldozer was not such a risk."

"You're that sure of your alleged magical powers? Or perhaps you were expecting the faeries who supposedly live in that tree to rescue you?"

"No," she said equably. "I was that sure of Brian. I've known him all my life. When we were nine years old, I watched him tend to a bird he'd found on the sand. The poor wee thing had broken his wing flying into the cliff in a storm and Brian carried him in his own two hands to my grandmother for a bit of healing powder. He never would have run me down."

"What about the horse? I realize you don't want to

admit it, because it might suggest a flaw in your breeding, but in case you haven't noticed, he's crazy."

"Not crazy. Merely afraid. He also knows that I'm the only one who can help him."

"I suppose he told you that?"

"He didn't have to. We understand each other, Legends Lake and I. I was the first human he saw after entering this world. He remembers that I care for him. And more importantly, he remembers that *he* cares for *me*, as well."

Alec was irritated as hell that she was managing to remain calm while he couldn't recall ever being so scared. Not even that time when he'd been seven, abandoned by his mother on a darkened street in a city that was as foreign to him as Oz, and a pervert who'd reeked of whiskey had tried to drag him into his van. He'd slashed the back of the bastard's hand with his pocketknife. Later, his father had whipped him for having lost the knife in the dark.

She secured the door to the trailer and had walked around to the driver's door, when Alec stopped her. "I'm not finished talking to you, yet."

Kate slanted a pointed look at the hand he'd slammed against the door beside her head. "Wouldn't that be a shame for you, then." She reached past his arm to the chrome handle that showed a touch of rust. "Since *I'm* through talking with *you*."

Alec was all too aware that the others had stopped loading their own horses and were watching them with not a little interest. Unwilling to create a scene in front of witnesses, he backed away, allowing her to open the door while he marched around to the front of the truck and threw his body into the passenger seat.

* * *

"How much farther do we have to go?" Zoe complained as she followed Jamie O'Sullivan on foot through a cemetery of high stone crosses.

"It wouldn't be far now," he assured her.

She stumbled over a fallen grave marker, then glared down at the high platform heels. She should never have come out here in these boots. She should have worn a pair of sneakers. She should have just stayed home.

"Are you all right?" Shea stopped beside her, concern on her freckled face.

"Yeah, sure." Zoe pushed herself to her feet. "Other than a broken ankle, I'm just dandy. . . . Look, why don't we do this some other day?"

"But what about the Lady?" Brigid asked.

"Your brother can tell me all about her on the ride back to the farm." The temperature was dropping. She looked up at the sky, saw the dark-rimmed clouds beginning to gather and remembered none of them had brought an umbrella.

"Oh, it wouldn't be the same thing at all," Jamie and Rory said together.

"It's a grand story," Jamie said. "But best told at the lake itself."

Personally, as fire shot through her ankle, Zoe didn't give a damn if she went the rest of her life without hearing the stupid story. But there was something about his earnest face. Something in the eyes—weird as it was, since she had not a single thing in common with this little Irish kid who sort of reminded her of Opie Taylor—that Zoe thought she recognized.

"This had better be worth it."

"It will," Jamie assured her.

"It will," Brigid echoed.

On the ride over here from the farm, Zoe had noticed that the little girl adored her big brother, echoing nearly everything he said. If she had a little sister or brother, would it look up to her?

"Stupid question," she muttered. She didn't have any brothers or sisters and now that her mother was dead, never would.

"Sister Mary Joseph says there are no stupid questions," Rory volunteered.

"Then Sister Mary Joseph needs to get out more. The world's full of stupid questions. And even stupider answers."

"Do you have a boyfriend?" Celia's question came from out of the blue.

"I don't know." Zoe didn't want to think about the possibility of Jake taking some other girl to California when he got out of jail. "Why?"

"Because our sister, Mary, is a teenager. And she gets out of sorts the same way whenever she's having boy trouble. Nora says it's just part of growing up."

"Thank you for the advice, Dear Abby."

The sarcasm flew right over the curly red head. "You're welcome to it. But my name is Celia," she reminded her. "Though there are two girls named Abby in my class this year," she tacked on helpfully.

Zoe just shook her head in mute frustration, then stopped as they reached a towering hedge. The brambles looked impenetrable, like ones that had kept any princes from rescuing Sleeping Beauty for a hundred years.

"If you think I'm going to become a human pincushion trying to get through this, you need your head examined."

"Don't worry. There's a secret passageway," Jamie assured her.

"It's a shortcut everyone uses to get to the lake." Brigid put her hand in Zoe's. "I'll show you."

As her fingers closed around that small hand, Zoe decided against pointing out that if everyone used the shortcut, it couldn't be all that secret. They emerged from the hedge to a view that was admittedly pretty cool. The reed-fringed lake was as smooth as blue glass until broken by the splash of a fish jumping. Two swans, a black and a white, floated on the surface. The gray stone castle stood on the far bank, crumbling, but dignified.

"Isn't it grand?" Jamie's face beamed with childish pride at having shown her such a special place.

She shrugged as she watched another swan glide in from the sky. "I've seen better." When the lie caused his small shoulders to droop, Zoe felt an unaccustomed prick of guilt. "But yeah, I guess it's pretty grand."

A huge smile wreathed his freckled face.

"A beautiful queen used to live here," Shea told her. "With long hair that went all the way to the ground."

"It was as yellow and bright as a leprechaun's gold," Brigid piped up.

"But she wasn't only beautiful." This from Rory.

"She was kind, as well," Jamie took up the story. "So the ancient ones—the gods who lived here a long, long time ago before St. Patrick brought his Catholic God to Ireland—gave the kingdom a very special gift."

"Gold, I suppose." She'd secretly always been a sucker for fairy tales. Hadn't she spent years fantasizing about Alec as a knight in shining armor?

"Oh, better than that," he said.

"Guess again," Brigid nearly shouted.

Zoe shrugged and played along. "Diamonds?"

"Better!" they all said.

"It was" —Jamie paused dramatically— "a spring!"

"That's all? A lousy spring?"

"It was a magic spring," Rory said. "Anyone who drank from it never got old."

Zoe still thought that was a pretty useless gift. "I can't wait to get older. Then no one can tell me what to do."

"That's what Mary says, too," Celia said comfortingly. "But Nora says that nobody gets to do exactly what they want in this world."

"We're getting away from the story," Jamie complained.

Zoe turned back to him and gave him an exaggeratedly bored, go-ahead gesture.

"The thing was, you see, the spring had to be capped with a magic stone every night so that it wouldn't overflow and flood the valley. It was the king's job to do that. But there was also a wicked faerie who lived in the glen."

"This is my most favorite part," Shea confided, smiling benevolently back at Jamie when he shot her a frustrated look at having been interrupted yet again.

"She was as ugly as a boar, as sharp as a brier, and as evil as the devil," he forged on.

"So no man would ever fall in love with her," Shea interrupted again. "But then, guess what?"

"She fell in love with the king."

"Would you be knowing this story?" Jamie asked.

Once again Zoe felt a little guilty at his crestfallen expression. She wasn't used to caring about anyone else's feelings except her own. "I just guessed. Don't women always fall in love with handsome kings in fairy tales?"

"Oh. I suppose so. Well, the problem was, you see, he didn't love her back."

"Because she was so ugly, right?"

"That's what the faerie thought!" Shea called out.

"Who'd be the one telling the tale?" Jamie asked.

"Sorry." Her guileless smile even had Zoe's lips reluctantly quirking. Jamie O'Sullivan may only be eight years old, but he was still a male, susceptible to a beautiful female, even if she was still a child. He stared at Shea Joyce's sunshine bright smile a moment longer, seeming a bit dazed, then continued doggedly on.

"Well, since she thought the problem was because she was so ugly—"

"Ugly as a boar," Zoe remembered.

"Aye." He didn't seem disturbed by her interruption; Zoe guessed he was just pleased she was actually listening to him. "She made a magic spell that turned her into the most beautiful woman in all the kingdom."

"And then the king fell in love with her back," Zoe guessed.

"Oh, no." They all shook their heads. "The handsome king loved the queen more than anything, and no matter what female wiles and clever tricks the faerie used against him, he stayed faithful to his wife."

"Yeah, right." *This really was a fairy tale.*

"He really did," Shea said earnestly. "Because they had a special kind of love. Just like my da and Erin have."

"And Nora and Quinn," Celia said.

Jamie wasn't as quick to jump in this time. In fact, he didn't respond at all. Remembering what Kate had said about her husband not living with them, and watching the shadow move across his eyes, Zoe decided that he wasn't all that familiar with happy marriages. *Join the club, kid.*

"So what happened next?" she asked in an attempt to get the subject back on track so he wouldn't look so damn miserable. "Did the wicked faerie turn the king into a toad?"

"No. Worse than that." Jamie seemed to perk up a little. "She put a magic potent in his goblet at the summer solstice celebration, which had him getting drunk so he fell asleep without putting the cap on the stone and the water flowed and flowed all night long until it flooded the whole valley and became this lake."

"Everyone but the evil faerie drowned? Even the king?" Zoe didn't think drowning the guy you loved was a real good romantic ploy, but she could definitely understand wanting revenge.

"No. That was the grand part!" Shea shot Jamie a "sorry" look and immediately covered her mouth with her hands.

Jamie sighed. Shook his head with resignation. But the corners of his lips curled ever so slightly as he pulled those small white hands away from those rosebud lips. "Why don't you finish up telling it?" he suggested magnanimously. "Since you're the best storyteller anyway."

Shea beamed. There was no other word for it. Zoe almost laughed.

"The water was magic," she reminded Zoe. "And the Ancients loved the good queen so much, they made it so the people could live the same way they always had, but beneath the lake. Of course the queen had to give up wearing her beautiful gowns because silk and satin aren't waterproof, but that was all right, because, you see, the gods also gave her some beautiful green scales that gleam like emeralds.

"And sometimes, if you come here at night, and go out on the lake when the moon is full, you can look over the side of your boat and see the castle and all the people, living just like they always did before the water flooded the kingdom. But I've never seen that," she tacked on, as if feeling the need for full disclosure.

"Rory has," Celia said.

Zoe shot him a look. "You have not."

"I've not seen the kingdom," he said, a bit defensively. "But I *have* seen the Lady." His chin went up a notch. "I've talked to her as well. And her to me."

"Really." Zoe wasn't buying a word of it. What'd they think? That she'd just fallen off the potato truck?

"It's the truth." He crossed his arms over the front of his jacket and looked up at her, inviting her to call him a liar. "And if you'd be asking her nice enough, she'll grant your wishes. Didn't she bring me Quinn, when I wished for a da?"

"Did you like the story?" Jamie, jumping in as peacemaker, asked.

"It wasn't exactly *The Bold and the Beautiful*, but it was okay."

"But the prince was very bold," Rory argued.

"And the queen very beautiful." This from Shea.

"I'm talking about a soap opera. It's a television show," she elaborated at their blank looks.

"I like television," Celia said. "We have one that takes up a whole wall."

"Quinn bought it for us after he and my ma got married," Rory backed up his aunt. "It has a sound system that makes you feel that you're right there with the actors, and we also have video games—"

"And Aunt Nora bought a big popcorn maker just like the ones in the theaters," Shea broke in yet again. "That's my favorite thing in the whole room."

"Perhaps you can come over and watch it with us someday," Rory said.

"Thanks a lot, but I think I'll pass." Being stuck on the O'Sullivan farm while Jake could be riding his Harley to California was bad enough. Hanging out with little kids was just too pitiful to contemplate.

"Oh, you have to visit," Brigid insisted. "You're our

new pro—mmph." Her brother slapped his palm over her mouth.

"Your new what?" Not one of them would meet her eyes. "Well?"

"Our project," Jamie admitted reluctantly, color flooding into his freckled face.

"What kind of project?"

Another long silence. Then . . .

"Our angel squad project," Shea finally offered.

"What the hell is an angel squad?"

"Exactly what it sounds like." Celia's temper flared, just a little. Of all of them, Rory's aunt appeared to have the shortest fuse. "And you ought not to be cursing."

Zoe folded her arms and tossed up her chin. "I'll do and say whatever the hell I want."

Jamie leapt into the lurch again. "Mary Margaret told us to practice acts of kindness. So that's what the angel squad does."

"Who's Mary Margaret?"

"I told you. She's my guardian angel," Shea reminded her helpfully.

"Let me get this straight. You all have some invisible imaginary guardian angel who talks to you?"

"She's Shea's angel. Which is why she only talks to Shea," Rory explained as if there was nothing at all weird about talking angels. "Then Shea tells us."

"Like a medium." When she got only blank stares in return, she tried again. "A channeler. You know, one of those crazy people who claims to talk to the spirit world." Thinking of Kate, who'd been pretty nice to her and had shared that cool story about her dead brother coming to say good-bye, Zoe felt another unfamiliar little stab of guilt at having inadvertently included her in that group.

"Shea isn't crazy!" Celia's face turned nearly as red as her fiery hair.

"That's true," Shea said easily. "Some people thought my da was mad, but they were wrong."

"The same way they were wrong when they said you were possessed," Rory reminded her.

"That's right." Bright curls bounced as she nodded her head energetically. "I only had my brain tumor. And my da may have seemed a wee bit mad for a time, but then I came to live with him, and he fell in love with me—"

"And Erin," Jamie reminded her.

"I was getting to that. My da used to take pictures of wars and people dying, so he was real sad and wanted to be alone all the time. But Grandmother McDougall brought me from Belfast to live with him after me mum was shot dead by the Unionists, then Erin came from America, and we both loved him so much and he loved us so much, he got happy again."

She beamed another of those smiles that reminded Zoe of the cherubs smiling down from the ceiling in the Swiss convent church. "And now he smiles all the time and takes nice pictures to show people what life in Ireland is really like. But he says his favorite pictures are the ones he takes of my new mum and me."

Zoe guessed those photos on the bedroom wall must have been taken by Shea's father. As she rode back to the O'Sullivan farm in the pony cart, Zoe also decided that she'd just hit a new personal low when she actually found herself horrendously envious of a nine-year-old brain tumor survivor whose mother had been murdered.

Kate was silent on the drive back to the stud, appearing to be deep in her own thoughts. Her scent, an intriguing blend that had him thinking of ancient spice routes, warm summer rain, and mysterious incenses burned over pagan fires, bloomed in the warmth blowing from dashboard heating vents.

"Pull over," he said when they reached a cross-roads.

She took her eyes from the narrow, twisting lane long enough to flick him a glance. "What?"

"I said, pull over."

She hesitated, then pulled the truck over to the far left side of the lane, cut the engine and turned toward him. "Is something wrong?"

"Yeah." Dammit, he still wanted to throttle her. "Don't ever do that again."

"Do what?"

"You took a damn-fool risk today. I don't want to ever see you do such a stupid thing again."

Her eyes flashed like blue fire. Displaying a bit of temper of her own, she tossed up her chin. "It isn't your place to be telling me what to do or not do."

"Someone has to. Since you don't seem to have enough sense to come in out of the rain."

"Ha." She tossed her glossy dark head with blatant disdain and not a little scorn. "If I were to stay out of the rain, I'd never be going anywhere. This is Ireland, after all," she reminded him pointedly.

"I was speaking metaphorically. You know very well what I meant."

"If you're referring to my little exercise with the horse—"

"You're damn right that's what I was referring to." He took hold of her upper arms, but refrained from shaking some sense into her as he wanted to. "You could have been killed."

Her eyes were now chips of blue ice, vibrant in a

complexion that had turned ghostly pale. "Take your hands off me," she said in a furious, low tone. "Now."

She'd turned as stiff as stone beneath his touch. Her scent—half smoke, half spice—became edged with a tang of fear. *Hell.* He should have remembered what O'Neill had said about her husband. "Look, I'm sorry, but—"

"Your hands."

Alec released her and held his hands up, palms out in front of him. "Okay." He drew in a deep breath and wondered what it was about this woman that evoked such primal emotions. "I apologize for manhandling you. But only that. I still think you're crazy as a damn loon and the best thing for all concerned here is for me to just take Legends Lake back to the States and tell Mrs. Tarlington she's going to have to retire him."

"And how would that be helping the horse?"

"This isn't about him."

"Isn't it?" She arched a winged, dark brown eyebrow.

"No. It might have been, in the beginning. But I've only been here a few days and things are already getting too complicated."

"And you're not a man who cares for complications."

"Got it on the first try."

"Then perhaps you should consider getting into another line of work. But whatever your feelings, things haven't changed. This is still about Legends Lake." Her voice and her expression softened. "You were right. He's very distraught. Distraught and frightened."

"Frightened of what?" Now she had him talking as if he actually believed she could read the Thoroughbred's mind. Which was, of course, flat-out impossible.

"Ah, wouldn't it be lovely if understanding were

that simple? I wouldn't be knowing where his fear is coming from. Not yet. But I do believe I can help him."

"I'm not letting you near that horse alone."

"Let me make one thing very clear, Mr. Mac-Kenna—"

"Alec," he reminded her.

"Fine. Alec it will be." She let out a breath. "It is not your place to tell me what I may and may not do. You may not have noticed, but the last man who attempted to control my life is no longer in it."

"I'm only trying to keep you from getting hurt. From what I hear, with your husband, it was just the opposite."

Hell, he'd definitely pushed the wrong button that time. She flinched, almost as if he'd struck out at her with his fists, rather than mere words. "You've been listening to gossip."

"Then it's true?"

She turned away, refusing to meet his eyes as she pretended vast interest in the crumbling ruins of the Castle Joyce. "That would be none of your business."

"Then why does it feel as if it is?" Alec was as surprised to have asked the question as she was to hear it. She glanced back at him, her exquisite eyes shadowed, wary.

"I wouldn't be knowing what's in your mind where I'm concerned."

"*You're* the one who inherited Biddy Early's gift of sight."

"Aye. But I can't pull it out on demand, like some bloody parlor trick. Besides . . ." She turned away again. Crossed her legs and folded her arms.

"Besides?"

She shot him a frustrated look. "It doesn't work that way. I may be able to see things about other people, but when it comes to my own life, I've always been mind-blind."

"Inconvenient." Despite that little incident in the field, which he'd just about managed to convince himself was a coincidence—a random meteorological event like an earthquake or a tsunami—Alec still didn't buy the idea of second sight and magic powers.

"Haven't I thought so, myself, from time to time," she murmured.

"Perhaps, deep down inside, you don't want to see your own future."

"I suppose that's one possible suggestion." Her tone was mild, but something in her eyes told him he'd hit close to the mark. "And now that we've settled that, I believe it's time we were continuing on to the stud. Legends Lake could do with a rubdown before his muscles stiffen up."

"I don't care what you think of me, Kate," Alec said as she twisted the key in the ignition. "You can call me controlling, arrogant, or chauvinistic. Or all three. But there is no way in hell that I'm letting you alone with that horse." He firmed his jaw, prepared for her argument.

"Fine."

He shot her a look. "Fine?"

"Fine," she repeated mildly.

Having always been suspicious of things that came too easily, Alec didn't quite trust her sudden acquiescence, but neither was he prepared to challenge it.

They'd nearly reached the stud when a small blue car sped past on a tight, blind curve, the rusty back bumper seeming to be held onto the car with equally rusty wire. A faded bumper sticker read: REALITY IS AN ILLUSION CREATED BY A SHORTAGE OF ALCOHOL. The words, which he supposed were meant to be humorous, but weren't, had him thinking of his own current reality. There was Zoe, who was continuing to both aggravate and worry him. And Kate O'Sullivan, who kept stimulating complex, unbidden feelings that were becoming more and more difficult to ignore. And then there was Winnie, who'd already called twice since he'd arrived in Ireland, and would undoubtedly be calling this evening, as well, wanting a progress report on a plug-ugly horse that probably never could be trusted on any racetrack.

Christ, Alec thought as the truck pulled into the driveway of the stud, *could my life get any more complicated?*

13

THEY ARRIVED BACK at the stud just in time to see Zoe coming down the driveway in a small wagon pulled by a pony and driven by Kate's son. Alec wondered what miracle had occurred to get his daughter out of the bedroom.

"So, I see you've been playing tourist," he said mildly.

"We took Zoe to the lake and told her the story of the Lady!" Brigid O'Sullivan's eyes laughed.

"The Lady?"

"The lough beastie." Her brother's tone was a great deal more subdued.

"Oh, yeah. From the movie."

"You have it the wrong way around," Kate corrected. "The movie was about our beastie. Though, as exciting as that story was, Quinn used a great deal of creative license, since there'd be not a soul in Castlelough who'd permit scientists to hound the poor creature to her doom, as happened in the book."

Alec was not at all surprised to learn that she believed in some fanciful Loch Ness creature.

"The Lady used to be a queen," Zoe surprised him by entering into the conversation.

"Did she now?" He couldn't decide whether her accepting the faerie tale was good or bad news. Then decided that anything that could get her to open up to him, even a little, couldn't be all bad.

"Aye," the pixie in the sunshine yellow jacket said joyfully. "But a bad faerie cast a spell, so now all the people live beneath the water in their magical kingdom."

"That's quite a story." The cherubic child's enthusiasm had him smiling.

"It's true enough," her brother said in a quiet, but firm tone. Jamie O'Sullivan's eyes were a bit wary, which made sense, Alec considered, if the remark about his father's abuse was at all true. But his back was as straight as a rod and his steady, unwavering gaze possessed a familiar inner strength. In their own ways, each of Kate's children bore a striking resemblance to their mother.

"So, did you see the Lady?" he asked Zoe.

"No." She crossed her arms in an argumentative gesture he'd come to recognize all too well. "But that doesn't mean she doesn't exist."

"Of course it doesn't," Kate agreed in a warm voice intended to soothe the tension. "The Lady is a wee bit shy. But if you're very lucky, and open your mind, you may just catch a glimpse of her before you return to America."

Adult skepticism warred with a desire to believe the impossible in Zoe's raccoon-rimmed eyes and on her painted face, reminding Alec yet again that she was at that painfully awkward age between childhood and adulthood.

"It'd be cool to see her," he said when she remained silent. "Wouldn't it, Zoe?"

She drilled a hard look at him. "What do you care? You don't believe in her."

Just like you don't believe in me. She might not have said the words out loud. But Alec heard them, all the same.

"I'll admit it's difficult to suspend disbelief." He wanted to touch her, just a stroke of a fingertip against her cheek, or a hand to her spiky hair, but the no-trespassing signs had gone up all around her again. "But I still think it would be neat if the Lady did exist and even better yet if you were fortunate enough to catch a glimpse of her while you're here."

"Wouldn't that be lovely?" Kate agreed. Whatever else he might think of her, Alec was grateful to Castlelough's witch for backing him up. She turned toward her son. "Jamie, darling, why don't you take Zoe and Brigid in and cut them some of your aunt Nora's lovely spice cake that's waiting on the counter?"

"I have to put away my pony—"

"Don't you be worrying about that. I'll take care of it. Just for today."

"Thanks, Ma." He threw his arms around her waist and hugged her. Brigid, not to be left out, grasped hold of her mother's legs and held on tight.

Alec watched Zoe watching the little group hug, saw the sheen in her eyes and once again experienced an almost painfully overwhelming urge to reach out to her. But while he was trying to decide exactly how to do that, she shot him a look of pure disgust, turned on her booted heel and began marching toward the house.

"Zoe!" Seeing her new friend go, Brigid unwrapped herself from her mother and began to run after the teenager. "Wait for me!"

Alec stood there with Kate, watching as the children disappeared into the cozy farmhouse. "Thank you," he said.

He was grateful when she didn't pretend not to understand what he was referring to. "Isn't it difficult to be a teenager?" She shook her head. "I wouldn't be reliving those years for all the tea in Ireland."

"Neither would I."

"And no wonder," she agreed. "Seeing how you were but a boy when you were forced to grow up too soon and too fast."

Before he could question how it was that she knew what few others did, she went to work unhitching the pony. Deciding that it was just a lucky guess, perhaps helped out by some track gossip she might have overheard, Alec didn't pursue the subject and instead helped her put away the tack and rub down her son's pony.

"Well, now," she said when the pony was in its stall, happily munching its feed, "I suppose I'd best see if I can determine what's bothering our dear colt."

Apparently word had spread throughout the stud. A half-dozen workers filed into the barn, bringing with them an air of expectancy. She'd introduced Alec around the day he'd arrived. From what he'd been able to tell, they were dependable, hardworking and absolutely devoted to their employer.

Legends Lake's ears flattened when Kate shut the stall door behind her.

"I think it would be best if you stayed outside," she suggested.

"No way, lady. If he goes off again, you could be hurt."

"As could Legends Lake." She combed her hand lingeringly, lovingly, through the colt's sleek mane. "And we wouldn't want that to happen, would we, darling boy?"

There was something about the way she was stroking that long chestnut neck that caused heat to surge into Alec's loins. Annoyed to discover that he hadn't entirely outgrown thinking with his glands, he yanked open the door again and joined her in the close confines. "Might as well get this show on the road."

The stall had been cleaned after they'd left for the track. The straw Kate knelt down on was dry and yellow and fragrant with the scent of the fields. Reluctant desire quickly gave way to apprehension. It was bad enough that the stallion towered above her. When she pressed her cheek against the horse's flank, a fist gripped Alec's gut.

"What the hell do you think you're doing?"

"Hush," she said softly, then began murmuring Irish words obviously meant to soothe. Her gaze grew distant. She and the horse could have been all alone, in a private world of their own.

Tension built; there was a tingling, like lightning about to strike, beneath his flesh. It appeared he was not the only one to feel it. Legends Lake grew skittish. When the Thoroughbred's hooves began to prance dangerously near Kate's bent legs, a murmur of anxiety skimmed through the onlookers.

"Okay, that's it. You're getting out of here. Now."

Alec reached to drag her out of the stall, but Kate shoved away his arm. "You mustn't be spoiling things when we're so close to the answer."

"Dammit, Kate—"

"Please, Alec." She tipped her head back to look up at him with solemn eyes. "I know what I'm doing."

A storm had begun to roll in from the sea. Outside, lightning flashed across the sky; inside, Legends Lake fretfully tossed his head and rolled his huge brown eyes as Kate continued to whisper to him through her fingertips.

She could feel his blood churning beneath his skin. She sensed his building fear; tasted the acrid tang of it on her tongue, as he whinnied and pranced.

Kate was vaguely aware of Alec's voice, harsh and demanding, no doubt repeating his earlier warning. A warning she could not, in good conscience, heed.

She'd been drawn to the American horse trainer from the moment she'd sensed him striding toward her across the meadow, as bold and brash as one of Ireland's ancient warrior kings. He could have been Finn mac Coul, fearless leader of the famed Fenians of old. Or Brian Boru, the strongest, bravest, wisest man in all Ireland, who came from this same place and would, as The Lion of Ireland, lead his country to its golden era in the late tenth century.

The attraction to the MacKenna had grown, forging new links with each passing day, binding her to him in ways she'd have to think about later. When she could slip away to the sacred grove and clear her head and open her heart.

But now, consumed by a need far more vital than that of her own womanly desires, Kate closed her mind to the man and opened it to the colt.

It was hot. So hot. Sparks skittered along her nerve endings, licked at her arms, raced like wildfire up her spine and across her shoulders. Orange flames with blue centers flickered beneath her closed eyelids.

Legends Lake's nervous whinnies turned to screams of primal fear. As she breathed in the acrid scent of smoke, Kate held on tightly to him and merged his tumultuous thoughts with hers.

There was fire. Red hot and rising. It surrounded her, blazed its way beneath her skin, scorching her from the inside out.

There was noise. Harsh and deafening, the thunder

of stampeding hoofbeats, the roar of flames racing through the hayloft overhead, the screeches of trapped animals, the shouts of humans, the wail of sirens in the distance.

Remembered traumas poured from the horse in painful heat waves, rising higher and higher, until Kate was engulfed in the conflagration.

Pain sparked between them, electric surges from Legends Lake to Kate and back again, as both became trapped in the terrifying memories. Refusing to give in to the torment that would have knocked her off her feet if she hadn't already been kneeling, Kate continued to run her hot and blistered hands over Legends Lake's neck, his side, his flanks and down his legs, absorbing his nearly insufferable misery, taking it beneath her skin, deep into the very marrow of her bones, which were threatening to melt.

Horrifically, there was more. Remembered fear was flowing through her veins in boiling molten rivers; terror exploded behind her eyes like a newly born star. Heat roared around her, in her.

Alec watched Kate's breathing become faster, shallower. Her eyes were glazed and unseeing as she chanted strange and lyrical words he could not understand.

Prayers to ancient gods? Reassurance to the horse? Or both? Her complexion, naturally the color of cream, turned ashen. Her skin glistened even as Legends Lake became lathered, making them both appear to have run a long and hard-fought race. As impossible as he knew it to be, as Alec watched in disbelief, whatever fear the horse was experiencing appeared to become a living, breathing thing the colt and Kate were suffering together.

The horse lashed out with a hoof, the sharp kick just

missing her head and splintering the side of the stall. Alec had tried to humor Kate, but no longer gave a damn what the fool woman wanted. The time had come to get her out of the stall before she got herself killed.

The colt threw back his huge head. The cords in his neck stood out in harsh relief as he let loose with an ear-splitting, heart-shattering scream. A scream that was echoed by Kate. Her clouded blue eyes rolled back into her head. Then she went limp.

Alec scooped her into his arms just as the colt's strong legs folded beneath him and he crumpled to the straw where she had been kneeling.

The world was spinning. Kate's flesh turned to ice, even as the flames of pain she'd drawn from the horse continued to burn through her.

Hot and cold.

Dark and light.

Good and evil.

The contrasts warred within her, clashing with wicked, killing blows that reverberated inside her head. She felt herself lifted into the air. She was vaguely aware of her face being pressed against the unyielding wall of the MacKenna's broad chest, of inarticulate words that sounded as if they were coming from far beyond the mortal realm.

She tried to open her eyes, but her lids were as heavy as anvils. Attempted to speak, but the smoke had burned her throat and her cracked lips were unable to form the words.

She was struggling to remain conscious, to return to her own world, when a sooty black mist floated over her eyes. Her strength depleted, her will sapped, Kate ceased fighting and surrendered to the darkness.

14

K ATE WAS FLOATING through the Other World like a white feather dancing on a spring zephyr. The land in which she traveled was filled with miraculous wonders designed to dazzle both eyes and soul.

Ancient kings and queens she recognized from childhood tales rode in flower bedecked chariots pulled by white horses with gilt ribbons woven through their flowing manes. Faerie palaces boasting bowers of sparkling crystal and lime-white walls rose on the banks of a sapphire ocean, where sea horses glistened in the glow of the summer sun that was being pulled across the world in the gold sun-ship of myth.

Gilt- and copper-leafed trees, crowned with frothy pastel blossoms and heavy with fruit so ripe and sweet it could make the gods weep, bent low to hilly fields where white cattle grazed in abundance; gossamer winged faeries drank mead from the mouths of fragrant flowers.

Silver salmon leapt in rivers that poured forth honey and mead; on glassy loughs charmed, snowy-winged swans became beautiful golden-haired princesses in the wink of an eyelash, while in the shadows of tall, round towers, wispy-haired frail men, their stooped backs bent over hawthorn walking sticks, were reborn into the warriors of their youth.

Enchanted music strummed on three-string gilt harps drifted on perfumed air, entertaining the revelers as they feasted at tables groaning with magic platters kept continually full, and toasted with hammered goblets that never went dry.

It was a glorious place. A welcoming land, free of the cares or strife of the mortal realm. Were it not for her children, who had remained on the other side of the filmy curtain, Kate could have happily lingered there forever.

A raven, bright-eyed and glossy-winged, flew down from the top of an apple tree and landed on her shoulder. "It's not your time, Kate O'Sullivan. You must return to your own world. To those who need you."

All those in that glittering emerald and gilt land echoed the black bird's words. "To those who need you." The god-king, a bold, strong giant with hair and beard the color of flame, lifted his tankard. "Go home, Kate." His voice, which boomed like summer thunder, was not unkind. "To your wee ones. And the new life that awaits you."

"Aye." What a glorious thought that was: a new life. Glorious and, she thought as she felt herself being pulled back through the misty realm, frightening, as well. "I'll go."

The curtain lifted. Then, as in the barn, everything went black.

When Kate opened her eyes again, she was in her bed. The room was draped in the deep purple shadows of dusk, suggesting that she'd been asleep for several hours. The growing dark seemed particularly hard to penetrate after the sun-drenched visions of her fanciful dream and Kate blinked several times to clear her vision.

"It's about time you woke up," a deep voice, not unlike that of the red-haired god-king, rumbled nearby. She turned her head and viewed the Mac-Kenna sitting in a nearby chair.

"I'm sorry." She pushed her tumbled hair back from her forehead and hitched herself up in bed. She was wearing one of her nightgowns, a chaste enough garment, white with hand-tatted lace at the rounded neckline, an ankle-length hem and long sleeves. But the intimacy of the situation made her feel exposed. "How long have I been sleeping?"

"I wouldn't exactly call it sleeping." His expression was a great deal more grim than that of the dream king's. "But you've been out like a light for twenty-nine hours and"—he glanced down at his leather-banded watch—"forty-eight, no, make that forty-nine minutes."

"Surely that's not possible?"

"Surely it is."

"Where are my children?"

"Safe and sound at your sister-in-law's. She assured me that slipping into a coma isn't normal practice. Even for you."

"Of course it's not. How could you be thinking such a thing?"

"When it comes to you, sweetheart, I'm not sure what to think."

The word may be an endearment, but his grave tone suggested he'd not meant it as such.

"The doctor was here, too. I wanted to send you to the hospital in Galway, but she assured me, over several house calls, that your vital signs were strong and that you'd recover from whatever spell you were under in your own time."

"Erin's an excellent physician."

"That's pretty much what all the doctors I called in the States said."

"You investigated her?"

"Hell, yes. Castlelough, as charmingly quaint as it may be, isn't exactly the center of the medical universe. You were unconscious; how was I supposed to know whether or not she was competent to deal with the situation?"

"She must have been livid." Kate had never seen Erin lose her temper. But she also knew how seriously she took her profession.

"On the contrary. In fact, she was the one who suggested I call for references and gave me the names."

"Oh. Well." Feeling oddly exhausted for someone who'd slept around the clock, Kate sank back against the pillows. "That was nice of you to care."

"Nice had nothing to do with it. I told you, my immediate future depends on getting Legends Lake fit to race. Since you seem to hold the key to that, it's in my best interests to take care of you."

His tone was gritty, his face closed and shuttered. Even so, Kate did not have to read his mind to know that he was confused, frustrated and angry. She also considered the fact that she was not afraid of this very vexed man hovering over her bed was proof of how far she'd come since her separation.

"What about your daughter?" Her mind labored to return to reality.

"She's with the other kids. She and Nora's sister Mary hit it off right away. Apparently they share the same taste in teenage boy bands."

"Isn't that nice?"

"You've obviously made quite an impression on

Zoe. I had a helluva time convincing her to stop hovering in your doorway and go over to the Gallaghers'."

"She's a lovely girl."

"She was. And could be again if her life wasn't so screwed-up."

"She has her father. Which is more than many children do."

"I'm her stepfather."

"So she insists. But it's obvious that her words and feelings do not agree. You're the father of her heart, which is what's important."

He shrugged again, appearing uncomfortable with such personal conversation. "You must be hungry. Nora brought over some food when she picked up the kids. I'll go heat it up. And make a pot of tea."

She tried to remember the last time a man had cooked for her—had even merely heated up a meal— and realized that no man had ever stepped into her kitchen except to be fed. "You needn't bother, I'm feeling much better."

"Good for you." He raked his hand through his hair. "Look, I don't know what the hell happened out there in the barn, but you scared me half to death and since I don't want to have to deal with you passing out on me again, you're going to stay right here until the doc says you're strong enough to get out of bed."

"Don't you think that's a bit of an overreaction?"

"No, I don't. Are you always this argumentative?"

His question brought back Brian's accusation and had her taking a moment to think about it. "Only when I feel strongly about something."

"Like the faerie tree and Legends Lake."

"Aye."

He gave her a long, unfathomable look.

"I believe I know what happened to him," Kate said.

"I suppose you expect me to believe you discovered the truth during that mind-melding session?"

"If I recall my American television programs correctly, it's Vulcans who mind-meld. My sense of Legends Lake's problems is more of images than specific, detailed knowledge. But I believe it may be a start."

He stared at her for another suspended moment, during which time Kate nearly forgot to breathe, then he shook his head and left the room.

It was goddamned impossible, Alec assured himself as he put the kettle on to boil. He took the pot of soup Nora Gallagher had brought over out of the refrigerator and turned the heat up under it. He didn't believe in psychics, magic, or things that went bump in the night. And he damn well didn't believe in witches. Even ones who looked like faeries and smelled like enchanted forests.

He'd found the tea earlier, on a shelf above the stove in a milky white porcelain canister shaped like a unicorn.

The black wall phone rang. Knowing it was the only one in the house, he scooped it up so she wouldn't go leaping out of bed to answer it.

"O'Sullivan residence."

"So, how's it going?" Pete's gravelly voice was a welcome familiarity.

Knowing that he was referring to the horse, Alec opted not to mention the unnerving incident with Kate. "He ran some test trials like a champ. Then took to the air."

"Shit."

"My feelings exactly."

"So the Irish horse whisperer isn't working out?"

"Not yet." Steam began to whistle from the copper dragon-shaped spout. Alec pulled the kettle from the burner and cut the blue flame. "She says she may have a handle on what turned him glitchy."

"I'm guessing she's not blaming her breeding."

"She may be right. This isn't any nickel and dime operation. The woman's damn good at her work."

"So what's the problem?"

"It's complicated." His old friend was salt of the earth, a practical, down-to-earth man. Alec wasn't about to share the news that the woman who held the key to both their futures in her slender white hands believed herself to be a card-carrying druid witch.

Despite having instructed her to stay in bed, Alec sensed Kate enter the kitchen behind him, bringing with her a fragrance of soap underlaid with her own mysterious, enticing scent that would allow him to recognize her in the dark.

He turned, and skimmed a look over her, taking in the long skirt that swirled around her calves and a soft sweater the color of heather that clung in all the right places. She'd obviously showered but hadn't taken time to dry her hair; it fell in a sleek wet slide down her back nearly to her waist.

"Gotta go," he told Pete. "I'll call you tomorrow when I've got a better handle on things."

He hung up just as she retrieved two cups and a pair of deep bowls from an open shelf painted sunshine yellow. The pottery was a soft green and blue that echoed the shades of land and sea. He caught a glimpse of ivory flesh between the hem of her sweater and the waistband of her skirt when she reached up for the dishes, and he was not at all pleased when it caused his pulse to jump a few beats.

"That was my partner," he informed her. "Pete Campbell."

"The trainer who was elected to the Hall of Fame two years past?"

"That's him." He took the bowls from her hands. "Sit down and I'll dish up supper."

"You needn't—"

"Lord, you'd try the patience of a saint. Would you just plant that curvy butt in a chair before I'm forced to tie you into it?"

The words, which she understood he didn't mean literally, caused her knees to turn to water. A chill hit her, like a shower of sleet.

"Hell, I knew you should have stayed in bed." She hadn't realized she was swaying until he'd taken hold of her and lowered her to the rush-seated chair. "You've gone as white as a damn ghost."

"It's nothing." There was a buzzing in her head, like a swarm of angry wasps. "Just a memory."

"Must not have been a very pleasant one."

"No. But it wasn't from my own past. I believe it was yours."

His fingers tightened ever so slightly on her arm. Then relaxed. "Sure it was," he said in an outwardly disbelieving tone. "But the past is easy. You can read all about me in any old *Sports Illustrated*. So, how about we try something a little harder? I'll cross your palm with silver and you can tell me my future."

"Even if I were to foresee your future and share such insight with you, would you believe me?"

"Not in this lifetime." He released her and went back to dishing up the soup. "Unless you tell me Legends Lake will sweep the Triple Crown this year."

"I'm not able to see what lies ahead for him."

"Too bad."

"Sometimes it's best not knowing."

"I'll take your word for that."

He put the meal on the table, along with a loaf of crusty dark bread and sat down across from her. For a while neither spoke.

"You know," she said mildly, "it's nothing to be ashamed of."

He glanced up from spreading butter on a thick slab of the bread. "What?"

"What happened to you. The fault lies with your parents. Not yourself."

His hands stilled and Kate, who was watching him carefully, saw his fingers tighten around the handle of the knife. His knuckles were white, his expression a smooth, unreadable mask.

"You don't know what you're talking about."

"I'm talking about a child." Knowing from experience that it would do no good to turn away from the painful image still lingering in the shadows of her mind, she closed her eyes and focused. "A boy. No more than four or five. He's all alone in a cellar. No." She shook her head. "That's not quite right. But it's a closed-in space, dark and musty—"

"A closet." He'd gone as still as stone. His voice was tight.

"Yes." She knew. Heaven help her, the boy's helplessness was flooding her senses. Along with a very unchildlike anger and an icy determination to escape his fate. "His father was away, as he often was, and his mother was going out for the evening. The last time she'd left him alone, he'd gone over to the neighbors'—"

"Only after three days of not having any food in the house."

"Aye." Her own stomach clenched in empathetic hunger. "The neighbors called the sheriff, who threatened to arrest her if she continued to abandon her son for days at a time." Her head was throbbing. Tears stung behind her eyelids. "So, this time she made him bring in the clothesline from outdoors and she . . ." Kate could not say the words out loud.

She opened her eyes again. "How could any mother treat her own flesh and blood in such a fashion?" Just the thought made her want to weep for the boy he'd once been, even as Kate knew the man he'd become would hate being the recipient of her pity.

"Not every woman is born with strong maternal instincts. Not every child is born into a loving, protective environment."

"And isn't that a shame." She reached across the table, lifted a palm to his cheek and felt the muscle tense beneath her fingertips. "Everyone, no matter how lofty, or powerful, or beautiful, is damaged in some way. We all carry the wounds and scars of mortality on our souls and those experiences, as painful as they were, are what shaped you into the man you are today."

His laugh held not an iota of humor. "Some people might not exactly consider that a plus. Considering the way I turned out."

"Some people would be wrong. I think you turned out quite well."

"Maybe you haven't heard, but the reason I'm stuck with that crazy bag of bones currently boarding in your barn is because there's not a Thoroughbred owner in the country who'll hire me. Because I put my former employer in the hospital."

"With a broken jaw. I know."

"Punching out your boss is not a way to win points."

"You were standing up for a poor defenseless animal who couldn't stand up for herself."

"Too damn late."

"Unfortunately that's so. But short of horsenapping Lady Justice, what could you have done beforehand?"

The muscle clenched again. His jaw tightened. The chair legs scraped on the wooden floor as he stood up and moved away. Watching him standing at the window, seeming so very alone, Kate was suddenly reminded of a young groom she'd hired last winter.

Barely out of his teens, Donovan Burke had undergone ten plastic surgery operations in as many years. Erin, who'd done the most recent one herself, had recommended him to Kate, assuring her that he was a hard worker who just needed a chance to prove that the flawed outer package did not represent who he was inside.

His story had been a tragic enough one: His father, a widower, had gotten drunk one night, fallen asleep with his pipe burning and set the house on fire. The boy, who'd been ten at the time, had managed to carry his three younger brothers and sisters to safety. It had been when he'd gone back into the house in an attempt to rescue his four-year-old sister's pet kitten that the roof had fallen on him, leaving his face and body horribly scarred. But his spirit and huge heart remained intact.

Indeed, she knew that nearly every cent she paid him was being sent to an elderly aunt who'd taken the younger children in.

Unlike her groom, Alec MacKenna's scars might not be visible to those who didn't take the time to look closely. But they were there just the same, encasing his heart, which she knew to be a great deal more caring than he'd admit.

He turned back, his jaw set, his eyes shuttered. "Too bad I didn't know you the day Lady Justice went down. I could have had you cast some sort of protection spell. Or better yet, a spell to make the sun shine, so the filly could have won on a dry track."

"I explained—"

"Yeah, yeah, I know. You don't believe in tinkering with fate."

"Every action sets forth a series of unseen consequences no one can foresee. For instance, suppose I could have cast a spell that day so Lady Justice would win. Which you say you would have wanted."

"It sure as hell would have been better than what happened."

"Aye. But what if, by shifting the universal destiny, the horse that did win . . . what was her name?"

"You're going to love the irony here—Destiny's Darling."

"That is ironic," she allowed. "But getting back to my point, for *your* horse to win, her main competition, Destiny's Darling, would have to lose."

"That's the way it usually works."

"So, what if, on the flight from her own stables, the plane went down in a storm, causing the death of not only the racehorse, but Destiny's Darling's trainer and owner. As well as the owner's wife and two little daughters. Would you be wanting that?"

"Hell, no, but don't you think you're overstating your point here?"

"Nothing in life happens in a vacuum. Everything we do stirs the universe in unseen ways. Ways that are better left to forces far more powerful than we."

"Even if that's true, and I'm sure as hell not going to claim to begin to understand how the universe works, this conversation doesn't have anything to do with Legends Lake's damn problem. Which is what we should be talking about."

"He's afraid of fire." The appealing aroma of Nora's nettle soup faded, replaced by the stench of remembered smoke that seared her nostrils.

"I've never met a horse that isn't. It's a primal survival instinct that probably goes back to the birth of the breed."

"Aye." The furious sound of flames eating their way across the hayloft roared again in her ears. Her eyes stung. Watered. "But this isn't a general fear. It's specific."

Her hands trembled as she lifted the swirled blue and green cup to her lips. The tea, answer to all problems Irish, was rich and strong. Kate took a long drink that burned the roof of her mouth even as it soothed her tangled nerves.

"Legends Lake was in a fire. That's why he runs."

"That doesn't make any sense." But she could tell he was considering her words seriously by the way he'd begun to pace. He reached the door, shoved his hands deep into the back pockets of his jeans and stared out the lace-framed window at the sea, which was bleeding red in the glow of the setting sun. "There's nothing that could remind him of a fire out on the track."

"You wouldn't think so." The images were too clear to be false. "But there's a connection. We just have to find it."

He spun back toward her, frustration etched on every line of his rugged, handsome face. "You're the witch. Why don't you save us a lot of time and trouble by just looking in your crystal ball?" He shook his head. Cursed. "Sorry."

"That's all right. You're upset." How many times had she said those words to her husband? Thought them? Used them to excuse behavior that went far beyond the pale?

"Yeah. But it's still no excuse to take my frustration out on you. I was out of line and I apologize."

"And I accept your apology."

She'd never received one from Cadel. Not even the morning after their wedding night. The night he'd gotten drunk, taken her with a fury that frightened her, then afterwards struck her—a single sharp slap to her cheek with his rough open hand and called her a slut for carrying another man's child in her belly.

There had been more blows over the years, and the open hand had turned into a fist. Yet she'd taken them along with the insults, hiding her secret as one might conceal an oozing sore. Until that day she'd feared he would murder her. That same day Quinn Gallagher had, in turn, nearly killed him.

"There's something else you need to know," Alec said, jerking her mind away from that terrifying, humiliating, yet ultimately freeing day.

"Oh?"

"I'm not always an easy guy to work with. I expect perfection, not just from myself but everyone else around me. I can be, on occasion, single-minded to the point of shutting everyone and everything else out. I speak my mind and, as you've already pointed out, on occasion I can be rude. But despite what happened in Louisville two months ago, I would never—ever—lift a hand to any woman or child."

"Of course you wouldn't."

"Okay." He blew out a short breath. "So long as we've got that settled. I'm going to go check on the horse."

With that he was out the kitchen door, leaving his supper untouched. As she watched his long-legged stride eating up the ground between the house and the barn, Kate found herself wanting to call him back. Wishing that they'd met in a different time, under any other circumstances.

She pressed the warm cup against her temple where a headache had begun to pound.

"I wish—" she whispered, then immediately cut off the errant thought.

Hadn't she just given the MacKenna a lecture on the folly of interfering with the Fates?

What if she *had* met Alec before she'd made the mistake of her life and married Cadel? What if they'd become acquainted before she recklessly gave not just her virginity, but her young and vulnerable heart to another dashing American horse trainer? She would have escaped a great deal of physical and emotional pain.

However—and here was the key issue—Brigid and Jamie would not exist.

Even as she firmly reminded herself that she was too old for wishes, Kate desperately wanted to go back upstairs, pull the lace-trimmed sheets over her head, and weep.

15

—

ZOE COULDN'T STAND it another minute. Oh, the Gallagher family, with whom Alec had sent her to stay when Kate passed out after reading that horse's mind, was friendly enough, but that was the problem. They were too damn nice. She figured that if she didn't get out of the house that smelled like vanilla and lemon oil populated by aliens who genuinely seemed to like and care about each other, she'd end up with a mouthful of cavities from a sugar overdose.

Fortunately, she'd always had an excellent sense of direction, which was how, on the way back to the O'Sullivan stud, she'd managed to find her way to the lake where the kids had claimed Castlelough's own Loch Ness monster lived.

Not that she believed in such things, of course, she thought as she sat down on the bank of the lake and wrapped her arms around her bent legs. Hell, she'd stopped believing in the tooth fairy when the silver dollars stopped appearing beneath her pillow after her mother had dragged her to Switzerland.

"I wish she'd never met that stupid duke." She

blinked furiously to stem the tears that were threatening to flow. "I wish she'd stayed married to Alec."

She remembered what Rory had said about coming here to wish for a dad. Then actually getting one. Zoe didn't believe some enchanted lake creature made that happen, but even if it had, there was no way it could bring her mother back to life so they could redo the last six years.

She picked up a smooth white pebble and threw it sidearm across the lake, the way Alec had taught her so many years ago. It skipped twice, creating ripples in the blue water before disappearing below the surface.

"I wish we hadn't had that fight." She picked up another stone, turned it over, then discarded it, selecting a flatter one. "I wish I hadn't told her that I'd rather be an orphan than have her for a mother." Three skips. Four. Five. A personal best.

"I wish I'd never been born." This time she didn't try to skip the stone, but threw it as far and as hard as she could. It landed close enough to send the swans into the red-streaked sky.

Zoe watched them soar over the dark castle ruins, then lowered her forehead to her knees. She squeezed her eyes shut, this time wishing instead that she'd been born a witch like Kate O'Sullivan. Then she could just cast a magic spell so that men and women would fall madly in love like in the fairy tales, and love their children, and everyone would live happily ever after.

Continuing to fight back tears of self-pity, she left the lake, walking back up the path toward the so-called secret passage. With her mind still on her problems, she failed to hear the faint, barely perceptible ripple on the surface of the water. Nor did she see the huge sea horse-like creature rise from the lake, water streaming off iridescent green scales that flashed emerald in the molten glow of the setting sun. The Lady's gentle gold eyes shimmered with sympathy. She tilted her head, considering the matter. Smiled. Then, with a flick of her tail disappeared beneath the glassy water.

Following the directions given to him by a friendly young groom whose scarred pink face was mute evidence that he'd been tragically burned, Alec found Kate on the beach with her children. A touch of spring rode on the salt air, reminding him that the Derby was not that far away.

He stood beside the hawthorn faerie tree at the top of the cliff and looked down at the little family scene. The boy, Jamie, was holding onto the red plastic reel of a long-tailed kite, his young face a study in absolute concentration as he focused on letting out just enough string to allow it to soar higher, without sending it crashing into the surf.

The little girl's hair blazed like wildfire in the lowering sun as she danced barefoot in the lacy sea foam. For not the first time Brigid O'Sullivan reminded him of one of those mythical faeries Kate had risked her life to protect. She was singing, in Irish, her small voice rising over the soft roar of the surf like silver bells.

Kate was seated on a rock, her skirt wrapped around her bent knees, her hair tumbling down her back, her smiling face lifted to the sun. She appeared more at ease than he'd seen her since arriving in Castlelough.

He made his way down the steep stone steps to the beach, realizing that she'd sensed his appearance when her shoulders stiffened ever so slightly.

"Nice kite," he said as he stopped beside Jamie. At the center of the kite, a picture of a sea horse shimmered emerald against the blue sky.

"It's the Lady."

"The one in the lake?"

"Aye." He nodded and smiled shyly. "Would you like to fly her?"

"Perhaps later." Without thinking, he ruffled Jamie's hair and felt him freeze much as his mother had when she'd sensed his approach. Understanding childhood fear all too well, Alec didn't immediately take his hand away, but left it there for a heartbeat, as if to prove he meant no harm. "You seem to be doing a bang-up job yourself."

The kid beamed, reminding Alec of how a boy can yearn so for the slightest word of praise from an adult male.

"Alec!" He was suddenly tackled around the legs by a whirling dervish of four-year-old energy. "Come dance!"

"It's Mr. MacKenna to you," Kate corrected her daughter in a smoky voice that slipped beneath his skin. "And I'm sure he'd be having better things to do than dance with such a flirt as you, Brigid girl."

"Wanna dance!" the little girl repeated firmly. Ignoring her mother's prohibition, she lifted her arms.

Since it seemed the thing to do, Alec bent down, lifted the sprite into his arms and began waltzing across the sand.

"You needn't humor her," Kate insisted.

"Hey, it's not every day I get a chance to dance with a beautiful red-haired lass." He grinned at Brigid, who smiled right back at him. When he spun her she squealed with pleasure, and when he dipped her she giggled.

"You're a good dancer," she said, once she was upright again. "Almost as good as Uncle Quinn."

"Almost? Well, I guess I'll just have to practice some more."

"With me!"

"You've got yourself a deal, pumpkin." Needing to speak to her mother, he began to lower her to the ground when she wrapped her arms tighter around him. "Uncle Quinn always kisses me after we finish dancing."

"He does, does he?"

"Aye!"

"Well, then." He brushed a light kiss on the tip of her nose.

"No! Not there. Here." She touched a pudgy finger to her petal pink lips. The familiar purple polish glittering on her tiny fingernails revealed that he wasn't the only one who'd fallen under this sprite's spell. "Like they do on the telly."

Alec laughed at her exaggeratedly pursed lips. Then glanced over at Kate, silently asking permission. With a resigned expression, she nodded.

He touched his lips briefly to Brigid's.

"That's good," she declared, wiggling in his arms. "Now you can put me down."

He did as requested.

"Now dance with Mama."

"Oh, Brigid," Kate protested, "doesn't Mr. Mac-Kenna have much better things to do than dance around the beach with an old married woman?"

"Dance!" Brigid insisted.

"Actually," Alec said, enjoying the faint bloom of roses beneath Kate's cheeks, "I think your daughter's on to something." He skimmed a thumb along the faint blue shadow beneath her eye. "Anyone ever tell you that you work too hard?"

He'd viewed the light in her window late into the night. And he'd already discovered that she was up each morning before dawn.

"The stud doesn't run itself."

"True enough. But from what I've been able to tell, you've hired yourself a good crew. So, what's to stop you from taking a little twirl around the beach?"

"Dance!" Brigid continued to insist.

"Yeah, Ma," Jamie entered the conversation. His kite, now high enough to soar on its own relatively free of danger, was a sparkling green dot in the sky. "You haven't danced since Dr. Erin and Michael's wedding."

"You're all ganging up on me," she accused.

"Absolutely." Alec held out his arms. "Mrs. O'Sullivan, may I have this dance?"

Appearing to know when she was licked, Kate sighed and went into Alec's arms. Her soft curves felt so good against his body that if her children hadn't been watching so closely, he would have drawn her a great deal closer.

He hummed a Celtic tune he'd heard on his bedroom radio only this morning. It was slow and typically Irish, a tragic tale of loyal home boys being slain by enemy swords on rolling fields of golden corn.

" 'Tis a sad song," she murmured. Her breath was warm against his neck.

"True." To please himself, he drew her just a bit closer, so that her calf-length, crimson wool skirt flattened against his thighs. "Most of your Irish songs are, I've discovered. What is it they say about the Irish? That all your wars are merry and all your songs sad?"

" 'Tis a foolish saying. And not at all true, since there'd be nothing merry about war. Or violence of any kind."

"Good point."

Because he hated to ruin what was a surprisingly enjoyable moment, he did a series of three quick turns across the sand that had her arms tightening around his neck ever so slightly and caused her hair to fly out like a black silk flag.

"Mama's dancing!" he heard the small voice call out with obvious childish glee.

"And very well," Alec murmured as he rested his chin against the top of her head and drew in the mysterious fragrance that surrounded her like a sensual cloud. From the various bottles and jars he'd seen lining the shelves of the bathroom, he suspected it was a potion she'd concocted herself.

"Aye," she responded when he asked her about it. "I've an herb garden in back of the house. Some of the plants are on rootstock from Biddy Early's own garden."

"Would that make them magic?" Magic or not, they were certainly having an effect on him.

She laughed lightly. "Now, isn't there no proper answer to that question? Since you don't believe in magic, if I respond *aye*, you'll accuse me yet again of having a too vivid imagination."

"And if you answer *no*?"

She pulled back just enough that she could look up at him. "Then I'd be telling a falsehood. Though the magic is not so much in the plant itself, but in the intent to which it's harvested and used."

Alec still didn't buy the witch story. But he did admire her refusing to back away from what she was. What she professed herself to be.

"It could be that my mind is a bit more open," he admitted. "After my call to the States."

The bright laughter in her eyes was instantly replaced by interest. "Did you find out something about Legends Lake?"

"Yeah."

"What?"

Her scent was tangling in his mind as they swayed

on the golden strand of sand, stimulating thoughts that had nothing to do with horseracing and everything to do with Kate.

"Later." He ran his hand down her back, settled his fingers at her waist.

When he'd first sought her out, concerned about getting Legends Lake ready for the May Classic, he'd been all too aware of the ticking of the clock. Now, enjoying the feel of her in his arms, Alec was in no hurry to leave the beach.

Feeling more ridiculously, foolishly carefree than he could ever remember feeling in his life, he spun her in a dizzying series of circles that made Brigid giggle and had Kate clinging tightly to him. Then, as he had with her daughter, he dipped her so deeply that the tips of her raven hair nearly touched the sand.

"Kiss Mama!" Brigid called out.

"Don't be a foolish girl," Kate said. Alec took some satisfaction in the fact that neither her tone nor the hotly curious look in her eyes echoed her negative words.

"Alec danced with me. Then he kissed me." The sprite was standing there, hands splayed on her hips, her head tilted back as she looked up at them, red hair cascading over her shoulders in a tumble of riotous curls. "Now he's dancing with you. So he needs to kiss you, too," she insisted with rigid, four-year-old logic.

"Sounds reasonable to me," Alec said.

"A man who is a parent himself ought to be knowing that there's very little reasonable about a child Brigid's age."

"Kiss!" Brigid shouted again.

"I don't think she's going to give in that easily."

"She's a stubborn lass," Kate murmured. She was looking at his lips, seeming as fascinated as he was with hers.

"Sounds as if beauty isn't the only thing she inherited from her mother," he said. "We're only talking about a kiss, Kate. No more intimate than the one I gave your darling daughter. The type 'kissing cousins' might share back home."

"Since I'd like to be standing back on my own feet sometime in the next century, I suppose I have no choice."

"You always have a choice, Kate. At least with me."

Her gaze met his and held. "Aye." It was barely a whisper floating on the sea breeze, but a world of meaning—and acceptance—shimmered in the soft tone.

Smiling, satisfied, Alec refused to accept the idea that what he was about to do could complicate both their lives. He lifted her back up so she was standing on her own power, directly in front of him. Her lake blue eyes were both wary and expectant as he threaded his fingers through the ebony silk of her hair, pushing it away from her face.

"Like cousins," she reminded him.

"Absolutely," he promised huskily.

With his eyes on hers, he slowly lowered his head. He watched her gaze go a little soft-focus. Heard her faint intake of breath. It crossed his mind that the same expectancy that was written across her exquisite features was currently humming through his own body. Since the chemistry between them was in danger of mucking up his mission here, the best thing to do was just get the damn kiss he'd been thinking about too much lately over with. Then they could get back to business.

One taste. With her children standing by as chaperones. Two pair of lips meeting. Like cousins, he reminded himself. One kiss, then they could both satisfy their curiosity and move on.

He was still assuring himself that this was the logical way to handle the problem that had kept his mind wandering off business too much since his arrival in Ireland, when he made the fatal mistake of touching his lips to hers.

And immediately forgot to think.

16

LATER, LOOKING BACK on the kiss, Alec would realize that he'd known, in the suspended moment when his lips had hovered a breath away from hers, that he was wandering into dangerous waters. At the first taste of her sweet and succulent lips, he realized that he'd dived in over his head.

She felt it too. Her eyelids, which had drifted partway closed, flew open. She drew in a short, sharp breath and her fingers, which had been curved around his upper arms, dug into his skin through the denim of his shirt.

It hadn't even been a true kiss, little more than a whisper of a touch without pressure. Far more promise than passion. But it was obvious from the stunned look in her eyes, which had darkened to indigo, that no cousin's kiss had ever had such an effect on her.

Join the club, sugar.

She reminded him of a wild bird, poised on the verge of flight. But Alec was not prepared to let her escape quite yet.

"Let's try that again." He splayed his hands at the back of her head, gently holding her captive as he brushed his lips lightly, tantalizingly against hers.

Kate was vaguely aware of the cry of gulls circling overhead, the steady muffled sound of the surf washing onto the sand, her daughter's delighted laughter ringing out like the silvery tones of a faerie's flute.

Her mind clouded as she allowed her lips to cling. For that glorious, suspended moment, Kate refused to consider that what she was doing could be reckless.

It was only a kiss. They were, after all, on a public beach, with her children. Alec would do nothing she didn't want to do. How dangerous could a mere kiss be?

The problem with that reasoning, Kate realized, as the tip of his tongue skimmed along the seam of her lips and made her feel as if she were levitating right off the sand, was that with this man there was no such thing as a mere kiss.

Her body went fluid. She heard a soft moan of surrender and realized it had come from her own throat. A sweet tenderness uncurled from somewhere deep inside her, lacing its way through the initial shock of passion like a silver ribbon woven through a crimson tapestry. She sighed. Offered. Opened for him, lips, heart and mind.

"Alec is kissing Mama!" The sweet voice of her daughter broke through the lovely mist fogging her mind.

Alec eased away, but seeming unwilling to entirely give up contact, touched his forehead to hers. "My guidebook didn't say a thing about earthquakes in Ireland."

"They're not unheard of." Her breath was labored, as if she'd been running along the beach. "But I suspect this was something entirely different."

"I suspect you're right." He sighed, then straightened to his full height. "I suppose we should talk about this."

"Oh, I'm sure there's no need." Because she was so shaken, Kate was determined to keep both her tone and her attitude light. "It was, after all, just a kiss. Like an American cousin, didn't you say?"

"Kiss!" Brigid echoed like a small dear parrot who'd learned a single word she was inordinately proud of.

"Kiss, indeed." Forcing a laugh, Kate bent down and scooped up the child clinging to her knees. "The tide's coming in. We'd best be getting back to the house before the selkies claim my darling girl to come live beneath the sea with them."

Seeming delighted at that idea, Brigid giggled as they waited for Jamie to reel in his lake beastie kite. On the way back up the cliff, she regaled them all with a fanciful story about a little girl who dwelt beneath the sea and swam with selkies, combed her hair with sea shells and danced with lobsters.

While Kate managed to respond at the appropriate times, her mind was not focused on her daughter's mermaid tale, but on the silent man who was following close enough behind.

Zoe had just returned to the house when she looked out the kitchen window and saw Alec walking across the fields. Kate was walking beside him. He was carrying Brigid piggyback, and Jamie was tagging along a little behind, carrying a huge green kite almost as big as he was and gazing at Alec with a goofy adoring look she figured had probably been pasted on her face back when she'd been the kid's age and living at Inverness Farms.

They looked good together. Almost like a family. No. *Exactly* like a family.

Hot moisture burned at the back of her lids as jealousy pricked her heart. Not wanting them to see her crying, she streaked up the stairs and managed to get inside her bedroom just as the kitchen door opened.

Kate had known she was being reckless. Just having Alec MacKenna staying here at the stud was a temptation she'd been having more and more difficulty resisting with each passing day. Even without her ability to sense moods, she would have known he wanted her. That his interest in her went beyond what he was hoping she might be able to do for his poor wounded horse was all too obvious. The tension had been building for days, like the dark and dangerous storm clouds she'd gathered together to halt Brian's bulldozer. The primal forces between her and the MacKenna had become so electrified, she'd been feeling it sparking beneath her skin.

As bad as the days had been, the nights had proven even worse. From that first day Quinn Gallagher had forced Cadel to leave their home, Kate had reveled in her solitary life with her children. One of the best parts of that new life had been not having to share a bed with a husband who'd felt the privilege of taking her whenever he pleased, with no more foreplay than drunkenly jerking her out of a restless, fearful sleep, covering her body with his thick and heavy one, then taking her swift and hard with no thought of anything but his own release. Which was why Kate didn't miss sex. It was impossible to miss something both painful and degrading.

She'd been relieved to see the back of him, yet ever since the MacKenna's arrival, the double bed she'd been born in had become lonely and cold.

Surely it was only natural desire that had her tossing and turning and tangling the sheets as if caught in the grasp of a fever night after night. She was, after all, a woman in the prime of her life; she should be worried if she weren't experiencing a surge of hormones while living in such close proximity to a virile, intense male. The solution, she'd managed to convince herself, was to stop fighting the attraction. After all, weren't forbidden temptations the most appealing? Hadn't they both been avoiding the subject, playing individual games of hide and don't seek?

Kate had always considered herself an honest person. While she'd never flaunted her gift, neither had she hidden it. Such frankness had cost her occasionally, but she could not live any other way. While the Irish might be known for their penchant for talking circles around any topic, Kate had always preferred a straightforward approach to conversation and to life.

She was not one to play games, which was why she'd made the decision that the next time Alec looked as if he wanted to kiss the very breath out of her, she'd let him, and gladly, taking her own pleasure, then moving on. As intriguing as he admittedly was, a kiss was, after all, merely a kiss, and surely his would be no different from any other man's.

How wrong she'd been! The merest touch of his mouth on hers had sent a force like a tidal wave surging through her. A roaring like storm-tossed surf had pounded in her ears, and all the breath had left her lungs in a rush that had left her drowning in a sea of emotions more tumultuous than any she'd ever experienced. Afraid of being swept off the face of the earth, it had been all she could do not to fling her arms around his neck and cling to him, as a shipwreck victim might cling to a piece of driftwood.

When they entered the house the sound of the door closing upstairs caught Alec's attention. "Zoe's home."

Kate wondered if he realized he'd called her house home. Then worried that she liked hearing him refer to it that way. "So she is," she responded with a calm that cost her.

"Zoe!" Brigid cried with open glee, wiggling so that Alec slid her off his back. She was dashing out of the room, her shoes clattering on the wooden stairs the moment her feet touched the floor.

"Your daughter appears to have made a fan."

"If the purple nails are any indication, Brigid's doing a helluva lot better job of getting through to her than I have."

"The child could wear down a stone. If her soul had only inhabited an Irish lass in the seventeenth century, our entire sad history would have been altered, for I have not a doubt at all that she could have melted even Cromwell's black heart."

"You won't get any argument from me about that."

"I suppose I should have asked you first, but I mentioned to Zoe that I could be using her help with the horses. Only after she finishes her lessons, that is."

"What did she say?"

"That she was afraid you wouldn't let her."

"Christ, she has such a positive view of me," he muttered.

"You needn't worry. I assured her that I'd handle you."

"And how, precisely, did you plan to go about 'handling' me?"

"I thought I'd try logic. Then, if that didn't work, appeal to your American Protestant work ethic."

"And if I still proved difficult?"

"Oh, I was planning to, as you Yanks say, pull out all the stops."

"Were you, indeed?" The faintly wicked gleam in his dark eyes suggested each and every one of the things she'd spent last night dreaming of. And more.

"Aye." She gave him a bland look. "I suggested casting a spell on you."

"I thought you didn't cast spells."

"And isn't that what Zoe said, herself?" Kate smiled. "And as I told her, there's always a first time."

"Thank you." His smile was easy and warm. "It's generous of you to help."

"It's she who will be helping me," Kate corrected. "And if working with the horses gives her a bit of pleasure, as well, isn't that lovely for everyone."

"Lovely," he murmured as his gaze drifted over her face in a way that had her thinking that he might not be referring to her clever plan to ease the rebellious teen's troubled heart.

"I'd better go upstairs and see if anything happened to make her come home from the Gallaghers' before I could get over there to pick her up. Then I want to tell you what I learned about Legends Lake."

"I'll be wanting to hear it." She glanced over at Jamie, who was pouring himself a glass of milk. "Darling, would you please go amuse your sister so Mr. MacKenna can be having a private chat with his daughter?"

"Sure, Ma," he said around a mouthful of chocolate biscuit. He gulped down the milk, then left the kitchen.

Once they were alone, another thicker, decidedly awkward silence settled over them. Kate searched her mind for something—anything—to say, but found it difficult to think when he was looking at her mouth in a way that suggested he was thinking neither of his daughter nor the horse, but of those two brief, but oh so devastating kisses they'd shared on the beach.

"I'll be out in the brood barn with Nora. Her time is getting near."

Alec didn't respond. Just nodded and, seeming as torn as she, left the kitchen.

When she heard his boots on the stairs, Kate let out a long shuddering breath she'd been unaware of holding. Then, dragging her mind back to the one thing she had been able to count on all of her life—the stud—she went out to check on her pregnant mare.

17

Zoe was sprawled on the bed, her nose stuck in a book. Not a textbook, Alec noted, but a worn, leather-bound book entitled *The History of the Irish Horse*.

"Finding out anything interesting?" he asked casually, raising his voice a little to be heard over the sound of sugary male harmony coming from the boombox she'd insisted on bringing to Ireland with her.

She slammed the pages closed. Her face closed up. "I finished today's assignment."

"Good for you." Her eyes were puffy, a sign she'd been crying. Alec decided to take a roundabout approach. "Have you gotten to the Connemara pony?"

"Yeah. The very first chapter calls it Ireland's native horse."

"So it is, and a great one. They're small, but muscular with strong bones. They've managed to retain their iron constitution along with foraging ability. Partly, I'd imagine, because the stallions are often turned out to survive on their own each fall, then rounded up again for breeding in the spring. The amazing thing is, despite maintaining so much of their wild ways, of all the horse breeds, they seem to bond the best with humans."

"They sound kinda cool."

"They are *way* cool." Inspiration struck. "You know, the Connemara's only a few miles north of here. If you'd like, we could take a drive up there and you can see some for yourself."

"I figured you'd be busy."

"I am busy. But it'd be a shame to come all this way and not get in some sightseeing. I'll bet Kate even knows people who own some ponies she'd enjoy introducing you to."

"Kate says that I can help her around here with the horses."

"So she told me. What do you think about that?"

She shrugged. Her mouth pulled into a tight line, but there was a yearning in her tear-reddened eyes, come and gone in such a quick flash that if he hadn't been watching her so closely, Alec might have missed it.

Her answer was a while in coming. "I might as well, I guess. There's nothing else to do around here." She paused and began picking at her fingernail polish. Sensing that she had something else on her mind besides Irish horses and teenage boredom, Alec waited her out.

"Why didn't you adopt me?" Her face had crumbled as she'd finally asked the question Alec had been half-expecting for the past six months. She could have been six years old. It broke his heart.

"It's complicated."

"Didn't you want me?"

"Bunches. But there were legal considerations in the beginning." Alec didn't reveal that Liz had been holding out in hopes of Zoe inheriting big wine bucks from her father's French wine fortune. Something his family, who'd never approved of his flashy American wife in the first place, had not allowed to happen. "I figured, since we were already a family, and the paperwork was just a formality, there'd be time to take care of it."

"But Mother left before you could."

She was looking out the window, toward the lake. Alec figured it was more a case of her not wanting him to see her hurting than any avid interest in the Irish scenery.

"Yeah. She left."

"With Philippe."

"Yeah." Surprisingly, he'd forgotten the guy's name. "And you."

Oddly, by the time Liz had left, that was the loss he'd mourned the most. Alec had never given any thought to becoming a father; Lord knows John MacKenna certainly hadn't been anything resembling a role model. But during his brief marriage, he'd discovered that not only was fatherhood far more fulfilling than he ever could have imagined, he'd actually been fairly good at it.

"Philippe was an asshole."

"Was he?" Alec responded mildly, deciding that this was not the time to work on cleaning up her language.

"Yeah. Just like all those other guys she ran around with after she dumped me in the Alps with those Nazi nuns."

"They were Swiss."

"Close enough." She glanced back over at him. "Mother was always falling in love with bastard creeps. I hated every one of them. But you were okay."

Okay wasn't much, but at least he ranked higher than the no-account duke and all the European playboys who'd come after him. "Thanks. So," he asked, almost afraid to push his luck, "how were things at the Gallaghers'?"

"They're nice. And they've got a cool media room. Nora Gallagher's sister, Mary, is about my age. She likes 'N Snyc, too. Her favorite guy is Lance."

"He's the youngest, right?"

"How did you know that?" She couldn't conceal her surprise.

"Hey, you're not the only one who's done her homework."

She smiled, just a little, at learning he'd gone to the trouble to learn something about her favorite pop group.

"I'll let you get back to your reading," he said, deciding to quit while he was, if not ahead, at least not lagging as far behind as he had been. "I want to talk to Kate about Legends Lake." Unable to leave without some physical contact, he touched a hand to her hair. "Want to come with us when we breeze him again tomorrow?"

Her shoulders lifted and fell in that teenage shrug he was getting used to. But she couldn't quite hide the expectation lighting up her eyes. "Okay."

Alec decided that they'd made enough progress for one day. "Great." He touched his fingers to his lips, then to hers.

They don't hear the words you long to say, 'N Sync was crooning.

Even as he thought the swoon-inducing kids sure as hell had that right, as he went out to the barn, Alec considered that no matter what happened with Legends Lake, perhaps Ireland would prove to be good for both him and Zoe.

He found Kate in Nora's stall. "How's she doing?"

"It won't be long now," she said, as she rubbed her hands over the heavily pregnant mare's sides. She took an apple from her pocket, along with a pocketknife she used to quarter it and fed one of the red-skinned segments to the horse. "As many times as I've done this, I always worry."

"She'll be fine."

"And here you'd accused *me* of having a crystal ball."

"I wasn't making light of your concern. Merely trying to remind you that you're damn good at your work and there's no point in borrowing trouble."

"Aren't you right about that?" The horse nipped another piece of apple from her outstretched palm. "Since I've already got enough in my life to deal with."

"Like having a crazy horse, a temperamental teenager and a rude Yank all showing up on your doorstep."

"The horse is a challenge. The teen, a sweet girl beneath that prickly armor she's taken to wearing. As for the Yank . . ." She absently caressed the mare's wide back. "I can't deny that he's livened things up a bit around here."

He caught her hand and linked their fingers together. "You don't sound real happy about that."

"My life was . . ." She paused, searching for the right word. "Difficult," she decided upon, "for several years. Calm and quiet days were an appealing change."

Alec was tempted to suggest that she might think about livening up her nights, at least, then reminded himself that she wasn't the kind of woman to indulge in a short, passionate affair. Which meant that she was pretty much off limits.

"Makes sense to me." Not quite ready to relinquish possession of her hand, he lifted it to his mouth and nipped lightly at her knuckles. "Though, since we're being entirely honest here, I'll have to admit that under any other circumstances, I'd seriously be considering seductive ploys to entice you up into that hayloft."

He waggled his brows in a mock seductive way that won a light laugh. "Under any other circumstances, MacKenna, you wouldn't be needing any ploys."

He shook his head. Untangled their fingers. It was his turn to sigh. "I think I've figured out your plan."

"And what plan would that be?"

"You're out to save money on your electric bills by forcing me to take cold showers."

"Sure, you've found me out." She returned his smile and the mood lightened again. For now. "So, why don't you be telling me about what you found out about your horse?"

"You were right about there having been a fire."

"Ah." She did not appear the least bit surprised by that revelation.

"However," he continued, "it wasn't that big a deal, according to the guy who was at the track at the time. A short in the electrical system started a small fire in the washroom. There was a lot of smoke, but very little flame and all the horses were gotten out safely."

"Still, I imagine they were terrified."

"Probably. But that still doesn't explain why he should be having a problem on the track. So I dug a little deeper, talked to more people who were there that day and discovered that the fire occurred shortly after Legends Lake was returned to his stall after a disappointing morning breezing."

"Was he treated poorly for not running to expectations?"

"According to a groom I spoke with, Jenkins was nursing the mother of all hangovers. After the breezing, he whipped Legends Lake with the exercise rider's crop. The guy said the lashes hadn't been hard enough to leave physical scars but—"

"Surely such mistreatment could cause mental

scars." The roar of out of control flames thundered inside her head. When the screams of terrified Thoroughbreds nearly shattered her eardrums, she went light in the head.

When she swayed, Alec pried her fingers off the top of the stall door and half-dragged, half-carried her outside, where a cool mist had begun to fall. "Sit down."

"I'm fine."

"Sure you are. But there's no way I'm going to risk a repeat of the other day." He shoved her onto a bale of hay beneath the wide eaves. "Sit. And put your head between your knees."

"Really, I'm—"

"Shut up. You're white as bone. If you don't get some blood into your head you'll pass out." When she hesitated, he put his hand on the top of her head and pushed.

She muttered something in Irish he took as a curse, but when she lifted her head again, the color was back in her cheeks. "I'm all right now. Truly," she insisted at his skeptical look. "It was only a flash of a vision. Come and gone in seconds."

"Are you saying you saw the fire?"

"And heard it as well. Was it sparked shortly after Legends Lake was whipped?"

"Yeah. About thirty minutes."

She granted him a faint smile. "Isn't that clever detective work on your part."

"You're the one who suggested the fire in the first place."

"It wasn't *I* who suggested it."

"Yeah, that's right. Legends Lake told you."

"Aye."

She thrust out her chin a bit as she continued to look up at him, silently daring him to argue. Something he was no longer prepared to do. Because, while the idea of some sort of equine/human mind-meld between this self-proclaimed Celtic druid and his glitchy horse didn't make a lick of sense, there was also no logical reason for her to have known about the San Diego fire.

"Okay, I'll reluctantly accept you knowing about that time I was tied up and locked in the closet when I was a kid, along with being aware of Legends Lake's experience with a fire, points to some sort of telepathic connection. But if your head starts spinning around, all bets are off."

"It's those who are possessed who have such difficulty, I believe," she said matter-of-factly.

Alec stared at her. "Whatever. The thing is, it's a very large mental leap from extrasensory perception to believing in witches and goblins and things that go bump in the night."

Overhead, thunder rumbled across the darkening sky, as if mocking his words.

"You've already come a long way since our meeting on the cliff. I'll not be pushing you beyond your limits."

"I appreciate that."

She smiled serenely. "No problem."

Since there wasn't any rational answer for what seemed to be her preternatural powers, Alec stuck to what he did know rather than what he couldn't understand. "The first time he jumped in a race was the day after the fire."

"Was he whipped that day, as well?"

"It took a while to track down the jockey, but he insists that he wasn't."

She was silent for another long moment. Alec waited.

"What about the other horses? Was the crop used on them, perhaps?"

"Yeah. The guy I talked with said Legends Lake broke like a rocket, the same way he usually does, but in the final stretch he was running nose to nose with the favorite, when the other jockey gave his horse a push in the stretch."

"With his crop."

"Got it on the first try."

"So it's possible that Legends Lake has linked those two things together—the crop and the fire—together in his mind."

"That'd be my guess."

"Which means that he'll run as free as the wind without any problem so long as some other jockey within his visual field doesn't pull out a crop during the race."

Which was highly unlikely since such a tactic wasn't necessarily cruelty, as some might think. Many horses benefited from a light touch of the leather crop as a signal that it was time to go into their final stretch run.

"I'd guess that's pretty much the case. Though I suspect it's more complicated, because the first time I saw him at Tarlington Farms, he was wearing full cup blinkers, and they sure as hell didn't work that day."

"His hearing must be acute enough that he can hear the sound. Or, perhaps he just senses it."

"That's what I was thinking."

"Well then, there's no choice." She decided what he'd already considered. "Since there'll be no curing his problems until we can trigger them, we'll have to be racing him again. Under controlled circumstances."

It was the only option he'd been able to come up with. An option that, while a long shot, could possibly work. Unfortunately, it was also rife with the potential for disaster.

18

LATE THAT NIGHT, Alec slipped upstairs to check on Zoe, who, though she'd finally joined the rest of them for supper, had remained, for the most part, silent all evening. It was more than obvious she'd been deep in thought. About what, Alec had no clue.

As restless in sleep as she was when she was awake, the teenager had kicked off all her covers. One slender white arm was hanging off the mattress, the other flung above her magenta head, which was no longer lying on her pillow, since sometime after falling asleep, she'd knocked it onto the floor.

She'd scrubbed her complexion clean before going to bed and with all that makeup she'd been spreading on her face like spackle now gone, she looked nearly as young and as innocent as the day when, dressed in a pink dress and ribbon-trimmed straw hat and carrying a white basket of rose petals, she'd served as the flower girl at her mother's wedding.

She'd been such a happy child that long ago sun-gilded afternoon, he mused as he straightened her sheet and retrieved the pillow from the floor. Zoe muttered a faint, inarticulate protest when he slipped it beneath her head, then rolled over with a muffled humph and buried her young face in the soft down.

As he'd watched her making her way down the white satin runner, her smooth forehead furrowed beneath her blond bangs as she scattered her petals with such fierce concentration, obviously intent on performing her role perfectly, Alec knew that he never could love a child of his own blood more than he loved Liz's daughter.

He covered her with a quilt made up of fabric Celtic circles, then bent down and brushed some fluorescent hair off her smooth young cheek.

Touching his lips to her temple, he whispered, "Love you, honeybunch."

As deep in sleep as she was, Alec didn't believe she'd heard him. But needing some positive sign, as he watched her mouth curve ever so slightly as she snuggled deeper into the pillow, Alec allowed himself a moment of fleeting parental pleasure and hoped to hell that she wasn't dreaming of that tattooed, pierced, Harley-riding felon he'd brought her across an ocean to protect her from.

He'd just left the room, closing the door behind him, when Kate appeared in the hall. She was wearing a robe the warm rose color of sunrise. It was heavy flannel and tied at the waist, but as she walked toward him he caught a glimpse of bare leg that struck him as more erotic than any *Penthouse* centerfold could ever be. It also had him wondering if she was wearing anything beneath it.

She froze like a startled doe. As they looked at one another in the muted nightlight illuminating the hallway, there was another suspended moment of awareness.

"I was checking on Zoe," he offered.

"Isn't that part of being a parent? I can never go to

sleep without looking in on my children one last time." In deference to the sleeping children, her rich voice was soft in the hush of the darkened house. "I had a thought."

Her seductive scent was stimulating a few vivid thoughts of his own. Alec wanted to touch her, to drag her into her room and untie that loose knot at her waist so he could feel her skin beneath his hands, taste her lips, watch those incredible blue eyes as he drove her over the edge.

Because *want* was becoming dangerously close to *need*, he shoved his fists deep into his pockets to keep them out of trouble.

"A thought?"

"About Legends Lake." Obviously flustered by what he suspected was an expression of sheer, unadulterated lust on his face, she lifted a slender hand to her throat. "Shall I make tea? Or, if you'd rather, coffee?"

What he wanted was her. Hot, naked, and bucking beneath him.

"Tea's fine."

"Fine. I'll brew a pot and we'll share it as we discuss my idea about how best to test your horse."

Tea was definitely way down on his list of things to share with the luscious Mrs. O'Sullivan. But since she already had him too edgy to sleep, Alec decided he might as well take her up on the offer.

He leaned back in the chair and watched her bustle around the kitchen with brisk domesticity. On the counter a blue bowl covered with a linen dishtowel held fragrant, rising dough. Outside, a soft rain was streaking down the windows, misting the insides and creating an intimate sense of being cut off from the rest of the world.

"I haven't decided which one I like best," he murmured.

"Which what?"

"Which Kate O'Sullivan. There are quite a few of you, aren't there?"

"I wouldn't be knowing what you mean." The earthenware rattled, just a bit, as she took the cups down from a shelf.

"Of course you do. There's the horse breeder and businesswoman, who's as hard a worker as I've ever seen and obviously well respected by all who work for her and those who bring their horses here to the stud for breeding.

"There's the druid who stands up to the Irish roadway department in order to save a faerie tree. Then there's the loving mother and homemaker, who's created a warm and inviting atmosphere where her children can feel safe and protected."

"I'm afraid it wasn't always so."

"Bygones. What's important is that Jamie and Brigid are obviously well adjusted, and the fact that it hasn't always been easy for you makes that even more of an accomplishment. I wish I'd been able to be half as influential on Zoe."

"Your situation is a delicate one." The kettle whistled. Kate pulled it off the flame and poured the water over the tea leaves she'd spooned into a pot painted with Celtic animals. "Although I'm not one to be telling tales, you should know that she feels guilty about an argument she had with her mother shortly before her death."

"Hell, I didn't know that." But it explained a lot, Alec considered. Including why Zoe had seemed so determined not to allow herself to enjoy anything since he'd brought her home. "It doesn't say much for our relationship that she'd share her concerns with a virtual stranger and not say a word about it to me."

"Isn't it often easier for a child to talk with someone

who isn't family? It was certainly that way when I was a girl. My parents tried to warn me about . . ."

Her voice drifted off as she reached into a jar and took out some shortbread cookies which she arranged on one of the small plates she'd placed on the table.

"About what?"

She shrugged and went over to the refrigerator to retrieve a small pitcher of milk. "The typical teenage things parents fret so about. Drinking, late nights, boys."

Despite what she'd said about Father What-a-Waste being afraid to kiss her, Alec decided that there had probably been a great many teenage boys from the village her parents would have been wise to worry about.

"It's a bit different, being a teenager in a small town like Castlelough," she said mildly. "Where everyone lives in each other's pockets and the boys and girls all grow up together. There's not so much mystery involved in courtship."

He wondered if she'd grown up with her husband. Wondered if the now absent Mr. O'Sullivan had stolen kisses on the beach. Had he sat in this very chair, enjoying the sight of her fixing him a late-night snack?

Had he ever noticed how sexy her bare feet with their high slender arches could be? Did he get hard as a stallion just watching the movement of her body beneath her robe? Had he ever taken her here, on this table, with the moonlight silvering her flesh and the homey aroma of burning peat tangling with her rich, womanly scent? That idea conjured up images that caused his already rampant libido to spike.

When she bent to place the cup of tea in front of him the robe gaped open just enough to allow him a glimpse of milkmaid pale flesh. Alec snagged her wrist and pulled her down onto his lap. The robe parted, revealing smooth bare thighs.

"The children—"

"Are all tucked away safely in their beds." He brushed a kiss against her temple and drew in her scent. "It's time for the grown-ups to relax."

Kate laughed at that and surprised him, just a little, by settling more comfortably on his lap. "No offense intended, Mr. MacKenna, but I find very little about you that's relaxing."

"No offense taken, Mrs. O'Sullivan." He ran his lips along her jawline, nipped at her chin. "Since I've been churned up since I saw you standing on the edge of that cliff, facing down that highway crew."

"I was afraid."

"You damn well should have been. If the lightning bolt hadn't hit when and where it did, that bulldozer might have rolled right over you."

"No." She shook her head. "There was no reason to be afraid of Brian. It was you who worried me."

"Me? I'd never hurt any woman."

Kate knew Alec honestly believed that. But she also knew that he was bound to hurt her before he returned with his daughter and Legends Lake to America.

Oh, he wouldn't strike her with his fists, or toss hard, hateful words at her like a shower of stones, the way Cadel had. No, his way would be unintentional, but harm her he would. As she looked deep into his eyes, Kate rashly considered that the reward could well be worth the risk.

"If I were to be telling the absolute truth, I suppose I was more afraid of myself. Of how you make me feel. I'm a married woman," she reminded them both.

"You're a legally separated woman," he reminded her back. "If you lived in any other country in the Western world, you'd already be free."

"That's true enough." She sighed and allowed her

head to rest on his shoulder as she remembered that day walking back from the beach with Jamie and Brigid when she'd been buffeted by the winds of change, little knowing that they'd be bringing this man to her doorstep. And into her heart.

"Have you ever been tempted to do something you know you shouldn't?" she asked quietly.

"How do you think I ended up here? I knew punching out Douglas Wellesley wouldn't be a real wise career move. But it seemed like a good idea at the time."

"Isn't that the way of it?" she murmured. "Yet ideas that may seem appealing at the moment often end up being something we regret."

"I don't regret my actions for a minute. I've never been one for wallowing in the past. Besides, if I hadn't lost my temper, Wellesley couldn't have effectively blackballed me in the horse world, which means I wouldn't have been so desperate I had to take on the training of Winnie's crazy horse, which, following that line of reasoning, means I never would have ended up here, in a kitchen that smells of rising yeast, peat, and very sexy woman, about to kiss the luscious witch of Castlelough."

She closed her eyes as he skimmed his thumbs along the sensitive skin of her jawline. "We shouldn't be about doing this."

"Give me one reason why not."

"Because," she moaned softly as one of those treacherous thumbs skimmed across her lips, creating a trail of sparks, "I'm not ready for such things." She drew in a long, steadying breath, opened her eyes and found herself drowning in his. "I'm not ready for you."

"I'm not real sure I'm ready for you, either, sugar. But here we are." He touched his lips to hers, rewarded when she shivered. "The peat's still glowing in the fireplace." He trailed a fingertip down her throat. "And your skin is warm."

She had to press her lips together to keep from moaning when the tantalizing touch skimmed down the triangle of flesh framed by the lapels of her robe.

"Yet you shiver when I do this." His lips followed the trail his fingers had made. "And your nipples harden when I do this." There was a rasping sound as he brushed callused fingertips against the decidedly unsexy flannel covering her breasts. Taking hold of her waist, he shifted her a bit on his lap in a way that revealed she wasn't the only one affected.

Even as much as Kate wanted him—and by all the ancient gods and goddesses she did—she couldn't quite overcome that final mental barrier. "You don't understand." Her brows knit. "Once, a very long time ago, I allowed myself the luxury of mindless pleasure. And paid dearly for it."

"I'm not looking for mindless pleasure." He took hold of the hand she was pressing against his chest. "When I make love to you, I want your mind fully engaged, so you'll be aware of everything I'm doing to you."

He touched the tip of his tongue to the center of her palm and made her heart skitter. "*With* you." His lips cruised up her cheek and set her trembling.

"Sex would complicate things."

"Things are already complicated."

She felt herself melting as he nibbled on her earlobe. Her head fell back, offering even what she kept insisting she did not want.

"You don't understand," she repeated weakly.

"I understand that I want you." When he touched his mouth to hers again, once, twice, a magical third time, she allowed herself to sink into the kiss. "And unless every instinct I've got has gone on the blink, you want me." He combed his fingers into her hair, pushed it back from her face and took the kiss deeper. Darker. "Tell me I'm wrong."

His mouth was hot and certain. His hands, strong and sure. Oh, the man was good at this, Kate thought as he pulled her closer. Their bodies were pressed so tightly together she could feel his heart beating, in a hard and fast rhythm that matched her own.

"No. You're not wrong." She shifted, straddling his thighs. "I do want you. But it's not safe." In so many complicated ways.

He drew back and gave her a long, measuring look. "Let me worry about that. It's probably the most over-used line by men trying to talk a woman into bed, but you really can trust me, Kate. I wouldn't put you at risk."

She knew he was talking about her body, about sexually transmitted diseases, which even here in Catholic Ireland, she'd heard all about. Or leaving her with a child, something she knew about firsthand.

"I do trust you."

Slipping free of his embrace was one of the more difficult things she'd ever done. She began to pace, afraid that if she didn't keep moving to use up some of the energy that was sparking beneath her flesh like lightning, she'd throw caution to the wind and fling herself back into the MacKenna's arms.

"I trust you and I want you. And if it were only the two of us involved, I'd probably take the risk. But I've the children to think of."

"There's no reason for them to be involved. I'm capable of control. I don't have any intention of ravishing you in front of them."

The thought of being ravished by this man set

rivers of flames coursing through Kate's veins even as she struggled to resist the primal urges battering away at her.

"Of course you wouldn't. But Jamie can be wiser than his years, and I believe Brigid has inherited The Sight. If either of them were to have even an inkling that we were . . ."

She struggled for the word. "*Together* in such an intimate way, they could be hurt when you went back to America. Haven't they already lost their father—"

"Which, from the little I've been able to gather, was the best thing that could have happened to them."

"Aye. That's true enough. So far as it goes. But to be a child of divorce is not a common thing in Ireland, as it is in your own country. I know it's difficult at times for Jamie. It's all too obvious that the lad is relieved his da is no longer living with us, yet there are times, when there's an event at school, like the annual father and son trek, or a football game, when it's so very difficult for him."

She was pacing like a nervous cat in an electrical storm. Sensing that it was important to let her state her mind, he managed to tamp down his hunger. For now.

"Michael or Quinn always volunteer to play the part of a da, but it's not the same thing for a boy, is it?"

"No," he agreed, thinking back on how many events his own father had missed during his childhood. "It's not."

She shook her head, shoved her hands through the heavy silk of her hair and pushed it back from her face. "I adore my children. There is nothing I wouldn't do for them." Her hand fisted against the front of her robe, over her heart. "I'd kill for them, if need be."

She was a mother lioness defending her cubs, and Alec had not a single doubt that she'd do exactly that.

"They've been harmed enough because of my poor and foolish choices," she said. "I'll not be risking them falling into a trap of desperately hoping for something that won't happen."

"Believe it or not, I know something about having childhood hopes dashed."

He thought back to his long ago seventh birthday when he'd waited for his mother to return to the theater, as she'd promised she would when she'd dropped him off to see *The Exorcist*. When they couldn't find his father, who turned out to be on a drinking and gambling binge in Hot Springs, he'd spent the night with the sheriff and his plump, motherly wife, who'd done her best by putting a small blue candle in a Twinkie and wrapping up one of her own son's Hot Wheels cars in hot pink Barbie wrapping paper, the only kind she'd had in the house.

"There's no way I'd hurt your kids, Kate."

"I do believe you mean that. But . . ." She shook her head, turned away.

She'd wrapped her arms tightly around herself in a gesture of self-protection. She no longer appeared to be the determined druid witch who'd stood up to an entire road-building crew. She looked as delicate as spun glass and unexpectedly vulnerable. Alec wanted to go to her. To hold her, not to seduce, but to soothe. But sensing emotions he couldn't quite decipher, not wanting to make things harder for her, he forced himself to remain where he was.

" 'Tis so complicated," she said on a sigh. "I'm not exactly saying no, mind you. Because there's a very strong part of me, that, despite my own past experience, still believes that we regret most of the things in life we never risked doing, rather than things we did. Even if they do turn out to be mistakes."

"You sure as hell won't get any argument from me on that one."

"But I take intimacy very seriously. And while I'm working things out in my own mind, I'm asking that you be patient with me."

"I'm not exactly known for my patience. But I also believe that some things—and one lovely Irish druid in particular—are worth waiting for."

She smiled at that. Then relaxed: her face, shoulders, spine. "Thank you."

The tense mood lifted, like morning fog. Kate O'Sullivan might appear to be calm personified, but Alec realized that she was far more mercurial than she'd have people believe.

"So." He leaned the wooden rush-seated chair back on its hind legs. "Why don't you tell me about this idea you have for Legends Lake?"

Enthusiasm lit her eyes as she sat back down across from him and shared her thoughts. And as he tried to keep from noticing the way her robe gaped open just a bit whenever she leaned toward him to press a point, Alec began to consider that her plan just might have merit.

It was, granted, a little off the wall.

But then again, wasn't everything concerning Winnie's crazy horse, including Kate's mind-reading episode that had somehow given them the clue to Legends Lake's problems in the first place? With the clock quickly ticking down to the May run for the roses, Alec decided they may as well give the idea a shot.

Later, as he lay on his back, alone in the dark, staring up at the shadows moving across the white swirls of the plaster ceiling, listening to the patter of rain on the roof, Alec forced himself to focus on tomorrow's experiment rather than to wonder if Kate were lying in her bed, thinking of him.

Zoe felt it at first. The faintest touch, like a whisper, against her cheek. Thinking it was Alec, coming to check up on her again, she kept her eyes closed.

"Zoe?" The familiar voice startled her for a fleeting moment, then, realizing she was merely dreaming, she relaxed.

"Go away," she muttered. "You interrupted my wedding to Justin." He was her favorite of the 'N Sync singers and though she was far too mature to do such things now, last year she'd practiced writing Mrs. Justin Timberlake all over her notebook cover. "He thinks I'm special."

"So do I."

"Yeah, right." It was bad enough losing the threads of her romantic dream. Losing it to argue with her dead mother was the pits.

"You *are* special. . . . I've missed you so."

"I've missed you, too." It was the truth.

"It's nice to know you haven't forgotten all about me."

Zoe heard the need, along with the surprise and pleasure in her mother's soft Southern drawl and mumbled something that could have been a response.

"How are you doing, dear?"

"Oh, great. Being an orphan's a lot of fun."

"You don't have to be sarcastic. I certainly didn't mean to fall off that yacht. Drowning isn't exactly a piece of cake, you know."

How like her mother to make this all about her. Which, Zoe admitted, now that she thought about it, it was. "I guess it wouldn't be." She didn't want to think about the details. "What are you doing in my dream?"

"You're not dreaming, darling."

"Yeah, sure." As if to prove to herself that she was still asleep, Zoe opened her eyes, hitched herself up in bed, turned on the lamp and jumped when she viewed the still gorgeous blond woman perched on the end of her bed. "This can't be some weird drug flashback. I've never done drugs."

"Well, that's certainly a relief." Her mother's smile was brighter than the stars shimmering outside the window. "I've always said you were an intelligent girl."

"I don't believe in ghosts."

"Oh?" She lifted a perfectly arched blond brow. "Isn't it a rather selective belief system that embraces witchcraft but refuses to accept ghosts? Especially when they're your mother?"

"I don't embrace witchcraft."

"You believed Kate O'Sullivan drew that lightning bolt from the sky. You also believed she had a visit from her brother after he died."

"Yeah, but—"

"But you didn't believe her when she told you that you could talk to me?"

Well, they were certainly falling back into their old conversational pattern of arguing over every damn thing. "Her talking to her brother is different. Because she has powers. I don't."

"Of course you do." Zoe knew her skepticism must have shown on her face when her mother added, "You have the power of love."

"Yeah. Right. Look, I don't want to hurt your feelings or anything, Mom, but this is just too freaky. So, if you don't mind, I'm going to turn the light off and go back to sleep, okay?" She reached out, pitched the small bedroom back into darkness, rolled over onto her stomach, squeezed her eyes shut and slammed the feather pillow over her head.

Even through her closed lids, she could see the lamp flash back on.

"Why did you do that?"

"Because we need to talk."

"Why can't we talk in the dark?"

"Because I need you to look at me so you'll remember what I'm about to say."

"Geez." This was definitely the weirdest dream she'd ever had. Zoe wondered what kind of crazy, hallucinogenic herbs Kate had baked into that bread of hers. The pillow fell to the floor as she sat up again and stared at the white satin evening gown that fit her mother's firm curves like a glove. Zoe had always felt like an ugly duckling next to this perfect, long-necked swan. It had been bad enough not to measure up while her mother had been alive; you had to be a real loser when even a dead woman looked better than you.

Testing, she leaned forward and touched the bare golden arm that felt like warm silk against her fingertips, then jerked back. Could you touch a hallucination? "If you're dead, how come my hand doesn't go right through you?" she challenged.

"Because if I hadn't appeared to you this way, I couldn't put my arms around you. And you're a girl in desperate need of a hug."

Zoe found it ironic that her mother was proving a lot more perceptive dead than she'd been while alive.

"I may be dead," the woman said when she didn't respond. "But I'm still your mother. And I have a mother's instincts when my baby's in trouble."

Mother's instincts? Get real. Now Zoe *knew* she was dreaming.

"You never cared before." Zoe hated the way her

voice went up a little on the end, turning what should have been a simple statement of fact into a question. Worse, she detested how she sounded like a sappy, needy little kid.

"I did care. I just never knew how to do anything about it." Her mother's sapphire blue eyes swam. Could a ghost really cry? Zoe wondered. "I know it's no excuse, but I wasn't as old as you when my own parents died in that plane crash. I was sent to Atlanta, to live with my father's mother, a stiff old harridan who never forgave her son for marrying, as she was always putting it, "beneath him." If there was one thing she taught me, it was that emotions were messy and must be kept reined in. I don't want to get into a long tear-drenched therapy session here, but I never really had a chance to learn how to appropriately handle my feelings. Which was partly why I was always messing my life up. With men and with you."

Hell. Now *she* was about to start crying. Zoe swiped the back of her hand beneath her nose. "I'm sorry." She had to push the apology past the painful lump in her throat. "For what I said about wishing you'd die."

"Well, of course. I knew that at the time."

"I didn't . . . I mean, I couldn't . . ." She still couldn't voice the fear that had wrapped icy tentacles around her heart ever since Mother Superior had called her to the office to tell her that her mother had drowned.

"Cause my death by wishing?" Liz asked gently.

Zoe couldn't answer. She could only bite her lip and nod as tears trailed hotly down her cheeks.

"Oh, of course not." Her mother held out her arms that gleamed like porcelain in the starshine streaming through the window. Zoe went into them and as she felt herself folded into the embrace, like a baby bird wrapped in its mother's wings, a strange peace like nothing she'd ever before felt washed over her. Flowed through her. "That's not how it works. It was simply my time, darling. You had nothing to do with it."

"Mom?"

"Yes, darling?" Liz brushed the pinkish brown hair off her forehead and pressed a light kiss atop her head.

Zoe sniffed. Somehow, in a magic way she wasn't even going to try to understand, she accepted that this really was her mother holding her in her arms, just like she'd always wanted to be held. "I love you."

"I love you, too, sweetheart. I always have and always will. Forever and always." She pulled back a little, her smile warming Zoe, melting that last little stubborn bit of ice that had lingered deep down inside her. "Now, you'd best be getting back to sleep."

"But—"

Liz put a perfectly manicured finger against Zoe's lips. "Don't worry," she answered the unspoken concern. "I won't be going away this time. You might not be able to see me in the future, but I promise I'll always be there for you."

"Really?" Now it was Zoe's voice that trembled with need.

"Absolutely." Her mother kissed her again. Smoothed a hand over her hair. Zoe felt her eyes grow heavy, her body lax as she slid effortlessly back into sleep.

Liz sighed. Then touched her fingertips to her daughter's cheek. "You won't remember me coming here tonight," she murmured as she removed the memory from Zoe's mind. "But you *will* remember that I'll always love you."

Tears sprang to her eyes once again. At first Liz had been surprised that she could cry after death, but it had been explained to her that all the emotions she'd kept bottled up while alive were no longer restrained. In truth, although her heart was aching, as it had been for months as she'd watched Zoe's struggles, oddly, crying was proving a release of sorts.

She brushed her lips against her daughter's smooth young cheek. Then faded away, back into the world where she'd finally found peace.

19

LEGENDS LAKE

KATE SPENT ANOTHER RESTLESS NIGHT, unsuccessfully chasing sleep. She'd thought she'd put worry away when she'd gotten Cadel out of her life and her house, but concerns kept circling endlessly in her mind, like a bit of seaweed caught in an eddy.

She fretted about Legends Lake. The horse had been born and bred to run; to ban him from doing what he so clearly loved to do could well crush his beautiful spirit. Yet if she and Alec couldn't break him of his unfortunate tendency to bolt during a race, that's exactly what would happen.

She worried about Jamie. He'd seemed to be doing so much better lately, coming out of his self-protective shell, no longer so obviously fearful of life. But she'd seen him casting wistful glances at the MacKenna and knew, not from any gift of telepathy, but merely a mother's natural instincts, that he was fantasizing how life would be if only the Yank horse trainer were his father.

All the more reason to avoid temptation, which was proving a great deal easier said than done. Especially since during those short periods of time she did drift off, her dreams were filled with the man. Kate suspected that were she to look up the definition of a "near occasion of sin," in the catechism from her days at Holy Child School, she'd see Alec MacKenna's face looking right back at her.

Of course he'd be wearing that cocky smile, and there'd be that same devilish gleam in his eyes that had undoubtedly coaxed more than his share of women into bed. And his mouth . . .

When just the memory of what that mouth had been doing during her hot, erotic night visions made her skin feverish and caused her blood to thicken and pool between her thighs, Kate groaned and pushed herself out of her lonely bed. There'd be no more sleep tonight.

After dressing quietly in the dark, Kate slipped outside to a dark world draped in a cloak of misty white. She worked in the barn, cleaning out stalls by the faint yellow glow of the electric lantern, and discovered yet something else to fret about. What if the fog lingered and ruined her plans for the day? Alec was right; he was running out of time if he were to have Legends Lake cured, trained, and ready to race in the American Derby. Now that she'd given him the answer as to why Legends Lake bolted, what if he put the horse onto that jet plane and took him back home?

"Where you knew all along he'd be going," she reminded herself firmly. "No matter what might happen between you."

By the time a rosy glow arose over the peaks of the eastern mountains, the morning fog was starting to lift. Kate decided to take it as an omen that the rest of their day would go well.

"Don't we have a treat for you this morning, darling boy," she crooned to Legends Lake, who returned her greeting with a whinny. She stroked his long face, scratched behind his pricked ear. He returned the affection by nibbling on her shoulder. "Shall we take you down to run on the beach, the way you did when you were a baby?"

She often ran her yearlings on the strand, as her father had before her, and his father before him, because the exercise was good for building muscle. Kate did not think it was mere good fortune that for as long as anyone could remember, no horse bred and trained here for its first year had ever broken a leg.

"Just remember," she said, as she began to saddle the colt, "neither Alec nor I would ever do anything to hurt you."

"I sure as hell hope he can understand that."

Kate turned to glance over her shoulder, her smile dying half-born as all the air left her lungs in one giant *whoosh*. She'd felt this way before, the first time she'd had the wind knocked out of her after falling off Finnegans Wake when she was no more than four years old. She could still remember lying on her back in high meadow grass, convinced she was going to die, and the way her da, kneeling beside her, had taken her childish hands in both of his strong large ones and assured her she wouldn't be leaving them anytime soon.

"I'd be wishing the same thing," she managed to say over the pounding of her heart.

Fragrant steam rose from the mug he was carrying. "I still don't know why you can't just boil up some eye of newt and cast us a fire exorcism spell."

"I told you—"

"Yeah, I know, you don't do spells." He entered the stall with her, plucked the bridle from her hand and shoved the mug into it, then slipped the bridle over Legends Lake's head.

She sipped the tea, which no man before Alec had

ever brewed for her, watching as he finished saddling the horse, who was in his laid back, half-asleep mode that could prove so deceptive.

"And far be it from me to call you a liar, sweetheart," he said. "But I'm not sure I believe that, since I've definitely been feeling spellbound lately."

Despite her need for some distancing in their relationship, Kate simply could not be this close to him without touching. She reached up a hand to his cheek. He hadn't bothered to shave and as her fingertips scratched against his face, she fantasized the scrape of that dark, sexy morning beard against her breasts and felt something warm and delicious flowing through her veins.

"Would you be suggesting that I'd be needing magic to appeal to you?"

"Hell, no." He took hold of her hand by the wrist. His fingers were dark and long and easily spanned her bones. When he lifted her hand to his lips and, with his eyes on hers, began kissing the tips of her fingers, one at a time, her thoughts began to swim. "If I actually believed the effect you're having on me was magic, it might be easier to ignore."

She was melting. Bone by bone. Cell by cell. Kate tugged her hand free. "I shouldn't have done that. Touched you in such a way," she responded to his arched brow.

"Sugar, if you haven't figured out that you're free to touch me anywhere, anytime you want, then you're not nearly as clairvoyant as you claim to be."

"It's wrong of me." She pretended a sudden, intense interest in one of the barn cats—a huge, obviously well-fed orange tabby who was taking a bath in a small pool of stuttering sunlight. "All these mixed messages I keep giving you."

"Don't worry." He tipped a finger beneath her chin and turned her gaze back to his. "I'll sort them out."

He dipped his head and touched his mouth to hers. Unlike his earlier kisses, which had felt like lightning bolts striking from out of a clear blue summer sky, this kiss was infinitely gentler. Softer. But unmistakably seductive.

Her lips yielded beneath his. Parted. His tongue dipped in, teasing hers into a sensual dance. Desire rose, slow and smooth as silk. Her mind began to float and her body felt as light as one of the bright helium-filled balloons Mrs. Monoghan down at the mercantile gave Brigid each and every shopping day. If she hadn't spent several childhood years trying unsuccessfully to levitate, Kate might have believed that they were floating several inches above the fragrant straw.

"We'd better get going." He nipped at her bottom lip. "Before I forget my vow to behave like a gentleman. Especially since Zoe could come looking for me and it wouldn't set a real good example if she discovered me tumbling you in the hayloft."

Kate knew she was in serious trouble when the idea of being tumbled in the loft sounded absolutely grand. "Would Zoe be coming with us, then?"

"Yeah. The munchkins are coming, as well."

"Munchkins?"

"Little people. It's how Zoe thinks of your kids."

Kate smiled at that. "She's beginning to fit in."

"Yeah. Which worries me about what's going to happen when it's time for us to go back home."

Kate didn't want to think about Alec returning to America. Not now. Not while she could still taste his kiss on her lips.

"Well, won't we have to make sure she takes home many happy memories?"

Kate's plan, as she'd explained it to Alec, called for them to run another series of races, but this time on the beach, where there'd be less chance of Legends Lake getting injured by leaping a fence, or stumbling in a foxhole while tearing wildly across the rocky meadow adjacent to the turf track. She'd rung up the same group of men, who arrived with their horses, looking even less eager to participate in the mock event than they had the first time.

The fog, which had been as thick as soup when he'd first walked out to the barn, was burning off as the west awoke to the first rays of the sun. A bit of vapor still floated in the salt air like silent ghosts and curled around the horses' fetlocks like wispy gray ribbons. The white sands still held a strange glimmer of moonlight.

"They don't look real happy to be here," Zoe murmured as she stood beside Alec, watching the men unload their Thoroughbreds from the trailers.

Overhead, a flock of glossy black choughs with vivid scarlet bills soared off the edge of the towering cliff, riding the thermals, seeming to play in the air with consummate ease, their cheerful cries belying the serious intent of the humans on the sands below.

"Whether they're happy or not isn't important. I'm just grateful Kate managed to talk them into showing up."

"It's hard to say no to her."

"Yeah. I'm discovering that for myself." He put his arm casually around her shoulder and decided they were definitely making progress when she didn't pull away. She seemed oddly different this morning. More approachable. More at peace.

They stood in comfortable silence, as wading birds scurried busily at the receding wavelets. The tiny stints seemed oblivious to the action around them as they single-mindedly snatched breakfast from the sparkling sea foam.

"I like Kate," Zoe volunteered. "A lot."

"Yeah. Me, too."

"Duh." She flashed him a grin.

"Is it that obvious?"

"I watch you watching her. When you think no one's looking." Her eyes, lacking much of that heavy makeup this morning, were wise, fond, and gently teasing, reminding him of the best of her mother.

"She's nice to look at."

"She's beautiful."

A gray heron stalked on spindly stilt legs through the ebbing tide, its gimlet gaze focused intently on the foam as it patiently waited for an unwary mackerel to swim within reach of its stabbing beak.

"So," Zoe said after another brief silence, "if you married Kate, do you think you'd stay here in Ireland?"

The insecure child was back. Alec could hear the hunger in her voice, and even understanding how desperate she was for what he suspected she considered a real home, with a mom, dad, and two-point-five kids, he loved her too much to lie.

"That's probably a moot point. Since she's already married."

"She's getting a divorce."

"These things take longer in Ireland than they do in America."

She thought about that for a long moment. "Maybe sometimes that's a good thing."

Alec suspected she was wondering if her mother hadn't been able to get that quickie Dominican Republic divorce, if they'd still be together. They wouldn't have been. But how to explain that to a teenage girl who couldn't yet even understand her own heart?

"You can't dwell on the past, sweetheart." He squeezed her shoulder and dropped a kiss atop her hair, which, while still fluorescent red, was softer this morning, revealing its natural curl rather than the punk spikes he'd reluctantly come to tolerate. "All that gets you is a stomach twisted up in knots. And worse yet, it keeps you from moving forward."

"I know." She sighed. "But I still wish . . ." Her voice drifted off. "I didn't know Kate was going to ride Legends Lake."

"She isn't," he ground out as he followed her gaze to where Kate had just climbed onto the colt's back. "Not if I have anything to say about it."

Why was it that whenever he seemed to be making headway with one of the troublesome females in his life, another decided to take up the slack? *What did they do?* he asked himself as he marched across the sand to where Kate was seated high atop Winnie's glitchy horse. *Have secret meetings beneath the full moon and decide whose turn it was to drive him nuts?*

"What the hell do you think you're doing?" Legends Lake sidestepped nervously at the harshness of his voice as he grasped the bridle.

"I'd say that should be obvious." She leaned down and patted the distressed Thoroughbred's neck. "I'd also be asking that you not upset the horse while I'm sitting on him."

"That's the point. You don't belong up there." Way up there. Christ, he'd known the horse was tall. But looking up at her now, Alec's blood ran cold at the idea of exactly how far Kate would fall if Legends Lake took it into his head to explode. "You're not a jockey."

"Perhaps not. But I began riding before I could walk. I can certainly handle a little morning breezing."

"Excuse me, but I seem to recall that you were the

one to come up with a cockamamie plan to make the horse take off."

"I did. And you didn't call it a cockamamie plan last night."

"Last night I was distracted and forgot about your suicidal tendencies."

"I'm not suicidal. Don't you see?" She was still stroking the now quiet horse's neck who, if he'd been a cat, would have been purring. "If we're to trigger instinctive fears, it's only right that I be the one to be riding him. So I can assure him that he'll be safe."

"What about *your* safety?"

Her eyes softened. Her lips, which he'd continued to taste long after they'd each gone to their separate beds, curved. "Would you be worried about me, MacKenna?"

"Of course I am." As he'd be worried about anyone under similar circumstances, Alec lied to himself, reluctantly acknowledging that he hadn't been this concerned when he thought a seasoned jockey would be putting Legends Lake through the upcoming test.

"Don't worry." She sat up straight in the saddle. Clicked the colt forward. "I know what I'm doing."

How could any woman who looked like a faerie and smelled like heaven be so damn intransigent? As he walked back to where Zoe and Kate's children were watching and waiting, Alec remembered what Brian the bulldozer operator had said about her husband and understood, for just one fleeting second, how Kate O'Sullivan could prove frustrating. But brute force was never the answer. Not with horses, troubled teenage girls, or stubborn Irish witches.

"You're going to let her ride?" Zoe asked.

"I'm beginning to realize that no one *lets* Kate O'Sullivan do anything."

Kate and the others were lining the horses up at a

place designated on the hard packed sand near the water's edge. Alec hadn't realized how narrow this strand of beach was. If Legends Lake decided to take off in the direction of the towering rocky cliff . . .

Hell. As nerves tangled in his gut, he considered his chances of tying Kate to the four posters of her antique bed to prevent her from getting into yet more dangerous trouble.

20

K ATE WATCHED THE EXCHANGE between father and daughter—she would not consider Alec Zoe's step-father, wasn't paternity more a matter of love than blood?—and smiled. She, more than most, knew the magic that was Ireland, and hadn't it woven its charmed spell on those two?

Alec at times seemed like an entirely different per-son from the cynical, taciturn man she'd met on the cliff. Oh, he was still ambitious—and surely there'd be no sin in that—but she'd also discovered he could be warm and caring. He still drove her to distraction, but in a way that wasn't altogether unwelcome.

Legends Lake snorted, reminding her that they hadn't come here this morning so she could moon over the Yank like some foolish young girl.

"All right, darling." After lining up with the others, she bent low over his head and stroked his neck in the way he liked to be touched. "Shall we be showing them what a champion is made of?"

Alec lifted his arm and shot the starter pistol into the air. When the crack sounded over the soft sighs of the surf, she pressed her heels into Legends Lake's sides. The colt took off like a bullet, streaking down the beach, long legs stretching, hooves drumming. Wading birds, usually oblivious to anything but their constant search for food, scattered. Laughing, Kate bent lower over the racehorse's neck.

"That's a grand lad," she urged him on. "You're the king of all Ireland today, darling."

Even if he hadn't been concerned about Kate's safety, Alec wouldn't have been able to take his eyes off her. Since she'd grown up with horses, he wasn't surprised she rode so well. But he hadn't expected such a forceful ride. Or such a joyous one. She was laughing as she and Legends Lake, two free spirits, sped across the line that had literally been drawn in the sand.

He took hold of the bridle. "You continue to surprise me, Mrs. O'Sullivan."

Her laughter was warm and low and breathless. "As you do me, Mr. MacKenna. We'll have to race, you and I. Just the two of us, here on the beach."

"Sounds like a plan. Got anything in mind for the stakes?"

"Oh, won't we be thinking of those later." She glanced around as one of the men called out to her, asking if she intended to try the next stage of the experiment. "I'd best be getting back before the lads escape." She made a clicking sound and was turning the Thoroughbred back into the direction they'd raced down the sand, when Alec touched a hand to her leg.

"I may not be able to read the future, but I know which of us is going to win."

"Oh?" She arched a challenging dark brow. The wind was tangling her hair into an ebony riot. "And who would you be thinking that might be?"

He squeezed her calf, resisting the urge to pull her off that horse and roll around in the surf with her until she was limp and soaked and throughly satisfied. "Both of us."

Her eyes darkened from a sparkling lake blue to the color of midnight. He'd been expecting her to blush, but instead she surprised him with a slow, potent siren's smile that caused the breath to back up in his lungs.

The next race went as well; Legends Lake streaked down the sparkling gold sand, lengths ahead of the others, seemingly unaware that behind him, the young female jockey astride Kevin Murphy's Claddagh's Prize had applied a light touch of the whip to her mount's backside.

"We'll try it again," Kate announced. "This time, Eithne," she said to the jockey, "I'll hold him back, so you can be nearer when you use the crop."

"Hold him back?" Murphy challenged. "Would you be suggesting that Claddagh's Prize isn't a proper match for your horse, Kate?"

"Not at all, Kevin," she soothed quickly. Expertly. "It's just that since this is an experiment, it's best to control as many factors as we can."

He grumbled, but didn't argue.

They were off again. Midway down the beach, Claddagh's Prize caught up with Legends Lake, who was obviously straining for more speed even as Kate tightened the reins. Thundering hooves threw up sand as they streaked neck and neck toward the finish line. And then, as he'd done before, Legends Lake suddenly cut to the left and went plowing into the surf, Kate leaning so low it took no imagination at all to envision her flying over the colt's head.

Later, Alec would realize that the entire event only lasted seconds, yet his feet seemed to have been mired in quicksand as he ran after them. He was up to his thighs in the icy water when he managed to grab hold of the reins.

"I knew this was a goddamn stupid idea!" He pulled her from the horse, hauling her against his chest. "That's enough. There's no race under the sun worth this."

Kate's head was spinning. Even having expected Legends Lake to bolt when Eithne had pulled out the crop, she'd been more than a little afraid when he'd gone crashing into the sea. But he'd listened to her. Even through his obvious terror, he'd listened to her. With not only his ears and mind, but with his heart.

"Would you be putting me down, Alec MacKenna." She pushed against his shoulder. "You'd be crushing my bones."

"You're lucky they're not all broken." Instead of releasing her, he held her tighter still, so she wasn't sure which wild heartbeat she was feeling. Her own or his. "That's it, Kate. I'm taking the horse back to Winnie and telling her that she wasted her money."

"Now wouldn't that be a shame," Kate insisted, finally managing to free herself from his tight embrace. She placed her hands on her hips, tilted her head back and met his frustrated glare straight on without so much as a flinch. "Since he has such grand potential."

"He's flat-out nuts."

"No. He's still a wild animal who spooks a bit too easily. But take a good look at your horse, Alec."

Her calm words managed to make themselves heard over the static buzz of lingering panic in his head. Following her gaze, he saw the Thoroughbred watching them as if they were putting on a show for his entertainment. "He's not trembling."

"No. He's not." She held out a hand. The colt hesitated, then walked forward, lowered his head, and nuzzled her palm. "See what a darling boy he is?"

She'd charmed him. That was the only answer Alec could come up with. Despite her continued claims that she did not do spells, it was obvious that she'd pulled off some druid hocus-pocus.

"We can work with him, Alec." She put her free hand on his arm. "It's not his fault that he's the way he is. Nature has made him a flight animal; the single element in his life is to survive by escaping everything that frightens him. Until a horse is taught otherwise, *everything* frightens him.

"Legends Lake isn't bad, only confused. Because of unfortunate timing, the poor horse believes that whenever he smells or sees, or even hears the crop anywhere near him, he's caught in a life and death situation again, as he was that day at the track. What else should he do, but run? He's tangled up the sound and smell and sight of the crop with the fire in his cellular memory. All we have to do is prove to him that he has nothing to fear from it."

"Pete was training a yearling in Louisiana when I was still a hot walker," Alec mused out loud. "Great configuration, dynamite bloodlines, and the horse could run like the wind. But for some reason we never did figure out, he was scared to death of just about everything."

"What happened to him?"

"He ended up winning about four million dollars over his career, but it wasn't easy. Pete started out getting him used to the blanket by hanging it on the stall door until he became accustomed to the sight and smell of it and figured out it wouldn't hurt him. He went through the same procedure with every bit of tack. Then there was the starting gate. And the track loudspeaker. It took two years before he started earning any money. But it sure turned out to be worth it."

"For the horse as well as his owner," Kate pointed out. "We can do the same thing with Legends Lake."

"We don't have that much time." He said the words that had been echoing over and over again in his mind like a mantra.

"Then isn't it fortunate that the only thing he fears is one small leather whip?"

"I think you ought to do it," a new voice entered into the argument. Alec turned around and noticed that Zoe had waded out into the water, as well. "Everyone needs a chance to straighten out their lives." She reached up and combed her fingers—which today were tipped with glossy turquoise polish—through the silky mane. "Even a horse."

Alec wondered if she was comparing Legends Lake's problems to her own. Then decided it didn't really matter because the Thoroughbred was the first thing she'd shown any real interest in since coming to live with him.

"That still isn't much time to prepare a horse for a race like the Derby."

"It's not a great deal of time, to be sure. But how prepared do you think the horse will be for your Kentucky Derby if you don't at least try to rid him of his fear?"

"Good point."

It was the lilt in her voice that did it. More than the reason, with which he couldn't argue. Alec still had no idea whether Legends Lake could be cured. But watching Kate's lips curve into that soft, pleased smile, he decided that before he returned to Kentucky, he and the witch of Castlelough would be lovers.

It hadn't been easy, convincing Alec that since she was the one the Thoroughbred trusted most, it was only logical that she be the one on Legends Lake's back. Kate had known, without looking into the

MacKenna's mind, that the best way to win with the man was by appealing to logic. American he might be by circumstance of birth, but his blood was of the Highlands, and the Scots were, after all, in their own often inexplicable way, a canny and practical race.

During the last years, she'd become so wrapped up in the logistics of the day-to-day running of the farm and keeping up her proper mating notes, always looking for the perfect match that would result in that champion every breeder dreamed of, she'd forgotten how much she enjoyed the glorious freedom found in racing the wind.

She'd have to keep it up after Alec took Legends Lake back to America, she thought as she lay in bed five nights after running those races on the beach, listening to the *tap tap tap* of the rain on the roof. Riding cleared her mind of the little cobwebs of concern that would begin to gather whenever she thought about Cadel, which was much more often since Alec had come to Castlelough. Try as she might, it was impossible not to compare the two men.

"There's no comparison," she murmured as she rolled over and tried to pound her pillow into a more acceptable shape. Her nerves were on edge tonight. There was something in the air. The premonition was not of anything bad or harmful. Not at all like all those nights spent awaiting Cadel's drunken return from the pub. No, this was more . . . expectation, she decided.

Still, she went to check on her children, beginning in the attic, in the room that Jamie had been so excited to claim when he'd heard the Americans were coming to stay at the house. It was a small room, but she'd made it cozy, with fresh paint and new curtains on the dormer windows that brought in light and offered a lovely view of the lake and castle.

He was sleeping peacefully, the X-Men action figures Quinn and Nora had brought back from a recent trip to California scattered over the quilt. She gathered them up and put them in the sally—willow—basket on top of the chest to keep them from accidentally getting caught up in the sheets and possibly damaging the washing machine. His notebook, which he was never without, was on the bedside table, pencil and flashlight lying beside it in the unlikely event he'd need to take notes during the night.

He was such a precious child. Such a special gift. He may have complicated her life a bit, but no more than she had made his more difficult by turning her back on the easier solution of adopting her infant son out to some loving family in America—and keeping him for herself. It had been, admittedly, a selfish decision on her part, compounded by a foolish, hasty marriage to a man she knew didn't love her. A man she knew she could never love.

Hoping, as she so often did, that her absolute love would make up for the sins of her youth, Kate bent down and brushed a soft kiss against his freckled cheek. Then she slipped out of the room and went back downstairs to check on her daughter.

Brigid was, as usual, turned around in the bed, her small bare feet at the headboard, her bright head down at the foot rail. Unlike Jamie, who was quieter and much more deliberate, her daughter seemed unable to remain still even while sleeping.

Kate lifted her gently, turned her around, then drew the covers over her. The waxing moon drifted by the window, bathing the room in a pale white light. Kate's lips curved as she viewed Brigid's small pixie face.

There was seldom a time when her darling daughter wasn't smiling. Even in her sleep. Kate still found it difficult to think of Cadel fathering this child, who'd been born sunshine personified.

After kissing her daughter as well, she opened the door to Zoe's room, just a crack, enough to see that Alec's daughter was also sound asleep. Everyone was safe. Which, since there had been so many nights over the years when that might not have been the case, Kate viewed as a major life improvement.

Still restless, she threw on a heavy sweater, jeans, wool socks, her barn coat, and boots and went out to the brood barn to check on Nora. When nothing proved amiss, she was headed back to the house when she saw Alec coming out of the barn where Legends Lake was stabled.

"Looks like I wasn't the only one who couldn't sleep," he said by way of greeting.

"It's an odd night."

"Edgy."

Kate looked at him, surprised that a man who claimed to be so resistant to any form of clairvoyance, could have sensed the energy in the moist air. "Aye." She glanced over at the barn. "How is he?"

"Seems fine. Though this damn cold is working against his metabolism." He glared up at the sky which, having cleared, was studded with stars that looked like pinpricks on black velvet. The moon lit the landscape with an unearthly glow. "It's hard enough to keep weight on him. He's using all his caloric energy to stay warm."

"Perhaps the weather will warm up."

Alec toyed with a silky tendril that had escaped her loose braid to curl down her cheek. He was flat-out crazy about her hair. "I don't suppose you'd be willing to boil up some toad tongues and lizard tails, toss in a little moondust, and cast a weather spell for me?"

"Magic is not my gift," she reminded him. Her eyes twinkled merrily.

Because it had been too long since he'd tasted her, he tugged a bit harder on her hair, coaxing her toward him. "Do you know, that when you laugh, your eyes fill with little gold lights? Like newborn stars gleaming down on a sparkling lake."

"You've obviously got some Irish blood in you, MacKenna. Because that's definitely the thickest blarney I've heard in some time." Even so, she couldn't keep from smiling. "Isn't it a good thing I'm wearing my Wellies."

He'd prefer to have her wearing nothing but starshine, a smile and her alluring scent. "It's not blarney." He moved closer, until their thighs were touching, his black denim to her faded blue.

He slowly lowered his head, giving her time to protest. To back away. Instead, her lips parted, just a whisper, in invitation and acceptance.

His mouth was a breath from hers, when Kate jerked out of his arms. "Oh! I knew it!"

"What's wrong?"

"It's Nora." She spun around and began to run through the silvered light and shifting shadows toward the brood barn. "It's her time."

A flick of a switch flooded the barn in incandescent light as bright as a summer day, revealing the mare lying on the straw in her oversize foaling stall. She was panting heavily, sweat streaming down her swollen sides.

"Poor baby." Kate dropped to her knees beside her and caressed the swollen stomach that clenched beneath her hands. "I know, it hurts like the devil, doesn't it?" The horse rolled her eyes, showing white, in apparent agreement. "But I promise, darling, you'll be just fine."

"Naturally, she chose the middle of the night to go into labor," Alec said.

"Aye. Isn't that always the way? Both my children were born between sunset and sunrise as well." Her hands continued to soothe the mare through the contraction. "It's going to take a while."

"It usually does. Especially with a first one."

"It feels as if the foal's upside down," Kate worried.

"Do you want me to go wake up someone to help? Or will I do? I'll admit I haven't taken part in that many births, but so long as you tell me what to do, I promise not to faint."

Despite her concern, Kate smiled at the idea of this man fainting in any situation. "Some men might be uncomfortable with taking orders from a woman."

Despite this being the twenty-first century, Alec knew that time moved a lot slower in Ireland. Especially in the rural west. He had not a single doubt that she'd encountered a great deal of masculine prejudice since taking the stud over from her father.

"Some men aren't real secure in their manliness."

"But you are."

"You bet." He beamed a wicked smile as he leaned over the heaving mare's back and murmured in her ear. "And once we finish up here, I'm willing to show you exactly how manly I can be."

"You'd best be watching out what you're promising, MacKenna," she said with a light laugh. "Because one of these days I may just take you up on that."

"Anytime, sugar." His gaze heated, intimately touching her. "Anywhere."

As they sat with the horse, able to do little but soothe her with words and hands, and watch as her contractions gradually grew longer and harder, they took the rare opportunity to talk. For the first hour, they stuck to safer topics—the weather, the type of music they preferred. Kate enjoyed Celtic ballads, Alec, American country, both of which, they agreed, they enjoyed because they told stories of ordinary people and everyday lives they could identify with.

Then, as time passed, Alec found himself opening up to her, sharing things he'd always kept locked deep inside him. Some he'd never even told Pete.

Her eyes shone when he told her about how his mother had dumped him at a theater on his birthday and taken off, never to be seen again. She turned pale when he brought up the closet incident again, paler yet when he told her about Fortissimo, but when he held out his arm, showing the small round scars from a lit cigarette the year he'd turned twelve, a sympathetic tear trailed down her cheek.

"Oh that poor, dear lad," she murmured, touching her lips to the puckered white skin. "Why didn't he leave?"

Alec thought it interesting that Kate so easily disassociated the child from the man. As he himself had done for so many years. "Because his roots were in that land. Because he loved the farm and the horses and the mountain, and he was damned if he was going to let any damn alcoholic son of a bitch run him off it."

"But he did leave."

"It was over when my father murdered that horse in cold blood. I didn't want any part of him. I changed my name for a while. To John Smith."

She smiled just a bit at that. "Isn't that original?"

"Thanks to my father, the MacKenna name was infamous in racing circles. I never would have gotten a job if I'd used my own name. Besides, at that point in my life, I just wanted to blend in."

"Disappear."

He was not surprised she understood so quickly. "Yeah."

She lifted her hand to his face. Bent forward and touched her lips against his.

"It's glad I am you decided to come back, Alec MacKenna. It's especially glad I am that you decided to come here to Ireland."

"That's where destiny comes in."

"I wouldn't be arguing with you about that."

He half smiled. "I gotta admit, when I first saw Legends Lake at Winnie's, I sure as hell didn't think I was looking at destiny."

"Appearances can be deceiving. It's glad I am that Mrs. Tarlington rang you up."

"Make that two of us. She really is one terrific woman. And the only person in Lexington who believed in me when everyone else was betting I'd end up no better than my father.

"I was in the clubhouse dining room one day, shortly after first returning home, having lunch with an owner whose horse I was hoping to train." Alec could still remember it as if it were yesterday. "The place went silent as a tomb when I first walked in and during the entire lunch, I could sense everyone staring at me. Then Patsy Camden, whose father ran Black Oak Farms and most of the county as well, made a point of saying, just loud enough so everyone could hear her, that it was a crying shame, given my talent with horses, that I'd have that wild MacKenna Scot blood running through my veins, so of course no one would ever hire me, since there was no telling what I'd do."

Alec shrugged, not adding that after that initial statement, she'd lowered her voice to an exaggerated stage whisper and gone on to say, "Why, once I caught him looking at my lips as if he was considering ravaging me."

What Patsy hadn't said was that the week earlier, she'd actually come on to him while slumming with her society friends at the Final Stretch bar where he was making some much needed extra bucks working as a bartender and had been miffed—as only a Southern belle can be miffed—when he'd turned her down.

"That's a horrible thing to say!"

While he liked her being angry on his behalf, Alec shrugged. "My father did the unforgivable; he killed a horse for money. In that part of the country, he probably would have been better thought of if he'd killed another man."

"Well, it's still hateful."

"It's life."

"But you forgave him."

Had he, really? Alec had to think about that for a moment. "Yeah, I guess I did. But only because grudges get too heavy to carry around." Plus, he'd been working too hard for too many years to save the mountain and reclaim the MacKenna name to have time to dwell on the past.

"Ah, wouldn't I be knowing something about that," she murmured.

He heard the sorrow in her voice, saw the shadow in her eyes and was about to delve into their meaning when the mare, which had been standing during Alec's tale, let loose with a deep groan.

"We're getting close," Kate said, as the mare's water broke, soaking into the straw. "Could you please wake the children for me? I promised them that they could take part in the birthing."

"Sure."

As he left the barn and was immediately swallowed up by the dark, Kate heard the distant caw of a crow, felt the flutter of wings nearby, and was rocked by a sudden, almost irresistible urge to go running after him.

21

THE FINAL STAGE of the mare's labor did not take long. Less than ten minutes after the children arrived in the barn she whinnied loudly, then pushed with an effort that racked her body. Two small feet emerged, confirming Kate's concern that the foal was upside down.

The mare whinnied again, louder this time, and rolled her eyes all the way back in her head. If it were possible for a horse to look pale, this one did. Remaining true to her placid nature, she managed to stay calm.

"All right. That's my darling girl." Kate waited for this latest contraction to subside, then slid her hands into the birth canal.

Alec watched those slender hands which, at first glance, appeared delicate enough to be strumming a gilt faerie harp. They were also gentle enough to soothe the mare's distress with a healing touch that had him believing in Biddy Early's gift. But there was steel beneath, strong enough to rein in a runaway colt and to bring new life into the world. For not the first time since arriving at the stud, he considered what a complex woman she was. Every day he was discovering a new intriguing facet of Kate O'Sullivan.

"He's too big for me to be pulling out by myself," she said. "I'll try to turn him a bit. You take hold of his legs and when she pushes, you pull."

"Got it."

The mare began to shake violently. Painfully. Alec grasped the two thin legs and working nearly as hard as the mare, grit his teeth and began to pull.

"I have his head." Kate was panting as if she were the one about to give birth. "If I can just . . . a wee bit . . . ah, there we go."

They were kneeling, side by side in the blood and manure and fluid that could not all be soaked up by the now filthy straw. Alec had the left leg, Kate the right, and they continued to pull and pull and pull until Alec feared they might yank the poor mare inside out.

A dark nose suddenly appeared. Just as suddenly, the mare stopped pushing.

"That's all right," Kate gasped, rocking back on her heels. Her hair had come loose and was clinging in thick wet strands to her face. Her bottom lip was bleeding where sometime during the labor she must have put her teeth through it. "We'll all just take a little breather, shall we, darling girl?"

"She's not going to die, is she?" Zoe asked, clearly concerned.

"Oh, no. Isn't she doing just fine. Nora's a brave girl, she is."

"If having a baby is that hard, I'm never going to be a mother," Zoe decided.

"It isn't easy, that's true enough. But—" Kate's gaze was fond as it swept over her son and wee daughter, whose eyes were as wide as saucers. Kate had just begun allowing Brigid to attend the foalings this year, at the same age she herself had been when she'd first watched her father bring a newborn horse into the world. "I'm sure dear Nora would agree that a miracle is worth a bit of trouble."

As if on cue, the horse grew alert again. Her eyes widened, huge and dark in her long face. She gave one last final push. The foal shot out of the birth canal with a force that had both Kate and Alec falling backward. Nora, exhausted from her efforts, dropped her head to the straw. The foal lay limp and still beside his mother.

"Wow," Zoe said, as the foal slid into the world. "That's really awesome."

"Aye." Kate thought it said a lot about Alec's daughter that she saw the gift, rather than the blood and fluid that had accompanied the birth.

"Do we have to get it out of that wrapping?" Zoe asked as they watched the foal struggling inside the wet and gleaming birth sac.

"The baby can do it," Jamie assured her. "If not, his ma will help. Or my ma." He smiled up at Kate, looking like a proud father himself. All he needed was a box of cigars to be handing out.

A vision flashed before Kate's eyes, of her son, no longer a boy, but a man, standing beside the bed of a red-haired young woman whose smile belied the fatigue in her eyes. Kate blinked. The scene shifted, ever so slightly, revealing the two infants she was holding in her arms, one wrapped in pink, the other blue.

Twins. Kate felt the sting of happy tears. She was going to be the grandmother of twins. When she saw Alec looking at her curiously, she managed a watery smile and shook her head, assuring him that she was all right.

"See," Jamie was telling Zoe, as Kate returned to the present. The foal had, as nature intended, broken free of his birth sac.

"It's a boy," Alec announced.

"A beautiful one," Kate said.

Zoe tilted her head, observing the small wet animal with open skepticism. "He doesn't look much like a horse."

His long spindly legs were attached to a painfully thin body. His feet were white and soft, nothing like the strong firm hoofs he'd be needing to run. His ears were flopped back, wet and seemingly useless on a too large head, and his lips and muzzle were covered with what appeared to be curly whiskers.

"He's just born," Jamie said, defending the colt. "You probably didn't look all that beautiful when you first came sliding out of your mother."

"His mother thinks he's beautiful," Kate observed as Nora gamely pushed herself to her feet, breaking the umbilical cord, separating mother from baby for the first time. She went to work cleaning her newborn, nickering encouragingly to the foal, who, after a time, nickered back.

"What's she doing now?" Zoe asked, as Nora began nudging the baby with her front feet.

"She's telling him to stand up," Brigid said, seeming pleased to be able to share her knowledge with the teenager she so obviously looked up to.

"So soon?"

"Horses aren't like people," Jamie informed her, as Nora began to kick her offspring. Not hard, but with definite authority. "They get started a lot faster."

"Are you sure this is all right?" Zoe asked Kate when the mare moved on to nipping at his flanks. "Won't she hurt him?"

"I think this is probably a case of mother knowing best," Kate assured the worried teenager. She handed Zoe a towel. "Why don't you help her a bit by rubbing the baby down."

Zoe looked over at Alec, who gave her an encouraging thumbs-up. She began gingerly drying the colt's neck.

"He's not glass. You won't be breaking him." Jamie grabbed a towel from the pile. "Rub him hard, like this." He vigorously massaged the colt's head and face.

Zoe followed suit, quickly becoming more self-assured as the foal began to stir, then squirm. He lifted his hind end up in an obvious attempt to stand, but his wobbly legs folded beneath him and he fell back down to the filthy straw.

"Come on, boy," Alec said encouragingly. "You can do it."

For the next few minutes, they all offered encouragement to the struggling foal, including Nora, who kept nudging at her baby and nickering her own equine words of encouragement. Finally, as if tiring of being pummeled, he kicked out at the humans who were pestering him so. As he struggled again to stand, succeeding on his fourth try, Kate unconsciously reached over and grasped Alec's hand.

There were cheers when he finally, gamely, made it to his feet and tottered the few steps to his mother, obviously seeking breakfast. The mare and her human helpers were drenched in sweat. Since the midnight air in the barn was a great deal cooler, the foaling stall had grown as steamy as a sauna.

"You're right," Zoe said.

"About what, darling?" Kate asked.

"A miracle is definitely worth whatever trouble it takes."

Kate and Alec's gaze met. "Absolutely," they said together.

22

THE DRAMA OVER with for the night, the children returned to the house, Zoe promising to make certain Kate's son at least ducked beneath the shower before returning to bed.

"She's a fine girl," Kate murmured as she stood in the open doorway of the barn with Alec, watching the lights come on upstairs in the house. "You should be proud of her."

"I am proud of her. But I sure as hell didn't have anything to do with it."

"Of course you did." She smiled reassuringly. With her eyes and her oh, so sweet mouth. "You're the only father she's ever known. She lived with you for four very important formative years, and you've stayed in touch since then—"

"Not as close as I would have liked. As I should have."

"Possibly." She impressed him once again with her honesty, answering him truthfully when a pretty lie would have been easier. "But parents aren't perfect and children don't arrive on the doorstep with instruction manuals." Her weary gaze warmed. *She really does have incredible eyes,* Alec thought. *The kind a man could drown in.* "Isn't that what second chances are for?"

Alec figured Kate knew a lot about second chances. "I'll take your word for that."

The night had remained clear. And cold.

He braced a hand on the wooden wall beside her head. "Where were we before we were interrupted? Oh, yeah. You were about to kiss me."

"*You* were about to kiss *me,*" she corrected.

"You weren't exactly running away."

"Would it have done any good if I had?"

"Probably not."

His rough voice made her smile. "Good."

Satisfaction glittered in Alec's eyes. Then his head swooped down and claimed her mouth with a force that stole Kate's breath away. Passion hit with a speed and power that made her head swim. As his roving hands reached beneath her sweater and cupped her breasts, she dived into the greedy kiss, matching heat for heat, hunger for hunger, then demanded more.

All the dreams she'd suffered, all the desires she'd been repressing, burst free with the force of a volcano. Needing to touch him, as he was touching her, Kate struggled with the stubborn buttons of his shirt. How was it that the same hands that had delivered a breech foal could not manage to unfasten a simple bloody button? "I can't . . . I need . . ."

"Rip it," he ground out against her mouth. His breathing was harsh. Ragged.

Wondering why she hadn't thought of that, she wildly yanked at the front of the shirt, sending buttons flying. "Oh, aye," she moaned as her hands streaked over hot damp flesh.

His mouth greedily ravaged hers, then moved down to savage her throat while rough hands plundered. When he pressed her against the wall with his hard male body, a bubble of panic rose from some deep dark place inside her. Kate pushed against his chest, but she might as well have been trying to move the cliff.

"Alec." She managed to choke out his name, but mistaking the ragged tone for desire, he didn't back away, but took the kiss deeper. Darker.

He caught both her wrists in one hand, braceleting them like a pair of steel cuffs with his fingers as his other hand deftly unfastened the button at the waist of her jeans, and suddenly she was no longer in the barn, but on the floor of her own bedroom, her hands held helpless above her head as her huge, hulking husband knelt over her, his free hand opening his trousers.

Terror was a cold, sharp thing, ripping through Kate like an icepick. "No!" Head spinning, knees shaking, heart pounding, she abruptly pulled away, yanking her hands free. Curled them into tight fists.

"Don't touch me!" Her voice was high, edging toward hysteria.

Alec blinked. Once, twice, a third time. "What the hell?"

She pressed a hand against her breast and wondered if a woman her age could have a heart attack. "You've no right to take what isn't offered."

"Isn't offered? I'm not the one who sent buttons flying."

"I apologize for that. I'll sew them back on tomorrow."

"Fuck the damn buttons. I'm just trying to figure out what just happened."

"A mistake is what happened."

"A mistake." Frustration and disbelief rang in his voice.

"Aye. A mistake I won't be making again."

Oh, bloody hell. She was going to start in weeping. She never wept. Not since that last day with Cadel. The day she'd feared she was going to die.

Kate pressed her fingertips against her temple and tried to remind herself what Erin had told her. That on those rare occasions deep-seated terrors were tapped into, they, in turn, could trigger other emotions she was trying to avoid.

She didn't experience the terrifying flashbacks all that often. At least not anymore. Only when she was exhausted. Or emotionally unsettled. As she'd been since first encountering the MacKenna at the cliff.

"You wanted me," he insisted stubbornly, "as much as I wanted you."

"I thought I did," she admitted. "But that was before I thought—" She shook her head with mute frustration, grabbed up a shovel and began furiously scooping up the soiled straw. "Never you mind."

"I do damn well mind." When he reached out a hand, she instinctively flinched.

"Aw shit . . . I'm not him, Kate." The sharp edge was gone from his voice. The pity she thought she heard in those words only added to the humiliation she was feeling from her overreaction.

"Kate." Her nerves screamed when his hand shot out again, but he was only after the shovel. "I'm not him," he repeated.

"I wouldn't be knowing who you're speaking of."

"Your husband." His tone remained mild; his eyes were not. "I'm not a saint. I get angry. Hell, as I proved with Wellesley, I've even been known to lose my temper. Especially when I'm filthy, exhausted, and flat-out frustrated. I wanted you earlier, before Nora had her foal, which damn well isn't anything new, and you were sending out some pretty powerful signals that you wanted me, too.

"But you don't have to worry, because even if you weren't looking at me like I was the Castlelough rapist, I'm so dead on my feet, I probably couldn't do anything about it anyway, and only end up humiliating myself. Which, to be real honest, isn't even a little bit easy for me to admit.

"So, here's the deal. If you don't want to go to bed with me, fine. I've never forced myself on any woman. Nor have I lied or used pretty words I didn't mean to get a woman into my bed. I'm not going to apologize for wanting to touch you, Kate. Everywhere and often. But I told you that I'd never—ever—lay a hand on any woman in anger. And I meant it."

"Well." Kate let out a long breath. He wasn't alone in his exhaustion. Now that the adrenaline rush of birthing the foal had worn off, she felt as if her legs could well collapse on her. "I owe you an apology."

"Nah." He shook his head and managed a half-smile. "We're both not at our best right now. How about we put whatever it was that just happened behind us, get this place cleaned up and hit the sack. Alone," he said quickly, as if afraid she'd misconstrue his meaning.

Anxiety faded into the background. "Thank you. Perhaps you don't want an apology. But I'd be needing to give you an explanation." She took in the stall that looked as if the Anglo-Irish war had been fought in it. "Later."

"Later," he agreed.

That settled, at least for now, he began shoveling up the straw. Grateful for his assistance, Kate set in gathering up the towels, putting those worth salvaging in a pile to be washed. While he scrubbed down the walls, she prepared a new feedbag for Nora, who'd labored so hard to bring her baby into the world and now appeared famished.

Finally, they were done.

"God, I need a shower," Alec muttered, grimacing as he took a sniff at his filthy shirt.

"You're not alone in that."

"I'll walk you back to the house."

"No." Her eyes lifted to his. In those weary blue depths he saw trust. And something else. Some emotion that at any other time might have sent him running in the other direction. "I don't want to spend the night there."

Jesus, the woman could be frustrating. What kind of female could be on the verge of bawling one minute, then turn right around and start arguing when it was obvious she was dead on her feet? PMS, he decided. That was the only answer since from what he'd been able to tell, except for the witch thing, she wasn't normally all that nuts.

"Look, if you're worried about the mare, I can stay down here with her and—"

"That's not necessary. What I was meaning to say was that I want to spend the night upstairs. With you."

Hell. Timing, Alec told himself, was everything. Earlier, he would have taken her up on the offer without a moment's hesitation. But it was more than obvious she was exhausted. And there was something else going on here. Something that had turned her emotions into live wires.

"Look, sweetheart, it's not that I'm not flattered. Hell, I'm grateful. But you've had a long night and an emotional one and—"

"Would you be saying that you've changed your mind? About wanting me?"

"Of course not. It's just that . . . Hell . . ." Surprising them both, he mustered up enough strength to scoop her off her feet. "Why don't we sort it out tomorrow? After we get a decent night's sleep."

"All right." He felt her go lax in his arms. Compliant. "I've never had a man carry me to bed before," she murmured. She rested her head against his shoulder as he carried her up the stairs, cuddled closer in a way that stimulated more tenderness than passion. "It's even more romantic in real life than it is in stories."

"You want romance?" He brushed his lips against hers, nearly walking them both into the wall of the stairwell when her lips heated again and clung. "I can do that."

"I'd not be needing romance, Alec. Only you." Her smile was soft and sweet and unbearably trusting.

As he opened the door to the apartment, Alec decided that one of the most appealing things about Kate O'Sullivan was that she had more facets than the Hope diamond. He carried her straight into the bathroom, bypassing the bed, which took up most of the small room, with rigid discipline.

"Why don't you take your shower," he suggested, after depositing her on the closed toilet and turning on the water. "While I run over to the house and get you some fresh clothes. Meanwhile, if you want, you can wear one of my T-shirts."

He tossed a dark green T-shirt, embroidered with the Keeneland horse and jockey logo, onto the top of the closed hamper and, because he didn't dare kiss her, skimmed a fingertip down her nose. "I'll be back in five."

The kids had gone back to bed, the towels on the floor evidence that at least they'd cleaned up first.

After checking on them, he went into Kate's bedroom and as much as he was in a hurry to get back to her, he took some time to look around.

The view from her window was spectacular. Even now, at night, he could see the silvered shimmer of the sea and lake and the castle ruins, the mica in the stone glittering like ice in the moonlight.

She'd painted the room a soft green that brought the rolling fields indoors and the windows were framed with traditional white curtains. Photographs of Kate and her children, which he assumed had been taken by Michael, adorned the walls. The bedroom was as tidy as a nun's cell, yet there were touches of whimsy that were uniquely Kate. A small metal faerie with gossamer wings smiled down from above a door at a porcelain wizard dressed in blue robes emblazoned with gold stars who held the moon in his hands atop Kate's dresser.

Alec picked up a smoky globe sitting beside a twig basket of fragrant dried herbs and flowers and stared into it for a moment, then laughed when he realized that a part of him had actually been expecting to see his future.

He retrieved a pair of well-worn, but neatly pressed jeans from the closet and a heather-hued sweater from a heavy five-drawer chest that was obviously an antique. The brilliant display of silk and satin lingerie in another drawer might be an unlikely choice for a woman in rural Ireland to favor, but perfectly suited the sensual woman he knew her to be.

He considered telling her that he'd forgotten the underwear, but figured she'd never buy that story. So, feeling a bit like a pirate sifting through a treasure chest, he selected a pair of scarlet-as-sin panties so skimpy it was a wonder that she even bothered to wear them. "No point getting carried away," he said, deciding to skip the bra.

She was in his bed when he returned to the efficient, but cozy little apartment above the barn. Just as he'd imagined her too many times to count. She was also sound asleep, her long wet hair strewn across his pillow in a way that brought up that fantasy he'd been having too often lately about those same jet silk strands draped across his thighs.

Biting back a groan, he tossed the clean clothes onto the chair in the corner, went into the bathroom and took a long hot shower, enjoying the feel of the needles of hot water stinging against his skin as the night's grime and blood and fluid washed down the drain. Then, gritting his teeth, he twisted the faucet, willing his mutinous body to respond to the icy onslaught.

She murmured something as he joined her in bed. Rolled over and put her hand on his bare chest. Alec drew her closer. As perfect as she felt and as much as he ached for her, Alec had only time for a long, satisfied sigh before he, too, dropped like a rock into dreams.

23

STARSHINE WAS STREAMING THROUGH the window, casting the room in an unearthly silver glow. Feelings flooded into Alec as he turned his head and looked down at the woman who was snuggled against him. Drawn by something stronger, more complex than mere desire, he touched his lips to her tumbled hair.

She sighed. Her lips curved in a faint, unconscious smile.

There were rules, Alec reminded himself as desire returned, settling hot and heavy in his loins. And taking advantage of a sleeping woman was undoubtedly up there at the top of the list.

Just a touch, he promised himself as he skimmed a feather light caress down the slender white column of her throat and felt the vibration of her sleepy purr against his fingertip. She pressed closer. Her breath was warm against his bare chest. When she draped a long leg over his thigh, Alec knew he was lost.

At first Kate thought she was dreaming. Hadn't she dreamed of the MacKenna this way, every night since he'd come to stay at the stud? Even before that, she mused sleepily as the dream of riding the big horse into the sun shimmered in her mind. She'd dreamed of him, and he'd come. To Ireland. To her.

Needing to be closer, she flung a bare leg over his and felt a shock of sheer pleasure as bare flesh met flesh. No dream had ever been so vivid. Or, so . . . solid. Her eyes flew open, her gaze colliding with his.

Before she could pull away to gather her tumbling thoughts, he touched his mouth to hers.

Awake now, Kate braced herself for passion.

But he surprised her. Beguiled her. Without words, he stroked her through the cotton T-shirt, wet her breasts with his mouth, took her nipple between his teeth, and when she began to move restlessly on the mattress, shifted onto his side and continued the leisurely exploration of her body, seeming fascinated with every curve and hollow.

His mouth was as soft as thistledown, his touch as tender as a wish. Her mind relaxed, then began to float; muscles strengthened by a lifetime on horseback grew lax as he coaxed her deeper and deeper into the swirling mists.

The room filled with the shimmer of starlight, with soft sighs and, impossibly, music. Kate heard the strum of harp strings, sweet as summer, sad as tears.

Time slowed as he seemed willing to caress her endlessly, as if her pleasure were the most important thing—the only thing—that mattered in the world to him. The T-shirt she'd worn to bed, the one that had wonderfully smelled like him, somehow drifted away, as if by magic. The moon floated across the black velvet sky. And still he lingered, lazily taking his time, apparently determined to touch and taste every inch of warming flesh.

How could any man be so strong, yet so gentle? So passionate, yet so impossibly patient? The mists thickened; her mind and body grew heavy, as if he were wrapping her in warm honey.

The bedroom filled with a pearly predawn light. Her eyelids grew heavy, as if weighed down by faerie dust; her body melted, flowing through his seductive hands like hot candle wax. Kate surrendered to him openly. Willingly. Blissfully.

He touched a soft kiss to each of those closed lids, encouraging her to open her eyes, which, though it took an effort, she did. His smile was as slow as his hands, his eyes warm with those same emotions that were swelling inside her, making her feel as if she'd swallowed the sun.

Steeped in him, Kate sighed as their lips met. They watched each other as he silkily slid into her. Filling her. Completing her. It was, they both thought, like coming home. It was magic.

It was the dream that jolted Zoe out of a sound sleep. She'd been riding Legends Lake, just the two of them galloping across rolling green fields, past the castle and the lake where the Lady supposedly dwelt in her underwater kingdom, down to the beach. As she rubbed her eyes with her fists, she imagined she could hear the pounding of the horse's hooves and feel the icy spray of the sea water in her face.

She got out of bed and went to the window, where the world was lit in the soft lavender and silver glow of approaching dawn. Legends Lake was grazing in the pasture, but as Zoe pressed her forehead against the cool glass, he lifted his head and looked up toward the house, as if sensing her presence.

Kate had proven true to her word. Ever since the race on the beach, she'd been letting Zoe work with the horse, walking it after his morning workouts, currying it; yesterday she'd even let Zoe saddle him for his breezing. Alec had worried about that, but Kate had assured him everything would be fine. Which it was.

The one thing Zoe had been secretly wanting to do, but hadn't dared ask, suspecting that Alec's answer would be a flat "no," was ride Legends Lake.

As if he'd heard her thoughts, the colt tossed his head. *Come on*, he seemed to be saying. *The world's still asleep, there's only you and I up and about and sure, it's a grand morning for a run.*

Zoe didn't hesitate. She threw on the Santa Anita sweatshirt she'd filched from Alec for working in the barn, tugged a pair of jeans over her hips and a heavy pair of striped wool socks onto her feet, then crept downstairs, avoiding the stair she'd discovered squeaked. The boots Kate had loaned her were by the kitchen door. She pulled them on, grabbed a handful of sugar cubes from the bowl in the center of the table, then, holding her breath, left the kitchen and went out into the soft day.

As she practically tiptoed toward the pasture, Legends Lake came trotting toward her; they met at the white fence.

"Hi." He pushed his nose against the front of her sweatshirt, searching for the treat she always brought him. "You big baby." She held out the sugar cube, which his large yellow teeth nipped with amazing delicacy from her open palm. She stroked his long face. "How would you like to go for a run?"

She'd said the magic words. His ears lifted. He tossed his lush mane and whinnied what Zoe took for an answer.

"Shhh." She touched her fingertips to his velvety nose. "It's got to be our secret."

He nodded slowly, soberly, as if he understood her perfectly. Then stood as still as a stone as she climbed up on the fence, and half climbed, half threw herself, onto his back.

Unfortunately, she overestimated the force needed and slid back down the other side, landing in an ungraceful heap on the wet grass.

He snorted, but remained still so as not to step on her.

"You don't have to laugh," she muttered, pushing herself to her feet. She glanced around and was relieved to see that the house—and Alec's windows over the barn—were still dark, which meant that no one had witnessed her fall. She considered going into the barn to get the saddle and tack, but worried that by then Kate, who seemed to get up with the sun, would be awake.

"It's been a long time since I've ridden a horse and I'm not going to be as good as Kate. But you're just going to have to adapt."

Zoe climbed up on the fence again. "Now hold still." She grabbed hold of the silky mane and held on tight, this time managing to stay put. "Good boy."

She'd forgotten how tall a horse could be. It was a little scary up here. Remembering how Alec had soothed her fears the first time he'd put her on the back of that mare he'd bought her so many years ago, she leaned down and patted Legends Lake's neck. Then fisted her hands in his mane and took a deep breath.

"Okay, let's go for it."

And go for it, they did. Zoe bent low and pressed her knees against the racehorse's sides, the way Alec had taught her. The sea breeze ruffled Legends Lake's mane and her short hair and as they ran together—horse and girl—in the misty dawn, over emerald fields, Zoe felt as free as the birds that were beginning to sing their morning songs. The air from the colt's wide nostrils looked like puffs of smoke.

"Dragon smoke," Zoe decided fancifully. And for the first time in a very long while, she laughed.

Kate woke early. Partly because it was her custom, and partly because some deep-seated maternal instinct responded to her desire to keep the children from knowing where she'd spent the night. In truth, she didn't want to leave the warmth of this bed and the glorious comfort of Alec's arms. But responsibility called.

They were curled up together like two spoons in her cutlery drawer. She'd known people slept this way, but had never experienced the pleasure herself. In a way, it was like when he'd filled her last night, making them seem like two individual parts of a perfect whole.

Sighing with regret, she lifted his arm, which was lying heavily, but not uncomfortably so, across her breasts. He muttered a complaint, then, without waking, rolled over onto his back. Kate slipped from the bed and found the clothes he'd brought her lying on the chair. She lifted a brow and smiled when she realized he'd left the bra back in her underwear drawer.

She was about to pull on her sweater, when she saw the green T-shirt hanging on the top edge of a framed photograph Michael had taken of Jamie and Brigid beside the lake. That was strange. She vaguely remembered Alec taking the shirt off her, remembered how it had seemed to dissolve, as if by magic. Considering how far he'd flung it, Kate now realized how much control he must have utilized in order to keep his touch and his kisses so blissfully soft and unthreatening. Unlike Cadel, who'd never given a thought to her comfort or pleasure.

Even Andrew Sinclair, Jamie's father, who'd introduced her to passion, had been more interested in satisfying his own needs than pleasuring her. When the dashing American horse trainer had passed through

Castlelough on his way to the Irish Derby at the Curragh in County Kildare, she'd been only a bit older than poor confused Zoe.

Looking back on it now, Kate could not fault the naive country girl she'd been for being thrilled that such a man had chosen her, out of all the girls in Ireland, to warm his bed. The moment she'd sensed him staring at her across the Irish Rose, she'd felt as if her heart had sprouted wings and flown straightaway out of her breast. Sure that only love could make her feel so deliciously warm and damp in those private places that were never discussed in polite company, Kate had not hesitated to go on a summer's eve drive with him. And when he parked at the edge of the cliff and kissed her until she was breathless and so thrillingly, achingly needy, she hadn't given two thoughts to accompanying him back to his room at the inn.

Kate had come to realize that while the American had introduced her to the mechanics of sex, he'd taught her nothing about love. He'd never written, as he'd promised. Never dropped by the stud when he was in the country, which, given his occupation, she'd assumed he must be from time to time. For years, whenever she'd attend one of the larger, internationally known horse fairs, she'd surreptitiously keep on the lookout for him, fantasizing that he'd sweep her into his arms, declare himself thrilled to be a father, and rescue her from the war zone of her marriage.

The years passed; memories faded. As Kate accepted the idea that she'd been little more than a pleasant diversion for the man, and learned to sleep in the cold and often harsh bed she'd foolishly made, there was not a single day that she wasn't grateful for the son born of that stolen night.

She plucked the T-shirt from the frame and, on impulse, pulled it over her head, covering it with her sweater. It would be her little secret, she decided. A private way of keeping Alec close by her all day long.

Kate was in the kitchen, frying up a rasher of bacon and eggs for the children when he walked in. His eyes were heavy-lidded from lack of sleep, there was a sexy stubble of dark beard on his face, but the sparkle of moisture in his hair revealed that while he hadn't shaved, he had showered.

Kate could see him, hot water sluicing down his hard male body, looking outrageously sexy in the clouds of steam. She saw the curtain pull back, and there was herself with not a stitch on, her skin all rosy with desire and expectation. There was a buzzing somewhere in the room, like a trapped wasp trying to escape, but drawn by the seductive power of the man, Kate ignored it.

He smiled a welcome. Pulled her into his arms, lifted her up, braced her against the tile wall and entered her with one strong, deep thrust.

"Ma?" The buzzing proved to be Jamie talking to her.

Kate blinked, clearing the vision. "What is it?" Her voice was a bit sharper than she'd meant it to be.

"The bacon." He nodded toward the iron skillet. "It's burning."

"It's well done," she corrected, waving away a bit of smoke as she took the pan off the burner. "It's healthier that way."

"I like black bacon," Brigid assured her with a huge sweet smile. "It's crunchy, like the outside of black marshmallows."

"Yuck," Jamie said.

"That's the best kind," Zoe entered into the argument. "When you stick them right into the flames and they're all crunchy on the outside and soft and gooey on the inside."

"Aye." Brigid enthusiastically nodded her bright head. "Gooey is the very best part."

"You're both daft," Jamie decided with a shake of his head. "Shall we have marshmallows at my birthday party?" he asked his mother.

"I don't see why not," Kate agreed as she placed the plate of bacon in the middle of the table. "I'll put them on my list."

"Good." He nodded, pleased. "I like marshmallows. When they're cooked the right way," he tacked on as he bit into a piece of charred bacon.

Kate smiled at that, glanced over at Alec and noticed that he was smiling as well. "Sit down and I'll pour you a cup of coffee." She'd begun making it when he'd finally admitted he preferred it to tea but hadn't wanted to make extra work for her.

"Thanks." He snatched a piece of bacon, crunched it and said, "Delicious." But the way he was looking at her, the same way he had the last time they'd made love this morning, assured Kate he was not referring to the burned pork product.

Brigid got down from her chair and without waiting for an invitation, went around the table and crawled up into Alec's lap. "Jamie's having a birthday."

"So I just heard."

"Will you be coming?"

"I suppose that depends on if I'll still be here in Ireland."

"You will," Kate said quickly. Too quickly, she thought as she felt some embarrassed color rise in her face. Could she have sounded any more desperate?

"It's two days before the Castlelough May Day fair," Jamie offered, hope blazing in his eyes.

"Well, then, you can count on me."

"Will you bring a present?" Brigid asked. "Everyone has to."

"Bri!" Jamie turned beet red. "That's not polite. Mr. MacKenna doesn't have to buy me a present."

"I want to," Alec assured him. "In fact, Zoe, maybe as the time gets closer, you and I can go shopping together in town."

"Sure."

"Great. We'll make a day of it. Maybe have lunch at the pub."

That settled, the conversation returned to last night's events, Nora Barnacle's new foal. Kate was surprised by how easily it flowed, and how, after all those hours tangling the sheets with the MacKenna, she felt no discomfort or embarrassment. Indeed, having him here, in the heart of the house with her and their children, felt absolutely right, making her worry about what the Fates might have in store for her, to exact payment for so much happiness.

24

—

"So," Nora Gallagher said as she put her infant daughter down for a nap, "how are you getting along with your Yank these days?"

"He's not my . . ." Kate's voice drifted off. She sighed even as she smiled down at the black-haired baby who was gazing up at her with those solemn blue eyes. "Do you remember when I asked you the same question about Quinn?"

"Of course. We were having tea at O'Neill's Chicken and Chips. I assured you that there was nothing at all going on between us, that he was only my boarder."

"Which was a lie."

"More of a sin of omission."

Kate laughed softly as she bent down to kiss the satiny pink cheek and inhaled the scent of warm milk and baby powder.

They closed the door to the nursery that Nora had decorated for a princess and went downstairs to the bright, cheery farm kitchen. Since marrying Quinn Gallagher, Kate's sister-in-law was undoubtedly one of the wealthiest women in all Ireland. But money hadn't changed her. Other than Quinn's office, where he wrote his internationally best-selling horror novels, the wonderful media room, and the nursery, the rest of the house Nora had grown up in hadn't changed. It was still every bit as warm and inviting as its owner.

"Alec isn't really my Yank," she said as she bit into an oatmeal biscuit still warm from the oven.

"But you'd like him to be." Nora poured tea into cups and placed them on the table. The older children were at school and Brigid was upstairs in the media room, happily watching *The Little Mermaid* for the umpteenth time.

"Liking something, or wishing it were so, doesn't make it true."

She took a sip. It was perfect. Like everything Nora did. If they hadn't been best friends forever, if Nora wasn't godmother to her children, Kate might, at times, become a bit envious.

"There's no way anything could come of it," she told her sister-in-law what she'd been telling herself for days.

"Isn't that what I said?"

"You were a widow and free to fall in love. I'm married."

"For the time being only," Nora reminded her. "I also remember how, that day, you didn't believe you could leave Cadel. You said you owed him loyalty for having married you when you were carrying Jamie."

"And didn't I pay that debt, a thousand times over?"

Nora patted her hand. "The important thing is that you're out of a terrible situation. And you're moving on with your life."

"Aye."

"May I ask you one thing?"

"Aren't you my best friend? There's nothing we can't say to one another."

"Do you love him? Your Yank?"

"I tried not to. But I believe I just might." Kate

sighed and bit into another biscuit. "How can you not love a man who makes you fly?"

"Fly?" There was a click of china as Nora lowered the cup that had been on the way to her lips back to the saucer. "Kate Fitzpatrick," she said, refusing, as she'd done since the separation, to use Kate's married name, "are you saying that you and Alec MacKenna have made love?"

"It was probably sex on his part." Kate was no longer the wide-eyed virgin who believed that every romance came with a happily-ever-after ending. "But whatever it was, it was wonderful." Her lips twitched. "Every time."

"Every time? And you didn't tell me?"

"It was only last night. What would you have had me do? Pick up the phone in the office and ring you up right away and say, "I'll be over at three for tea and biscuits, and by the way, I just discovered that multiple orgasms are no myth?"

"Oh, they're grand, indeed," Nora agreed on a merry laugh. "And I can understand you not ringing me from bed, but you've been here for over an hour and we've only talked about your new foal, Legends Lake, and Jamie's party."

"I wanted to tell you as soon as I walked in the door. To tell the truth, I wanted to stand on the rooftop this morning and shout it out to everyone in the county. But Brigid was with me, and while I believe children should be taught far more about sex than in our day, I felt that four years of age was a wee bit young to be learning that her mother can come by a man biting the back of her knee."

"No!" Nora's hand went to her breast. She leaned forward, her eyes wide and fascinated. "Can you, really?"

"I can. And did. Several times." Kate had never felt

so smug. "Alec believes I'm particularly sensitive there from all the years of riding horses."

"Well, that does it," Nora decided. "I'm definitely going to be spending more time on that mare Quinn bought from you."

They laughed, enjoying the jest, enjoying each other.

"Kate?"

Nora's eyes were moist.

"Is something wrong?" It was not like her friend to weep. Indeed, despite having overcome the tragedy of being widowed, Nora was the most optimistic person Kate had ever known.

"No." Nora shook her auburn head, sniffed, and offered Kate a watery smile. "It's just that I'm so happy for you."

Kate felt her own eyes mist as she smiled back. "I'm happy for me, too."

Kate had always been easily able to compartmentalize. Wasn't it the only way she'd survived her marriage, after all? In her work she was required to live in not only the present, but the past and future, as well. How else to determine what stallion and dam to bring together, melding the best of them both in hopes of creating the next Red Rum or Arkle, whose bones were on display at the National Stud.

In her personal life, she'd learned to live not only day by day, but often minute by minute. Cadel had never been an easy man, but there were those weeks, and even months, when the worst she could say about him was that he had an unfortunate fondness for the bottle, an aversion to work and a sour disposition he appeared to have been born with, which he'd managed to conceal from her that day he'd suggested rescuing her from the plight of unmarried motherhood.

But his moods could turn on a dime, which was why she'd spent the years until his leaving tiptoeing on eggshells. She'd never looked toward the future because having to face the prospect of spending the rest of her days with such a man would have ground her natural optimism down to dust.

She couldn't have imagined that such behavior could prove useful in love, but it did. It allowed her not to look forward to when the time would come—which it must—for Alec to leave Ireland and return home with Legends Lake.

Her days were spent with her usual work, along with breezing Legends Lake, who was becoming less whip nervous with each session. Despite what she secretly admitted was a less than stunning outer package, he definitely had championship potential.

The hours between sunrise and sunset were also spent with family. Zoe had blossomed, like a Burren wildflower that had finally gotten water to its roots, showing more and more promise of the lovely young woman she would soon become. Her way with Legends Lake also had proven Kate right about her being a born horsewoman. It was clear to everyone that she and the Thoroughbred had bonded.

Kate felt a prickling of concern about the way Brigid and Jamie were becoming so close to Alec, but they both so obviously adored him, it would have taken a harder woman than she to deny them such pleasure.

Pleasure. Her nights shimmered with it. Glowed. It was true, she'd told Nora and Erin on their monthly girls' lunch at O'Neill's Chicken and Chips, what they said about the entire world being brighter when you were in love. Surely the sun was warmer this year? The yellow of the primrose starring the hedges brighter? The birdsong sweeter?

They'd laughed at her, with affection, but Kate hadn't cared that she was in danger of becoming a walking cliché. She was going to grab this glorious stolen time with both hands, revel in it, and if it turned out to be all the Fates were willing to grant her, she'd celebrate it, and gladly, then have memories to keep her warm for all the rest of her life.

Ireland had, over the centuries, resisted the mechanical dominance of clock and calendar, yet in the end there was no escaping the tyranny of time. It was the day before Jamie's birthday; in only a matter of days, it would be Beltane, when the village May Day festival would take place, after which Alec would be returning to America with his daughter and Legends Lake. While Kate didn't have any fears about the horse performing as he was born to do, the idea of spending her life reliving happy memories was not nearly so appealing as spending that life with the man she loved.

25

On THE DAY BEFORE HIS BIRTHDAY, Jamie was in the barn currying his mare when a remarkable thought occurred to him.

He wasn't afraid.

The mare wasn't all that tall—only fourteen hands—but she still towered so high over him that he was forced to carry a three-legged stool around to climb up onto her back. There had been a time when even being in the same stall with one of his ma's horses would have started his knees to trembling, made his heart pound like an Orangeman's drum, and his lungs feel all tight.

Jamie had once been afraid of everything . . . the horses, the big boys on the bus that took him from the stud to Holy Child School in the village, the Brennans' border collies that nipped at his heels whenever he'd pedal his bicycle over to his best friend Rory's house, which he did most days, rain or shine.

But that had been when his da still lived in the house. His big strong da who was more often than not drunk, always angry at the world and everyone in it. Cadel O'Sullivan would return home late from the village, larger than life, like Goliath in the story Sister Immaculata told in morning Bible studies class.

BANG! The front door would slam shut, followed by the sound of his big boots clomping a warning on the bare wood of the stairs. Whenever Jamie dared to crack open his bedroom door and see his da swigging from a bottle of whiskey, he'd run back to bed, pull the covers over his head, close his eyes, and try to pretend that he didn't hear the next *BANG!*—another slamming of the door to his parents' bedroom, the terrible names his da would call his ma, who would try to hush him, reminding him of their sleeping children. His da's answer to her tearful plea would be the unmistakable smacking sound of a hand against flesh.

After Brigid was born, the moment the first door slammed, his little sister would crawl from her trundle bed and hunker beneath the covers with him, where Jamie would hold her tight and try, as best a big brother could, to protect her from the demon fears while the terrible shouting and the bad words, that the nuns would have washed his da's mouth out with soap for saying, got louder.

His ma had always tried her best to pretend that things were fine. Even on those days when she'd come downstairs to make breakfast with new bruises blooming like ugly blue roses on her face and her eyes redrimmed and swollen, she'd quietly, but firmly, insist that some conversations were not for children. That when Jamie was a grown man, he'd discover that marriage was not an easy sacrament to keep, day by day, year after year. Then she'd hasten to assure him that he needn't worry. Because she'd never—ever—allow his da to lay a hand on him.

When he'd been younger, Jamie had accepted her words at face value. She was, after all, his ma, and everyone knew that a mother would never lie to her children. Even after he finally realized that she was being less than truthful to him, that her words were born more of hope than fact, Jamie never brought up the subject of what he'd hear in the lonely, frightening darkness of the night. Just saying the terrible words out loud would have made them too true.

But then one afternoon, which would become the day Jamie began believing in miracles, his father was magically gone, his cruel, threatening dark presence blown away as if by a fresh Atlantic Ocean breeze.

Perhaps, his best friend Rory had suggested, the faeries had come and spirited him away. Or more likely, Jamie had overheard Mrs. Sheehan, the butcher's gossipy wife, say to Mrs. Murphy, the devil had come and collected Cadel O'Sullivan to sharpen pitchforks in hell.

Jamie hadn't exactly known what had happened to cause such a miraculous event. All he knew was that one day he'd gone into the village with his aunt Nora for ice cream and when he'd returned, his ma had been in his aunt's bed, instead of home in the barn, tending to the horses as she should have been.

He heard rumors of Quinn Gallagher beating his da to a bloody pulp down at the Irish Rose, but none of the grown-ups were talking, except to tell him that his da had gone to live with family in Dungarven and to assure him that he wouldn't be back and Jamie needn't ever worry about him again.

There were times when Jamie considered that if he'd only been a spy back then, he could have discovered what had happened to his da. But most of the time, he didn't want to think about the man who'd terrorized his family, and he certainly didn't want to fill the pages of his notebook with writings about him, either.

At first, after his da had left the house—and Castlelough—Jamie had lain awake nights, fearful that the slam of the door and the shouting and the fighting would start in again. But miracle of miracles, his da stayed gone and his ma began to smile and laugh and tell him stories about when she'd been a little girl growing up on the farm, learning the secrets of the horses from her own dear da, who apparently had been a kind and warmhearted, gentle man who'd never lift a hand to an animal. Or, though she'd never said it, Jamie guessed, against any other person.

Jamie hadn't inherited his mother's magical gift with horses. But at least, he thought, as he carried the stool around the front of the mare and climbed up on it to begin combing out her mane, he wasn't afraid of them anymore.

And then it happened.

He felt it first. An all too familiar prickling at the back of his neck, followed by a skim of ice up his spine. The barn was suddenly cast into deep shadow. Tightening his fingers on the curry comb, Jamie glanced nervously over his shoulder and viewed the huge hulking shape that took up the entire doorway of the barn, effectively blocking out the lowering daylight.

"Where the fuck is your mother?" The giant's all too familiar roar had Jamie quaking in his boots.

"I d-d-don't know." Jamie continued currying the mare, hoping his da wouldn't notice how badly his hands had begun to shake. He wondered if he'd somehow conjured up his father by thinking about him.

"You wouldn't be lying to me now, would you, boyo?" His da took a swig of the clear *poitín*, then tossed the empty whiskey jar onto the barn floor. The horse, sensing danger, grew skittish; her ears flattened against her head, and she danced a bit in place as if preparing to bolt at a moment's notice.

Jamie knew exactly how the mare felt.

His da began slowly, threateningly, unfastening his leather belt. "I'll be asking you again, where is that whore who thought she could be kicking me out of me own house?"

"It's not your h-h-house. Ma inherited it from G-g-grandda Joe."

Jamie hated the way he'd begun to stutter again, something he hadn't done since his da went away. He also knew his trembling voice gave away his fear. His da was a bully and like all of his kind, could smell weakness like a shark sensed blood in the water. "And she isn't a w-w-whore."

He wasn't certain what, exactly, a whore was, except that Jesus forgave them and just yesterday he'd heard Mrs. Sheehan telling Mrs. Kelly that Kathleen O'Shaunnessy, who'd recently separated from her husband, and who, according to Mrs. Sheehan, dyed her hair too blond, wore her skirts too short and too tight, and went home from the Irish Rose pub with a different man every night, was a whore.

Jamie's mother might be separated from his da, but she'd never dyed her hair, and as for other men, the only ones who ever set foot in the house were his uncles and Father O'Malley, who'd drop by on occasion for a cup of tea and a chat. And Alec. Jamie desperately wished his ma's Yank was here now.

"There are things you don't know about your precious sainted mother," Cadel O'Sullivan said on a silky slur more dangerous than the loudest shout. Ireland might not have any snakes, but if it did and if one could talk, Jamie figured it'd sound a lot like his da right now. "You'll be finding out the hard truth yourself one of these days, but I'm not here to be wasting time having a fucking conversation with the likes of you."

"Why *are* you here?" Jamie dared ask as he judged the distance to the door of the barn, trying to determine whether or not he could outrun his tormentor.

"I had a run of bad luck at the racetrack and I need money to pay off me debts. So, lad, you've got yourself three seconds to tell me where your ma would be, or you won't be able to sit down for a month."

Watching the leather belt slowly slip free of the loops of his father's tweed trousers caused icy fingers to squeeze Jamie's heart, which only moments earlier had felt so carefree. Looking at his father's beet-red face and viewing the dark murder blazing in his narrowed eyes, Jamie had never been more frightened. Not even the moonless night he and Rory had been camping out on a school trek and he'd momentarily mistaken the moan of the wind for a banshee.

But then he remembered bruises darkening his mother's pale skin and the way she'd kept her face to the wall that day his father had disappeared from Castlelough, as if *she'd* been the one who'd done something to be ashamed of, and Jamie knew that he'd die before telling this bully that she'd gone to his aunt's where he supposed they'd be planning his birthday celebration.

"I told you," he lied unconvincingly, "I d-d-don't know."

For such a large man, and drunk to the gills as he appeared to be, Cadel moved with surprising speed. Before Jamie had gotten the last word out, he was yanked off the stool by his collar and flung across the stall into a pile of straw.

"I warned you, ye little bastard," his da roared,

sounding just like Hawthorn, evil chief of giants from the old Celtic myth Brother John had read the class only yesterday. He towered over Jamie, beefy arm raised.

Jamie put his arm over his face to shield it as the belt whipped through the air.

Crack! It missed its target and hit the door of the stall. Crack! This time it whistled past his ear before curling around a wooden post.

"Tell me, you fucking little spawn of a slut!" As the belt slashed through the air once again, Jamie finally began to react and rolled over, out of harm's way. The buckle instead grazed the foreleg of the mare, who whinnied a loud protest and backed into a far corner of the stall.

"Tell me where she'd be off to, or I'll be killing you!" From the evil expression darkening his eyes, Jamie feared it was no idle threat.

"Go to the d-d-divil," he shot back, determined that it would be better to die fighting for principle than die a coward.

After all, he thought, as he rolled out of the way of the slashing belt once again, weren't the nuns always talking about how beloved the martyrs were in God's eyes? Being whipped to death by your father might not be on the same level as being stoned by Pharisees, but surely it must gain some points in heaven?

"Cadel O'Sullivan!" His ma's voice suddenly rang out as clear and strong as church bells proclaiming the Angelus. "If you threaten my son one more time, I swear on St. Peter's holy ring, that it will be the last thing you ever do."

Jamie's da slowly turned. His furry caterpillar-like brows plunged down toward his crooked nose, which had been broken more than once in pub fights.

"Since when did the likes of a pagan witch such as yourself believe in the Pope? Or his fucking ring?" he sneered. "And would ye be threatening your own husband?"

"I'd be warning you that if you lay a hand on my child, you'll be a dead man."

His ma's blue eyes were as icy as sleet in February, her voice steel. If he weren't so terrified, Jamie would have cheered. Even the much revered Irish pirate queen Maeve, who stood up to the first Queen Elizabeth, could not have been braver.

"Talk's cheap enough. We both know that you wouldn't dare fight me. Aren't I your husband, after all? Your lawfully wedded husband, despite your pitiful attempts to make it otherwise," he stressed with supreme confidence.

"We're legally separated."

"The Church doesn't recognize it," he reminded her.

"Our marriage is a state affair, having nothing to do with your Church."

"And isn't it that same state who might be interested in knowing that you're giving a bad moral example to the boy"—he jerked his head in Jamie's direction—"by having some oversexed Yank staying beneath your roof."

"He's not staying beneath my roof, but in the room above the barn."

"Why don't you be telling that to the divorce court?" he suggested evilly. She was used to him roaring curses at her. But the way his voice turned soft, nearly a whisper, proved more deadly than the loudest shout. "Perhaps I'll be asking it to take the boy away from his slut mother and return him to his da, where he belongs."

The threat was like a sledgehammer slamming into her chest. She couldn't breathe. Could barely stand.

No, Kate vowed. There was no way she was going to allow this man to control her or her son any longer. Besides, if pushed to the wall, she could prove Cadel was not Jamie's father.

"Over my dead body."

"And can't that be arranged?" Again with surprising speed, Cadel grasped a handful of Kate's long black hair.

"Jamie, run!"

Terrified, Jamie watched as she clawed at her brutal husband's ruddy face with her short fingernails, witnessed his father backhanding her, once, twice, then a third time, slamming her head back and forth like the sock doll Jamie's great-grandmother Fionna had made Brigid for Christmas. Blood began to flow from her nose in terrifying rivulets.

Jamie's blood was rumbling in his ears like the roar of the surf during a December storm as he crawled up onto his knees, then managed, on legs as wobbly as a foal's, to stand. His feet wanted to flee like the wind, to race away, over the fields and never stop, until he'd reached some faraway place his da could never find him. At least to the cave on the beach where he'd hidden other times when his father had gotten drunk and mean. But those very same feet seemed to be nailed to the barn floor. He could only stand there, frozen.

"Save yourself, Jamie!" His mother jammed a knee into his da's crotch, causing him to howl in rage. "Run away from here," she cried as the next slap sounded like the crack of gunfire. "Now!"

Cadel dodged another of her wild kicks, then tore her blouse, exposing the lacy bra Jamie had only ever seen hanging on the clothesline.

Jamie had been raised on a stud. He knew about sex; not only had he seen the results of his mother's breeding, he'd also witnessed stallions covering mares. But as he watched those brutal, hairy-backed hands rip apart that lovely blouse adorned with Celtic animals his mother had embroidered herself, he knew that she was in danger of something far worse.

Screaming like an ancient warrior king, he launched himself onto the evil giant's back, hitting and kicking for all he was worth. When he managed to bite down on his da's ear, hard enough to draw a bit of blood of his own, Cadel roared. Reaching behind him, he flung Jamie all the way across the stall where he landed beneath the mare. As she reared up on her hind legs, Jamie feared that if his father didn't kill him, the horse's hooves surely would.

But his distraction worked. His mother scrambled to her feet, grabbed the nearest weapon—which happened to be the scoop shovel she'd used just this morning for the grain—and swung it with all her might. The shovel was not one of the modern aluminum ones sold in feed stores, but a heavy metal shovel with a thick oak handle that had been made by her great-grandfather Fitzpatrick.

Thwack! It hit her husband against the chest, which only seemed to make him angrier. She swung again, this time connecting with the side of his head with a sickly *thump* that sounded like a melon being dropped from the top of the barn.

Appearing shocked by the way the tables had turned, Cadel crumbled to his knees. His dark eyes slowly rolled back in his head. Then he toppled to the floor.

"Ma?" Jamie cautiously crawled out from under the terrified mare, who was violently shaking her head, but had stopped kicking at her stall door. "Did you kill him?"

"Oh, darling!" Kate scooped him into her arms and

held him so tight, he thought she might squeeze the air out of his lungs. "Are you all right?"

"I'm f-f-fine," he gasped. It was more lie than truth, but he wanted to reassure her. Together they stared down at the blood that was soaking into the yellow straw from the split in his da's head. "Jaysus, do you think he's dead?"

"I don't know." Trembling, she touched her lips to the top of his head and hugged him tighter. "But I suppose I'd best check." She knelt in the straw that was quickly turning the color of rust and pressed her fingers against the monster's throat. "I feel a pulse. So he's alive."

Jamie couldn't decide whether to be happy or sad about that. He certainly didn't want his ma to be imprisoned for murder. But to never have to worry about his da again . . .

"Jamie." Amazingly, his mother's voice had regained its usual calm tone. "I want you to go into the house and ring up the surgery. Tell Dr. Erin what's happened here. Ask her to come as quickly as possible and to bring her medical bag."

As if unable to bear touching her husband any longer than necessary, she rocked back on her heels. "And you'd best be ringing up Sergeant O'Neill, as well."

"Jaysus, Ma!" Bringing the Guards into this was, in Jamie's mind, a foolish thing to do. If Sergeant O'Neill came, wouldn't he have to arrest her?

"Don't be using the Lord's name in vain," she said absently, which even through his shock and distress, struck Jamie as a strange thing for his mother, who openly followed the ancient religion, to say. "Now please, darling, do as I ask. Then stay in the house. I put your sister down for her nap when we came back from your aunt's. She shouldn't be alone."

Jamie desperately wished Alec was here. His ma

would listen to the Yank. But he'd taken Zoe into town. As he'd watched the car disappear down the road, Jamie had been pleased they'd be about buying him a gift. Such foolish childish things no longer seemed important.

"But Ma—"

"It'll be all right, Jamie," she repeated what she'd told him so many other times over the years. "I promise."

Jamie didn't want to leave. But he also knew his ma would be in even more trouble if his da bled to death while he stayed here arguing. So he gave her a quick, hard hug, wishing he was grown up enough to take care of her as she'd always taken care of him, then raced toward the house to make the telephone calls.

If he'd looked back, he would have seen Kate exchange the shovel for a pitchfork. She stood over her unconscious husband, the sharpened tines pressed against his broad chest. Just in case.

26

~

CADEL HAD REGAINED CONSCIOUSNESS enough to begin cursing a blue streak by the time he'd been put on the ambulance stretcher and taken away to the hospital in Galway. Although her nerves still felt as numb as the stones in the nearby ancient circle, Kate nearly wept with relief when Sergeant O'Neill assured her that since she'd been acting in self-defense, and in the defense of her young son, he wouldn't think of pressing charges against her.

"Now Cadel," he said with a meaningful glance toward the ambulance pulling onto the road from the driveway, "is another matter altogether. He'll be charged with assault, which should be keeping him away from you and your children. For a time, at least."

He didn't sound all that convinced that her husband wouldn't be back. In truth, neither was Kate. But having been granted a reprieve, she decided to be grateful for small favors.

Shortly after arriving and ensuring that her patient would live, Erin O'Halloran Joyce had rung up Nora, who'd come straightaway from her farm to ensure that Kate was truly all right.

"Why don't you take a nice shower to wash off the barn dirt and calm your nerves," Nora suggested as she took in the smears of drying blood. Kate silently blessed her for refraining from mentioning the scarlet handprints she knew from past experience would be staining her face. "Then take Jamie for a relaxing stroll on the beach."

"Brigid might wake up from her nap."

"I believe I can take care of one wee little girl," Nora said dryly. "Having practically raised my younger brother and sisters as well as my own children."

Grateful for the opportunity to talk with Jamie without interruption, to assure him that such horror would never be repeated, Kate quickly showered and changed her clothes—tossing the blouse away so she'd never have to look at it again in this lifetime. Soon she and her still shaken son were walking together, hand in hand, on the beach.

The tide was coming in, rolling onto the sand in long breakers that would retreat, leaving a sparkling silver trail of shattered shells and sea foam in their wake, only to return, even stronger. As she had, Kate mused.

Despite today's setback, her little family had grown secure in the past years since that awful day of the rape, when Nora's Yank had tracked Cadel down at the Irish Rose, beat him to a bloody pulp, then convinced Cadel that it would be a great deal safer for him to move away from Castlelough.

There had once been a time when Jamie couldn't dare look any adult man in the eye; now today, he'd had the strength to attack the very same man who was infamous for bullying everyone who had the misfortune to cross paths with him.

"I was proud of you today," she said as they walked side by side, barefoot through the rising water. "What you did was wonderfully brave. Though," the mother in her felt obliged to point out, "extremely reckless. And dangerous."

"He was hurting you," Jamie responded simply. "Since I'm the man of the family now, it's my duty to take care of you."

"Oh, darling." Her heart turning over so that it felt like a three cornered stone in her chest, she knelt on the beach, mindless of the sea foam dampening the spirit-lifting long scarlet skirt she'd changed into.

Holding him by his slender shoulders, she looked her young son straight in the eye. "You're a fine, brave lad. But a lad nonetheless. It's my responsibility to take care of you."

He thought about that for a moment as a trio of breakers washed over them, nearly up to his knees, dampening the legs of his jeans. "Perhaps we can take care of each other," he decided, seeking compromise.

"We'll argue about the matter later," she decided, not wanting to get sidetracked. She stood, inhaled the healing tang of the sea and took his hand in hers again. "For now, let's go sit up higher on the rocks before we get washed out to sea and end up in America."

"That might not be so bad," he said as they scrambled over boulders draped with moss and wet green kelp to higher ground. "I've always wanted to go to America. Rory said it's a grand place."

"So I've heard."

She and Jamie found a perch midway up the cliff, out of the wind. "As brave as you were, I'm sorry Cadel behaved so horridly." Despite having taken out his frustrations on her for years, today's terrifying incident was the first time her husband had actually physically threatened one of her children.

"I hate him." The hand she wasn't holding curled

into a small tight fist. His voice, which Father O'Malley assured her was the finest in the Holy Child School's boys' choir, was low and tight and strained with resentment.

"I know." She uncurled the small tense fingers, one by one. "And I suppose your feelings are perfectly natural, given the fact that Cadel is not the easiest man to get along with—"

"He's a bully."

Kate couldn't argue with that. The sad truth was that in her desperation to protect her family from the shame of her unwed pregnancy, she had married an ill-tempered bully whose naturally cruel temperament was made even worse by his affection—nay, his overwhelming need—for whiskey.

"But hating anyone is a waste of energy, darling. It hurts you more than it does the person you're directing all that emotion toward."

"I don't understand why you don't just cast a spell on him and turn him into a snake."

"Now, you know very well that I wouldn't be doing that kind of magic."

She had, admittedly, secretly, been tempted to try over the years. But ever aware of the natural law that whatever you did to another returned many times magnified, Kate had avoided giving in to temptation where her brutal husband was concerned.

"Besides, there aren't any snakes in Ireland. I'd certainly not want to be the one responsible for changing that."

She'd hoped to coax a bit of a smile out of him. Instead, his scowl only darkened. "But if he *were* a snake, we could cut off his head, so that would be the end of him *and* the snake."

His child's attention momentarily drifted. "Do you

believe St. Patrick really drove all the snakes in Ireland into the sea the way Sister Mary Immaculata says?"

"Well now, that's one popular story."

Grateful for a momentary change in subject, Kate leaned back on her elbows and watched a pair of seabirds building a nest high on the cliff. She'd have to remember to bring the children back here when the eggs hatched.

"There is, however, an even older one. Going back to the Ancients."

"The one about the River Barrow." It was certainly not the first time Jamie had heard the tale, yet interest lit up the small face that was so gloomy only moments earlier. Kate decided her son was as eager for a respite from thoughts of Cadel O'Sullivan as she was. "Will you tell it to me?"

"I suppose we have a wee bit more time before we need to be getting back." She knew that Nora would stay as long as she was needed. "Some say that there never were snakes in Ireland," she began.

"Because they didn't make it across the land bridge before the water turned Ireland into an island," Jamie offered with a nod.

"That's what I learned in Brother Sebastian's science class when I was a bit older than you are now. The nuns, being of a more traditional and fundamentalist mindset, preferred to tell the legend of Patrick, as they seem to still be doing.

"Yet many of the old timers believe that Diancecht, the ancient god of medicine, is the true reason we'd be having no serpents in this fair land."

"Because of Morígú."

He'd heard the story at least a hundred times and never seemed to tire of it. Kate suspected he could tell it as well as she. In another age, when there was only one true way, she might have encouraged him onto the druid path in hopes he might become a bard, one of the keepers of the Celts' oral history. Since he was a lad born into modern times, she tried to ensure that he had knowledge of both Catholicism and the old ways so he'd be free to choose his own path.

"Aye," she said, returning her mind to her tale. "The way I heard it from me own grandmother Fitzpatrick, who first told me the story when I was a girl, was that the fierce wife of the heaven-god had borne a son whom Diancecht recognized as being cursed from birth. He counseled that the wee infant's heart should be opened on the spot."

"So he did. Even though he had to kill the baby."

"And wasn't that the saddest part of the business, even though he knew that the babe's innocent spirit would go to the Otherworld and be reborn."

Kate sighed, thinking, as she always did when this tale came up, how tragic it would be for any mother, even one as fierce as the wife of the heaven-god was alleged to be, to lose a child.

"Still, I imagine it grieved him to declare such a sentence on a child who'd yet to have his naming ceremony. But his diagnosis proved true, because within that wee heart, he found three infant serpents which Diancecht, with his godly wisdom, understood were malevolent spirits who would be capable of eating every single person in Ireland if allowed to grow to full size."

Jamie's confrontation with his father was momentarily forgotten as he considered that unsavory possibility. "If I were Diancecht," he declared, with the youthful self-confidence that had first begun to bud after Cadel had left their home, "I'd quick take my sacred knife and cut off their heads."

"Well, now, I believe he did just that. But then, to

avoid the evil which even their beheaded, dead bodies might do to our people, he burned them into ashes, then flung those ashes into the nearest river."

"Because the ashes might carry their spirits and be evilly charmed."

"Aye, that was his reasoning. And, once again wasn't he proven right when indeed, the ashes were so venomous the water boiled up and destroyed every living creature in it? Which is why, ever since that day, the river has been known as the River Barrow."

"Because barrow means boiling."

"Aye." She smiled and ruffled his windblown hair. "Your Irish is improving day by day."

"I know. Brother John says that I have the best pronunciation in the class. But that's because I have you to practice with. A lot of the parents don't speak the old language."

Or practice the old religion, he did not say. There had been a time when Kate had worried that by being so open in her druidic practices, she might cause her son difficulty in such a small parochial community as Castlelough. However, the secret truth was, that even many of those who showed up every Sunday morning to hear Father O'Malley say the Roman Mass, secretly clung to more than a few of the old beliefs. Tradition, as even Cromwell himself had discovered, did not die easily out here in the Irish west.

"If you made a spell and turned my da into a snake," Jamie suggested, returning the conversation to its original track, "we could do like Diancecht and cut off his head, then throw him in the river."

"But we're not gods. And wouldn't that be murder? Since we'd be killing a man and not a snake?" she asked gently.

He sighed, surrendering the suggestion. "I'd mostly

forgotten about him after he went away." He fell silent as they both watched a seabird dive into the waves and come back out with a sparkling silver fish in its beak. "There's something that's been worrying my mind."

She put her arm around his small slumped shoulder. "And what would that be?"

"I'm afraid that I'll grow up to be like him."

"Of course you won't." Kate was quite honestly shocked that her son might have been troubled by such thoughts.

"He's my da. Maybe getting drunk and mean is in my blood. Aren't you always talking about bloodlines?"

"For horses," she said quickly. "It's different with people."

"Are you sure?" The small, earnest freckled face that looked up at her was filled with a desperate hope that nearly broke Kate's heart.

"Positive." She deliberately did not mention Biddy Early's genetic contribution to the family bloodline, which had made such an inescapable difference in her own life. She dampened her fingers with her tongue and smoothed down the unruly cowlick at the front of his head that was a replica of his father's.

Kate realized that this was the perfect time to tell Jamie the truth about his parentage, but the words she'd been practicing for so many years in her head would not come to her tongue. *Coward.*

"You're a fine lad, a wonderful son, and Brigid couldn't be asking for a better big brother. You've no need to ever worry about behaving like your . . . that man."

Jamie's jaw tightened. He turned away and stared out over the sea, which was beginning to be gilded with copper and gold. As she did each day, Kate took a moment to sing a brief, silent farewell to the setting sun.

"Ma?"

"Yes, darling?"

"He wouldn't be doing it, would he? Taking me away from you, that is?"

"Of course not. You know how your father says things he doesn't mean when he's been drinking."

His relief was palpable. "Good." He turned back toward her. "I don't want to talk about him anymore."

"Then we won't," she agreed. "We'd best be getting back to the house. It's time for me to start supper and your sister will be waking from her nap."

As they walked back along the cliff, near the circle of stones that had once belonged to the Ancients, Kate wished she could only have foreseen today's events and prevented her son from being traumatized.

When Cadel had first left, her flashbacks had been nearly constant. Indeed, there'd been occasions when she'd not been quite sure what was real and what was memory. But until Alec MacKenna's arrival, she'd gone months without a single instance. And even on these recent occasions with him, she'd managed to keep a hold on reality. She was proud of her progress, but a new fear that she may have caused the same problem in her child was chilling.

"I love you, Jamie lad." Swept by an immense wave of emotion, even stronger than the tides below them, she pulled him into her arms, and hugged him tight, daring to risk the Fates by wishing she could keep him forever safe from harm.

"I love you, too, Ma," he said when she'd finally loosened her grip enough that he could breathe. "You're the best ma in Castlelough. In County Clare. Even the entire world."

She laughed as he flung his thin arms out in a broad gesture meant to encompass that world. Then sent a small silent prayer to those ancient, hopefully benevolent gods who dwelt in the Otherworld that Jamie would still believe that when he discovered she'd been lying to him his entire life.

"Do you think he'll like the book?" Zoe asked as she and Alex drove back from the village.

"Sure. *James and the Giant Peach* is a classic. You sure got a kick out of it when you were his age."

"Yeah." She smiled at the memory. "I remember liking it because of how it began."

"You liked the idea of parents getting trampled by a runaway rhinoceros?"

"Not because of that. But most of the stories written for kids are really sappy. When the writer started out that way, then had James have to go live with terrible Aunt Sponge and Aunt Spider and become the saddest and loneliest boy you could find, I figured he wasn't going to talk down to me. And that he'd tell a really good story."

"You figured right." Alec smiled over at her. Zoe smiled back. It was, he thought, one of those rare Kodak moments he'd have to freeze in his memory to enjoy again later. "Mrs. Monohan says Jamie's got all the Harry Potter books, so it stands to reason he'd like this one, too."

"Yeah. He's going to freak when he sees what else we bought."

"You think so?"

"Are you kidding? There's not a kid in the world who wouldn't want to eavesdrop on grown-ups."

"Yeah." He hadn't thought of that until the friendly shopkeeper had already wrapped the Spy Kit in the colorful dinosaur paper. "That's what worries me."

Zoe shrugged. Not sullenly, but uncaringly. Which

was, Alec thought, a huge difference. "Jamie's a good kid. He won't get in any trouble. Besides, Mrs. Monohan said he'd been looking at it every time he's come into the shop for weeks."

"That's another thing that bothers me. If Kate had wanted him to have it, why didn't she buy it for him?"

Another shrug. "She already bought him the night vision spy goggles. Maybe she figured that was enough. With all his relatives, he's probably going to get a huge haul anyway."

"That's possible." Alec decided that just in case, he was going to ask Kate about the gift before taking it to the party.

"Thank you for the sweater set."

"It looks great on you." The hot pink color clashed a bit with her hair, but since the color seemed to be fading, Alec hoped it would eventually wash out.

"Better than my other clothes?"

It was his turn to shrug. "At your age you should be allowed to wear whatever you want. Within reason."

Zoe put her feet, clad in zebra striped, platform soled sneakers up on the dashboard. Alec figured he'd made real progress when he was no longer bothered by the blue and red butterfly tattoo on her ankle.

"Jamie really likes you a lot."

"I like him."

"I think he misses having a dad."

"I suppose there are times when he does," Alec said mildly.

"I'll bet, when he blows out his birthday candles tomorrow, he wishes that you could be his dad."

Alec didn't quite know how to answer that one.

"I know Kate's married," she said, while he was still fumbling around for a safe response. "But if she wasn't, do you think you'd marry her?"

"Hypothetical questions are hard to answer," he hedged.

"Okay. Try this one. Do you love her?"

He shot her a dry look. "How old are you, anyway?"

"Older than my years," she shot back. "Leaving a kid to fend mostly for herself tends to make her grow up fast."

"Yeah, I suppose it does." Alec certainly had.

"So?"

"So how about it's not really any of your business." Her eyes narrowed. "You do, don't you?"

"Zoe, I love you. Lots. I think you're beautiful, inside and out, and sharp as a tack. But I think this is where I point out that you're a bit nosy."

"Don't you think it'd be cool if Kate was part of our family?"

Alec's irritation was soothed by the fact that she actually considered the two of them a family. "That's not as easy as it sounds."

"I know she's not going to be able to be divorced for a long time. But couldn't she if she moved to America?"

Alec wasn't about to admit the idea had flashed through his mind on more than one occasion. "I don't know the law, sweetheart."

"Even if you couldn't get married right away, you could live together. Everyone does these days."

"Kate isn't everyone. And Castlelough might be a little more conservative than what we're used to."

"So, she could move to Kentucky," she said again.

"No." He'd thought about this, as well. "Her roots are here, Zoe. It's where her family is. It's where she belongs."

"If I loved a man, I'd want to be with him."

The conversation was definitely getting too sticky.

"And a lucky man he'll be to have won your heart," he said.

"I still think you could work it out," she muttered. She reached behind her into the backseat, retrieved the kelly green-and-white striped shopping bag and began digging through it. "I know there's a box of candy in here somewhere . . . Hey, I didn't buy this."

He didn't have to glance over to know what she was talking about. "I did."

"*You* bought nail polish?"

"It's not mine. It happens to be for Kate."

"Kate doesn't even wear nail polish. Why would she ask you to pick up a bottle of Scandalous Scarlet high gloss?"

Alec thought about lying, then realized he'd un-doubtedly get caught as soon as they got back to the stud and Zoe opened her big teenage mouth. "It was just an impulse, okay? I noticed she's started wearing clear polish lately, so I just thought . . . perhaps . . . Hell, it seemed like a good idea at the time." He wasn't about to mention his hot dream the morning after the foal had been born in which her nails had been exactly the color of the red in the bottle he'd just bought.

"Wow," Zoe breathed.

"Wow what?"

"You really do love her, don't you?"

His fingers tightened on the steering wheel as he shot her a look. "Where did you come up with an idea like that?"

"You bought her nail polish."

And was beginning to regret it. "So?"

"When a man buys a woman something that per-sonal, it's a sure sign he's in love," she said blithely, with all the wisdom of her fifteen years.

"It's not all that personal." He'd bought the stuff in

the pharmacy department, for Chrisssakes, where it was across the aisle from the cold remedies and arthritis rubs. How personal could that be?

"Don't worry, Pop." She shot him a saucy look that reminded him that this woman-child was growing up at warp speed. "I won't say a thing." As if to emphasize the promise, she crossed her fingers—tipped in lemon yellow today—over her heart.

He lifted a brow. "Did you just call me Pop?"

She shrugged and popped a Cadbury chocolate into her mouth. "Daddy's for little kids."

"Well, since you're so mature these days, you should realize that adults can have relationships that don't necessarily involve love."

"Sure. Sex. But that's not what you've got going with Kate."

He knew he was going to regret not just cutting this ridiculous conversation off right now, but had to ask. "How would you know that?"

"Because she's not that kind of woman. She may be getting a divorce, but anyone can tell she's definitely into forever-afters."

Despite having had no personal experience with long-term marital relationships in her own life, somehow, Zoe had managed to hit it dead on. He reached over and snagged a piece of chocolate from the cardboard box. "How did you get so wise?"

"I'm a woman. We're born knowing these things."

He was wise enough not to laugh at that lofty pronouncement. As they continued home in companionable silence, Alec allowed himself a little fantasy of painting Kate's toes Scandalous Scarlet.

27

Nora Gallagher came out the kitchen door as soon as Alec pulled into the driveway. Her expression was as sober as it had been the day she'd come over to fetch the kids after Kate had collapsed.

The premonition squeezed his gut like an icy fist. He was out of the car in a flash. "What's wrong? Where's Kate?"

"She's down at the beach with Jamie."

"Then she's all right?"

"Yes. Now." She briefly closed her eyes and shook her head.

"Dammit, what do you mean, *now*? What the hell's happened?"

"I'm sorry." There were seeds of worry in her moss green eyes as she looked up at him. "Cadel was here."

"Her husband? Here?" He looked around as if expecting to see the guy who'd caused Kate so much pain standing behind him.

"He's gone now. Sergeant O'Neill came and arrested him, but they've taken him to hospital . . . Damn." She shook her head again. "I'm telling this badly."

Alec felt the same way he had watching Legends

Lake galloping toward Kate. His blood froze. But this time a white hot rage flashed beneath the ice. He rubbed the heel of his hand against his rib cage, reminding the air to keep going in and out.

"Why don't you just start at the beginning." He suddenly remembered they weren't alone. "Zoe, go into the house."

"I want to hear what happened, too." Her face settled into frustratingly familiar stubborn lines. "You're not the only one who loves her, you know."

Nora was looking at him hard and deep. Alec might have been uncomfortable at being so thoroughly analyzed were he not so concerned for Kate. "You were saying?" Knowing this woman was not only Kate's sister-in-law, but dearest friend, he managed to keep his tone civil when what he wanted to do was to grab her arms and shake the words from her.

"Apparently Cadel came here while Kate and Brigid were at my house, doing some last minute planning for Jamie's party," Nora began again.

Alec managed—with effort—not to interrupt her halting recital of events, so far as she knew them, but when she got to the part about Cadel attacking Kate, temper streaked through him.

"That's all I know," she finished up apologetically.

"So he didn't—" He shot a careful glance toward Zoe, who'd gone pale as glass.

"I know the word," she said, with a touch of teenage disdain he was actually grateful to hear. "He didn't rape her, did he?" she asked Nora.

"No, thank God. And, I believe, Jamie had a great deal to do with that. It seems he attacked Cadel, just before . . . well, in time."

"Christ." Alec scraped both hands down his face. As bad as the things he'd survived when he'd been

Jamie O'Sullivan's age, none of them came close to being forced to rescue your mother from being raped by your father. "Where is he now?"

"Jamie? I told you, he's—"

"No. O'Sullivan." He'd kill him, Alec decided. Slowly. Deliberately. So the bastard would know the same terror she must have felt. Not just this afternoon, but for all the years she'd been trapped in a marriage made in hell.

Nora looked at him carefully, reminding him of the way he used to study his father, trying to judge the level of violence simmering beneath the surface. But it wasn't the same, Alec assured himself.

"They took him to hospital. In Galway."

"Which one?" His voice was low and uneven.

"I wouldn't be knowing that." There was a tremor in her voice that told him he was frightening her. Which, dammit, was the last thing he wanted to do.

"That's okay," he said with a mildness that cost him. "It's not important."

Castlelough was a small village. The kind of place where gossip was the coin of the realm. He'd go to the pub, buy a few rounds of pints to get folks talking and find out for himself where they'd taken Cadel O'Sullivan. Then he'd go there. And make certain the bastard never bothered Kate or her children again.

At the moment, however, Alec was torn between going down to the beach or trying to remain sane while waiting for Kate here, allowing her to deal with her son in her own way, when he saw the relief flood into Nora's expressive eyes and turned to see the pair approaching the house.

Even from here he could see the bruises on her face. They were already turning as dark as his thoughts. He felt a light pressure on his arm, glanced down and saw Nora's hand resting on his sleeve.

"I can handle it," he said between his teeth. "My way."

"And isn't that what worries me," she murmured back. "I've been through this, Mr. MacKenna. With my own husband, who, if he were here, would tell you that he understands your feelings. But I *can* tell you that the last thing that Kate would want would be for you to destroy your life for the likes of Cadel O'Sullivan."

"I'll try to keep that in mind." Neither was looking at the other. Both their attention—and Zoe's—was directed on mother and son.

"I dearly hope you will."

Alec wanted to run to her. To pull her into his arms and hold her tight and assure her that he'd never let anything happen to her again. But uncertain what the kid's reaction would be to see another man's hands on his mother so soon after what had to have been a nightmare, he forced himself to stay where he was.

"Hey," he greeted them as if it were only another day. As if Kate wasn't looking as if she'd just gone ten rounds with Mike Tyson.

She managed a faint smile but her eyes were still shadowed. Jamie looked a bit better than his mother. Shaken, but Alec decided the anger lingering in his eyes was only natural. It was also something he could identify with.

"Hello," she said, her voice subdued. She wouldn't look at him. Not straight on, anyway.

"You're back," Jamie said.

"With gifts for tomorrow's gala celebration."

"Thank you." His voice was as flat as his mother's eyes.

"Jamie," Nora said with forced cheer. "I'm so glad

you're home. Brigid has been after me to make my famous chocolate chip biscuits, but she told me that we couldn't begin until you got back because your job is to grease the pans. And lick the spoon."

"There's nothing better than chocolate chip cookie dough," Zoe said with feigned brightness, earning Alec's lifetime gratitude.

He scuffed the toe of his sneaker in the pea gravel of the driveway. "Ma doesn't like us to have snacks so close to supper."

"Oh, I'm sure we could be making an exception in this case. Since it is, after all, your glorious birthday eve," Nora assured him. "Couldn't we, Kate?"

"Aye." Her voice was choked. Almost as if it were still being cut off by those dark purple fingerprints framing either side of her throat.

Jamie didn't immediately respond. Just kept pushing that gravel around without looking at any of them.

"I never told you about my trip to the lake," Zoe coaxed into the heavy silence. "I think I may have caught a glimpse of the Lady."

He didn't respond. But he did lift his gaze at that.

"I'm not sure. But I did see a sort of green shimmer."

"Really?"

"Yeah. I can tell you all about it while the cookies are baking."

He considered that for a moment. "Okay." They were on the step when he turned to Kate. "Ma? Are you coming?"

"If you don't mind, Jamie, I'd like to talk to your mom for just a bit. About Legends Lake," Alec lied.

He'd half expected Jamie to protest, but when the small freckled face cleared, Alec realized that he'd not been wanting his mother to stay with him for his sake, but for hers. Obviously he still felt a responsibility to protect her.

"Okay," he repeated.

Alec caught Zoe's arm just before she went in the door. "Thanks."

"Hey, I like chocolate chip cookies."

Despite the seriousness of the situation, he grinned at that because he was so damn proud of her. "I owe you one. Big time."

"I'll remind you of that when I bring you the permission slip to get my nose pierced." He knew his knee-jerk horror about that showed on his face when she flashed a quick grin of her own. "Chill, Pop. I was just kidding." With that she went into the kitchen, closing the door behind her, leaving Alec and Kate alone.

Because it was difficult to speak with his emotions tangled like a ball of poisonous snakes, Alec merely held out his arms.

Without hesitation, Kate walked into them, welcoming the way he held her tight, her cheek on his shoulder, his against her hair. She felt some of the tension ease out of her as her body adjusted to his. Not as it had those times they'd made love, but in a different way. Oddly, a more intimate way.

Sex, as marvelous as it had been, was easily had. Hadn't more than one eligible man—and a few married ones—in the village let her know that they were more than willing to help her out in that department since her separation. She'd turned them all down, of course, having believed more honesty occurred in the breeding barn than ever in bed. Alec had changed her mind about that. As he had changed so many other things. It felt good to be able to lean on him, to rely on someone other than herself for a change.

"How are you?" he murmured against her hair. "Really?"

"Better now." Now that she was with him, surrounded by his strong arms.

"Want to talk about it?"

"Aye." She sighed and closed her eyes and held on a little tighter, as if borrowing a bit of his courage.

She'd never been one to talk about Cadel. Not even to Nora, who'd certainly tried to breach the stone wall of family secrecy enough times over the years. But she'd learned from therapy that bottling things up inside her could be more harmful than the things she was trying to ignore. Besides, while Kate wasn't exactly certain what was happening between herself and the MacKenna, she did know that to not tell him about the reasons behind her marriage would be to hide some important part of herself from him, the last secret that explained so much of the woman she once was. And, more important, the woman she'd worked so hard to become.

Neither of them spoke as they returned, hand in hand, to the beach. There was no need. Kate couldn't remember the last time she'd been so comfortable sharing silence with a man.

They sat on the same rock she'd been sitting on the lovely day she'd watched her daughter dance and her son fly his kite. The day she'd danced with Alec. The day he'd kissed her and stolen not only her breath, but her reawakened heart.

The breeze, tinged with salt and seaweed, ruffled her hair and cleared her mind. The surf washed onto the sand, then retreated, leaving behind scattered shells and sparkling sea foam. Other than a fishing boat chugging along on the horizon, they could have been the only two people in the world.

He went to put his arm around her shoulder, then paused.

"Don't," she said quietly.

"Don't touch you?"

"Don't *not*. I like you to touch me."

He blew out a breath. "Well," he said, as he drew her a little closer. "I guess I'll just have to do a lot more of it." He brushed some wind tangled hair from her face. "I like it when you touch me, too."

"I enjoy it as well. Touching you."

They shared a smile. "It's getting warmer."

"Aye." She could smell the sweet scent of spring wildflowers about to be born.

Kate sighed, wishing she had the power to freeze the sun, which was lowering in the sky for just a while, so she could enjoy this stolen time with Alec. But the sea continued to roll in on long breakers; if she didn't get this over with soon, they could be stranded here when the tide rose too high.

"You're going to think I'm a terrible person." She'd come to accept her reasons for doing what she'd done, but still feared that others—Alec most of all—might not understand.

He laced his fingers with hers. Lifted them to his lips. "I want to do this your way, Kate. In your time. But there's one thing you have to know right off the bat."

"What's that?"

"There is nothing you could tell me that could ever make me believe you were anything but warm and loving and wonderful."

His eyes were dark. Stormy. Unnerving. But when his intense gaze also caused the now familiar little quickening inside her, Kate felt a flood of relief that Cadel hadn't managed to ruin this for her. Even after what had happened today, she could still want a man. No, she corrected. Still want *this* man.

"I'm flat-out crazy about you, Kate."

Surprise had her lifting a hand to her throat. When she felt the tenderness where she knew there'd be bruises, she reminded herself that she'd brought Alec here to get the truth behind them. Not that she knew where they were going, where they *could* go, so long as Cadel was still legally in her life.

"I'm rather crazy about you, as well," she said, deciding that had to be the champion Irish understatement of all time. "I might as well say it straight out." She took a deep breath. Blew it out. "I didn't love my husband when I married him."

"I get the feeling no one could."

"He wasn't that bad before we were wed. Truly," she insisted at Alec's openly skeptical expression. "Oh, he wasn't one to be quoting poetry or bringing me posies or fancy chocolates. But he never raised his voice to me. Nor struck me."

"Now there's a reason to marry a man."

"It was enough at the time. In truth, it was I who came to the marriage with baggage which *he* had to overcome." She closed her eyes briefly, gathering strength. "I was pregnant with another man's child."

"Jamie."

"Aye."

"Did you love this other guy?"

"Didn't I think so the night I gave him my virginity?" *Foolish, foolish girl,* she thought now, with a mingling of affection and sadness for that starry-eyed romantic. "I think I was mostly bedazzled. He was one of you Yanks. Handsome, dashing, rich. At least more so than anyone in these parts. I was flattered when he took me to his bed the night before the Derby.

"He was a trainer," she said before he could ask. "Not as famous as you, because he was just getting started. But everyone said he showed great promise." A promise he must not have lived up to, since she'd never heard his name come up in racing circles since that stolen time they'd spent together.

"What was his name?" Alec winced. "No. Forget I asked. That's none of my business."

"I wouldn't mind telling you. His name was Sinclair. Andrew Sinclair."

She saw the recognition in his eyes. "Please tell me he wouldn't be a friend."

"I only met him once and our paths haven't crossed in years. I figured he got out of the business."

"Oh." Kate actually found that idea a bit of a relief. After she'd stopped hoping to run into Andrew at some county horse fair, she'd begun to dread the possibility that she might.

"The next morning he asked me to go to America with him. But I didn't believe he meant it, and even if he had, it was a bad time for me, with my da having just been diagnosed with cancer, and him needing me to take over the work at the stud."

"It must have been tough."

"The decision was not difficult at all. The illness was harder. And took longer than the doctors predicted."

She sighed. How many times over the years had she replayed that pivotal morning in her mind, wondering what would have happened if she'd followed her heart? Which would have meant, of course, turning her back on her family. Something she could never have done.

"Andrew promised me he'd ring me from his travels. And come back for me at the end of the racing season." By then she'd been a bride. A bride who was already discovering she'd jumped out of the frying pan into hell.

"I never heard from him again. But I'm certainly not the first girl to make such a mistake and I doubt if I'll be the last."

"I'm afraid not," Alec said, thinking of Zoe and the predatory Jake. He skimmed a hand down her hair, which was damp with sea mist. "It was his loss."

"Aye," she said, thinking of the son he'd missed out on knowing. "I didn't know Cadel all that well," she continued her story. "His family was from Dungarven. His father was a fisherman who, I later learned, spent nearly as much time in gaol for drunkenness and assault as he did out at sea in his boat. I met him—Cadel, not his father—when he took a job at the feed and began delivering hay to the stud. We'd talked from time to time, enough for me to know that he was ambitious, which is no sin."

"Not in most cases," Alec allowed obligingly.

"I was frantic when I realized I was pregnant. My da was in treatment in Galway and my mother was worrying herself to death over him when she wasn't at church saying her rosary and making novenas, trying to bargain with God for a miracle. The last thing they needed was to have their only daughter disgrace them with a bastard."

"Jamie's no bastard."

She smiled, just a bit, at that. "No. Of course he's not. But even today, tongues wag when a girl gets herself into such a situation. I didn't want to put my family through such gossip. I didn't want to put my *child* through it. And, while it may sound selfish, I didn't want to have to face such hurtful talk myself.

"It was bad enough, when I was young and cared what people thought about me, to have been born with The Sight. I could well imagine the truly hateful stories people could invent about who actually fathered the child of the witch of Castlelough."

"You'd probably get some *Rosemary's Baby* plotlines."

"Didn't I think that myself? Even now, with people knowing both Cadel and myself, there are those in the village who whisper that he left me because of my practice of sex magic. Which is, of course, ridiculously false."

"Oh, I don't know." He smiled at that and kissed her again. "You certainly bewitched me, sugar. Anytime you want to practice some more, just let me know."

That earned a light, surprised laugh. Then she immediately sobered again, drawn back to the grim story. "I lied and told my parents that I was going to Dublin to look at a mare I was thinking of buying, but in truth I went there to talk with an order of nuns who took in pregnant unmarried girls. The babies were sent to Irish American families in the States, which served both parties' needs. But the logistics were impossible, since I couldn't live at the convent and run the stud. Besides, even knowing I was being selfish, I couldn't imagine giving my child away."

"You couldn't be selfish if your life depended on it. Are you saying you actually asked a hay-truck driver you barely knew to marry you?" Christ, surely there'd been some other single guy in town who would have found marriage to Kate no hardship.

"No. Cadel was the one who asked me. When he discovered me throwing up in a bucket behind the barn. He's the eldest of eleven children. He recognized right away that I was pregnant."

"So he offered to solve your little problem." And marry his way into a tidy income and respectability.

"Aye. I was grateful for the offer. For a time."

"Until he started hitting you."

"Aye."

"When?"

She bit her lip. Moved her shoulders. Looked out toward the sea where the boat had now disappeared over the horizon. "The first time was on our wedding night."

"Your wedding night? Christ, Kate—" He held up a hand. "Okay. Sorry. I promised I'd let you tell this your way and not make judgments."

"He'd had too many pints at the reception, and it vexed him that he wasn't getting a virgin bride."

"Which he already knew," Alec pointed out. "Besides, that old adage about men wanting virgins is a myth."

"Would you be saying you wouldn't have wanted me, if I'd never been with another man?"

"I told you, sugar, I'd want *you* any way. Any time."

Kate believed him. A warm little flame flickered inside her, burning away the chill that had taken hold of her when she'd come home and found her child in peril.

Although it wasn't easy, Kate forged on. "Later, I began to excuse his behavior by accepting the idea that my having slept with another man—had a child by him—was damaging to his self-esteem."

"You don't still think that?"

"No."

"Good." He touched his lips to her temple. "Nora said something," he said carefully. "About Gallagher somehow getting involved."

"Oh, wasn't that a terrible day." Her breath feathered out as she remembered the cruel fists. The harsh, painful invasion into her dry-as-dust body. "But freeing in its own way. It was before Nora and Quinn were married, but it was obvious to everyone that they were very much in love.

"I don't want to be telling tales, but Quinn had grown up without any family, and I believe Nora's horde was a bit difficult for him to absorb at first, but of course it wasn't long before he'd fallen in love with each and every one of them. He'd embraced her family as his own, which was why, when he showed up at my door and discovered Cadel had raped me, he took it upon himself to get revenge."

Alec's eyes iced with a cold and deadly fury. "He should have killed him."

"From what I've heard, if Brendan O'Neill and the others at the pub hadn't pulled him away, he might well have."

"Too bad." Alec made a mental note to thank Gallagher.

"No." She shook her head. "Cadel would not have been worth Quinn going to prison. Besides, I would have felt terribly guilty."

"You?" He stared at her. Of all the things she'd said, this was the most astounding. "How the hell do you figure that?"

"It was not the first time such a thing had happened. Indeed, that's how my darling Brigid came to be born. By allowing it to continue all those years, I put Quinn in that situation, don't you see?"

"Now we're back to every deed stirring the universe."

"Aye." Her eyes were dry and clear and firm in this belief.

"Why wasn't he thrown in jail?"

"You have to understand, this isn't America. A man isn't as likely to be charged with the rape of his wife, even if she were willing to air her shame before the entire village."

"It's O'Sullivan who should be ashamed. Not you."

"Well, don't I realize that now? But even so, it was a family matter and I preferred to keep it that way."

"Christ." He plowed his hand through his hair. "I hate that you had to go through any of that."

"Don't we all have trials to overcome in this life?" She managed a faint smile that amazingly, after all she'd been through today, was obviously meant to reassure him.

"The other night? When you held my hands above my head . . . You were right. It wasn't you I was upset with. I was remembering. It doesn't happen that often. At least not anymore. My therapist in Galway, a lovely woman who reminds me of my mother and always serves tea and scones after our sessions, assured me that I'd eventually overcome the flashbacks."

"Are you talking about post-traumatic stress?"

"Aye. And after today I'm going to be arranging a session for Jamie. Just in case."

"That's probably not a bad idea."

He'd had the nightmares and flashbacks himself for years, finally burning them out of his brain by working so hard and so long he was too tired to dream, and staying focused on racing so no other thoughts could filter through.

"Does Jamie know O'Sullivan's not his father?"

"Not yet. Cadel never confirmed what gossip there was, because he didn't want people thinking he was less than a man, marrying used goods, as I was."

"Please tell me you at least realize that's garbage."

"Aye."

"Good."

"I keep wanting to tell Jamie, but it's difficult. I was also concerned that he'd get angry someday and throw the truth up at Cadel, which could be a dangerous thing for him."

"Yeah. I can see how it would be. But did it ever occur to you that it's more difficult for the kid to believe that brutal bastard is his father?"

"Not until today. When he told me that he was afraid he might grow up to be like Cadel. Because of having his father's blood."

"That's not an uncommon notion. I used to worry about it myself. But no longer. My father was born with a great many gifts. It was his choice to become a drunk and throw them all away."

"Still, it must have been hard for you."

He shrugged. "I survived. And so will Jamie. In fact, he's a lot luckier, because he has you." He smiled down at her. His eyes darkened in that way she'd come to recognize. "You are so astonishingly lovely." He touched his lips to the darkening bruise at her temple. "Just looking at you takes my breath away." The scrape on her cheek. "And makes me believe in magic."

I love him. The words, which she could not quite dare admit, even to herself, shimmered in Kate's mind with all the brilliance of a rainbow after a storm. In that stunning moment of realization, she would have shared that wondrous thought with him, and gladly, if his sweet, silken kiss hadn't left her speechless.

It seemed the MacKenna would kiss her endlessly. His lips were patient as they skimmed up her bruised face, kissed her eyes shut, lingered on her with a reverence that nearly made her weep. Mists and dreams clouded her head as he told her, with soft murmurs, how beautiful she was, how special, how exquisite. Showed her, with heartbreakingly delicate touches that he was nothing like the man who'd so terrorized her. In his own miraculous way, Alec was as much a healer as any of the Ancients who'd first settled this wild, tempestuous land. A healer of hearts. Of souls.

Lost in him, unable to discern whether the soft sighs that drifted in the air were his or hers, Kate sank bonelessly into the kiss, her mind swimming, her body seeming to float on gentle wavelets of pleasure.

The world fell away. Time ceased to have meaning. There was no past, no future. Only this glorious, delicious present where her entire universe swirled inward, growing smaller and smaller until it became centered on this one man.

"More," she whispered against the mouth that was drawing helpless sounds from deep in her throat.

He tilted his head, changed the angle, soothed the broken skin of her bottom lip with his tongue. "More," he agreed. His voice was husky, but not at all rough, wrapping around her like warm and soothing velvet.

It was like a dream. No. Something better than a dream. A wish she'd never dared whisper. It was magic, and she was marveling in the pleasure of being spellbound when a towering splash of icy surf poured over the rock.

Alec cursed. Kate gasped. He looked down at her; she looked up at him and they laughed. Hand in hand, they scrambled back over the rocks before the incoming tide cut them off from the steps cut into the cliff.

When they reached the top, Alec took hold of her shoulders and skimmed a thorough, masculine look over her. "You look damn good wet, Kate."

It was her turn to treat him to the same slow perusal. "As do you," she replied, biting back the groan as her gaze focused on the obvious sign of arousal straining against wet denim.

He looked down. Shook his head. "See what you do to me?"

"It would be a bit difficult to miss."

"Well, there's only one answer for it."

"And that would be?"

"You're going to have to make love with me." He flashed that wicked, wonderful smile Kate knew would still have the power to thrill her when she was a hundred. "All night long."

She traced his smile with a fingertip. "Aye."

28

THE NEXT DAY DAWNED BRIGHT and clear and sunny and a great deal warmer than it had been during Alec's time in Ireland.

He sat on the same rock where only yesterday he'd been tempted to make love to Kate, watching her dance barefoot near the edge of the sea, surrounded by a circle of adoring children. Her toenails, which he'd surprised her and pleased himself by painting, flashed like rubies on the glittering sand.

Whatever doubts he'd had about her alleged supernormal powers—and he still couldn't quite shake them all—there was admittedly something different about her. Some forces swirling beneath the surface that touched everyone around her.

"She's something, isn't she?" The words were underscored with a hint of humor.

"All that implies and more," Alec answered Nora's novelist husband, who'd joined him. He took the bottle of stout Quinn Gallagher was holding out to him. "A lot more."

"Kate's important to me." Quinn took a long pull from his own bottle as he watched her strike a pose for

Jamie, who'd been clicking away all morning with the spy camera Michael had bought him for his birthday. "When I first arrived here, it was like I'd landed on the moon. The laws of physics had been suspended, gravity repealed. From the moment I met Nora, I didn't know up from down."

His gaze shifted to his wife, who appeared to be pointing out a flock of noisy seabirds to their baby daughter. Love and a barely restrained passion surrounded the novelist like an energy field. Alec realized that he'd been sensing more things like that since coming to Ireland. It was as if there was something in the air that lifted the veil between conscious and subconscious and allowed him to better read emotions. Or, he considered, perhaps the magic was that the land intensified feelings, making them more visible.

"Our Kate provided a calm haven in the midst of all the storms," Quinn was saying when Alec returned his mind to the conversation.

"Calm is not exactly the word I'd use to describe the effect she has on me."

"I know the feeling. Only too well." He waved at his wife who smiled and waved the baby's hand toward him. "Want a word of advice from a veteran of the Castlelough romance wars?"

"I'm always open to advice."

"You can run," Quinn advised, masculine sympathy in his deeply set eyes. "But you cannot hide."

Alec laughed. "I figured that out for myself by the second day."

They fell silent for a time, watching the dancing. The brilliant sunlight of high noon allowed Alec to view Kate's long firm legs through the gauzy blue and green skirt she was wearing today; the memory of the way she'd screamed his name when he'd made her come by biting the back of her knee was enough to make him hard again. Which, after how many times they'd made love last night, was amazing.

"I care about Kate. A great deal." Quinn's tone was mild, yet there was no mistaking the warning that flashed in his nearly black gaze. "We all do."

"I'm not her bastard of a husband. I won't hurt her."

"If I thought you'd lay so much as a hand on her, I would have dragged you out into the surf and drowned you by now."

Alec sensed it was no jest. Quinn Gallagher had earned his millions writing horror stories; with his newly discovered intuition, Alec had the feeling that not all the man's monsters were fictional. "What worries me, and the rest of Kate's family, is another matter. The woman you know now is not the woman she was three years ago. Nora tells me that until O'Sullivan ground away at her like that tide turns a boulder to sand, Kate used to be the happiest, most fun-loving, confident girl in Castlelough. It hasn't been easy, but she's managed to recover that girl, along with the strength of a woman who knows her own mind and desires. Which is why, if she wants you, and it appears she does, we're all happy for her. So long as—"

"I don't screw it up."

"That's more blunt than Nora asked me to phrase it, but yeah."

"She's special," Alec said, weighing his words.

"I believe we've already determined that. And I hate like hell to sound like her father, but as I said, I care about her and since her brother and father are dead, the womenfolk have named me her designated protector. So," he drew in a breath, "you got any intentions?"

"Yeah."

"I don't suppose you'd care to elaborate a bit on

that? Not for me, you understand. But Nora and Erin"—he tilted the neck of the bottle toward the reed slender physician with the short curls and gamine grin who'd offered Alec continual reassurance while Kate had been in her coma, or whatever it was—"are going to be cross-examining the hell out of me and it'll be a whole lot easier for both of us in the long run if I can give them some answers."

"I've got intentions," Alec repeated, more firmly this time. "I just haven't figured out what the hell they are."

Quinn snorted. "Boy, have I been there." He shook his head with chagrined humor. "Don't worry. I'll tell them something that should put them off for a while. Until you can get things sorted out."

"Thanks."

"No problem. Women are fabulous creatures. And they smell damn good, too. But in times like this, we guys have to stick together."

They talked a bit longer, during which time Alec told Quinn that he'd enjoyed his novel about the ghost horses, and Quinn, in turn, surprised Alec by admitting that much of the characterization of the trainer who'd been haunted by the horses from the other world, had been taken from articles he'd clipped about Alec over the years.

"That's quite a coincidence," Alec said. "Not so much that we'd admire each other's work, but that we'd both end up here, from entirely different parts of the States, on an Irish beach, with two women who've been best friends all their lives."

Quinn tossed back his beer. "Like Kate always says, you can't escape your destiny."

Alec knew that at the end of his life, when he looked back over the months and years, this day would stand out as one of the highlights. The perfect weather, the bountiful food, the haul the beaming birthday boy was obviously tickled with, the companionship, all contributed to a pleasure he'd not known in a long time. But even that enjoyment was dampened whenever he'd look at the angry bruises no makeup could begin to hide on Kate's exquisite face, and feel a stir of barely restrained rage.

After Jamie had blown out his candles and the cake and ice cream had been served, Alec sought out Brendan O'Neill, whom Kate had introduced as the owner of the Irish Rose pub, her late brother Connor's childhood friend, and, more important to Alec, second cousin to the Garda sergeant who'd arrested O'Sullivan and sent him off to the hospital in Galway.

"Did you ask my cousin what hospital he'd been taken to?" Brendan answered Alec's question about Cadel's whereabouts in the Irish fashion, with one of his own.

"Yeah, but he said that he didn't feel right about giving out police information."

"No doubt because Cadel has made a great many enemies over the years who would be crowding the hallways, wanting to see the man finally on his back," Brendan supposed. He rubbed his chin and eyed Alec thoughtfully. "Kate likes you."

"I like her."

"Aye. Isn't that obvious for anyone with two eyes in their head?" He glanced over to where she was taking her turn flying her son's green lough beastie kite. "When she was a young girl, not even in her teens, she thought herself to be in love with me. Followed her brother and me all over the place, she did. If she'd been any other girl, we would have found her a bother. But it's difficult to resist our Kate."

"So I've discovered."

"I was older than her by a few years, which meant more at that age, so I never thought of her as a female. Only my best friend's sister. In later years, our little circle of three changed: Connor died, I moved to Dublin and took up the law for a while, and Kate, well, she wed herself to O'Sullivan." The iced hatred and regret that had slipped into his easy tone were feelings Alec could identify with, all too well.

"When I returned to Castlelough, to take over my father's pub, I was stunned that the wee faerie sprite who'd once been like my shadow had grown into a goddess. Needless to say, I fell the moment she walked into the Rose to fetch her husband home my first weekend behind the bar. Hard, I did. But I kept such feelings to myself because while Cadel didn't love her, he was jealous of any man who might so much as glance at her, and I didn't want to be creating more pain for her.

"I did *not*," he stressed forcefully, "know that he'd been using his fists on her. If I had, I would have done away with him with no more thought that I might have crushed an insect beneath my boot."

"Since you're sharing this with me, may I ask what your feelings are now?"

"Oh, they're much the same. But while I'll admit to a bit of regret that by choosing to wait until she was legally free to make my case, I'm resolved to the fact that I've lost her to you."

"You seem to be taking it well."

He shrugged. "I love Kate. I only want for her to be happy, which you seem to make her. Besides, there's always the chance that now that she's grown up she might have outgrown her schoolgirl crush, and this way I can enjoy lovely thoughts of what might have been, rather than have to remember that she turned down any proposal of marriage, which may have harmed our friendship, which is as vital to me as breathing."

"That's very pragmatic of you."

Another shrug. "We're not so much known for it, but we Irish can be pragmatic when the situation calls for it. Isn't that how we've survived, after all, during all the centuries of others bringing change to our little island?"

His faint smile faded. His eyes became hard. His expression grim. It crossed Alec's mind that as friendly and easygoing a man Brendan O'Neill was on the outside—and wasn't that a necessary attribute in a bartender?—the inner man was far more intense. Still waters, he thought, with another flash of intuition.

"I did not tell you my little tale so you'd be concerned I was intending to move in on you. Or even to assure you that I'm giving you a clear field, since I doubt if I could influence her mind one way or another where you're concerned. I'm telling you this so you'll understand why a former friend of the Irish court is going to tell you where you can find O'Sullivan. And, while I'm not one to be recommending violence, mind you, if you happen to find your passion overruling your head, despite the fact that I'm running a pub these days, I've kept my license to practice law current and would be more than happy to take on your defense."

"And if I don't keep the bastard away from her?" Alec had every intention of doing exactly that, but he was curious how far O'Neill would go.

"I'll kill him," Brendan replied, proving that the Irish could, on occasion, be succinct.

After the party, Zoe went into the village for a movie and ice cream afterward with Mary Joyce and some of Mary's schoolmates. The long day had caught up with the younger children, who were already nodding off in the tub, although the usual tractable Jamie had given Kate a bit of an argument when she'd told him that he couldn't be wearing his new night vision goggles to bed. They'd compromised, by letting him keep them beside him, in the event he might feel the need to spy in the middle of the night.

"They fell asleep the minute their heads hit the pillow," she reported as she entered her bedroom where Alec had been waiting for her. She closed the door and latched it.

He was standing beside the bed he'd just turned down, backlit by the moon. His shirt was open, baring the rippling of muscles she loved to run her hands and mouth down, his feet were bare, his eyes hot. Kate heard a faint moan, not realizing it had escaped her own throat. Her mind went a little light, as it occasionally did when she'd experience a bit of vertigo while standing on the very edge of the cliff, watching the seabirds soaring below her.

"Alec . . ." She reached out a hand to him.

He came to her, predatory gray eyes glinting. "Do you have any idea how much I want you?"

No more than she wanted him. "Show me." She went up on her toes and twined her arms around his neck. "Take me."

Passion flared like a match set to dry straw. There was heat. And flame. And smoke. Kate had never realized that desire could be so primal. So thrilling. His mouth savaged hers, tormenting with harsh lips and teeth and tongue. His night beard scraped like sandpaper against her skin, his hands rough as they hiked up her skirt and grasped at her quivering thighs.

He rained stinging kisses over her face, demanding what she gave eagerly, his breath as hot as she imagined the winds must be in the Sahara. As hot as her blood.

She released her hold on him only long enough to lift her arms as he yanked her tunic over her head and unfastened her bra with a single quick flick of the wrist. With a half oath, half groan, he lifted her off her feet and took her breast in that ravenous mouth.

Kate shattered like a piece of Castlelough crystal, going so limp that if he hadn't been holding her up, she would have slid to the floor.

But he gave her no time to regain her breath. Dragging his mouth back to hers, he ripped away the lace panties she'd chosen this morning just for him, freed himself and plunged into her, swallowing her sharp, ragged cry.

"You're mine." He was huge and hard as stone.

"Aye." She was burning for him.

"Say it." When he began to pull out, she arched back like a bow in a silent, desperate plea.

"Yours," she gasped on a ragged sob of need.

His fierce eyes glimmered with satisfaction as he thrust deeper. Harder. He took her standing up, high against the door, muscles straining, heart pounding, so fast and furious Kate could only cling to him, her Scandalous Scarlet nails biting into his shoulders as climax after climax slammed through her.

He threw back his head. A rough, feral growl was torn from his throat as he gave into his own release.

"Jesus." He managed, walking like a drunken man, to carry her the few feet to the bed, where they collapsed together in a tangle of arms and legs. "Are we still alive?"

"From the thunderous messages my body would still be giving me, I'd say aye." She was blissfully, gloriously limp and would be more than happy to stay right here, with Alec sprawled on top of her, for the rest of her life. "Though I may never be moving from here again."

She felt him go absolutely still. Even his heart, which had been pounding like a bodhrán, seemed to pause for several significant beats.

"Christ." He rolled off her. "I'm so damn sorry, Kate."

"Sorry? What could you possibly be sorry for?"

"For the way I took you." He pushed himself up to a sitting position on the edge of the bed. "I was like an animal."

"Isn't it a coincidence that we'd be having the same thought." She smiled at the memory of how she'd imagined him metamorphosing, like an ancient Irish shapeshifter into that snarling, feral wolf she'd imagined him to be that first day, out on the cliff.

"My behavior was indefensible. Unpardonable."

Those words, muttered with harsh self-disgust, made her eyes fly open. "Sure, it was not."

"After what you went through . . ." He plowed his hands through his hair. Grimaced as he touched a fingertip to her breast. "Hell, I bruised you. The same way he did."

Kate was stunned he'd be thinking such a thing. "Alec." Unnerved by the self-loathing in his eyes, she went up on her knees and threw her arms around him. "You're nothing like Cadel. *Nothing,*" she repeated firmly.

"I didn't take any time. Any care. I ravished you, dammit."

"Aye, you did. I'll probably be stiff for a week." *And love every day of the erotic reminder.*

"Christ," he repeated. He shook his head. "You must hate me."

"Don't be talking foolishness."

She'd been on the verge of telling Alec that she loved him, but now that their conversation had taken this sudden, unexpected and thorny path, not wanting him to feel pressured to return the words out of some misguided sense of guilt, Kate kept her feelings to herself. For now.

"It's amazing enough that after your marriage to that bastard, you'd let any man put his hands on you," he ground out. "Knowing what I know—especially about yesterday—I should have treated you more carefully."

Kate didn't know whether to laugh or to weep at such uncharacteristic behavior from this man, who had seemed to possess a wealth of self-confidence, so much so, she could understand why so many in the racing world had described him as arrogant. "It's true that I wouldn't let *any* man put his hands on me, but you're not just any man." *Just the man I love*, she thought with wonder.

"I wanted your hands on me." She took hold of one of those hands, uncurled the tight fist one finger at a time, then pressed it against her body where even now shock waves continued. "This is what you do to me, Alec MacKenna. Why on earth would I be objecting to that?"

He didn't answer. But she watched a bit of the tenseness leave his shoulders. "There was a time when I wouldn't have been able to have even *you* touch me in such a way," she admitted. "A time when even Michael or Brendan's brotherly pats would have made my heart chill to ice in my breast. But thanks to therapy and time, I've moved beyond that. Don't you think I'd be knowing the difference between passion and brutality? Could you possibly believe that I was thinking about sex in the barn yesterday?"

"You were almost raped."

"Aye, I was, and as I told you, not for the first time. Which allows me to know firsthand that rape has nothing to do with sex or lovemaking between a man and a woman. It's an act of violence. Something I need never fear from you." She framed his face with her hands and kissed him hard. "It's not at all the same."

"No," he agreed huskily. She could feel him slowly surrendering to the kiss. To her. "It's not at all the same." The worrisome mood shifted, like the dark of night giving way to the brilliance of day.

"We did it fast." He touched his lips to hers, turned his hand and pressed a clever finger against her, fitting the flat of it to the curve of her body. "What would you say to trying it slow this time?"

"I'd say aye."

He kissed her more deeply, sweeping the interior of her mouth with slow swirls of his tongue while gradually increasing the pressure on that tender pink flesh between her legs.

"Alec . . ." Her senses had begun to swim.

"What, love?" With his eyes on hers, he slid his long middle finger into her slick wet sheath.

Her vision blurred; she was flowing over his hand. "I can't."

His grin was quick, dark and thrillingly wicked. Another finger went even deeper, drawing a wet sucking sound from within her. "Want to bet?"

To her amazement, he showed her that she could. Again and again as he drove her higher and higher to where she had the freedom to fly, and in turn, to make him soar as well, above the clouds, past the stars, into the heart and heat of the sun.

29

IT WAS STILL DARK when Kate lay amidst the tangled sheets, watching him dress. He really did have the most amazing body. And she should know, since she'd explored every masculine bit of it. At first she'd been hesitant about taking on a more aggressive role that was so foreign to her.

That first time, in Andrew Sinclair's suite in the stately Georgian Moyglare Manor, not far from the Curragh, where he'd stabled the horse he'd brought to Ireland to race, she'd played a passive role. The thrill of the forbidden, of being wanted by such a bold, brash man had proven more an intoxicant than whiskey.

While she'd never regret that night because of her son, Kate was discovering that love with Alec was so very different from that blinding passion she'd shared for that single night with Jamie's natural father. Instead of exploding outward, it narrowed, as if she were viewing this glorious new world through the wrong end of a telescope. She found herself fascinated by every little thing about him: the way he made eye contact with her children when they were talking to him; the way he'd never shave until after they breezed

Legends Lake, as if harboring some subconscious superstition; those little lines that crinkled outward from his eyes when he smiled, which was more and more often, even while they made love, which was another revelation, since she never would have imagined it was possible to laugh in bed.

She loved the feel of him, hard male angles to her soft curves. She loved the taste of him as she kissed her way down the rigid muscles of his chest that reminded her of her grandmother Fitzpatrick's old wooden washboard. She loved the scent of him, leather and saddle soap blended with natural male. She loved that part of him that made him so different, as smooth and hard as marble, but so much hotter. Hotter than the rest of him, as hot as she'd feel beneath her own skin.

"You realize, don't you," Alec murmured as he buttoned his shirt, "that if you keep looking at me like that, I'm never going to get out of here before the kids wake up." They'd agreed, early on, that he'd not be seen spending the night in her room.

"I like looking at you."

He laughed at that. A soft sound, in deference to his daughter sleeping across the hall, but it still slipped beneath her flesh and warmed her all over again. "Wench."

"Aye." She stretched like a sleek, smug, satisfied cat. "Which is coming as a great surprise. But I'm enjoying it quite a bit."

Her pulse spiked when he unbuttoned his jeans again in order to tuck in the shirt he'd finally found lying on the floor beneath the wing chair in the far corner of the room.

"Well, that makes two of us." The mattress sighed as he sat down on the edge of it and ran a hand down her flushed, sated body, from shoulder to thigh. "It'll be dawn soon. I didn't let you get much rest."

"Nor I you."

"Perhaps you ought to sleep in."

"That sounds lovely. But there's breakfast waiting to be cooked. Children to get off to school." His light, caressing touch made her want to sigh. "And Legends Lake to breeze."

"We could always put that off until later. Maybe after lunch." His tone was casual. Too casual.

"It's not like you to be changing his schedule. Especially since we didn't work with him yesterday because of Jamie's birthday party."

"It's no big deal." He shrugged. "Changing the time isn't going to make any difference."

"And what will you be doing while I'm supposed to be catching up on my beauty sleep?"

"Not much." He framed her face and gave her a light kiss. "This and that."

"Ah." She nodded. "I've been known to do a bit of that myself, from time to time. Tell me, Alec, would you possibly be doing any of either *this* or *that* in Galway?"

He'd been skimming his thumb along her lips, but at her words, he dropped his hands. "Read my mind, did you?"

The attempt at levity fell as flat as a stone off the top of the cliff. "No. I watched you yesterday, talking with Quinn. As well as Michael and Brendan. It was obvious from your expressions that you were not discussing such casual male things as horses or football."

"They love you. And they understand why I have to do what I have to do."

"And don't you sound just like one of your American western movies," she countered. "How interesting that they'd be understanding. While I'm not."

"The bastard hurt you, Kate."

"And I hurt him back. With the shovel. Which is why he's in hospital."

"But he won't be for long."

"Then he'll be behind bars, where he won't be able to bother me or mine."

"I only wish it were that simple. Quinn warned him once. And he came back."

"Aye. But I refused to listen to Quinn when he wanted me to call the Garda last time. This time I did."

"The police have to work within the law. They can only do so much."

"And you'd be working outside the law? Is that what you're saying?"

"If it comes to that, sure."

"Are you mad?" She hitched herself up in bed and stared at him. "Can't you see he's not worth putting yourself at risk in such a reckless way?"

"You're my woman, Kate. I'll do whatever it takes to keep you safe."

"Your woman?"

"You said it," he reminded her. "When I took you against the door."

She tilted her head and studied him. "Would you be considering me your property, then? Like a lorry or a horse you've bought at auction?"

"No. I'd be considering you the woman I love and I'm damned if that son of a bitch will ever—so long as I'm alive—lay a hand on you or Jamie. Is that clear?"

"Not entirely. Would you be referring to a love such as that of your kiss that day on the strand? A familial type? As you'd have for your cousin?"

"Sugar, what you and I have going for us is undoubtedly illegal for cousins, even in Kentucky." He blew out a long, frustrated breath. Flexed his fingers and looked about as uncomfortable as she'd ever seen him. "Okay, here's the deal: I love you, Kate. To distraction. I sure didn't come here looking for this and I don't have any idea if it's destiny, magic, or just plain good luck. But it doesn't matter, because whatever the reason, it doesn't change the fact that somehow, when I wasn't looking, I fell for you. Hard."

"You don't sound very pleased about that."

"I'm not pleased because I just realized it last night and wanted to tell you in my own way. And my own time."

"What a surprise you'd be wanting to control the situation."

Either her dry tone flew over his head or he didn't want to get sidetracked. "As I said, I haven't had time to think it through. But even before it sunk in, I'd decided to go to Galway. To make sure that O'Sullivan never hurts you again."

"I love you, too," she said. It should have been simple. But, of course, it wasn't.

"Well, isn't that convenient." He ducked his head again and kissed her. Harder this time. Longer. Until her breath was clogging up in her lungs and she'd almost forgotten what she'd wanted to say.

"I've nothing to offer you." She had a husband. A husband who would undoubtedly try to make her pay if he were to learn that she'd taken up with another man.

"Shut up." His gentle tone and the light touch of his mouth against her frowning one took the sting out of his words. "The woman I love is too intelligent to even think such a thing. You've already given me more than I dared ask for. If it's all I can ever have, you won't find me complaining."

He touched a finger to her lips when she began to open her mouth to argue. "I'm not saying it's going to be easy. But you belong to me, Kate. The same way I belong to you. So we can work things out, somehow. Okay?"

Unable to get the words past the lump in her throat, she could only nod. And sink into the long leisurely final kiss he gave her before slipping out of the bedroom and down the stairs. She stood in the window, watching as he left the house. She was still standing there, arms wrapped tightly around herself, as she watched him drive away from the stud, headed on the northern road to Galway.

Galway City was set like a jewel in a stunning and wild expanse of wide bay, stony hills and dark bog. It was a seaport town, where the past still lingered in its narrow alleys, cobblestone lanes, medieval arches and gates, which had once signified the "fourteen tribes of Galway," those Norman market families who'd ruled the strategic location on the salmon-silvered River Corrib like a private fiefdom deep in hostile Irish territory.

Following the directions Brendan had given him, Alec took the bridge over the river, driving past the cathedral that dominated the skyline. He supposed that had the day not been such a gray and soft one, the sun on those stained windows could be dazzling.

The hospital where Cadel O'Sullivan had been taken was a typical institutional building, though Alec did, on some absent level, admire the way the architect had incorporated replicas of the Gothic carved stone windows seen throughout the city. The varied languages he heard as he walked by the people sitting in the chairs lined up in rows in the waiting room were more diverse than was the norm in western Ireland.

The woman at the reception desk was occupied with a family of five, whose very vocal youngest child had fallen off his bicycle in Eyre Square and possibly broken his arm. Thanking Kate's Fates, he strolled past the sign asking all visitors to please stop and check in as if he belonged there, made his way to the bank of elevators and took one to the fourth floor.

Good fortune continued to be with him, as the nurses at the desk on this floor were distracted by a class of harried medical students following a physician around on his morning rounds. Thinking that Jamie would be proud of his spy abilities, Alec strolled the floor until he viewed an orderly rolling a cart filled with bed linens down the hallway to the supply closet. He followed him, then passed him by on a brisk, determined stride that suggested he had somewhere important to go. After making another circle of the floor, he returned to the closet.

Wearing a white lab coat he hoped would give him authority, he went straight to O'Sullivan's room. Kate's husband was lying on his back, his rattling snores making him sound like a bear in deep hibernation. He was a large man, with a florid face and a mean mouth that looked threatening, even in sleep. His head was bound in a white bandage; an IV drip ran from a bottle hanging from a metal stand beside the bed. He had huge arms the size of smoked hams and thickets of hair on the backs of his brawny hands, one of which was handcuffed to the raised rail of the hospital bed.

When Alec thought of those meaty hands striking Kate and her son, he was hit with a flood of dark and deadly emotions like those he'd experienced when Lady Justice had gone down, multiplied a thousand fold. The idea that he'd not been able to keep Kate safe from this monster was eating away at him like battery acid in the gut. For the first time in his life he fully understood the savage impulse to commit murder.

He considered the logistics of dragging O'Sullivan over to the rain-streaked window—which had a view of the cathedral's rose window—and shoving him out onto the tidy courtyard below. Was four stories even a far enough fall to kill a man?

O'Sullivan stirred. Then glared up at Alec. "You'd best be the doctor come to sign the fucking order for pain-killer."

"What's the matter, O'Sullivan? Got yourself a headache?"

His mean eyes narrowed a bit at the American accent, but he didn't dwell on it. "I've been telling those nurses since I got here that I need something for the pain. And I'm still fucking waiting for the fucking injection."

"You're not the only patient on the floor. I imagine the nurses have more important things to do than ease any aches and pains of a wife beater."

"Who the fuck are you?"

"You know, you really need to add some variety to your language," Alec replied mildly. "You're not doing your part to live up to the long tradition of the Irish as word artists." His voice was viciously pleasant. "As for who I am"—he curled his fingers around the thick neck and pressed his thumb against O'Sullivan's windpipe—"I'm the guy who's going to cut off your balls with a rusty knife and stuff them down your throat if you so much as think about Kate or those kids again. Understand?"

The bully's eyes bulged in his poppy-red face.

"I can't hear you," Alex said.

The natural meanness in O'Sullivan's eyes turned to fear. Then, as he began to gasp, choking for lifesaving air, to panic.

"Want to try that one more time?" Alec watched him carefully as he sunk his thumb deeper. "You realize, of course, that I could probably kill you right here, right now, and I doubt if anyone would care." Deeper still, past cords and muscle. "Because most people—decent people—don't give a shit about men who get off on hitting women and children. You'd serve a more useful purpose fertilizing flowers in the graveyard."

Those frightened eyes slowly rolled back in O'Sullivan's head, revealing the whites. Alec fought back his temper and reluctantly reminded himself that if he did what he wanted to do, he'd only succeed in bringing Kate more pain.

He removed his hands and as Kate's husband began choking and wheezing, leaned down over the railing. "The name's MacKenna. Alec MacKenna. Remember it, O'Sullivan. And remember this, as well." He pulled out a pocketknife, flipped it open, and skimmed the tip of the blade down the center of the sheet, over the other man's most vulnerable body parts. "If you ever show your face again in Castlelough, you're a dead man."

Alec heard a gasp from behind him and glanced back over his shoulder. A young brunette nurse was standing in the doorway, her hand to her throat. He shot Kate's husband, who was still struggling to breathe, one last warning glare. Then pocketed the knife and walked past the nurse out of the room.

She caught up with him at the elevator. "Excuse me, sir."

He sighed. Then turned, half expecting to see that she'd rounded up some security guards to put him away. But she was all alone.

"Yes?" he asked with a mildness that was exceedingly hard to come by, since fury still had him in its grip.

Her face was sober. Her eyes appraising. "Thank you."

"Thank you?" he repeated, surprised by the emotion in those two little words.

"None of us like taking care of the horrid man," she divulged, sweeping a hand back toward the nurses' station. "We have to give him the IVs, since to not do so would be to endanger his life, which we couldn't, in good conscience, do. But he won't be receiving any pain medication while he's here in hospital. And he'll be finding that the more those fluids start running through him, his light won't be answered quite as quickly as he might wish."

"Well, that's some good news." He managed a half smile. "Thank you. And the others, as well."

"No problem." She turned, as if to leave, then blurted out, "Me father beat me mother."

He saw the shadows in her eyes. Recognized them from the ones that had darkened his heart for so many years. "Mine too."

This time they both smiled. A secret had been shared, and in the sharing a bit of the stigma neither should have felt, but sometimes still did, was removed.

The elevator door opened. "Good day, nurse"—he glanced at the name tag pinned to her uniform—"Duggan."

"God Bless," she responded as he stepped into the elevator, his mind already on Kate.

30

A FULL, MILK-WHITE MOON rode high in the midnight sky like a ghost galleon, casting a silver light over the ancient forest, illuminating Kate as she slipped away from the house, headed toward a grove of oak trees that had managed to survive the axe when Richard II had plundered Irish woodlands for the timber to build the roof of London's Westminster Hall. Her hooded white cape glistened in the swirling mists of fog draped like gossamer silken veils over the moon, dimming its light.

It was Beltane, the Time of Brightness in the Celtic eightfold year, when the earth was reborn out of winter's icy death. The night was silent save for the soft sighs of the sea, the occasional sweet, lonely cry of an owl hidden somewhere in the treetops calling for his mate, and the stirring of about-to-be-born wildflowers beneath the earth. The familiar night sounds were primal music to Kate's ears, reaching into her soul, stirring the wildness that lurked deep in her heart.

It was music from an ancient time, a time when primitive man trembled with fear against the unseen denizens of the dark night. A time when the druids ruled with wisdom and power.

A time of magic.

The trees appeared black in the night. In the center of the grove stood the sacred circle of stones. She entered the circle and turned her face skyward, lifting her arms, palms turned upward, toward the spinning stars, and received a warm infusion of energy from Mother Moon.

Her greeting completed, Kate cast her circle with the ancient, singing words she'd learned in her mother's womb, who'd learned them from her mother, who in turn had learned them from hers, going back through the centuries to the Celts. Once the circle was completed, she began scattering the fragrant flower petals she'd carried to the grove in a sally basket. The powers of feminine clairvoyance of the sally would be strengthened beneath the mystical nature of the full moon. Especially tonight, on this first of the Celtic fire festivals.

She'd told the MacKenna that she wasn't one to be dancing nude in circles of stone. But since Beltane required her to be skyclad, Kate slipped off the hooded cape and let it fall off her shoulders onto the ground. The only thing she wore now was a silver amulet in the shape of a wheel, the three spokes depicting the trinity of Earth, Man, and the Otherworld. She opened the amulet, took out a small vial of scented oil, then sprinkled the oil over the wood she'd stacked in the circle that morning.

With the powers of midnight and Beltane vibrating through her, she held her hands over the wood, instantly igniting them in a *whoosh* of wind and flame. The wind picked up, catching her long hair, whipping it into a wild froth around her face.

Then, closing her eyes, still singing, Kate lifted her face and her arms to the moon once more and began to dance the ancient pattern.

*　*　*

Alec had followed her to the grove. Sensing, with his newly discovered intuition, that she needed some time alone, he stayed in the shadows of the trees, keeping her in view, but not invading her privacy. He'd seen other circles on earlier trips to Ireland. But none like this: sixteen man-size standing stones surrounding a huge recumbent stone on which lines and swirls had been chiseled. Alec could feel the powerful force protecting the circle; a low, humming sound vibrated from the very heart of the stones.

He watched Kate cast her circle, then strew her petals like a flower girl at a faerie wedding. She was singing a chant, her voice as clear and pure as a silver flute, rising on the breeze, drifting along with the distant roar of the sea and the sigh of the breeze in the treetops.

She was wearing a coronet of fresh flowers and had entwined narrow red and white ribbons through her wealth of black hair. The perfume of the blossoms wafted on the night air as she shrugged out of the robe, letting it skim over her curves like a silken waterfall. In the streaming moondust her body appeared to have been carved from alabaster, but Alec knew that it was much warmer. And worlds more yielding.

She lit the fire, causing sparks to fly upward into the black sky. He watched her sway the glorious female body that now glowed silver and orange from moon and firelight. As she danced to music only she could hear, the night around her began to sing as well. Alec could have sworn that he heard the melodic strumming of a harp coming from the overhead tree branches.

Her voice rang out over sea and wind and as he watched, she drew the moonlight down into her, swathing her in brilliance, making her glow from the inside out.

Alec could have no more resisted the sensual lure than he could stop breathing. He entered the sacred circle she'd cast, his mind clouded, as if it had been draped in gossamer cobwebs, but at the same time more alive than it had ever been.

Kate turned toward him, her warm and generous heart shining in her eyes and when he gathered her into his arms, the night sighed. Time took on a mystical, dreamlike feel as she slowly undressed him, blessing each bit of newly exposed flesh with butterfly kisses and tender touches. Freed of mortal trappings, they moved to the music of the night, bodies, minds, and souls in perfect unison and harmony.

Magic. It crackled around them like the electricity in the air before a summer storm; flowed through them like the River Shannon answering the age-old call of the sea, melted their bodies together in divine union, like a brilliant sun melts hot wax, making it impossible to know where she left off and he began.

"Read my mind," she sang softly in his ear. "As I read yours. Two minds, with a single heart."

Opening his heart to Kate had been the most natural thing he'd ever done. Now he opened his mind as well, tenderly reading her innermost thoughts as she was his, discovering realms of sensuality beyond anything either of them had ever known as the flames of the sacred fire danced around them, in them.

He was male to her female, the golden half of her silvery being. Their coming together, two parts of the perfect whole, was as it was meant to be, from the beginning of time immemorial. And it was wonderful.

The trees sang and the stars spun, welcoming the lovers who, entwined, rode the magic to soar and wheel and tumble in the midnight sky, finally returning to earth, safe and replete in each other's arms.

"That was," Alec said as they lay together afterward on the bed of her cape, "the most incredible experience of my life."

"Beltane is a special time." She was lying with her head on his chest. "It's a time of awakening."

"I've certainly been awakened to a lot of new things lately." He tipped a finger beneath her chin and lifted her gaze to his. "And Beltane may be special. But you, sweetheart, were incredible."

"As were you."

"It's the two of us. We're obviously magic together." He touched his smiling lips to hers. "I also now realize that being moonstruck isn't just an expression."

He drew her closer, ran his hand down her bare back. "I knew you were the most extraordinary person I've ever met, Kate. I just didn't realize how extraordinary."

He kissed her again, a slow sweet kiss that brought tears to her eyes.

"I dreamed of you," she murmured.

"I've been dreaming about you every night since I landed in the country. But believe me, sugar, as hot as they've been, they don't come close to reality."

"I dreamed of you before you came to Ireland. I felt the winds of change that brought you here before you rang me up about Legends Lake."

"That's what you were talking about that first day. My destiny."

"Aye. As well as mine. It was obviously our destiny to be together."

Although she was not eager to leave the circle, it was growing cold. As he dressed, she picked up the petals that were now infused with magic. She'd scatter them around the house as protection for her family.

A new day was dawning, the stars beginning to

fade beneath the superior light of the rising sun as they walked back to the house, hand in hand.

The festival grounds, located at the stone bridge on the outskirts of the village, were bustling with holiday revelers. Old men in tweed caps quaffed pints of Guinness and pointed out pretty young girls who, on this bright and sunny day, had cast off their coats and sweaters and changed into colorful spring finery. Young men flirted with those young girls, who flirted back in the spirit of the holiday. The air was filled with music and genial conversation.

The Travelers had arrived in their caravans with their horses and began making deals with the slap of hands, a bit of Irish earth smeared onto the horses' rumps to show that bargains had been struck, and a few pounds given back to the seller for luck. Children wearing flowers in their hair danced around towering maypoles, which, Kate told Alec, had actually begun their existence as phallic symbols of the pagan god whose emergence from youth to manhood was being celebrated.

Bright orange, white, and green flags flapped in the sea breeze, the blue sky was filled with kites, many in the shape and emerald green hue of the Lady. Farmers who'd come to town for the day's festivities competed in antique plow contests and in a nearby venue, money furiously exchanged hands as to which farmer's draft horses could pull the most weight.

Craftsmen proudly displayed their goods on wooden tables: Gold and silver gleamed while the rich leather scent of hand-fashioned tack mingled with the mouth-watering aroma of fried fish and chips and the sweet, pungent smell of manure.

Jamie had gone off with Rory, Shea and Celia to ride the amusement rides; Zoe was with Nora's younger sister, Mary, at the crowning of the May Queen. A former queen herself, Mary was part of the royal court.

"Look, Mama, a monkey." Brigid pointed toward a tinker who was entertaining a circle of onlookers with an accordion while a monkey in a red suit and hat deftly snatched coins flipped to him from the crowd. "May I have a penny?"

Kate handed the penny over to her daughter, who skipped over to the tinker's performing animal, but instead of tossing the coin, held it out on her palm with a smile. They looked at each other, red-haired sprite and monkey. And in a flash of an instant, something unspoken appeared to pass between them. Something that caused the monkey to reach out and touch his long thin finger to the center of her hand while she continued to smile.

"Jesus," Alec murmured. "You've got yourself another one."

"It appears so." Kate had suspected as much, but had never witnessed an actual sign of her daughter's gift before.

Brigid began chattering away to the red-suited monkey, who began chattering back while people gathered to watch the impromptu show. Even the tinker stopped playing his accordion.

"It's as natural to her as taking a breath," Alec murmured.

"Aye," Kate agreed. Hadn't it always been that way for her?

Her attention was drawn by someone calling her name. She turned around, lifting her hand to her forehead to block out the sun. Then smiled in a way that caused a sharp stab of jealousy in Alec's gut.

"Devlin!" She raced across the grass into the arms of a man built like an oak tree. When he lifted her off her feet and twirled her around, Alec's jaw clenched.

"Alec, I want you to meet the best horse breeder in all of Ireland," she said, as she dragged the man by the hand to him.

"Second best," he declared on a laugh. "Kate holds the champion's crown."

"I'm not the one employed at the National Stud," she said.

"True. But only because you refused to leave your own farm when recruited."

"You were offered a position at the Stud?" Alec asked.

"Isn't that just like our Kate," the man said with an easy smile her way. "Always hiding her light beneath a barrel. They did, indeed, invite her to join their lofty ranks, but didn't she wisely tell them that her roots are buried too deeply into our western bogs to transplant well to Kildare?"

Kate's brow furrowed at the slight edge to his tone. "Is something wrong?"

He shook his shaggy head. "Nothing I can't deal with. It's just more difficult than I'd expected, juggling the constant demands of the Stud, with my desire to be home occasionally with my wife."

He thrust out his hand. "I'm Devlin Monohan. I was in school with Kate and Nora. You'd be Alec MacKenna. Kate's Yank."

"That's me. MacKenna. Kate's Yank."

Hearing the faint challenging edge in the response, Devlin's gaze drifted down to her hip, where Alec had placed his free hand. *Taken*, that possessive touch said.

"It's glad I am to be meeting you, having heard so much about your training skills, Mr. MacKenna," he said. "I only wish my wife, Tara, were here. She's a little under the weather."

"Oh, dear," Kate said. "I hope she's not too ill."

"She's a bit sick of me hovering over her, but insists that it's nothing out of the ordinary for a woman who's going to be a mother by Yuletide."

"A baby!" Kate's face beamed with delight as she clapped her hands. "You're going to have a baby?"

"Well, I won't be the one having it. Thank God." He lifted his eyes skyward, then grinned at Alec, who, deciding the amiable bear was no threat, grinned back.

"Oh, it's such grand news. Does Nora know?"

"Not yet. I hoped I'd be seeing her and Quinn here."

"The last I saw them, they were headed to the baked goods pavilion. Nora won first prize for her spice cake."

"And no wonder, since she's the best cook in the county. Well, I'll be tracking them down so I can congratulate her." He brushed a kiss against Kate's cheek. "It's pleased I am to see the light back in your lovely eyes." He turned to Alec. "Good day to you, Mr. MacKenna. I hope our paths cross again soon."

"He seems like a nice enough guy," Alec said as he picked up Brigid, who'd returned from her visit with the tinker's monkey.

"Oh, Devlin's a dear," Kate said. "There was a time, when we were young, that we all thought he and Nora might marry. But that wasn't to be their fate. He'll make a wonderful father."

"Was your husband the reason you didn't take the job at the Stud?"

"No. I'm not saying he might not have given me a problem about it, because wasn't he always giving me problems anyway, but I didn't take the job for much the same reason the Stud is so highly regarded in the international racing world."

"What reason would that be?"

"They take tradition extremely seriously."

"That's not a bad thing. I seem to recall you saying something about the Fitzpatrick stud feeding Guinness to your pregnant mares for over a century."

"Ah, but see, isn't that my point." She smiled up at him. "Those would be *our* traditions. Which suit us."

"Makes sense to me," he said. Wasn't that why he wanted to establish his own stable?

31

THEY WERE HEADED ACROSS THE FAIRGROUNDS to the car park at the end of the day when they were approached by a man wearing the dark blue uniform of the Garda.

"Good day, Kate," he said.

"And a good day to you, Gerry. I believe you know Mr. Alec MacKenna—"

"We've spoken on the telephone." He shot Alec a look and did not hold out his hand. "I'm afraid I have to speak with you, Kate. It's official business."

"Official Garda business?"

"Unfortunately, yes. It's Cadel."

When the pleasure washed off her face, like a sidewalk chalk drawing beneath a torrential rain, Alec found himself wishing he had just thrown the bastard out that window.

"Oh, dear. You're here to tell me he's out of hospital."

"He was released yesterday to await trial. Either the hospital or the Galway Garda was supposed to contact me to let me know at the time, so I could inform you, for your own safety, but somehow that didn't happen."

"Well." She drew in a breath. Let it out. Combed a hand that only trembled slightly through her hair, then lifted her chin. "Thank you for warning me, Gerry. But you needn't worry. I'm sure the children and I will be fine. And if by any chance he does return to the stud, I'll be ringing you up right away."

"He won't be showing up at the stud, Kate." He paused, seeming to choose his words with care.

Before he could elaborate, Kate gasped. All the color drained out of her face as she reached instinctively for Alec's hand and clasped it tightly with her ice-cold one. "He's dead."

"Aye, that he is." The sergeant took a pen and a small notepad from the pocket of his shirt. "He was found floating in the River Corrib this morning only a few blocks from the hospital."

Interestingly, it was Jamie whose expression revealed the most emotion at the news. He looked, Alec thought, as if someone had just informed him that Father Christmas had arrived eight months early.

Responding with her newfound maturity, Zoe immediately scooped Brigid up and grabbed Jamie's hand and took them over to a balloon vendor several meters away.

"Since Cadel had been seen drinking at a nearby pub earlier," the officer continued, "it was first thought that he'd gotten drunk and fallen in. But an examination proved he'd been stabbed in the heart, so, if you don't mind, Mr. MacKenna, could you tell me your whereabouts last night?"

"He was with me," Kate said before Alec could respond.

"All night?"

"Aye." The color was back, as was the steel in both her tone and her spine.

He nodded. "Have you happened to have occasion to visit Galway recently, Mr. MacKenna?"

Alec was in no mood for Irish circumlocution. "I was there yesterday morning, as I've no doubt you've already discovered. Which means you undoubtedly have also learned that I threatened O'Sullivan."

The sergeant glanced down at his notes. "And the nature of that threat would be?"

"I told him that if he ever came near Kate or her children again, I'd kill him. With a knife," he went ahead and tacked on, suspecting the sergeant probably already knew that.

Alec heard a loud gasp and glanced over at the butcher's wife, who was standing nearby, her hand on her chest, staring with the fascination of a woman watching a snake devour a field mouse. Realizing that by trying to protect her, he'd inadvertently opened Kate up to more gossip, he gave her an apologetic look which she told him, with a brief shake of her head, was not necessary.

"I assume your words were meant merely as a figure of speech."

Despite the grim topic, Alec almost smiled at the way the cop was obviously trying to help him out for Kate's sake. "I suppose that would have depended on whether or not O'Sullivan was stupid enough to come back to Castlelough."

Sergeant O'Neill nodded. "Well, he won't be doing that, sure enough." His expression, as he turned back to Kate was sympathetic. "I'd hate to be asking you, Kate, but the Galway Garda will be needing someone to officially identify his body."

"I'll do that," Quinn, who'd walked back with them to the car park, said.

"I'm sorry." It was obvious he meant it. "But regulations state it should be, if possible, a relative."

"O'Sullivan was Kate's husband," Quinn argued quietly. Forcefully. "Nora was once married to her brother. I'm now married to Nora. Which, the way I see it, makes me related to O'Sullivan."

"It does, indeed." Alec was almost amused at how relieved O'Neill looked at this quintessentially Irish solution to a thorny problem. He turned back to Kate. "I'll inform the medical examiner that Cadel's body be returned to his family in Dungarven."

Relief that she wouldn't have to be dealing with this final problem flooded into her eyes. "Thank you, Gerry."

As if by mutual, unspoken agreement, no one spoke of the death on the way back to the stud. Brigid, still too young to fully understand how her life had just changed, was chattering away, reliving the events of the day, the bright red balloon Zoe had tied around her wrist with a white string bobbing on the ceiling of the van. A glance in the rearview mirror showed Jamie, deep in thought, staring out the window. Alec suspected he was not all that interested in the passing scenery, but was reliving scenes from his own life with his father. Or perhaps, Alec hoped, envisioning a life completely free of threat.

He reached across the space between them and took Kate's hand. When she turned toward him, he saw the faint trail of silent tears on her cheeks and did not have to read her mind to know that they were not born of grief, but of relief.

Finally wearing down like a seven-day clock on the eighth day, Brigid fell asleep before they reached the stud. Alec carried her upstairs and put her to bed, while Kate went into Jamie's room for a private talk with her son.

Thirty minutes later, she came down to the kitchen, where Alec was waiting.

"How's he doing?" He handed her a cup of strong tea.

"Better than I could have hoped. He's told me before that he wished Cadel was dead, but wishing and actuality are often different things." She sighed, then took a sip of tea. "It's a sad thing for a son to be grateful about his father's death. I feel horribly guilty for having put him in such a situation."

"Cadel wasn't his father."

"Aye. And don't I have even more reason now for telling Jamie the truth. Because I'd hate to have him someday feeling guilty for having wished such a thing."

"Speaking of which," Alec said carefully, still not entirely knowing how she'd react to his news, "I found something out yesterday. I was going to tell you last night, but we got sidetracked. . . . It's about Sinclair."

"Oh?" Her voice was calm but her fingers had tightened ever so slightly on the handle of the teacup. "Are you about to tell me that you looked him up?"

"Not because I felt threatened by any memories you might have of him." It was vital that she understand and believe this. "Or that I was worried about the guy showing up someday wanting to pick things up where the two of you left off. But it occurred to me that when you did tell Jamie the truth, he'd have questions. I thought it would be easier if you had some answers. I realize that you've a perfect right to tell me that I've no business interfering in your life—"

"Of course you have every right. You love me. As I

love you. And isn't that what we sometimes do for those we love and want to protect? What did you learn?"

"He died."

"Died?" She stared at him in disbelief.

"I know it's damn ironic that you learned that Jamie's natural father and biological father are both dead on the same day, but it turns out that Sinclair died in a car wreck at Sussex that same year you met him."

"The Glorious Goodwood festival begins in Sussex only weeks after our Derby."

Alec was not surprised she'd know that, since the twenty-one-day event, often referred to as a garden party with horses, drew some of the world's leading owners, trainers and jockeys to Great Britain's hallowed turf.

"It was sixteen days after the Irish Derby the year Jamie was conceived." He watched as realization dawned.

She turned to look out the window at the sky that was turning from the bright, bleeding colors of sunset to a soft dusk. "He may have been serious," she said slowly. Thoughtfully. But not, he thought, regretfully. "About me joining him in America." She turned back to Alec. "He may have come back, as he'd promised."

"I suspect, having made love to you, he wouldn't have been able to resist."

She offered a soft smile at that.

"I'm sorry, Kate. I wish things could have turned out differently for you."

"It would have been lovely if I could have been spared those years with Cadel. And I'm truly saddened to learn about Andrew's death. He was a man filled to overflowing with life. It's a shame his flame was snuffed out at such a young age.

"As for my life turning out differently . . ." She lifted a hand to the side of his face. "Aren't I here, at this time, in this place, with you, exactly where I belong?"

"No escaping destiny," he agreed, surprised by the amount of relief he was feeling. Obviously he'd been more concerned about her reaction to lost opportunities than he'd been willing to admit to himself. "There'll be talk," he warned her. "About what I told O'Neill. And about your alibi about us having spent the night together."

"Isn't that the least of my concerns," she replied mildly. "There are those few people in the village who've been talking about me my entire life." She took another sip of tea. "In truth, I feel sorry for them, that they lead such uneventful lives they need to be gossiping about mine to spice up their existence."

"Do you have any idea who could have killed him?"

"Cadel had a way of getting on the wrong side of people. But drinking and bullying people weren't his only vices. Jamie told me that he'd come here for money to pay his gambling debts. It wasn't the first time, certainly. The day Quinn sent him away, he'd torn the house apart, looking for my bankbook. I'd be suspecting that perhaps one of those gamblers finally got tired of not being paid."

"That makes sense. Especially if he was killed to set an example to other welshers." Alec reached across the table and linked his fingers with hers. "This changes things. Opens up more possibilities we need to talk about."

"Aye." Her eyes were both warm and weary. Alec was encouraged by the love he viewed in those lake blue depths.

"It's been a long day. And you didn't get any sleep last night." He skimmed his knuckles up her cheek.

"How about we table the discussion until tomorrow?"

He was leaving the day after. Sometime between last night and when he'd learned about Cadel O'Sullivan's murder, Alec had made the decision to take Kate with him.

Staying in the shadows and taking care not to step on the squeaky step, Jamie crept down the stairs. He suspected his ma wouldn't approve of him using his new birthday spy equipment to eavesdrop on her conversation with Alec. But his second thought upon hearing that his da was dead, right after relief that he'd no longer be able to beat on people with his big mean fists, was that now his ma could marry Alec.

Ever since the American had come to stay with them, Jamie had been slipping off to the lake on his way back from Rory's each afternoon to make a wish. Each day that wish was always the same. That somehow, Alec could become his new father. He didn't know about the law, only vaguely understood that it would still be a long time before his ma was free to marry again, but surely if the Lady could be bringing Rory a father, he'd kept telling himself, she could be making the same magic for him. Now it appeared she'd answered his wish, by getting rid of his da just like Diancecht had cut off the heads of the evil snakes, then rid Ireland of them by throwing their ashes into the River Barrow. Which was why he wanted—needed—to hear what the grown-ups would be saying about his father's murder.

He was wearing his night vision goggles. Since the lights were on in the kitchen, he didn't need to turn on the headlamp, but he felt more like a spy when he was wearing them. His ma and Alec were talking so quietly that he couldn't quite hear them. *No problem*, he thought with satisfaction, *thanks to Alec and Zoe*. He stealthily opened the blue plastic spy case they'd bought him at Monohan's, the same one he'd been wanting ever since Mrs. Monohan had first put it in the shop window, and pulled out the combination microphone, voice magnifier and tape recorder.

At first Jamie thought there must be something wrong with the transmission he was hearing in his earplug. There was more static than he suspected 007 had to deal with, but from what he could hear through the crackling, Alec didn't believe his da was really his da. Jamie waited for his ma to set the American straight.

But she didn't. Instead she was saying his father was someone named Andrew Sinclair!

Jamie wanted to burst into the kitchen and demand answers. But he still wasn't certain he'd been hearing right and didn't want to get into trouble for eavesdropping and have his spy kit taken away from him.

The thing to do, he decided, was to go down to the cave, where he could listen to the recording. As he tiptoed out of the house, Jamie told himself that he must be mistaken.

His mother would never lie to him.

Would she?

32

K ATE WAS EXHAUSTED. The day had been an emotional one, what with Cadel's murder and learning of Andrew's death, which brought with it the discovery that he'd not betrayed her as she'd believed all these years.

She checked on Brigid, who was lying crossways on the mattress, her red balloon resting on the ceiling above the bed, the stuffed purple elephant Alec had won for her shooting at a moving line of metallic ducks beside her. She didn't know it, Kate thought as she tucked her properly in and brushed a kiss against her cheek, but Brigid's life had changed greatly today. And all for the better. Knowing that her daughter was safe from Cadel O'Sullivan gave Kate's heart wings.

Next she climbed the stairs to the attic. At first, when she didn't see her son lying in his bed, Kate thought her eyes hadn't adjusted to the light. She bent and placed her hand on the pillow. Which was empty. Nerves skittering, she swept her suddenly ice-cold hand across the bed, from head to foot.

Nothing.

She turned on the lamp. A bubble of fear rose in her throat. *You're letting your imagination run away with you,*

Kate Fitzpatrick. Sure, he drank a great deal of lemonade and orange soda today. He's only downstairs ridding himself of a bit of it.

She kept telling herself that as she tore back down the steep, narrow stairs, her mind plagued by the fact that his spy kit was missing as well. She ran from room to room on the second floor. Then raced down to the kitchen, where Alec was slicing beef from last night's roast for a late-night sandwich. He glanced up as she flew into the kitchen, face paper pale, eyes frantic, appearing on the brink of hysteria.

"What's wrong?"

"It's Jamie! He's gone!"

"Gone?" She was trembling like a willow battered by a hurricane. "What do you mean, gone?"

"I mean gone!" Her voice rose, cracked. Her eyes were wild, circling the kitchen like a trapped sparrow seeking to escape. "His bed is empty. And his spy kit is missing, as well. But I found this on the floor right outside the kitchen door." Hand shaking, she held up the plastic pen filled with invisible ink.

"Shit." Alec shook his head. Of all the goddamn things to happen. "He heard."

"Aye." Tears began to stream unchecked down her cheeks. Her shoulders slumped. She looked more beaten than when he'd first seen her coming back from the beach with her son, her lovely face marred with angry bruises. "He heard."

It was true. Jamie sat on the sand in his secret spy hiding cave, still stunned after listening to the tape for the third time in the past ten minutes. Part of him was angry at his mother, for keeping such a secret from him. For bringing such a hateful man into their lives and pretending all these years that they could ever be a real family. Like the Joyces and the Gallaghers. But then he remembered all those times of bruises and silent tears his mother would shed when she thought he wasn't watching and knew that she'd suffered far more than he had.

"James Sinclair," he murmured, trying out the name he might have had if his real da hadn't died in England and his mother hadn't married horrid Cadel O'Sullivan. "Jamie Sinclair."

It was a nice enough name. But strangely, it didn't feel natural on his tongue or in his heart. He just didn't *feel* like Jamie Sinclair. He decided to try another name. The one that had been teasing at the back of his mind for weeks. The name he hadn't dared allow himself to say out loud.

"Jamie MacKenna." Better, he decided. "James MacKenna." He nodded. Definitely better. Deciding to write it down, just for himself, so he could see how it looked, he rummaged around in the blue plastic spy briefcase for his pen with the invisible ink that could only be seen when activated with lemon juice.

It was gone. He thought back. He'd had it when he'd first gotten home, because he'd written all about his da being murdered in his spy notebook. It must have dropped out when he'd taken out his secret eavesdropping equipment.

He thought about going back to retrieve it, then worried his mother might hear him sneaking into the house. From what he could tell from the taped conversation between his mother and Alec, they weren't going to talk about getting married until the morning. But from what Rory had told him about Nora and Quinn's romance, adults often said one thing and ended up doing another thing altogether when they were in love, so he didn't want to interrupt just when Alec might be proposing.

He'd give them a little while, he decided, hitting the rewind button again. Meanwhile, he'd listen one more time to the glorious news that he didn't have to worry about having Cadel O'Sullivan's blood, after all.

They all came: Nora and Quinn, Michael and Erin, Mary Joyce and Brendan, who brought along all the men and women who'd enjoyed the May Day party at the Rose when they'd gotten the word that Jamie O'Sullivan had gone missing.

Sergeant O'Neill arrived with other Guards, divided the area around the stud into quadrants and sent teams of police and volunteers out to comb the fields. The only bright spot in the night, if it could indeed even be called that, was his news that the Galway Garda had arrested a thug, known to work for the gamblers to whom Cadel had been so badly in debt, for her husband's murder.

Father O'Malley arrived to offer whatever comfort he could, and Mrs. Monohan from the mercantile brought baskets filled with cheese, crackers, bread and sliced meats to feed the army of searchers.

It took every bit of the persuasive skills Alec and the others possessed to talk Kate into staying behind in the house when she so desperately wanted to be out searching for her child.

"It's best you stay here," Nora soothed, "to welcome our Jamie home."

"He'll undoubtedly be wet and cold and frightened," Erin Joyce had backed up her sister-in-law. "He'll be wanting his mother."

"I should have sensed he wasn't taking Cadel's death as calmly as he seemed to be." The way Kate was dragging her trembling hands through her tangled hair reminded Alec of the stories he'd read of keeners, women hired to wail and tear their long hair out at Irish wakes. The wild panic in her eyes slashed at him.

"It'll be all right," he assured her. "Jamie will be all right."

"He thinks himself to be a spy. Why didn't I realize he'd be spying on us to learn more about the murder?"

"It'll be all right," he repeated, as if saying the words with enough strength would make them so. He ran a hand down her ice-cold arm. "I promise you, Kate. Nothing's going to happen to your son."

It was the splash of icy water that woke him up. Jamie jolted awake, realizing that he'd fallen asleep on the sand. The sky outside the cave was as dark as inside. Rain was falling like a thick curtain in the entrance. He didn't know how long he'd been asleep, but it must have been a while, since the torchlight radiating from his night vision goggles was not nearly as bright as it had been when he'd used the beam to find the cave and see the buttons on his tape recorder.

The sand, which had been dry when he'd first sat on it, was now wet. So was his recorder. Jamie pressed the play button, grimacing when nothing happened and hoped Alec wouldn't be angry with him for having broken his lovely present so soon after his birthday.

Another wave splashed over him, reminding him that as bad as ruining his spy microphone and eavesdropping device might be, he had a more vital problem to deal with. He stood up and was nearly knocked off his feet by another stronger, higher wave, that splashed all the way to his chest. He'd just told himself that he'd best be leaving, before the incoming tide cut off the way to the nearby steps that led to the top of the cliff, when the light atop his goggles flickered.

Once.

Twice.

A third time. Then flickered out, pitching him into a coal-black darkness.

"It's all my fault," Kate was moaning when Alec returned with the priest to receive a new search assignment after failing to locate Jamie at the Joyce castle ruins. She pressed a fist against her mouth, as if to keep from screaming. "If I hadn't married Cadel . . . I knew something would happen. I *knew* there would be a price to be paid for being happy again after all these years."

"That wouldn't be the way it works," Father O'Malley said quietly as he pressed yet another cup of tea into Kate's hands. The priest was a young man, tall and thin, with a bookish appearance. Behind the steamed-up lenses of his wire-frame glasses, his eyes were kind.

"Now I know you've chosen to follow the old ways, Kate. But whatever path one takes to the Creator, the one constant is that the Maker of all things seen and unseen is too all-powerful to stoop to petty behavior such as giving with the right hand and taking away with the left."

He squeezed her shoulder reassuringly with his long fingers. "God gave you a grand gift, with Jamie and Brigid. I've prayed every night since I first arrived in Castlelough that He'd also give you the strength to do what you had to do to keep yourself and your family safe. And weren't those prayers answered? I have every faith that God will keep your boy safe in His arms until he can be returned to yours."

Despite her pagan beliefs, Kate appeared to garner strength from the priest's words. When Alec gathered her close before resuming the search that thus far had proven futile, her tremors eased ever so slightly.

She clung to him. Then tilted her head up, the anguish in her eyes nearly breaking his heart. "Find him, Alec," she begged on a sob. "Please find my son."

After promising her yet again that it was only a matter of time when Jamie would be back home where he belonged, Alec left with the priest to take on their new assignment along the cliff.

"That was a nice thing you did," he said as they made their way across the back pastures that had already been throughly searched.

Father O'Malley slanted him a look. "You sound surprised."

Alec shrugged. "Well, you're Catholic. Irish Catholic," he stressed, implying that, although he hadn't given it a great deal of thought, if he had, he would have expected the priest to be more rigid about New Age religions than a more liberal American one might be. "And Kate's pagan."

"Aye, so she says. You know, religion was an intensely personal thing to the Celts, filled with the wonder of the Creator's daily miracles. It often seems to me that when God looks down on this miraculous world He's created, one of the things that makes Him the most sad, along with wars and hunger, would be the fact that His people have lost their wonder."

"Not Kate."

"And wouldn't that be my point," the priest agreed as they climbed over a stone wall. "Kate's life, like those of the old Celts, whose belief system she's embraced, is a ceaseless, endless prayer of nature, while too many of us have forgotten that no matter how powerful man is, we all live on this planet as guests in the divinity of nature.

"I only wish I could convince her that her beliefs and mine share a common ground, because I believe she could bring a great spiritual strength to our Catholic congregation. Meanwhile, I consider myself blessed to have her as a friend."

"I love her, Father."

"Of course you do, Mr. MacKenna. Isn't she an easy woman to love, after all? It's pleased I am that she's finally going to know the happiness that's eluded her for so many years."

He *would* make her happy, Alec vowed as he swept the flashlight in a wide arc. But first he had to find her son.

Jamie was growing more and more frightened. He no longer felt like an all-powerful international superspy capable of saving civilization; what he felt like was exactly what he was: a nine-year-old boy who'd recklessly gotten himself in a mess. He'd managed to scramble onto an outcropping of limestone up near the ceiling of the cave, but the pull of the moon was causing the tide to come in faster and higher and he knew that if someone didn't find him soon, he'd surely drown. Not yet prepared to give up hope, he assured himself that they'd all be looking for him—Alec, Quinn, and Michael, and the rest of his family. They'd soon be finding him.

The night grew colder. Somewhere in the distance he could hear the lonely tolling of the foghorn off Castlelough Point, warning ships of the dangerous rocks. The wind howled at the mouth of the cave, the water roared and tendrils of fog skimmed across his face like the clammy fingers of ghosts. When another wave splashed all the way up to his ledge, the icy spray drenching him, the salt stinging his eyes, it was the thought of how sad his mother would be if he drowned that started tears streaming down Jamie's face.

As the word of the lost boy spread, more and more people from the village and local farms showed up to join in the search. The kitchen of the farmhouse took on the look of a war room. But still the hours passed and they found nothing. Kate O'Sullivan's son appeared to have vanished from the face of the earth.

Remaining true to form, Mrs. Sheehan, who'd shown up more to gawk than to help, suggested that perhaps Jamie had fallen off the cliff and drowned in the sea.

"That's when our poor Kate, her nerves frazzled, slapped the old biddy," a still furious Nora related the incident to Alec later. "Despite the seriousness of the situation, I had the feeling everyone in the room wanted to applaud her for doing what so many of the rest of us have longed to do for years. Poor long-suffering Dermott took the woman away, of course, back to town, and good riddance to her."

Eventually Erin threatened to have Nora and Zoe hold Kate down while she gave her a tranquilizer injection if she didn't go upstairs and rest so she wouldn't be a wreck when they brought Jamie home needing his mother's comfort. Alec found her lying on her back on the bed where they'd shared so much love, her eyes staring blankly at the ceiling, her arms crossed over her breasts, hands curled into fists.

She turned her head toward him when he opened the door. Looked away again when she viewed the failure in his gaze.

"We'll find him," he said again. "I promise."

Nothing.

"Sergeant O'Neill has people checking all the buses arriving in Galway, Limerick and Cork."

"I suppose a boy who hates his lying mother might run away."

Her flat tone was filled with such self-loathing that Alec decided against telling her that the police had also put out an emergency bulletin for authorities throughout the country to be on the lookout for male adults traveling with young boys. If the possibility of Jamie being kidnapped hadn't yet occurred to her, he sure as hell didn't want to be the one to put it into her mind.

Feeling more helpless than ever before in his life, Alex took hold of her hand and unclenched her fist. As he smoothed the deep moon-shaped gouges her fingernails had dug into her palm with a caressing fingertip, his attention drifted up to the photograph of Kate, Jamie and Brigid holding hands while walking on the beach. They looked so happy and carefree, he thought with a deep inward sigh. He was almost glad that Kate hadn't been able to see this future moment. . . .

"Kate."

She didn't look at him.

He took her chin in his hand and turned her head toward him. "This is like Kevin Noonan."

"Kevin hadn't gone missing." That flat tone was downright spooky. If he hadn't known better, he would have thought Erin *had* followed through on the threat to drug her.

"No, but he would have drowned. If you hadn't seen him."

"You didn't believe me." She turned away again and stared out into the well of blackness.

"That was then. This is now. You can do it, Kate. You have Biddy Early's gift of Sight."

"It's obvious that you weren't listening to me that day, Alec. I'm mind-blind where my own life is concerned."

"No, you're not. You told me, in the circle, that you'd sensed my coming. Then later, dreamed of me."

"Aye."

"See? You knew."

"Sensing and dreaming are different things from seeing."

"I'll take your word for that. But the sergeant's running out of options, sweetheart. We've searched everywhere the kids suggested he might be and turned up nothing. The longer Jamie's missing, the colder the trail gets. He's your son. You carried him under your heart for nine months. You can do this."

"We've always had a close bond." Hope blazed in her eyes. "I used to think it was because until Brigid was born we only had each other. The only reason I had the courage to divorce Cadel was to make certain that Jamie wouldn't be physically or emotionally harmed. Or end up learning such brutal behavior from Cadel."

"Never would have happened," Alec said with confidence. "The kid's got the heart of a cocker spaniel puppy." He reached over and took the smoky globe from the dresser. "Will this help?"

"Perhaps." She reached out to take it. As their fingers touched, Alec felt a surge of warmth and knew that Kate had felt it, too.

"Maybe I'd better leave you alone," he offered, having no idea what the protocol might be for crystal-ball reading.

"No." She managed a soft smile that wobbled only slightly. "I feel stronger when I'm with you. And right now, I could use all the help I can get."

They sat there, side by side on the edge of the mattress, Alec watching as Kate stared into the smoky quartz globe. It had been a very long time since Alec had stepped foot in any church; as the silence spun out, he did what he'd been doing the entire time he'd been out searching the hillsides with Father O'Malley. He prayed.

Jamie felt it at first. A light touch of a hand against his cheek, as soft as dandelion down, the way his mother touched him late at night when she'd come into his room to make certain he was safe before going to bed herself.

He was curled into a tight, miserable ball on his ledge. As a wave washed over him, he smelled the kelp and salt and a wonderfully familiar scent that billowed in the cave like fragrant smoke from a friendly campfire.

"Ma!" He bolted upright. "Ma! I'm here!" Then he heard her. Over the roar of the surf, the wail of the wind, and the foghorn, he heard his mother's voice calling out to him. "I'm here, Ma!"

You can do this, Kate told herself. *If you can do it for others, you can do it for yourself. And your son.*

You never could before, a negative little voice pointed out.

Ah, but isn't that because you didn't truly want to look?

She concentrated, shutting out the external: the rain on the roof, the buzz of conversation filtering up the stairs, the cry of the wind, the squeaking of two-hundred-year-old rafters, the sad and lonely sound of the foghorn off the rocky shoals of Castlelough Point. Even, and wasn't this the hardest of all, the MacKenna whom she loved with all her heart. The man who'd just shown more faith in her than anyone she'd ever known.

The first time she'd accidentally practiced scrying, she'd been a child, too young to understand that what she was viewing in her mother's sterling silver hand mirror was not her imagination, but reality. After that, she'd practiced, at first using candles to light the crystal, and incense to attract positive vibrations. But eventually she'd gotten so she could see things in her great-grandmother's globe without such props. Of course, she still could not see things on demand, as Alec was suggesting. But she had no choice. What was the point, after all, of being born with this ability that was both gift and curse if she couldn't utilize it to save her own child?

She took a deep breath. Let it out slowly. Another. Focused on Jamie. On his darling freckled face, serious eyes and sweet shy smile that revealed the gaps of lost teeth.

She continued to breathe deeply, clearing her mind of all conscious thought, allowing it to drift as she looked into the crystal. Nothing.

Realizing she was staring into the globe, which would do little more than give her eyestrain, Kate blinked, lifted her gaze to the white plaster ceiling, and took another longer, deeper breath. Then, reminding herself that she could not help her son if she permitted her conscious mind to interfere with her subconscious, she returned her gaze to the small round crystal and let her thoughts drift.

A mist began to swirl, slowly at first, then faster and faster, growing thicker and thicker until the entire globe was filled with swirling white clouds.

Kate viewed herself walking out of the clouds, which had begun fading away. However, she was not a woman, but a girl in her teens, and it was not Jamie holding her hand, but Peter Quinlan, who'd cheated her of her long-awaited kiss and gone on to become Father What-a-Waste.

But in this vision, she was not only allowing him to

take her to the cave, she was actually laughing as she ran with him into the opening carved from wind and surf in the limestone cliff. The rising tide was chasing at their heels, but mindless of the danger, they'd no sooner entered the darkness when she held her arms out to him and . . .

"No!" Her cry was that of a wounded animal as the globe began to fill with clouds again. She blinked furiously, unwilling to cede control. Forced her heart to slow its rabbit rhythm, and forced the fear and clutter from her mind.

The clouds parted, allowing her to see Jamie. He was wildly waving his hands and calling her name. "Ma! Ma! I'm here, Ma!"

"I'm coming, darling," she promised as the globe turned misty yet again.

Even as the globe clouded, her mind cleared. "He's in one of the caves on the beach."

"There must be a dozen of those things."

He didn't state the obvious. That with high tide coming in there would be no way to reach—let alone search—them all.

It was then Kate understood her earlier vision. "I know which one." Wasn't it, after all, the very same one Peter had tried to lure her to all those many years ago.

"Every breath stirs the universe," Alec murmured, shaking his head as they both contemplated the fact that by wounding her heart all those years ago, the boy who would become a Limerick parish priest would be giving Kate the answer that would allow her to save her son's life.

33

WHILE MARY JOYCE STAYED AT THE HOUSE in case Brigid might awaken, the others moved to the edge of the cliff, where the massive floodlight Michael had bought for nighttime plowing lit up the ocean below them.

"Shit," Alec muttered when it was obvious that several of the lower stone steps were covered in swirling surf. Then grimaced when he remembered a Catholic priest was standing beside him. "Sorry, Padre."

Father O'Malley shrugged. "No need to apologize, Mr. MacKenna. I'll confess to sharing your viewpoint."

There was something else worrying Alec. The tide was so high, how could Jamie have possibly survived?

"There's a ledge near the roof of the cave," Kate answered his unspoken question. He was no longer surprised she'd read his mind. Whatever powers she possessed seemed to have gone into overdrive. "He's climbed onto it."

"Anyone happen to know the tide tables?"

"I do," Jack Feeny, a fisherman who'd come to the stud as soon as he'd heard the news on his radio, said. He pulled a laminated piece of paper from his jacket pocket. "We've got twenty-two minutes until high tide."

Twenty-two minutes, Alec thought grimly, exchanging a look with Kate. What would be eternity for a horserace seemed no more than a blink of an eye when it came to a young boy's life.

"I don't suppose the police have a helicopter we could use?" Alec knew the answer as soon as he'd asked the question of Sergeant O'Neill, but didn't want to leave any stone unturned.

"A rescue copter operates out of County Galway," he answered. "It's most often used to rescue hikers who overestimate their abilities or go astray while climbing the Maumturks." He frowned as he looked down at the surf. "But I doubt it would be able to get close enough to the cliff to serve our purpose."

"You can't just leave him down there to drown!" Kate's voice once again edged toward the hysteria Alec had heard when she'd first discovered her son missing.

"Michael," Quinn said, "what of that tractor you bought from Devlin Doyle last year? The one with the winch at the front you used to bring up your sheep that fell over the cliff onto that ledge last St. Brigid's Day."

"It's in Limerick," he said gloomily. "At Fintan Doyle's garage, where it's been for the past month awaiting repairs. I inquired about it just yesterday, and didn't he assure me the work will get done eventually."

Kate closed her eyes. Bit into her hand to keep, Alec guessed, from screaming. He drew her close. "It'll be okay," he promised her. He had no idea how. But there was no way he'd allow himself to fail her.

He looked over at Michael. "You used a winch to bring up sheep?"

"Aye. A lamebrained ewe and her lamb who'd tumbled over in search of a bit of green to eat." His eyes narrowed as he realized what Alec was getting at. "But I didn't go down on the rope, meself. I used the path. And I wouldn't even recommend that for any man with half a brain in his head."

Alec didn't answer. Instead he leaned a bit over the edge of the cliff, studying where, exactly the steps leading down met the water.

"How high is the mouth of the cave?" he asked Kate.

"Five feet. Perhaps a bit more. I seem to recall having to begin to duck down to go into it around my first year of secondary school."

"Piece of cake," he decided.

"No!" Although he would have thought it impossible, Kate went even paler. "I'll not have you risking your life."

"Not even to save your son?"

She stared at him and could only shake her head at the choice he was offering.

"I know the steps better," Michael said. "It's going to be next to impossible to see them even with the lantern, the way the wind is blowing the rain and water over them. If it's going to be done, I should be the one doing it."

"Jamie's going to be my son." Alec's tone offered no argument. "I'll be the one to retrieve him."

"Daddy?" a faint voice behind him said.

He glanced over his shoulder and saw Zoe, looking as ashen as Kate. "What is it, sweetheart?" he asked, bracing himself for an argument he didn't have time for.

"I know you can do it." She was looking at him the same way she had when she'd been four years old and had trusted him to lift her onto the back of a horse that outweighed her by more than a thousand pounds.

"Thanks, honeybunch." He bent down and kissed her cheek. "One of these days when you're a parent, you'll understand how much that vote of confidence means to me."

"Even if you were to do this daredevil thing," Kate said, obviously torn, "how would you be lowering yourself past the steps and bringing Jamie up? Without Michael's winch?"

"Easy." He pointed to the hawthorn tree that clung to the edge of the cliff at the top of the steps. "Looks as if it's time for the faeries to repay the favor."

Alec had no idea whether or not his plan would succeed. He only knew that with the nearest tractor a good fifteen minutes away on Dennis Murphy's farm and the tide rising by the second, they didn't have a helluva lot of choices. He also knew, as he fashioned the makeshift harness from the rope Devlin Monohan had retrieved from the barn, that he didn't dare fail.

"I'll be asking God for a miracle for you, Mr. MacKenna," Father O'Malley said.

"Thanks, Padre. So far, it's been my day for miracles." He winked at Kate, kissed her quick and hard, then began his descent.

Kate couldn't think. Her head began to spin and little white spots were dancing in front of her eyes.

"Take a deep breath," Erin instructed. "Good. Now slowly blow it out. . . . Again. It's called breathing, remember? We can't have you passing out and breaking your neck at the bottom of the cliff."

No. That would not do anyone any good. As Nora and Erin kept reminding her, Jamie would need her comfort when Alec brought him to safety. Something she had to believe would be happening because she could not allow herself to think otherwise.

The cliff was wet with rain and tide and slick with moss and gull droppings. Despite Alec being harnessed to the tree, despite a dozen men holding on to the rope they'd tied around the trunk of the hawthorn, there was always the chance that he could slip off the steep and narrow steps, slamming his body against the towering limestone wall. Not a single person said a word as he continued down the steps. Indeed, Kate suspected many of them, like her, had to continue to remind their lungs to keep the salt air coming in and going out on a regular basis.

Kate could barely hear herself think over the moaning of the wind, the roar of the sea, and the drumming of her blood in her ears. When she saw Alec land on the ground, after what had seemed an eternity, a sob of relief escaped her throat.

Brendan, who was gripping the rope nearby, glanced over at her with concern. "You okay?" he asked gently.

Kate nodded. She only needed a moment to compose herself before Alec began the terrifying journey back up again with her son.

"He's in the cave," Michael, who'd taken the lead position on the very edge of the cliff, called out.

Kate bit her lip and reminded herself that no good would come from screaming.

The trip down the cliff had been the longest few minutes of his life. Alec figured he'd have to wait until he got Jamie to the top, safe and sound before having the heart attack he'd thus far managed to stave off. He turned on the light on the helmet one of Kate's neighbors had provided, then ducked into the opening that had been carved into the cliff, momentarily blinded by going from the glare of the floodlight into the inky black of the cave.

"Hey, Jamie," he shouted over the water surging into the cave.

"Alec?"

Relief flooded through him. "Yeah, it's me. Keep talking, so I can find you."

He began trailing the beam along the wall near the roof of the cave.

"I came here to think," Jamie said. "But I forgot about the tide."

"That's okay. We're going to get you out of here." Where the hell was he?

"Is Ma mad?"

"Of course not. She's worried. But I told her you'd be fine."

"I was afraid I was going to drown. . . . I'm to the left," he tacked on helpfully. "And up a bit."

"Hey!" Another obstacle overcome. "There you are." He waded through the roiling surf. "Now, what we're going to do first is put this life jacket on you," he said, unfastening it from the fluorescent orange one Kate had insisted he wear in case the rope broke. Since he didn't want her to contemplate the very real possibility that if that actually happened, he'd break his neck and a life jacket wouldn't do him a helluva lot of good, he hadn't wasted time arguing.

"Good boy. Next we're going to tie this rope around you." He lifted the end of the rope that was around his waist and attached Jamie to him. "Now, put your arms around my neck and your legs around my waist and we'll go home to your mom."

Jamie did as instructed.

"Alec?" he asked as they waded back toward the entrance.

"Yeah?" Alec lifted him higher as a huge tidal surge plowed into them. "Did Ma cry?"

"Yeah."

"I'm sorry."

"I'm sure she knows that, sport."

"Do you think I'll be punished?"

"Maybe not. Since there are extenuating circumstances involved." They were back in the circle of light, which while offering a lot of illumination, was also blinding.

"What does that mean?"

"It means that some people might argue that you had a pretty good reason to need to get away to think. Still, you'll have a harder case to make for eavesdropping on your mom and me."

"I won't be doing that again."

"Well, she'll be glad to hear that." Thankfully, it was actually easier climbing back up than it had been going down. Or perhaps, Alec thought, now that he'd gotten Jamie out of the cave, his heart had slowed down enough that he could actually envision skipping the heart attack.

"My spy kit got washed away."

"That is a bummer. But perhaps it's for the best."

"I decided, while I was in the cave, that I didn't want to be a spy when I grow up, after all."

"Okay."

"Do you want to know what I'm going to be?"

"Sure."

"A racehorse trainer."

"It's a grand occupation. And I've no doubt you've got the talent for it in your genes."

"Because of my real da?"

"Well, yeah. Sure. And your mom's certainly no slouch when it comes to horses, either."

"I know. But they're not why I want to become a trainer."

"Oh?" His boot slipped. As he wavered a bit on the edge, Alec felt the hitch on the rope and was grateful that the men above him were paying close attention.

"I want to grow up to be like you."

He'd made it a good eight feet off the beach and was eager to get to the top of the cliff. But Jamie's declaration had Alec pausing for a minute. There was no other career that he'd want. But he'd never actually chosen the work, it had simply been what the MacKenna men of Inverness Farms did. He'd been expected to go into the family business the same way the sons of Sheehan and Sons had undoubtedly been expected to become butchers.

But Jamie was choosing to follow in *his* footsteps. Whether or not the kid actually became a Thoroughbred trainer remained to be seen, but right now, as they were getting pounded by rain, and buffeted by what felt like gale force winds, hearing those words felt damn good.

"I'd be proud to work with you, Jamie lad."

He continued up on a cautious snail-like pace, step by step, and had made it another two feet when a swift gust of wind came swirling up from the beach, like a small tornado. Alec muttered what was half oath, half prayer as they were thrown off the step to dangle in the air. He kicked his legs, struggling for purchase while Jamie's arms tightened around his neck in a near choke hold.

He felt the rope straining as the wind gusted at them, flinging them back in the direction of the cliff wall. Alec braced, then hit the wall with the soles of his boots, feeling every bone in his body jolt at the impact. He'd just managed to stand again when yet another, stronger gust threatened to blow them out over the water.

"Don't worry," he ground out as he struggled not to fall over backward and pull a dozen of Castlelough's best men down with him. "I'm not going to let you fall."

"I know," Jamie said with remarkable calm as they picked up the pace. "Are you going to marry her?"

"You bet. But let's keep that our guy secret for now, okay?"

"Aye." Jamie's face was pressed against Alec's neck, but he could feel the kid's smile.

When they finally reached the top, Kate was crying and laughing and hugging them both before Alec could even remove the rope.

"I told you," he said, feeling pretty damn invincible, as he put Jamie back onto firm ground, "piece of cake." This magical green island had gotten to him, he decided, grinning at his own outrageous Irish understatement. He tangled his hands in her wet hair and pulled her to him for a hard kiss.

The excitement over for the night, people left to return to their homes where, Alec figured, the tale would be told and retold and elaborated upon from now until doomsday. Fortunately, Brigid had slept through the entire adventure.

After a long talk with her son, Kate peeled off her soaked jeans and sweater, changed into a new short silk nightgown and robe she'd bought with Alec in mind and went into the bathroom where Alec was soaking his aching muscles and joints in a hot bath.

"How's he doing?"

"Fine. Thanks to you." She sat down on the edge of the bathtub.

"I didn't do anything any dad wouldn't do."

"You're not his dad."

"Funny. It doesn't feel that way."

"I can't thank you enough for saving my son." She shook her head, still marveling that he'd risked his life for Jamie. And for her. Tears she hadn't dare shed earlier filled her eyes.

"Hey." He reached up and brushed the moisture trailing down her cheek away with a damp fingertip. "Don't cry now. It's all over."

"I don't know how I'll ever repay you."

In an obvious ploy to lighten the mood Alec flashed her a bold, cocky masculine grin. "Don't worry, sugar. If we put our heads together, I'm sure we'll think of a few ways." He snagged her wrist and pulled her into the tub.

"We'll drown," she said on a laugh when he unfastened the now drenched silk robe and pulled the lovely new nightgown over her head. The frantic mother had vanished, and in her place was the gorgeous Irish druid witch who, despite her assertions that she did not cast spells, had certainly managed to bewitch him.

"Just hold your breath," Alec suggested as he captured her mouth. "And hang on."

34

KATE DIDN'T HESITATE when Alec asked her to go to America with him for the Derby. Fortunately, since she'd taken the children with her to the Glorious Goodwood last year, where a horse she'd bred had won the illustrious race, their passports were up to date and Devlin, declaring that a seaside holiday with his wife would be no hardship, promised to look after the stud while she was away.

Despite having grown up around racehorses, Kate discovered that the racing fever surrounding the Kentucky Derby festival was definitely contagious. The Derby was more than the two most exciting minutes in racing, as its promoters liked to boast. Much, much more. There were parties and balls, a parade, a glorious hot air balloon glow, which Kate suspected Brigid would still be talking about ten years from now, a balloon race, a fireworks display dubbed *Thunder Over Louisville*, which, as her ringing ears could attest, it indeed was, and Jamie's favorite event, a steamboat race that seemed to draw nearly as many bettors as the horserace that was, of course, the jewel in the gilded festival crown.

Kate felt as if she and Alec were in a fishbowl. Wherever he went, he was peppered with questions from reporters and racing fans. When asked about what the press all seemed to be referring to as "The Incident," Alec responded that he only regretted his actions because violence never solved anything. But the tragic death of Lady Justice revealed what could happen when people made the mistake of forgetting that horseracing was, first and foremost, all about horses, not profits.

He went on to answer the same old questions about Legends Lake's problems, assuring the reporters—and the viewers all over the world—that thanks to the talents of the Thoroughbred's breeder, Kate Fitzpatrick, that little glitch had been solved.

Kate could only hope that was true.

"Did you read this morning's paper?" one of the reporters called out as they left the trainers' dinner together.

"I've been a bit busy," he responded.

"The latest line has Wellesley's Litigator as the favorite," another revealed. "And your horse a thirty-five-to-one long shot."

Kate felt a spark of temper on Legends Lake's behalf, but Alec, she noted, remained steadfastly calm. "Now that doesn't much disturb me," he said on the slow drawl that had become more pronounced since returning to his home. "Since Legends Lake can't read."

Finally, the day they'd been waiting, and working for, arrived. Kate and the children were in the owners' box with Pete Campbell and Winnie Tarlington, whom Kate had taken to immediately. The elderly owner was wearing a watermelon pink suit with white piping—the color of her racing silks—and a matching pink hat swathed in clouds of white tulle. Assuring Kate that there were certain traditions surrounding the Derby that must not be violated, one of which was the wearing of a hat—the more spectacular the better—she'd taken her shopping at the Mad Hatter.

The red roses surrounding the crown of the wide-brimmed straw hat Kate had fallen in love with matched the flowers that bloomed on the cream silk sundress Alec had insisted on buying for her in one of the pricey boutiques in the hotel lobby. It had been terribly dear, costing more than Kate had ever imagined paying for a single dress, yet when she'd gotten ready for the race today, in her new Derby hat and dress, she'd known exactly how Cinderella must have felt just before she left for the ball.

"Riders up!" boomed the paddock judge over the loudspeaker, instructing the trainers to give a leg up to the jockeys and send them out through the tunnel onto the famed oval track. When the band struck up "My Old Kentucky Home," the entire crowd—from the lofty environs of Millionaire's Row through the quarter-mile long grandstand, down to those shorts and T-shirt clad spectactors lounging on the infield grass—began singing along, emotion riding with the notes on the warm spring air.

"I don't think Legends Lake is so ugly as you said, Dad," the high voice of a small boy sitting behind them piped up as the colt walked past in the post parade, a healthy, glowing sheen to his coat.

Zoe, who'd opted for a black and pink zebra-striped hat, turned around and speared the man sitting beside the boy with a look. "Of course he isn't," she said on a flare of heat. "He's beautiful. He's also the sweetest horse in the entire world. And the fastest." She turned around again and folded her arms over the front of her hot pink spandex top in a "So there" gesture.

Legends Lake paused, turned toward the familiar voice, and with a kind look in his gentle brown eyes—and although there'd be much arguing about the matter after the race—appeared to wink at his defender before continuing on.

"Jesus," a dark-haired man sitting in front of them said. "Did you see that? The horse knew what she was saying."

"He did, didn't he, Ma?" Jamie asked Kate.

"Why, of course," she agreed without hesitation. She turned to Alec, who, having done all he could to prepare the colt for the race, had joined them. "Wouldn't you say?"

"Sure. The horse is as smart as a whip. Brains *and* looks," he added, raising his voice to ensure it would be heard by the boy's father behind them, "is a winning combination."

Legends Lake moved into his position in the starting gate with ease.

"I wasn't this nervous when I went to see *Blair Witch Project Two*," Zoe muttered as the ten horses awaited their send-off.

"He'll do fine," Winnie assured her, patting her hand. "In less than five minutes, the darling will be wearing roses."

A hush came over the stands as everyone held their collective breath.

The field of the world's best Thoroughbreds exploded through the gate. "They're off!" the crowd shouted in unison, eager to watch history in the making.

Legends Lake had leapt forward the instant the gate opened and, long lanky legs stretching, led easily into the first turn.

"Come on, big boy." Alec was still secretly concerned with how the horse would do in an actual race situation, with the roar of the crowd, the distractions of the fluttering flags surrounding the racetrack, the press of the other Thoroughbreds straining to gain the lead.

"Come on, darling," Kate coaxed as well. Nerves had her squeezing her fingernails into Alec's hand.

When they turned into the backside stretch, Litigator, the huge jet-black colt Alec had once intended to take to the Derby, managed to draw even, then get a nose ahead.

"I can't stand this," Zoe moaned as she covered her eyes, continuing, nevertheless, to watch the race through spread fingers as the two silks—Wellesley Farms' royal purple and Tarlington Farms' white diamonds on a field of watermelon—broke away from the rainbow-colored pack.

"It's okay," Alec assured her. "So long as Legends Lake is in position by the track kitchen, he can win."

"The kitchen?" Kate's heart seemed to have taken up residence in her throat.

"The stretch is long here. From the kitchen on, there's a little less than half a mile to go. The key is to be in place there, with enough in the tank to come home."

"Go, Legends Lake!" Brigid was jumping up and down on her seat as their colt regained the lead. "Go, go, go!"

It wasn't proving easy. Litigator surged forward again and the two horses were neck and neck in the far turn.

Alec bent down to Kate's ear, to be heard over the roar of the crowd. "Did you see that?"

"Aye." Not only had she seen Litigator's jockey use the whip, within inches of Legends Lake, she'd feared she'd forgotten how to breathe. "He didn't bolt."

"He's ahead again!" Jamie shouted above the din of the crowd as the two horses thundered past the red brick building just outside the rail.

Again Litigator closed the lead. The two Thoroughbreds were now running stride to stride. As they tore down the stretch toward the finish line, Litigator's jockey continued to use the crop on the black stallion's flanks, but intent on winning, Legends Lake appeared to neither notice, or, Alec hoped, no longer care.

There was pandemonium as Legends Lake accelerated, putting an extra burst of speed, stretching, digging down deep inside himself to increase the distance to a neck. Then more. The crowd went apoplectic as he crossed the line a full length ahead of his nearest rival.

"The brave, darling horse won!" Kate threw her arms around Alec. She kissed him. Kissed the children. And Winnie, whose eyes were bright with tears of joy. Then kissed Pete. Then Alec again.

"I told you," a triumphant Zoe shot the words at the man sitting behind her, who had torn his betting stubs into confetti.

The rest of the day passed in a blur. Kate could barely remember standing in the Winner's Circle with Alec and Winnie as they accepted the tall gold cup topped with the horse and rider and Legends Lake received the famed blanket of fresh crimson roses. She had no memory of waiting out the results of the testing, or returning to the hotel. She'd merely sipped the frosty mint julep someone had shoved into her hand, but her adrenaline high was so strong, she didn't need the alcohol buzz.

"I can see why you do it," she said when they were finally alone in the living room of their suite. Winnie, demonstrating far more energy than those half her age, was making the rounds of post-Derby parties; Brigid and Jamie had fallen asleep the moment their heads had hit the fluffy down pillows, and Zoe, seeming to understand their need for some time alone, had declared a pressing desire to read the paperback romance novel she'd bought in the hotel gift shop.

"Watching Legends Lake win that race was nearly the most exciting thing I've ever experienced."

Alec lifted an amused brow. "Nearly?"

"Well, it doesn't quite come up to bringing my children into the world," she admitted.

"I shouldn't think it would," he agreed.

"Or making love with you."

His eyes darkened in that way that always made her feel warm all over. But he wasn't smiling. Indeed, Kate thought, with a little prickle of nerves, his wonderful mouth that could create such havoc to her body was drawn into a frown.

"Is something wrong?"

"I had plans for tonight. After we won, I was going to seduce you with candlelight and champagne, and music—"

"Haven't I had enough alcohol for one day?" A nondrinker, just a few sips of the mint julep had left her head spinning. "As for candlelight and music, I wouldn't be needing those things, Alec."

"Maybe not. But I wanted to give them to you." He reached into the pocket of his slacks and took out a small forest green velvet box. "Along with this."

Kate caught her breath, almost afraid to hope. It could, she warned herself, be just another lovely piece of jewelry to commemorate the occasion, such as the Pegasus Derby pin he'd surprised her with this morning before the race. But she knew it was much, much more.

"Oh, Alec." Her eyes welled up.

"Hey, don't get all soft and mushy before you see what it is."

"I already love it," she insisted. "Oh!" She opened the velvet lid and drew in a breath. Rather than the traditional diamond she'd expected, the ring was made of three stones set in a gold woven Celtic band. The tiger eye represented dawn, the silver hematite, dusk, and the obsidian, midnight.

"I picked it up at the Beltane festival while you and Nora were checking out the weaving booths," he revealed. "The craftsman who created it said the druids used those stones for divination."

"That's true." She slipped the ring on her finger. It was a perfect fit. "They're called Sky Stones, and I can't think of a more perfect gift."

"It's a bit more than just a gift." He swiped a hand through his hair. She'd never seen him this nervous, not in the beginning when they'd first begun working with Legends Lake, today at what could well have been the most important race of his life, or even when he'd been preparing to risk his own life to rescue her child.

"Look, I understand how much Ireland means to you. It's your home, and you've got your family, and your business, and centuries of family history."

"Aye, that's true enough."

"And I also realize that Kentucky might not have circles of standing stones, or faerie trees, and magic—"

"Magic can be found anywhere," Kate interjected quietly. "If you keep your heart open to it." As she'd opened her heart to him.

"That's true." He seemed encouraged by that idea. "Hell, I'm not any good at making speeches. So, I'm just going to say it straight out. You are going to marry me, aren't you, Kate Fitzpatrick?"

Kate refused to be coy. "Aye, I will marry you, Alec MacKenna. And gladly. On one condition."

"Name it and it's yours. If you want me to try to

move my training stables to Ireland so you can keep your stud—"

"That's not necessary. I understand it's important for your career to be based in the States, and I'll love making a new home with you in your Kentucky. As for the stud, I have a few ideas about that.

"But what I'm speaking of is my love for my children. And I love Zoe, as well, as if she were my own dear girl. But I've discovered I'm a greedy woman. I want to have babies with you."

"You've got it," he said without hesitation. "How many?"

"Oh," she said blithely, her ring catching the light and making the gold gleam as she waved her hand, "lots and lots."

"Sounds like a plan." He scooped her up and began walking toward the bedroom. Her full silk skirt flowed over his arms and one high heel dropped onto the lush cream carpet.

"Well now, aren't you the one for sweeping a girl off her feet?"

"Get used to it." She sank into a cloud of down as he dropped her onto the wide bed, then leaned over her, eyes warming her from the inside out. "Because if we're going to meet that lofty family goal you've set for us, we're going to be making a lot of love."

Her laugh was light and merry as she twined her arms around his neck and drew his mouth down to hers. " 'Tis quite a sacrifice you'll be making."

"Aye," he agreed, feigning exaggerated exhaustion as he lay down beside Kate and gathered her, heart to heart, into his arms. "But it's one I'll be making for us. And gladly."

* * *

From the *Castlelough Chronicle*'s "Around and About Our Village" page, nine months later:

> The new Sister Bernadette Mercy Hospital was christened in grand style this weekend when Castlelough's own Kate Fitzpatrick MacKenna gave birth to an eight-pound, six-ounce son, Connor Patrick MacKenna. Mrs. MacKenna had returned from her family's Thoroughbred farm in America—where she and her family reside nine months of the year—to give birth to young Connor in the same village where her roots go back so many centuries.
>
> Accompanying her were her husband, Mr. Alec MacKenna—whom loyal readers of the *Chronicle* will recall trained America's most recent Triple Crown winner, Legends Lake, bred by his wife at the newly named Monohan & MacKenna Stud established with Devlin Monohan—as well as the infant's brother, James, and sisters Brigid and Zoe.
>
> Dr. Erin Joyce reports that mother and son are doing well.
>
> The father is expected to recover.

Dear Reader,

When *A Woman's Heart* was published, many of you wrote asking for Kate's story. I'd always intended to tell her tale, but first she needed time to get her life in order. During the writing of *Fair Haven*, I watched her bloom like a Burren wildflower that had finally gotten water to its roots, and by the time I'd written THE END to that story, she was ready to embark on a future she'd never dared dream of.

Those who follow Thoroughbred racing may have noticed that I took a bit of literary license with the date of the Kentucky Derby. Well, as they say in Ireland, when God made time, he made plenty of it, so with that in mind, I borrowed two extra weeks to allow Kate and Alec their Beltane celebration.

I'll probably be returning to Castlelough one of these days, but in the meantime, I hope you'll come with me to the romantic Louisiana bayou, where fireflies twinkle like fairy lights in centuries-old oak trees, ancient ghosts hover like wisps of smoke over moss-draped cypress and still waters hide dark secrets. Destiny is about to grant Danielle Dupree and Jack Callahan a second chance at love. But first they must confront their past, then vanquish a new threat lurking in the shadows.

To write to me about any of my stories, or to subscribe to an electronic newsletter with contests and preview scenes from *Blue Bayou*, please visit my website at *www.joannross.com*